MARC STRANGE

Follow Me Down

AN ORWELL BRENNAN MYSTERY

ECW PRESS

Published by ECW Press
2120 Queen Street East, Suite 200, Toronto, Ontario, Canada M4E 1E2
416.694.3348 / info@ecwpress.com

LIBRARY AND ARCHIVES CANADA CATALOGUING IN PUBLICATION

Strange, Marc
Follow me down / Marc Strange.
"An Orwell Brennan msytery".

ISBN 978-1-77041-031-2
ALSO ISSUED AS: 978-1-55490-926-1 (PDF); 978-1-55490-687-1 (EPUB)
ORIGINALLY PUBLISHED IN HARDCOVER IN 2010 (ISBN 978-1-55022-926-4)

I. TITLE.

PS8637.T725F64 2012 C813'.6 C2011-906970-9

Cover and Text Design: Tania Craan
Cover Images: Winter Sunset © Hemera Technologies/Getty Images
Bow Hunter Aiming Compound Bow © Ron Chapple/Corbis
Typesetting: Mary Bowness
Printing: Friesens 1 2 3 4 5

The publication of *Follow Me Down* has been generously supported by the Canada Council for the Arts which last year invested $20.1 million in writing and publishing throughout Canada, and by the Ontario Arts Council, an agency of the Government of Ontario. We also acknowledge the financial support of the Government of Canada through the Canada Book Fund for our publishing activities. The marketing of this book was made possible with the support of the Ontario Media Development Corporation.

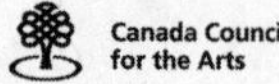

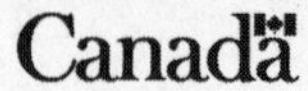

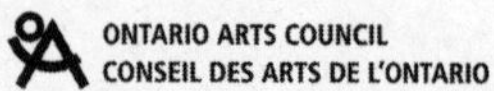

PRINTED AND BOUND IN CANADA

For Karen Petersen
researcher, editor,
first reader, best reader

Author's Note

To those who care about such things:

I have taken many liberties with longitude, latitude, distances and road signs in order to fit my fictional town of Dockerty into a particular area. There is no Snipe Lake or rivers in the Kawartha District and the surrounding region has been elbowed left or right when necessary.

This is a work of fiction and the people in the story live around Dockerty and nowhere else.

The hunter listened to the sounds of prey on the far side of the beaver pond — a cough into a gloved hand, the creak of canvas bearing weight, the tap of carbon fiber against aluminum. The hunter turned at the shadowy beat of a great owl's wings and glimpsed a grey ghost flickering between dark trees, banking up the slope through shafts of moonlight. Another killer in the night.

The moon was waxing. Nearly full. It was bright enough to stalk by, with shadows for concealment. It was the October moon; the Hunter's Moon. An assassin's moon.

The shooting place was across the beaver dam under the canopy of a wild apple tree with overhanging branches touching the ground. The hunter could smell the rotting apples underfoot. The quarry was in a poplar tree within whispering distance.

The hunter took aim. There was moonlight on the blades. The sound, when it came, was a deeper sigh than the whispers of the night forest, it was the sigh of the guillotine blade descending. It was the whisper of death.

The man in the tree said, "What?" and grabbed at the thing that was sticking out of his belly, pinning him to the trunk.

The hunter stepped closer.

"Hi, Jer," said the hunter, and nailed him to the tree a second time.

It is said that a hundred or so years ago, a man named Hermann Breithaupt was murdered in the woods north of County Road 17, near Dockerty, Ontario. His body was never found. There is no way of knowing for sure if there ever was a murder, or if Hermann Breithaupt was the victim. Certainly no one named Hermann Breithaupt had ever owned property in Newry County. But in the way of things, the forest has for many years been known as Breithaupt's Bush.

One

DAY ONE — Monday, October 11

Orwell Brennan rarely missed a sunrise. He figured any miracle you could set your watch by was worth proper observance. On this October morning the sun was scheduled to come up, if not actually appear, at 7:37 but it didn't look promising: the wind had picked up again, and the sky was thick with impending rain. Orwell was about to advise the dogs that their customary walk would be a short one, when a shaft of purest light kissed his face and he lifted his eyes to watch the sun come up over the rolling hills of Newry County under the hem of low-lying clouds hiked just high enough to reveal the brightness — whole, and perfect, and right on time.

Orwell allowed himself a brief look directly at the sun before turning to see how far his shadow might stretch across the pasture to the west, but in that instant clouds claimed the light and the course was set for yet another in a long series of dark, wet and moody autumn days. Nonetheless, he knew that he'd been blessed and he was smiling as he settled his hat on his big head, for he had doffed it to the dawn. It was something he did every time.

Dockerty's Chief of Police lived on a farm about ten klicks outside town, and a circuitous drive to work was another of his routines. His stately tour over the tar and gravel county roads afforded him time to think and showed him how things were going in what he often thought of as his parish. It was one of his conceits that he might have made a good priest, had he not been so fond of women and were he not so angry with the Catholic Church. He varied his route according to whim, but his speed remained constant. Orwell Brennan drove like a parade.

He took the River Road that morning. A glimpse of open water was always welcome, even when the ospreys were elsewhere and their forlorn jumble of sticks atop the telephone pole looked as inviting as a crown of thorns. RiverView Lodge too looked abandoned — the parking lot empty, three canoes and two aluminum outboards stashed under tattered blue tarps, a FOR SALE sign by the front entrance. So much for scenery, Orwell thought. He could feel winter lurking, waiting on the other side of Halloween. It had been the worst summer for a hundred years, the farmers said, and they said it as if they had all been around the last time a year had been as bad. "There's no hay," they said, meaning that what hay there was, was dear.

Orwell drove over the one-lane bridge by the boat launch and continued around the bend onto County Road 18, heading east toward the highway. It was raining again. Wet leaves wiped side-to-side across the windshield. He could feel the east wind pushing against the broad front of his old Ramcharger. He wondered, in passing, whose car that might be, sitting outside Dan Warren's place, with vanity plates that said "Stalker."

It was an electric blue Camaro. The driver's side window was fully open and Saturday's newspaper was soaked on the front seat. The car was parked outside Dan Warren's front gate, off to the side, under the big Manitoba maple whose yellow leaves were plastered thickly on the roof and hood.

Dan Warren wiped his breath off the cold front room window and went into the kitchen. "Heard the weather yet?"

Irene Warren handed him his sweet tea. "They just gave it," she said. "More of the same."

Dan sat at the kitchen table to drink his tea and wait for his eggs and toast. "That car's still out there," he said again. "Left the front window open."

"Bad day for it," Irene said without much sympathy. It was none of her concern if some city fool wanted to park his car in the rain with the window open. She called up from the foot of the stairs. "Terry? You want eggs?" There was no answer from above.

"He get to the south field yesterday?" Dan asked.

"Said he had other things to take care of."

"That spreader's got to get back to Fern Casteel's for tomorrow," Dan said.

"I'm not going to wake him," Irene said.

Dan grunted when he got to his feet. The weather wasn't helping his sciatica. He carried his tea into the front room and looked out again at the blue Camaro sitting in the morning rain and wondered about the driver.

"Expect he's still back there," he said.

Terry Warren hunched on the edge of his bed, scanning the lawn and the gate and the road. He had slept in his clothes and he was damp and chilled from sweating in his sleep, and from the wet socks still on his feet. He could hear his mother and father moving about downstairs, one or the other of them fiddling with the dial on the kitchen radio, searching for optimism. From his bedroom window he had watched Orwell's Ramcharger roll by, as he had watched every other vehicle since before first light. Terry looked at his hands. They were in need of a wash.

This is Terry's Law: See and not be seen, hear and not be heard, follow and leave no tracks.

He is a shadow, a movement of air, the fading echo of a sound half heard. In his high school yearbook he is hard to find, a blur on the back tier with a stroke of white where an eye might be. The picture on his driver's license too is vaporous. When Terry wants to, he disappears. He has the power. It is his gift, his faith, his calling.

He was five years old when he first heard his father chasten him for "sneaking around," "lurking." He was always angling for a glimpse of something he wasn't supposed to see — his mother's breasts, naked for the briefest flash as she got ready for bed — eavesdropping on whispered conversations, gossip, revelations, family lore. By nine, before he was old enough to know what he was finding, he had been through every drawer in the house, every closet, every top shelf and cubbyhole. The most mundane details consumed him, the cryptic particulars of old letters with illegible greetings and farewells, yellowing photographs of ancestors long dead, deeds and policies, birth announcements and death certificates. He had rifled through a hundred boxes filled with odd bits of clothing, broken tools, forgotten schoolbooks, keys to anonymous locks. He left no trace.

Terry's Grandpa Max had first taken him hunting in Breithaupt's Bush when he was six years old, and when he was nine, Max gave him a single-shot Cooey .22. "It's good to be able to put some food on the table once in awhile," Max said. "That way it doesn't look like you're wasting your time in here."

Terry was an apt pupil. By age seven he could skin a rabbit, set a snare, dress a deer and crawl, silent as a snake, to where the brown trout rose for flies in the heat of day. He had an uncanny talent for interpreting tracks and sign, and could read them like street maps. He knew where the animals were, and where they were going, and when they would be back. In time, he perfected his art of quiet, became a part of all around him, could merge with the atmosphere. Disappear.

"Animals know when you're sneaking," the old man told him. "They're not stupid, they can tell you've got evil intent if you're all crouched over and creepy. Just be naturally quiet, like a respectful person in a library, going about your business, calm, like you belong here."

Max walked without haste, stopping frequently to listen, eyes open, nostrils too, careful where he put his feet. He employed the tip of his hawthorn walking stick like an instrument, to lift a leaf or scratch the dirt or plumb a depth of mud. And Terry followed him, learning how to see through veils of foliage, how to sniff the earth and read the dark through his fingertips.

The swamp in Breithaupt's Bush stretched a mile or more in bog and silt, following the winding course of a beaver creek, one of the Snipe River's feeder streams, never named, forever flooding, branching, dammed and breached according to the dogged whim of a clan of beavers as destructive as they were industrious.

"Stick a body in that swamp, nobody'll ever see it again," Grandpa Max used to say, and before he died he made a list of all those who had done him a hurt or used him ill, and contented himself in his waning days with plots for the unmarked disposition of their worthless bones.

"Sink him so deep in mud he'll cease to exist in the world as we know it" were his dying words, but exactly whose worthless carcass his fast-fading mind was then disposing of was left to God to ascertain.

Grandpa Max had been searching for something. Often he would hint to Terry that there was buried treasure in the ground. In the spring, they would say they were foraging for fiddleheads and morels, or later in the year, berries and puffballs, but Terry knew that there was something else in Breithaupt's Bush. One time they found a silver half-dollar dated 1904, and another time they found a brass belt buckle crusted with verdigris, but whatever else the old man sought, he had not found it by the time he took to his bed for the last time and left Terry Warren, then thirteen, to hunt the bush by himself.

Terry believed that the bush was his. He owned it because he knew it, all of it, as no one else ever had, or would. He knew the beaver's skid roads, the wide deer highways, the tight passages and the half-buried fence lines. He knew where the iron-pin markers were sunken at the lost corners of the Warren property, and where the Coughlans' and the Footes' property lines lay to the west and south, unsurveyed in more than a hundred years. He knew all the ways to slip in and to slip out. Three hundred acres of tall, mixed hardwoods, steep wooded hills and sudden bogs in the dark bottomland where thick, gnarled cedars, as old as the valley they grew in, still held fast to the damp black earth with roots as long as country lanes. He knew the trees as if by name, and every foot of Breithaupt's Bush, in bright of day, or dark of night, was more familiar to him than his mother's kitchen.

The resentment he felt whenever his father and brother would invade his preserve to hunt or chop was visceral, and filled him with righteous irritation. He would watch the pair of them, hacking his garden like butchers, tearing up the earth, maiming the maples and scattering their limbs. He watched them from a shadowed ridge, or a dense thicket, invisible, embittered, hearing them shouting back and forth, never listening to the forest, oblivious to the shifting underbrush, to the quick evacuations of threatened burrows and nests. When finally they departed, dragging the next year's quota of firewood, they left behind a mess that was unbearable. He would clean up after them, drag the lopped and discarded branches into a neat pile for the beaver to use, pare the brutalized trunks close to the earth, blend the chips and sawdust into the living forest floor. It would take him weeks to return his property to its natural order. Neither Billy nor his father, from one year to the next, ever noticed that the bush had magically healed itself. To his father and brother the section of bush belonging to the Warren place was a hunting preserve, a source of lumber, firewood and occasional revenue.

It wouldn't always be that way, Terry knew. His father would grow old and die. Inevitably, Terry would own it.

Terry built his first fort when he was seven years old. It wasn't much, an extension of a deer blind that his grandfather had helped him locate. It was cramped and unfinished inside, but even at that young age, Terry grasped the essential principle — it was invisible.

A few years later Terry made a tree house that he still used from time to time. It was thirty feet up a first-growth eastern hemlock, a solid nest large enough for him to sleep in, sheltered by a roof of woven branches. It too was invisible. A bird watcher staring straight up from the base of the tree would have seen nothing more than a fan of living branches and a lightning scar ending at the scorched stump of a missing limb. Lightning had never touched that hemlock, and the living branches were attached to the tree beside it, carefully bent back year by year until they hid the aerie as artfully as a fan dancer veiled her privacy.

Terry relished being high in the air, scanning like an eagle, sleeping like a squirrel, his perch swaying with the wind. But the nest had its drawbacks — a limited field of view through the branches, restricted space, difficult access, no room to store his treasures. His treasures were mounting. Some were hidden in the barn, some in the root cellar, some in the attic, and in Terry's eyes they were all vulnerable and exposed. Worse, he couldn't touch them when he wanted to, couldn't handle them, inhale them, study them. So he dug a treasure cave to hold his collection.

The entrance to his tunnels had been a gift from the forest gods. The spring that Terry turned seventeen, the rains were unusually heavy. The clean, meandering trout stream became a muddy torrent, undercutting both banks along its length. Sometime in April, upstream of the largest beaver dam, a first-growth cedar, a hundred years old and four stories high, after hanging on through countless generations of beaver projects that weakened both its damaged roots and the earth they clutched, finally relinquished its hold and dropped into the surging water. Swept downstream, root-wad first, it punched a hole the size of a garage door in an overburdened beaver dam releasing half a million gallons of water. The sudden wall of water scoured away the accumulated silt and sediment of a century, laying bare the secrets of the riverbank.

Terry found the stream spanned in a dozen places and he crossed the swirling grey water on a haphazard bridge of toppled cedars and birches to the twisted fan of roots on the far side. The roots had not easily given up their hold on the riverbank upstream. Many of them were snapped and wrenched as arm bones from a shoulder socket. Through the broken tangle of roots Terry looked down and saw, half-buried in the deep and sucking wound of the riverbank, a broken, bony claw, a scapular and collarbone, shards of a rib cage, and, still under earth but for a mud-choked grin, the skull of a long-dead man.

Terry had grown up with the Hermann Breithaupt stories. The generally accepted version had his great-grandfather, William Warren, coming home from the Great War to find his wife Lillian in bed with a tractor salesman named Breithaupt and shooting him dead on the spot. In another account, Breithaupt was merely attempting to "interfere" with Mrs. Warren when he was dispatched. This was the preferred rendering insofar as the family was concerned. The fact that Breithaupt was known to have been in the area for some months diminished its credibility. The story no one inside the family spoke of, the story that pointed out that Max was born seven months almost to the day after Dan's return from the Great War, was common knowledge among those old enough to still care about local history. It had once crossed Terry's mind as he rifled a box of birth certificates and family documents how strange it was that in a family of Bobs and Davids and Williams, his great-grandparents had named their first child Max. And although his grandfather had never mentioned the matter, Terry was sure that what Max had been hunting for so many years was the body of his real father.

With the bones piled out of the way, a natural doorway was revealed, an entrance to a cave inside the riverbank, a space of dark wet odours, snarled with roots, littered with the droppings and leavings of creatures who live underground. That cave became Terry's vestibule. As the years went by he added a passageway deep into the belly of the ridge, widening it at intervals into chambers and alcoves, rooms large enough to sleep in and a stretch within the brow of the ridge in which he could stand upright and scan the forest below through a string of windows barred with rootlets and curtained with leaves. And after that he kept digging. The wooded ridge within the forest became a honeycomb of burrows and chambers, passages, compartments and bolt holes. There was a treasure room where he kept Trina's things, and the money, an armoury where he kept his .22 rifle and ammunition, his machete and axes and mattock and adze and Swede saws and blades. His stronghold inside the wooded hillside coiled like a great hollow worm with fat rooms and connecting passageways. Terry's bedroom in his father's house was Spartan, held little that was personal; he slept there when he had to, and only then. Terry's true home was with those burrowing creatures who frequented his lair and shared his reticence.

Two

"It's a dumb idea," Orwell told the mayor. He disliked being in her office. She had photographs of herself on every wall. "You just spent seven million dollars building a new station," he said. "What are you going to do, turn it into condos?"

"No final decision has been made," said Donna Lee Bricknell.

"On what? Hiring the OPP or retrofitting the station for human habitation?"

"One suggestion has been to lease it to the Provincial Police for their local headquarters."

"Good plan," he said. "Sounds entirely workable. The building was designed to accommodate fifty cops, you'd be lucky if ten OPP were stationed here."

"As I said, no decision has been made," she said.

"I trust the town will have an opportunity to voice its opinion," said Orwell, "rather than have this pet scheme of yours shoved down its throat."

"I resent your tone, Chief Brennan. This is not my pet scheme."

"Wave a few tax breaks at those trained seals of yours on the Knoll and they start foaming at the mouth."

Of all the things at which he was savvy, accommodating bureaucrats and functionaries, whether elected, appointed or tenured, was not Orwell's strong suit. He was neither clever nor careful when he dealt with officialdom; the insolence of office offended him, the lack of accountability exasperated him.

In many ways both big and small, Orwell Brennan failed to fit the template of Dockerty Head Cop cast during the long tenure of Chief Alastair Argyle, now gloriously dead and interred beneath a headstone which read, "Rectitude, Respect, Responsibility." These were the "3-Rs of police work" according to Orwell's predecessor. The great Argyle had been a spit-and-polish Presbyterian, Orwell was a conflicted Catholic; Argyle had been an embellishment to any civic function, Orwell was considered something of an embarrassment — arriving late, eschewing decorations, predisposed to speak his mind and vacate the premises without ceremony. The iconic Argyle had, with a great sense of theatre, died of a massive stroke while marching on church parade wearing his dress blues and all his laurels. If I die on a Sunday morning, Orwell thought, it'll be face down on the weekend crossword wearing a bathrobe.

But despite knowing full well that he had been third on the list of candidates and might well be retired or replaced before the conclusion of his contract, he had accepted the job because his wife Erika had her heart set on buying the old Robicheau place. And while he wasn't particularly looking forward to retirement, he had of late entertained a not unappealing notion that he might enjoy raising fancy chickens. He had a farm; he might as well do some farming. The fact that he knew almost nothing about the care and breeding of domestic fowl bothered him not at all. Orwell had no doubt that he could handle chickens.

He cut across Armoury Park in the direction of the new police building — ugly pink brick, bronze plaque by the flagpole, Alastair Argyle's inescapable visage keeping an eternal eye on the town. Orwell didn't much care for the new police building. Plans had been laid down during Argyle's reign and the structure had about it a palpably Presbyterian air — unadorned, standoffish, deliberately commonplace. Argyle's bronze likeness struck Orwell as out of place. It smacked of idolatry.

Staff Sergeant Roy Rawluck was custodian of a fine moustache of which he was justly proud. Orwell thought it would have looked good in a tintype. Rawluck had served with distinction for the final ten years of Alastair Argyle's stewardship and was staunch believer in "observing the form." That he disapproved of the Chief's casual approach to service attire was no secret. It bothered Orwell not a bit, although he could have done without the audible clucking from that quarter whenever he went out in public.

"What have we got, Roy?"

Rawluck checked a piece of paper on his desk but Orwell knew he had no need to. There was nothing going on in the department that his Staff Sergeant wasn't on top of.

"Three men still tied up in court. Willis on the hit-and-run, Generoux is on the witness list for the home invasion, Loesse still has a couple of traffic appearances to cover. The Bernier kid was transferred down to Juvenile in Toronto. They collected him about an hour ago."

"Good," said Orwell and headed for his office where Dorrie Burell, his diminutive and alarmingly efficient secretary waited with a cup of fresh coffee and the day's obligations.

"The Groton family have asked for an escort for tomorrow's funeral," Roy reminded him.

"What do they want, a parade?"

"Three cruisers should do it, Chief."

"I'm not expected to show up, am I?"

"It would be the right thing," Dorrie said. She was Orwell's advisor on all matters of etiquette and on more than one occasion had kept him from offending local custom. By now she no doubt had his pew location pinned down.

"Oh, Lord," he muttered, as he saw his last escape route close.

"Herb Groton was a descendent," she said. "One of the original families."

"Would that be the Iroquois or the Mississauga branch of the family?" Dorrie rarely laughed. Orwell sighed. "Where and when?" he asked.

"Zero nine hundred. St. Bart's," she said.

Roy said, "They'll have the pipes."

"Of course they will," said Orwell. "Been rehearsing 'Amazing Grace' behind the Armoury all bloody week. You wouldn't think you could get tired of a tune like that, but trust me, you can."

"Dress blues, Chief?" Roy suggested.

"I'll get my harness out of the closet."

"And take the Chief's car. Leave your old truck in the parking lot," Dorrie suggested.

Orwell was offended. "Bozo's not that old," he said.

"It would be out of place on parade," said Roy.

"I assure you folks, I will arrive in style."

"The family will appreciate it."

"I doubt that," said Orwell. "They would delight in seeing me canned. Wouldn't surprise me to learn they're the ones pushing this OPP plan."

"Did Her Honour say anything definite, Chief?" Dorrie asked.

"We are still evaluating options and considering what's best in the long run for the town and its citizens," he said, in a very bad imitation of Donna Lee Bricknell's nasal whine.

"So nothing's been decided," said Roy.

"The way things work over there I'd say we have a few months of bean counting and hedging before they begin the actual decision-making process."

"But they want to make it happen."

"Not if I have anything to say about it, Staff Sergeant."

Dan Warren was tired of the wet. His back ached all the time. He needed a hot dry spell at least once a year. Same as crops, he thought as he hauled himself into the green Dodge pickup and headed across the brown and yellow fields, sticking to the high sides of the track. Dan's place on County Road 18 had always been a "wet" farm. The Newry aquifer undulated within the hills at levels wildly variant to the surface contour. Dan's neighbour, Roland Coughlan, had drilled more than ninety feet before he got his well, while forty rods and one ridge east of Coughlan's farm, hillside springs were forever leaking into Dan Warren's fields, leaching topsoil down to bottomland too wet to cultivate.

A dark, wet summer on a steep, wet farm had brought forth patchy acreage of paltry hay, and Dan hadn't bothered with a second cut. The fields in mid-October were unruly and uneven. Through the long stubble blotched with pallid milkweed, goldenrod and blue vervain, he could trace the subterranean watercourse by following the swaths of water grasses marching downward to the cedar swamp that cut through both parcels of Warren land.

The hay fields were part of the "long hundred," a narrow tract running between County Road 18 at the north end and through the bush to County Road 17. Three working hayfields plus the "bottom field" where the stream cut through and the forest began on a north-facing slope. The sap always ran late on that side of the hill, Dan remembered. Years ago they had tapped the trees but it was too much trouble now with Billy moved away and Terry not much interested in farming. Too much for one man.

The pickup got its left rear wheel into a boggy patch and Dan had to gun it out. Ahead of him he could see the manure spreader parked where Terry had quit two days before. The sugar maples on the slope beyond were showing bare branches and what leaves were left were fading and turning from red and gold to the colour of mud. In one of the taller poplar trees was an unnatural patch of yellow and green and shiny black. A heavy pendulous shape like a wild bee swarm.

Dan drove along the fence line and crossed into the bottom field. In the old days they used horses to work this field, but it was too steep for a machine. It was shaped like half a bowl, sheer sides and a ridge in the middle, treacherous going in a high-wheeled tractor. He remembered the time Billy tipped the old Minneapolis Moline. Being an athlete saved his life. As soon as he felt the tractor lose balance, he jumped, bouncing off the hood, scorching his arm on the stovepipe exhaust and cracking a rib on the front wheel. The big orange tractor rolled all the way to the bottom of the bowl, twisting the cultivator into a piece of junk. That was the last time they bothered with the bottom field. The forest was reclaiming it now.

Dan stuck to the narrow track across the ridge and then almost straight down. It was wet in the bottomland, but the thick wild grasses provided a solid carpet and he wasn't worried about getting back. He half-opened the truck door to lean out and look up at the thing in the branches.

The man was hanging upside down, the back of his head against the trunk, mouth open in a silent moan, the toe of one boot caught in the crotch of a branch. He was fixed in place by the two hunting arrows that stapled him to the tree through his lower belly.

The Chief was writing, in longhand, on a yellow pad of lined paper. He was on his third sheet and there was much crossing out and marginalia. His handwriting was large and for the most part legible except where he'd been forced to cram in a word at the end of a line.

Roy Rawluck knocked once on the open office door. "Wanted me, Chief?"

Orwell looked up, picked up the pad and read aloud, "We serve at the pleasure of the Town Council, but we serve the citizens of Dockerty." He looked at his Staff Sergeant. "Am I correct?"

"Of course, Chief."

He continued: "Our brand of police work delivers significant advantages to the service this town would receive from the Ontario Provincial Police. Both in style and substance. You would agree?"

"You going to make a speech, Chief?"

"Just want to have all my cannons loaded and pointed in the right direction when I have to face the Town Council next time. They start throwing numbers at me, I want to be able to throw something back. I don't think we should go down without a fight, do you, Roy?"

"No, Chief."

"Town deserves better."

"Yes, sir."

"We're going to need someone to carry the ball." Orwell tossed his notes on the desk and rose to stand by the window. He wiped the glass distractedly, collecting his thoughts. "I definitely do not want the police department out politicking to save its ass; I want a grassroots movement, groundswell of public opinion, something spontaneous, albeit given a gentle nudge. People who've been here forever, people who like us."

"The merchants. The schools. Hospital."

The Chief grinned. "Now you're talking," he said. "Let's get a package together. Statistics, numbers, arrests, convictions — anything that makes it look like we're doing our job."

"We *are* doing our job."

"'Course we are. They know it, you know it, the town knows it. I want it in black and white."

"How far back you want to go?"

"Just my four years. My predecessor's record is already carved in marble." Orwell sat back down, straightened his papers. "Town Council certainly isn't going to suggest that Argyle didn't do his job." He smiled at his Staff Sergeant. "Are they?"

"No, Chief."

"I'm the chink in the armour, Roy; I need rivets."

"I'll get some people on it."

Dorrie's voice came through the intercom: "Chief Brennan?"

"Yes, Dorrie?"

"Call on line one. Says he's your neighbour, Mr. Warren."

"Who? Dan Warren? Put him through."

Dan sounded a bit distraught, his voice strained. "Chief Brennan, it's Dan Warren on 18," he said. "Could you come out t'my place? There's somebody hanging in a tree with a couple of arrows in him."

"Just sit tight, Dan, someone will be right along," said Orwell. "You say he's got two arrows in him, Dan?" He looked down at the notepad where he was unconsciously doodling arrows flying to the margin. Orwell shoved his notes into the top drawer. "Roy?"

"Chief?"

"There's been a fatality on Dan Warren's farm. Possibly a hunting accident. Get on to OPP Region, ambulance. Dorrie, who's on Dispatch? Get them for me, will you?"

"It will be Putnam, Chief. Mary." It was another of Dorrie's responsibilities to feed the Chief names.

"Mary? Hi, it's Chief Brennan. We got a cruiser anywhere near 18 and the Little Britain turnoff?"

"Stacy Crean's out there." She pronounced it 'Crane.' "She's hunting that grow-op."

"Reach out. Tell her to get out to Dan Warren's farm on County Road 18. Tell her to hold the front gate until the OPP gets there."

"She's not in uniform, Chief."

"That's okay, she's got a badge. Get her moving, and send a couple of uniforms too when you find them."

"Certainly, sir."

"Appreciate it, Mary."

Orwell grabbed his hat and coat.

"You going over there, Chief?" Roy Rawluck didn't care for breaches of protocol.

"Dan's a friend," Orwell said, somewhat virtuously. "Making sure he's okay."

"Taking someone?"

"No."

"It's outside city limits, Chief."

"I know the border, Staff. I won't step on any toes."

Had Dan Warren made a 911 call, it would have been routed directly to the Ontario Provincial Police Region dispatcher. OPP handled fatalities outside or inside Orwell's jurisdiction and he had no legitimate business sticking his nose in. Nonetheless, he saw the incident as a chance to get out of his office for a few hours. After all, he had received a personal call, he knew the family, and it was a neighbourly thing to do. All plausible excuses. In truth, he just wanted some fresh air. There was a war coming. If the Town Council wanted to throw Dockerty to the OPP, they'd have to go through him. They could fire him of course, but they'd still need someone to oversee the yard sale and he figured Mayor Donna Lee would rather see him stuck with the job of handing out pink slips, negotiating pension packages and writing recommendations. Whatever the outcome, she was in for a fight.

He cut across the top of Dockerty along the Old Slant Road. Joe Greenway's place was halfway down; twenty acres of bush that backed onto the upper arm of the Snipe River, known locally as Big Snipe, and on maps as Upper Snipe.

Joe was splitting firewood beside his cabin as the Chief arrived. Joe Greenway made physical things look simple and natural. A wiry, long-limbed man with powerful hands, and fingers that could bend a dime or tie a fly on a #16 Mustad hook, streamside, without a vise. Each arc of the heavy maul whacked a big piece of hardwood into two equal chunks. There was at least a cord split and ready for stacking and another cord of the big rounds waiting. For all Orwell knew, Joe might have felled the trees and bucked them into stove lengths as the sun was coming up. The cabin was made of squared timbers and had a shake roof and a roofed verandah that overlooked the woods and the river. Joe had squared all his own timbers and built his own fireplace and dug his own well. He was a self-sufficient man.

Joe's border collie, Maggie, wagged her tail and danced around on the verandah. The Chief was a particular friend of Maggie's, and his pant cuffs had stories to tell of cats and dogs from distant places. As Maggie bounced and sniffed at Orwell's trousers and shoes, Joe walked over, looking at his dog with amusement.

"She only acts like an idiot around you."

"Erika would say she recognizes another idiot." Orwell crouched and gave Maggie a scratch behind the ears and ruffled her thick black-and-white coat.

"You want coffee?"

"No. I'd like you to come with me to Warren's. There's been a hunting accident and somebody's dead over there." Orwell straightened up, flexed his sore knee twice. "That's all I know. Except the deceased has two arrows in him. I thought you could have a look, get a picture of what happened."

"Watch the house, Maggie babe."

Maggie broke off her inspection and trotted onto the porch and sat there smiling at him. Joe grabbed his jacket off the verandah and climbed into the big Ramcharger. He reached for the pouch of Drum tobacco in his shirt pocket, peeled off a Zig Zag paper and proceeded to roll himself a frugal cigarette.

"OPP show up yet?"

"Called. Ambulance and OPP Region. They're on the way."

Joe fired up his smoke with a wooden match, broke the match in half, and put it in one of the cavernous pockets of his complicated oilskin and leather jacket. He'd sewn it himself. If he were thrown from a plane into the wilds of the Temagami, he could survive on the contents of his pockets.

"Somebody ask for me?"

"Nope. Didn't ask for me, either."

Three

There were two cars waiting in front of the Warren place, a Dockerty cruiser with two uniforms inside, and an unmarked unit on the far side. Corporal Dutch Scheider was stuffing a half-eaten cinnamon bun into a Tim Hortons bag and trying not to look like his mouth was full. Orwell rolled down his window.

"No sign of the OPP?"

"No, Chief," Dutch said.

"Finish swallowing, Dutch."

"Yessir." Dutch wiped his mouth.

"Who's that with you?"

"Carlisle, Chief."

Orwell couldn't remember Carlisle's first name but he knew his rank.

"Morning, Constable," he said.

Orwell got out to talk to the woman who was looking through the open driver's side window of the electric blue Camaro.

"Morning, Stacy."

"Morning, Chief."

Detective Stacy Crean had dark hair, a wicked smile and black belts in disciplines with which Orwell was unfamiliar. He thought she was good-looking, and probably dangerous. She was his best investigator. "Saturday's newspaper," she said.

"See anything else in there?"

"Left his street shoes and socks in there. I could probably pop the glove box from here."

"Love to," Orwell said, "but not wise. They'll be here in a minute."

"Don't suppose there's any way I can work this, is there, Chief?"

"Work what, Detective? Hunting accident?"

She looked around at the three police cars awaiting more police cars. "Big turnout for a hunting accident," she said.

"I'll see what I can do."

"Appreciate it, sir," Stacy said.

"Dutch? Open the gate," Orwell said. "I want to talk to Dan."

"You got it, Chief."

Joe smiled at Stacy as they drove through. She smiled back. "It true she broke a biker's wrist last week?" he whispered.

"His elbow doesn't work too well either," said Orwell.

Dan Warren was coming out of the house as they pulled up. Orwell got out to shake his hand formally.

"Hiya, Dan. You know Joe Greenway, don't you?"

"Sure do. Hello."

"Morning," Joe said.

Orwell looked Dan over carefully. The man looked tired, but then he always looked tired, as if merely getting up wore him down. "Shakes you up some, doesn't it?" said Orwell. "Finding a body."

"It was a surprise, tell you that."

"Who else is home, Dan?"

"Irene, and Terry — he's still in bed I think. Didn't come down yet."

"OPP are on their way. They handle this kind of thing. I just wanted to make sure you were doing all right."

"Appreciate it, Chief. Thing is, I keep having this bad feeling that the man might still be alive and I just left him hanging there. The more I think about it, the more I think maybe I should've checked more close, but like you say, it shook me, seeing him up there."

"How far back, Dan?"

"Straight back. Just stick to the track, he's in the bowl, right at the bush."

"Okay. Joe and I will check. You wait here for the OPP and they'll probably send an ambulance. You can bring them back when they get here."

"Hope I didn't leave a wounded man just hanging there," Dan said.

Orwell got back into the Ramcharger. "Tell them I went back to render assistance if need be."

"Will do," said Dan.

"I'll probably get a reprimand," Orwell said to Joe. "Cluttering up a crime scene far outside my purview."

"I won't clutter," Joe said.

They got out at the top of the ridge. The forest began below them where the stream and beaver pond gave off a gunmetal gleam.

"Doesn't look like you'll have to render assistance," said Joe.

"I'll go take a closer look. You do whatever it is you do."

Joe Greenway went off at an angle making a wide turn across the face of the slope before heading for the bottom.

Orwell watched his step. It was steeper than it looked. His left knee had been acting up and by the time he reached the bottom of the bowl it was aching like a worrisome tooth. He looked up at the bundle in the tree. Whoever the man was, he was very dead. Big man, heavy shouldered; wearing a camo-suit of colours inappropriate to the time of year. The man's hat had fallen off and Orwell could see the beginnings of a bald spot on his crown.

Well now, Orwell thought, how'd you manage to get yourself in that position? Legs up, head down, arrows holding him like a bloody spindle.

He heard the slamming of car doors on the rim above. At the top of the slope he saw a military-looking man — creases, pleats, trimmed mustache. He was a Sergeant. Not anyone Orwell knew.

A young officer got out and stood by the open cruiser door.

"Chief Brennan?"

"Sergeant. Watch your step coming down."

Orwell looked around for Joe, spotted him a hundred yards away, quartering in from the west then gone from sight. He turned to face the uniformed cops.

"I'm Sergeant Paul Dean. That's Officer Rush. What have we got?"

"Dead man, Sergeant Dean. He's all yours."

"Got an ambulance and a couple of paramedics stuck in the mud back there." He looked up at the body. "But I guess there's no hurry."

Dean noticed Joe Greenway moving through the trees off to his right. "Who's that?"

"Friend of mine," Orwell said. "Joe Greenway. He's a tracker. I thought he might be of some help to you."

"Tell him to get back up the hill," Dean said.

"Will do, Sergeant. It's just that there's more rain coming. If there are any tracks down here they won't last long."

Dean thought about it for a moment. "Professional tracker, you say?"

"Got the best eyes in the county."

Dean gave Orwell a careful look. "You should all be heading back to Dockerty," he said. He checked to see which way Joe Greenway was headed. "Hell," he said. "You're first officer on the scene. I guess I'm stuck with you. For the moment."

Orwell stood back and watched as Dean and Rush moved closer to the tree. The bush was rank and unruly in the bottomland. Buckthorn, hackberry, scarlet hawthorn and wild apple trees were reclaiming the open ground. Dean shook his head.

"Okay, Rush, we're going to need a medical examiner, crime scene unit. See if those EMTs got their vehicle out of the ditch, that farmer's got a tractor. Tell Region they'll need 4x4s."

"Here," said Orwell, tossing Rush his keys. "That beast of mine will pull stumps."

"At least the body's still more or less fresh," said Dean. "Way back here, he might've tenderized for weeks before anybody found him."

"As you were coming in, Sergeant, there was a woman in a brown leather coat."

"I saw her," Dean said.

"Detective Stacy Crean. She's my best investigator. If you need any help . . ."

"That's okay, Chief. I think Region will want to run this one."

Orwell nodded. Well, he'd given it a shot.

"Looking to beef up her résumé?" Dean inquired.

"Her résumé's pretty impressive as it is. I'm just trying to hang onto her."

Dean said, "Well, if that thing that nobody's talking about happens, she won't have trouble finding a job."

"If that thing that no one's talking about happens, Sergeant Dean, it'll be over my inert carcass."

Dean was staring up at the man in the tree. "Be careful what you wish for," he said.

"Look like a hunting accident to you, Sergeant?" Orwell asked him.

Dean turned to look at him. "Once in the belly, maybe. Twice in the belly, that's pretty good shooting."

Joe was standing quiet and still. This was where the shooter stood. Under this tree, facing that way, waiting. Joe felt rather than heard Orwell coming up behind him.

"Stood here," Joe said. "Wood chips on the ground. Looks like he cut off a branch to get a clear shot. Took a few steps out into the open, stood there, probably took the second shot from there, then went around that way, back into the swamp."

"Big feet, small feet?" Orwell asked. "Male, female?"

"Could be either. No clear prints so far. Thick grass, everything's wet. There's a little bridge across the stream over that way.

Might have left some prints on the other side." He looked up at the wooded hillside rising beyond the beaver pond. "Big bush," Joe said. "This is only part of it. That stream runs into the Snipe. A couple roads cross it but it's all one piece mostly. Back that way too." He looked across the clearing to the dark shape in the poplar tree.

Orwell leaned his head to the sight line. "Sergeant Dean thinks it was pretty good shooting," he said.

Joe nodded. "But the second shot wasn't strictly necessary, was it?" he said. "The second one was pure hate."

OCTOBER — Five Years Ago

Terry Warren wasn't in Oshawa on the day the Securex truck was robbed. It had happened on a Thursday morning. Terry was in his woods, in his most secret place, the place where he kept his treasures, in a cave that could not be found, under a tree that was indistinguishable, through a door that didn't exist. Pencil shafts of illumination entered through a thousand pinhole skylights. Terry was curled inside the third room, the room where he kept Trina's clothes — the duffel coat, and three pairs of her underpants that he stole from her suitcase one Christmas at the farm, a jacket she had forgotten in some man's car one motel visit, and the shoes she had left behind in her own car one snowy day after changing into boots for a walk in the park with another man, the one who had the dog.

Terry was wrapping his treasures inside plastic bags to keep them safe for the winter. He heard the sound of an engine coming up the far hill from the direction of County Road 17, coming up the logging road. When the pickup stopped, he heard doors slam and raised voices. Terry squeezed himself out through one of his wormholes and hid himself inside a thicket.

His brother Billy got out from behind the wheel and staggered as if his legs were weak. Terry recognized his passenger. It was Bull

Hollyer. He was married to Trina's sister, Beverly. Bull was built like his name, thick neck, heavy shoulders, skinny hips. He had a full beard and his hair was long in back, thinning on top. Two other men were coming up the hill on foot. He heard Bull call out one of their names. "Hey, Jer, you believe it, man!? Do you fucking be-lieve it?" Bull was so high on what they had just done that he kept pumping his fist in the air and silently screaming *ahhhh* over and over, compressed air, like a death rattle, the only sound escaping his throat. Billy was shaking. He sat on a log with his elbows between his knees and his hands clasping his ankles above his boots and his heels were drumming in time to his accelerated heartbeat.

The man called Jer was heavyset, clean-shaven, dressed in a black track suit. The fourth man had a red beard. Terry didn't catch his name. Between them they were carrying a big athletic bag that sagged with weight. The red bearded man didn't stick around. After a few private words with Jer he departed on foot down the logging road. From the ridge, Terry caught a glimpse of a red Pontiac as it headed back in the direction of Highway 35.

The three who remained were behaving as though they planned to stay awhile. Locating a bottle, rolling dope, lighting cigars. Terry moved closer, a shadow on the hillside. He could smell the smoke; he thought he could smell his brother's sweat.

"Did it. Did it. Did it." Billy repeated it over and over.

"Want to count it?" Jer asked.

"Fuck yeah," said Bull. "Fuckin' A! Let's do some arithmetic."

Jer zipped open the bag. Terry could see it was filled with money.

"Holy shit!" said Bull, "Jeezus!"

"Gotta be two in there. At least two," Jer said.

"This'll take a while," Bull said. "We gonna have enough light?"

"We've got lights," Billy said.

"How you doin', big guy?" Jer said. "You okay?"

"I never thought we'd get away with it."

"Fuck!" Jer said. "I told you. You plan something right down to the last detail and you can get away with anything. Anything."

Terry watched them count out the money on the tailgate of Billy's truck. It took an hour. Two million, three hundred and fifty thousand dollars, all in cash. They put the cash into double green garbage bags wrapped tightly with duct tape around and around in both directions, stuffed that parcel back into the athletic bag, and wrapped two more garbage bags around the outside. More duct tape. They took a shovel from the truck and carried the loot further into the woods, over the first ridge and halfway up the second rise where they dug a hole under a cut bank and buried the money deep in the dark soil, forcing the bag between thick maple roots, filling the hole with dirt, rolling a heavy rock over the freshly turned earth, scattering leaves and dragging dead branches and camouflaging the hiding place until they were satisfied that no one could see that the forest floor had been disturbed.

And all the while that this was going on, Terry haunted them like a will-o'-the-wisp, moving from shadow to shadow, anticipating their destination and arriving before them, above them, always above them, like a bird of prey. Invisible.

The three men backed away from the place where they had stashed the money. They stood off, studying the place, making certain it was well hidden, making sure of the site, marking trees and rocks for the future. Terry smiled to himself that they would have to make such a big deal of the location when any fool could spot the mess they'd made from a mile away.

Back at the truck, Bull smoked a big joint of homegrown and Jer drank from a bottle of vodka and Billy had a drink and a toke and gradually began to relax and smile and take deep breaths. "Two point three-five," he said. "Two point three-fucking-five million dollars."

"Okay," Jer said, finally, "there it stays. I don't care what happens, it stays there, un-fucking-touched for five years from today." He looked at the other two. "Swear it. Five years. No matter what."

"No problemo," said Bull. He took a belt of vodka and proceeded to roll himself another doob. "Money in the bank."

"No new cars, no new toys, no quitting our jobs, no nothing. Anybody spends a nickel more than they usually do, anybody starts attracting attention, anybody screws this up . . ." Jer aimed his finger like a pistol at Billy and Bull.

"You electing yourself judge and jury there, Jer?" Bull's voice turned flat, his eyes narrowed. "'Cause I got a finger too." He pointed at Jer's chest and grinned.

"I'm just saying," Jer said, "we stick our heads up and the cops will be all over us."

"We pretend it isn't there for five years," Billy said.

"Fuck, I forgot about it already," Bull said, and started laughing. "I don't know what you're talking about."

"I can wait," Billy said.

"Good," said Jer. "Just so we're agreed."

And Terry, still above them, in one of his favourite places, under a log, half buried in dead leaves, could see them getting ready to leave, starting the truck, backing slowly down the logging road, and if he turned his head he could look behind him and see the place on the other hillside where the hiding place stood out to him like a scab on a woman's cheek. Terry had a much better place to hide all that money.

Four

Once or twice a week Chief Orwell Brennan took his lunch at the Kawartha Kountry Kitchen so that he could finish up with a slice of their excellent pie. Orwell was a connoisseur of pie and deemed it the pinnacle of baking. Today the banana cream looked especially good. Joe Greenway sat across from him, drinking black coffee and looking at a sheet of paper.

"Hot off the wire," said Orwell. "Interservice solidarity at its most inclusive."

Joe read aloud but not loudly. "Kramer, Jerome W., 'Jerry.' b. 1965. 21 Boxter Crescent, Haldane, Ontario." He looked up. "That's it?"

Orwell drained his glass and wiped the milk mustache from his upper lip. He said, without rancour, "I am not exactly 'in the loop,' as it turns out, although I will be 'shown all appropriate professional courtesy, including regular upgrades of my informational package.'"

"That's nice."

"One of the paramedics said he'd been up there for a while; probably happened last night."

"OPP's case?"

"Region thought it was theirs. But now, much to their chagrin, Metro Homicide has decided the case warrants an intervention."

"They think it's a murder?"

"They do, indeed."

Orwell munched his sandwich and looked out at the traffic on Vankleek Street, Dockerty's main thoroughfare. The air was wet, the street was shining.

"What do you know about deer hunting, Orwell?"

"Bugger all."

"With a bow and arrow?"

"Less than bugger all."

"Right." Joe handed back the paper. "Bowhunters are invisible. They wait in ambush for hours to let off one clean shot. I know a guy who doesn't bother shooting anymore, he just likes to get close enough to slap a big buck on the ass and watch him jump."

"That's invisible," said Orwell.

"Have to know which highway the deer are using, when they're moving, and then be waiting for them."

"Which is where the victim was," said Orwell, "hidden up a tree, ready to kill something at a moment's notice." He rubbed his big hand across his sparsely thatched dome. "Except, he's the one who gets shot." He shook his head. "You'd think whoever did it would have to be a bowhunter as well."

"The guy knew exactly what he was shooting at. Those two arrows were less than a thumb's width apart."

Orwell checked his watch. "I've got to welcome the Metro contingent and give them official permission to take over the investigation, not that I have any say in the matter."

"Will they be upgrading your informational package?"

"Nope."

"So what am I doing here?"

"I am indulging myself," Orwell said. "First murder in these parts in who knows how long. Everyone will be speculating. Why not me? Am I not entitled?" Orwell finished his sandwich and signaled for his banana cream pie and coffee.

"Your wife says two cups, Chief," Ethel said from behind the counter.

"This isn't the only place in town that sells coffee you know, Ethel." He looked back at Joe. "So," he said, wiping his fork, "Kramer, Jerome W., shows up Saturday, finds himself a tree and sets up. It's not his first time in the bush."

"He'd done it before."

Ethel arrived with the coffee pot and Orwell's dessert.

"There's a Country Style a block away gives me good coffee," said Orwell. "And none of them know my wife."

Ethel refilled Joe's cup. "But I *do* know your wife," she said. "And she isn't a woman to mess around with. If she says two cups, I pay attention."

Orwell adjusted his pie so that it pointed directly at his heart. "A fine slice of pie demands a cup of coffee, wouldn't you say?"

"Just don't tell her where you got it," said Ethel.

Joe shook his head in something like admiration. "Got close enough for a clear shot at his belly. That's stalking. Kramer's armed too, remember. Not like hunting rabbits."

"Kramer would've shot first if he'd seen the guy?" Orwell wondered

"Could have. Don't know if he would have," Joe said. "But he's got a wide field of fire. Alert for anything moving. Whoever shot him would have to be real good to get that close."

"Two guys out there with bows and arrows. Some kind of duel?"

"Except Kramer was hunting deer," said Joe. "The other guy was hunting Kramer."

As they left the Kountry Kitchen Joe stopped in the doorway to roll a smoke. The rain was thin and sharp and Orwell turned his collar up against the wind. He wouldn't have minded a cigarette himself, but he'd promised Erika many things recently — healthier eating, no tobacco — and for the most part he was living up to them. He did give in to an occasional illicit puff, an occasional slice of pie; he wasn't quite ready for sainthood yet.

"Something I can't figure," Joe said.

"What's that?"

"Deer hunting's illegal after dark. That Kramer guy could try for one before sundown, I suppose, he could try just after sunup, but why spend the whole night?"

"Outdoorsy type like that, maybe he was going to roll into a sleeping bag for a few hours."

Joe lit his smoke. Orwell sighed as the plume drifted by his nose. They started back toward the police building.

"Who's driving me back to my place?" Joe wanted to know. "You sending me home in a cruiser?"

"I'll run you back," Orwell said. "Probably a good idea for me to keep a low profile for the afternoon."

Easier said than done. The Chief enjoyed a high civic visibility. He was easy to spot. He took up a lot of sidewalk.

"Good afternoon, Chief," said Clara Rewald, outside her flower shop.

"Hi, Clara," Orwell said.

"I'm doing the wreath for the Groton funeral tomorrow."

"Splendid," he said. "You'll do the man proud."

"I'm trying," she said. "They do hate to spend money."

"Hey, Chief." Sam Abrams, managing editor of the *Dockerty Register* was in the middle of the street. He was shaggy and portly and surprisingly graceful as he dodged traffic and caught up with them.

"You know how I frown upon jaywalking, Sam," said Orwell.

"OPP says I should talk to you, they're too busy canvassing the countryside looking for a cold-blooded killer."

"As far as I know, Sam, the Dockerty force will not be involved in the investigation except if called upon, and so far we haven't been called upon."

"At least you can confirm that somebody was killed out in Breithaupt's Bush, right?"

"Copy this down," Orwell said, handing Sam the piece of

paper. "Better yet, keep it. I'm sure I can get another copy when they upgrade my informational package."

"Anything else you can give me?" Sam asked.

"Let's see, yes, I'm expecting someone from Metro Homicide to show up and take charge of the investigation."

"That'll pee off the OPP."

"I'm sure they'll all co-operate," said Orwell. "See you later Sam."

"You know that's the second murder in that bush," Sam called after him.

"Really?" Orwell stopped. "When was this?"

"Hundred years ago." Sam chuckled. "Maybe more."

"Donna Lee can't lay that one on my doorstep," Orwell muttered to Joe. "You ever hear that? Another murder?"

"Oh yeah, ancient lore around here," Joe said. "Lost in the mists of time, as they say."

"Just as well. OPP would no doubt tell me to keep my nose out of that one too."

Sergeant Dean was waiting at the entrance. Now that's what a cop should look like, Orwell thought. That's a first-class shine on those shoes. Pretty good considering he just got back from the swamp.

"Hi, Chief." He turned to Joe. "Mr. Greenway?"

"Joe."

"Joe. Hi." They shook hands. "Not sure we would have found the stuff you did, where the shooter was hiding, and where he came from." He looked at Orwell. "The Chief here tells me you're the best tracker around."

"Wouldn't go that far. If you need a real Hawkeye talk to Willie Peete over on Scugog," Joe said. "He's Mississauga. Track a fox through a dog show."

"Willie's up in Bancroft, after moose," said Orwell.

"Well, you probably shouldn't have been there," Dean said,

"but I'm glad you were, in a way. It took two hours to get the man out of the tree. Those arrowheads were buried in the wood; shafts had to be unscrewed before we could get him down. With the ladder and everything, the crime scene got a bit torn up."

"I can go back there with you," Joe said. "Show you what I saw."

"I was thinking, maybe you, me and my partner, before we get an army out there messing up all the sign, we could have a quiet look-see."

"Makes sense," said Joe. "Whoever did it either came straight in from the farmhouse, the way we did . . ."

"Not if he didn't want to be seen," Dean said.

". . . or he came up from 17. Through the bush."

"There's a logging road into the bush on that side." Orwell threw in. He looked hopeful for a moment, but no invitation to join the search party was forthcoming.

Just as well, Orwell thought, who wants to stomp through wet woods when he can deal with paperwork and fiddle-faddle? Roy Rawluck was waiting for him with barely concealed impatience. Orwell was sure the man was tapping his foot under his desk. "You may call off the search party Staff Sergeant, for I have returned," Orwell announced.

"Yes, Chief," he said. "Duly noted." Rawluck had the bad grace to sneak a look at his watch.

"Any luck finding somebody who'll go to bat for us?"

"I think we have the Downtown Business Association."

"That sounds impressive."

"They like the foot patrols, Chief."

"Who's the president over there?"

"Dinwoodie. Chrysler dealer."

"I'll have a chat with Mr. Dinwoodie. First name? Carl, isn't it?"

"Clare," said Dorrie.

"Clare. Right. Good. Okay. It's a start. A good start. Keep thinking."

"OPP likely to be hanging around for a while, Chief?" Roy wanted to know.

"Could be, Roy. Why don't you see if you can organize a better space for them? They might want a map, too."

"I'll take care of it, Chief."

"I know you will, Roy."

Sergeant Rawluck went off to organize the office and set up a command headquarters. He was already thinking about a hotline into the station.

"Chief?"

"Yes, Dorrie."

"Newspapers and TV are starting to call. You think we should put together a statement?"

"Let Sergeant Dean handle it. OPP's in charge of the investigation."

"He wondered if you'd be good enough to handle the press today. You know, the regular stuff, nothing to report, investigation is proceeding, like that."

"Oh, I can do that well enough. Since I know virtually nothing, I'd say I'm the ideal man for the job. Tell them to contact Sam Abrams at the *Register*. He's got all the details. Anything else?"

"Metro Homicide is here."

There was a tall, rangy woman, standing in his office. Square shoulders, long skull, short, unflattering hair. Well now, Orwell thought, and who are you?

"Detective Adele Moen," she said. "Metro Homicide."

Orwell shook her hand. It was almost as big as his. "Orwell Brennan," he said. "Pleased to meet you. You made good time."

"Happy to get out of the city," she said. "Raining worse down there."

"For a change. You on your own, Detective?"

"My partner is in the hospital. Idiot broke his leg. He says chasing a purse snatcher." She looked for a moment as if she'd like to smack someone. "He'll be out two months. Stupid bastard."

"Sorry to hear that."

She looked at the big aerial map of Dockerty on the Chief's wall. "Where'd this thing happen?"

Orwell pointed to the Warren parcel on Road 18. "North end of this big bush. Right around here."

"That's outside the town limits, isn't it?" she asked him.

"Just," he said.

"So how do you happen to be there?"

Orwell pointed to his own farm on the other side of River Road. "That's my place. Dan's my neighbour. He called me personally."

She turned from the map. "I guess we'll all have to get along, won't we? Durham Region wants a piece because the vic comes from Haldane, OPP says it's theirs, and I'm the trump card supposed to keep us all on the same page."

"Any help we can give," Orwell said with a generous gesture toward the outer office. "Just say the word. You need a command post, extra bodies, whatever."

"Any chance it's some kind of hunting accident and I can wrap it up?"

"Not my field of expertise, Detective, but from what little I know, it looks deliberate."

"What the hell. Be a change from the usual gang-bangers and wife beaters."

"I can pretty much guarantee it will be a change," he said. "Sergeant Dean has a small search party out there. Trying to find out where the shooter came from."

"That's a lot of ground to cover," she said. "Okay, I have to interview the family and look at the crime scene. I'll need somebody to show me the way."

Orwell tried not to grin. "Why, under the circumstances, Detective, and in the spirit of interservice collaboration, it would be my pleasure to escort you personally."

Orwell savoured the faint clucking he heard as he began his second unscheduled excursion of the day.

"There's a logging road along here somewhere," Joe said. "It's coming up soon. Right there."

Dean pulled the cruiser off to the south side of the road and the three got out.

"Let's see if anybody parked along here," said Dean.

Dean headed west, Rush went the other way. A blue jay gave them hell and a crow took up the alarm from a tree near the top of the hill. Joe pulled out his tobacco and surveyed the entrance to the logging road. He rolled a smoke with two flicks of his fingers, pinched off the excess and returned it to the pouch. The rain had backed off but the wind was picking up. He stood by the back door of the cruiser, smoking and looking up at the hillside.

"Over here." Dean was waving from up the road. Rush headed toward him. Joe pinched the coal off his cigarette and put the butt into his pocket.

"We'd better get a team out here," said Dean. "Get an impression of these before it rains again."

Joe crouched behind Dean and looked over his shoulder at the clear tire marks in the wet ground. "Somebody parked here a while," said Joe.

"Twice," said Dean. "Double sets of prints."

"A frequent visitor."

"Not a big car." Dean was using his hand span to take rough measurements. "You can see wheelbase, tread size. Michelins I bet. Probably an import. Honda, Toyota, something like that."

"That's pretty good," said Joe.

"Shit," said Dean. "Tire tracks are my life." He stood up, brushing his hands together. "Rush, you want to get on to Region, let them know what we need. And you better rope this off, mark our footprints."

"On it," Rush said and went to the cruiser to call in.

"Stick around 'til they get here. Joe and I are going to have a look in the bush." Dean looked at the wall of trees on the other side of the ditch. "Got any idea where he headed in?"

Joe straightened up. "Somebody went up the logging road. At least for part of the way. You can see the prints from here. They were in a hurry, slipped three or four times."

"Lead the way," said Dean.

"Use the running board," said the Chief.

"Oh yeah," Adele said. "This thing's as tall as a semi."

"Just about," said Orwell. "Got the aerodynamics of a billboard, but it'll go through anything."

"I guess you need something like this out in the country."

"It's an affectation," Orwell admitted. "I drive it to discomfit my Staff Sergeant."

"The one with the handlebars?"

"He thinks it's inappropriate transportation for a man in my position."

"It's a dinosaur."

"Yeah, but it'll get us to the crime scene," he said. "Lots of mud back there." He detected a sigh from the passenger seat.

The blue Camaro was still at the Warren's gate. A uniformed OPP officer was standing guard. Detective Moen climbed out and had a look at the Chevy.

She flipped her gold shield for the uniform's benefit. "We got the trunk key?" she asked.

"All that stuff was on the body, Detective," said the uniform. "They're bringing it back as soon as they do whatever it is they're going to do."

"Yeah, well get on the horn and tell whoever took him away to wherever they took him . . ."

"Lindsay, most likely," Orwell said.

"Tell them not to do anything until I get there. I want a look at the vic and his clothes and anything else he had with him, and I want it all in the same place so I don't have to chase it all over hell's half-acre."

"You're taking charge of the case, Detective?" asked the uniform.

"As of this minute," she said.

Orwell noted that he didn't have to shorten his stride as they walked through the gate.

Five

"Looks like somebody spent some time here," said Joe Greenway.

They were inside the forest, high on the slope; trees all around them, a whispering canopy above their heads.

"Found himself a little hideout behind this big stump and stayed for a while." Joe crouched by the spot. "Sat here, dug his heels in here." Joe pulled out a lock-back knife and snapped it open. He lifted a few leaves carefully, one at a time. "These were put here on purpose. This one is upside down, curled the wrong way." He turned the last leaf over with the blade of his knife to reveal a patch of brushed earth. "Ashtray," said Joe. He dug the blade into the dirt and turned up three cigarette butts and some ash.

Dean pulled a Ziploc baggie out of his back pocket and picked up the cigarette butts with his hand inside the plastic.

"Three smokes," said Joe. "If this is our guy, he must've known where Kramer was going to be."

"Or that Kramer wouldn't show up for a while," said Dean. "One smoke every twenty minutes you think?"

Joe looked at the butts again. "He wasn't sucking on them. They're not squished in. Round butts."

Dean said, "Even smoking fast he's here half an hour. He charges up the hill like he's late for work, then he has time to take a long break."

"Maybe the break was important," said Joe. "Get his breathing back to normal after that long climb. Get his mind right for what he was going to do." Joe stood up. "He dropped something over there." He pointed to a gleam of steel in the leaves at the bottom of a shallow crater formed by the decomposition of a huge first-growth hemlock stump.

"Bust him for littering," said Dean.

Joe lowered himself carefully into the depression and crouched on his heels. Dean handed down a fresh baggie and Joe picked up the piece of steel. It was a blade, like a small, triangular razor. He handed the bag up to Dean.

"This's from an arrow, right?"

"Replaceable broadhead blade," said Joe. "Puts the weapon in his hands, doesn't it?"

"If there's a fingerprint on this thing, he's toast," Dean said.

Joe accepted Dean's hand to haul him out of the depression. The ridge they were on was the highest point in the bush; long slopes fell away in both directions.

"Odd forest," Joe said.

"How so?"

"It's . . . tidy. Look at that pile of slash down there. The butt ends are lined up. Somebody's looking after this section."

"Should make our job easier," said Dean.

But after that they found no more sign.

"I kind of wondered what that fella was doing back there all this time." Dan Warren was sitting at his kitchen table across from Detective Moen. Irene was in the front room. Terry Warren was sitting against the wall, hemmed in by the kitchen table. The two Warren men had empty cups in front of them. Adele Moen had taken the chair on the other side of the table. She had her notebook open and her notes were neatly printed. Orwell could almost read them from where he leaned against the sink.

"When did this guy show up? Yesterday?" she asked.

"No, ma'am, day before. Saturday afternoon." Dan said. "Around three. I'd just come in the gate with the truck and he was pretty near right behind me."

"What'd he say to you?"

"Said, 'Hi, howareya.' Asked did I remember him from last year."

"He was here last year?"

"Yes, ma'am. I remembered him more or less. He was just here that one time before."

"You never used to let hunters on your land, did you, Dan?" Orwell said.

"That's right," said Dan. "My dad didn't like strangers on the place. Didn't trust them."

"How did you come to give this Kramer hunting privileges?" Adele wanted to know.

"I suppose I sort of remembered him. You remember him from last year, Terry?"

Terry shrugged. "The guy last year had a moustache. And a ponytail."

"That's right," Dan said. "There were two of them last year. This guy and a man with a mustache."

"Did you know the man with the moustache?"

"Nope. I didn't see them come in last year. I just saw them go out. Terry let them in last year."

"Did you know them, Terry?"

Terry shook his head. "Just a couple of guys from the city," he said. "Mum and Dad were over to the co-op. I thought they'd already talked to them."

She finished a page of notes and flipped to a fresh one. She numbered her pages.

"Okay, so the dead man was here last year with another man. You remember the other man's name?"

Dan shook his head. "Never heard it."

"Terry? You know the name of the other man?" Terry shook his head, pouted his lower lip. Adele lifted her head to look directly at him. He didn't flinch. Neither did she. "Did Kramer say anything about meeting up with his friend?"

"No, ma'am," Dan said. "Said he was flying solo this year. Those were his words, just come back to me. 'Flying solo.' I didn't put two and two together right away. I thought for a minute he meant he was separated from his wife or something."

Terry got up from the table abruptly and went into the living room, stood by the window. It was probably a trick of the light, but for an instant Orwell thought Terry had vapourized into the lace curtain.

Adele printed "flying solo" with neat little quotation marks, a 66 and a 99. "He's flying solo this time. Not expecting to meet up with his friend. Nobody showed up later, looking for him? The guy with the moustache maybe, or somebody else?"

"No, ma'am," Dan said. "He parked his car and changed into one of those hunting suits and headed back toward the bush by himself."

"What time of day was this?"

"By the time he got geared up and ready? Maybe half an hour after he got here. Say 5:30 maybe. Getting dark."

"Kind of late to be heading back to the bush."

"Joe Greenway says he might've tried for a buck before dark or wanted to be there this morning when the deer came down to the water," said Orwell. "He can't figure why Kramer wanted to spend all night in a tree."

"Long night," she agreed. "You didn't see him come back out did you, Mr. Warren? Come out and drive off to a motel or something? Maybe come back early this morning?"

"That car hasn't moved for three days," Irene said from the front room. "He parked right on top of my pansies and he never got off them."

"Okay now," Adele said, "he shows up Saturday afternoon and you didn't see him at all yesterday, Sunday. Didn't anybody wonder where he'd got to?"

"Terry was going to have a look for him when he was out there with the tractor."

"Terry? Yesterday? You didn't see him?"

Terry came back from the front room and stood in the doorway to the kitchen. Orwell was struck by how adult and physical he looked. Always considered him 'the kid brother,' Orwell thought, and there he is, man grown and just a bit threatening, taking up most of the doorway, long arms, big shoulders.

"I didn't work the fields yesterday," Terry said. "I drove out there but the tractor broke down so I parked it and walked back. Drove into town to get a part."

"What time did you get back?"

"When?" Terry said.

"You say you drove into town to get a part."

"It was just a coupling," Terry said.

"Would you mind sitting down, sir," Adele said. It wasn't really a request. "I don't like having to swivel my head."

Terry squeezed behind his father and resumed his seat. His face was expressionless.

"Okay," Adele said, "what time did you get back?"

"Dinner time."

"Fix the coupling?"

"Canadian Tire didn't have the right part."

"So you just left it."

"I was going to fix it today."

"That spreader's got to get back to my neighbour today," Dan said.

"He may have to wait," Adele said. "Terry? You stay in last night?"

"Watched TV, went to bed."

Irene was at the front window. "There's a tow truck here," she said. "Be happy to see that car gone."

"Was Billy here over the weekend?" Orwell asked.

"Who is Billy?" Adele.

"My older boy, William."

"Right." She made a note. "Was he around here over the weekend?"

"Not since before Labour Day."

"He lives here?"

"Oshawa. Works at The Motors."

"That would be General Motors?"

"Ayeah. That's what most of them call it, The Motors. He's been there near nine years I guess."

"He still working full shifts?" Orwell asked.

"He's lucky," said Dan. "They're haven't stopped building Camaros."

"That's good."

"What does your son do down there?" Adele wanted to know.

"Production line," Terry said. "Installs electrical components."

"Did he know Mr. Kramer?"

"I wouldn't know," Dan said. "I don't know many of his friends since he moved away. He doesn't come up here much."

"Terry, do you know if your brother knew Jerome Kramer?"

"He never said."

"And you never saw them together?"

"No."

"Unh-hunh. How about the other one, the man with the moustache and the ponytail? You ever see your brother and that man together?"

"Nope. Not him either."

"That's interesting," she said. "As far as you know, this man, Jerome Kramer, and the friend he hunted with the previous year, were complete strangers to everyone here and yet you gave them permission to hunt on your property."

"Well, ma'am, truth be told, he gave me a hundred dollars for the privilege," Dan said.

"Oh, now that makes a bit more sense," Adele said, jotting the figure in her notebook. "Same thing last year? A hundred dollars?"

"Yes, ma'am."

"Cash?"

"Yep. He had a good roll in his pocket."

She checked her notes two pages back. "Last year . . . you weren't here when Mr. Kramer and the unidentified man with the moustache and ponytail showed up, and I have it that you, Terry, let them in. Is that right?"

"Yes."

"Did he give you the hundred dollars, Terry?"

"He gave it to my dad when they were leaving."

"Did he say he was going to do it that way?"

"I don't remember," Terry said. "He might've, I thought it had been arranged or something."

"Had it been arranged, Mr. Warren?"

"No, as I recall, I was kinda surprised that they'd been back there, those two men. They were already on their way out, wasn't much I could do about it then."

"That's when he gave you the hundred dollars?"

"Ayeah. Said, 'Here's a little something for the hunting privilege,' or something like that."

"Do you remember what kind of car they were driving?"

"Not exactly. Don't believe it was that bright blue Chevy. I think I would've remembered that colour. I think it was more dark, like a pickup or a 4x4 or something."

"And did Jerome Kramer give you the hundred dollars the first time, or was it the other man?"

"No, it was the first guy, Kramer. The other man didn't want to talk. Got in his Jeep, that's what it was, one of those Cherokees, and said, 'Let's go, let's go.'"

"He was in a hurry you say?"

"I guess, but Kramer seemed friendly enough. Said it was a nice bush. Didn't get lucky, but it was worth a hundred dollars anyway."

"Same big bank roll this year?"

"Can't recall. First time was a hundred-dollar bill. I remember that."

"And this year? Hundred-dollar bill?"

"No, five twenties this time."

Adele wrote it all down. "Okay then," she said at last, "but you should've mentioned the money right off."

"Well . . ."

"I'm not the taxman, Mr. Warren. It's your land, your business what you do with it. I'm only interested in who shot the man."

"Well, ma'am, wasn't anybody here. I would've been happy to keep taking his money any time he wanted to hunt back there."

"I'm sure that's true, sir, but men who carry big bankrolls are tempting targets."

"I suppose," Dan said. "Wasn't the kind of man I'd go looking for trouble with, if you know what I mean."

"Somebody did." Adele closed her notebook. "I'll probably have some other questions later. And if you remember anything else you'll give us a call, won't you? Or call Chief Brennan if that feels more comfortable."

Adele handed Dan a card and placed another one deliberately in front of Terry. Dan turned his over to see if there was anything on the back.

Terry went to the parlour window to watch the departure of the Chief and the woman from Toronto. He replayed the conversation in his head, checking for things he might have let slip. There was nothing.

Adele was at the front gate engaged in what looked like a contentious discussion with the tow truck driver and the OPP officer as Orwell took his leave of Dan on the front porch.

"Appreciate you coming out, Chief. Makes it easier, knowing a familiar face."

"Be a lot of strangers around the next few days, Dan. Can't be helped," Orwell said. "Sooner we catch who did it, the sooner it'll quiet down."

"Hope so. It's hard on the wife; you know how it is."

Adele had evidently got her point across regarding the ultimate destination of Kramer's vehicle and was climbing into the Ramcharger.

"I s'pose it'll make the papers."

"It'll blow over, Dan. These things do."

"No, they don't, Chief. People just stop talking out loud. It'll still be there."

Adele Moen was checking her notes. "What's with that kid?" she said as Orwell got behind the wheel.

"Terry? Well, he's not a kid," Orwell said. "Got to be twenty-eight, twenty-nine."

"Still living at home."

"That's not uncommon," he said. He shifted into four-wheel drive and headed down the muddy incline behind the barn and up the rutted curve into the first field. "He's probably in line to take over the farm."

"Not married?"

"No."

She scrutinized the stubble going by as if for answers to questions she hadn't yet thought of. "He's younger than the auto worker one?"

"Billy's about three years older."

"He's a little odd don't you think?"

"Terry? I get the feeling he's a watcher," said Orwell.

"And trying not to look like he's watching," she said. "He knows more than he's saying. I think they all do, but mostly him. He knew that guy in the tree. I'd bet money on it. I'll get back to him after I talk to the widow."

They got out at the top of the ridge and looked down into the bowl.

"Where was the body?" she asked.

"That big poplar," said Orwell. "Watch your step going down. It's steep."

"Shit! Am I wearing the wrong shoes or what?" She put a hand on his shoulder as they made their way down the slope. He hoped his trick knee wouldn't decide to give out and embarrass them both. A perimeter of yellow crime scene tape was pegged from the poplar to the apple tree. They stepped over it. There was blood down the trunk from the shooting perch to the grass.

"How high up is that you figure? That seat thing? Twelve feet?"

"About that," Orwell said. "Dean probably measured."

"How is he?" she asked. "The Sergeant."

"Hasn't put a foot wrong so far, except for not reaming me out for sticking my nose in his crime scene, for which I was grateful."

"I don't like all this jurisdictional shit," she said. "I can work with OPP, Mounties, Durham . . ."

"Nosy, small-town police chiefs."

"Them too," she said. "As long as everyone knows who's in charge." She watched where she put her feet as she began exploring the ground. "You had a tracker looking around?"

"He should be back there with Dean," Orwell said. He called out. "Sergeant Dean! Joe!"

An answering call came from inside the bush. "Yo! We're coming down."

Orwell joined Adele near the apple tree.

"Joe says the shooter fired from right here, then took a couple of steps out to there and shot again."

"That's one serious fucking murderer," she said.

"Have to be."

"I mean serious premeditation." She took a few steps closer to the poplar, looking up at the blood smear high off the ground. "Shoot him once, claim hunting accident, probably get away with it." She raised her arms in an approximation of an archer's stance, hands pointed at the blood. "Twice? You *know* you're doing murder. You *want* to do murder."

"There they are," Orwell said.

Joe and Sergeant Dean were approaching the tree from the direction of the stream.

"Introduce me," she said.

"Detective Adele Moen, Metro Homicide, this is Sergeant Paul Dean, OPP, and that's Joe Greenway."

"Hi," said Sergeant Dean.

"Wish you hadn't taken the body down before I got here," she said.

"Didn't know you were coming," Dean said. "Region was supposed to be handling."

"Yeah, well, I've got it now. That's okay. You can work this end of things. I'll handle the rest. You got lots of pictures?"

"Oh yeah."

"See anything up there?" Orwell asked Joe.

Joe said, "Strangest bush I've ever been in."

"How so?"

"It's very tidy."

"Found these," Dean said. "Got a blade from a hunting arrow, and three cigarette butts. And we've got tire prints from the road."

"County Road 17," Orwell said to Adele. "Runs parallel. It's on the far side of those ridges."

She looked up at the dark forest rising. "That's it?" she said.

"And some boot prints," said Dean. "Like he said, it's a neat and tidy bush."

"Like somebody swept the crime scene?"

"More like Zen gardeners live in there," Joe said.

"Okay, let's see if we get anything off that stuff. Still, no way to pin down when it was put there, when the car was parked."

Joe said, "Prints were put down after the last rain, same with the tire tracks."

"Yeah," she said, "but at the time of the murder? The morning before? The day after? If there's a print on that blade thingy it might help. But it's not much."

"Could be DNA on the cigarette butts," Dean said.

"First we need a suspect," she said. "Then, if we can place them in that bush, if we can put any of that stuff in their hands, maybe we can *almost* connect them to the murder weapon." She shook her head. "Not much."

"You still have men working 17, Sergeant? Give you a lift back," Orwell said.

"I'll go back to the station with you, Chief," Dean said.

"Joe?"

"Maggie," Joe said.

"I hear you."

The four of them headed up the hill to the Ramcharger. Orwell lagged behind, favouring his knee.

"Somebody must've seen something," Adele said when they got to the top. "Small town, farming community, everybody knows everybody, everything going on. You notice an unfamiliar car going up your road, you notice strangers in town."

"I've got two teams out canvassing," Dean said.

Orwell climbed behind the wheel. "Fewer than thirty thousand souls in Dockerty, plus the rurals from about six hundred square klicks, plus the thousand or so cottagers and hunters and boaters and fisher folk and long-haul truckers and antique pickers and travelling salesmen who pass through most weekends. A stranger with evil intent is bound to stick out like a sore thumb." He beamed cheerfully at Moen and started the engine.

When they reached the gate Terry was holding it wide. Adele looked over her shoulder to watch him close it.

"Mr. Greenway?" she said.

"Joe."

"Joe. You know that kid, Terry?"

"Never had much to do with him," he said

Adele checked Terry's reflection in the side mirror. "That place where the body was hanging," she began. "Kind of remote, wouldn't you say?"

"It's back there," said Joe.

"Person would really have to know where they were going, wouldn't you say?"

"Definitely," Joe said.

"Maybe we don't need to worry about all the long-haul truckers and antique hunters," she said. "What do you think, Chief?"

Six

Terry cut across the fields behind the barn, moving like a shadow along a snake fence and a windrow thick with wild apples and buckthorn. The searchers hadn't been back there very long, most likely hadn't found anything, but he needed to see for himself. Downstream of the beaver dam he melted into the underbrush. There might be cops coming up the logging road from 17.

Along the eastern perimeter of the bush, where it ended and gave way to a pair of long-neglected fields, a thickly wooded ridge bent southward like the top tier of a vast stadium, curving high above the forest floor. Here and there, where first-growth hemlocks had been felled in ages past, thick hedges had sprung from the roots and there were good hiding places on the ridge and a wide view of the forest now that the trees were bare. Terry knew how to reach his vantage spots in ways no policeman on earth could find.

There were cops still down there. He could hear them calling back and forth, laughing. They weren't coming into the bush. He lay in wait, watching, waiting for them to leave. He'd been in almost the same spot last year when Bull got out of jail.

One year ago. Almost exactly.

He'd heard Bull Hollyer's voice before he saw him. And then the voice of Terry's brother, not as loud, placating, telling Bull to keep it down. They'd come up the logging road in Billy's new, black GMC Sierra.

Bull looked thinner than before he went to jail. His beard was streaked with grey and his long hair was getting wispy. He was pacing, kicking at the dirt and hunching his shoulders like a man with a sore back. Billy was sitting sideways on the driver's seat of his new vehicle with the door open and his feet on the running board. Only a few of Bull's words were loud enough to reach Terry.

"I don't give a good fuck!"

He couldn't hear his brother's response, it was something meant to be soothing, it had that sound, but Bull wasn't listening.

"I don't give a good fuck!"

Then Terry saw the other two, Kramer and the guy with the red beard. It had taken them that long to reach the meeting place. Terry had beaten them easily. Jer had his bow in his hand. The other one had his gear strapped to his back. The two men were coming down the slope of the second ridge. They weren't talking. Jer was leading.

"Hey, Bull. How they hanging?"

Bull looked up at the two men coming to meet them. "Fuck me, it's Robin Hood and Little John," he said.

Terry moved closer, low to the ground, using the rain gullies and brush piles. A pair of ruffed grouse exploded from cover and beat their way directly over the four men on the logging road who glanced up briefly but never thought to look where the grouse had come from. Hunters. Any real hunter knew you couldn't flush a grouse unless you practically stepped on its tail. It wouldn't have mattered if they had checked out the brush pile. Terry was now behind a tree, close enough to hear everything.

"Not much chance of seeing a deer with you yelling like that," Jer said.

"Yeah, well I'm not here to shoot Bambi's mother," Bull said. "Let's get this straightened out and you guys can go kill something."

"Okay," said Jer. "What do we have to straighten out?"

"I told you what I want. I want to get away, move on, start something new."

"I think that's a good idea."

"Where are you going?" The other guy wanted to know.

"Head west. I'm tired of the winters. Find somewhere quiet on the coast."

"Sounds good."

"So I'm gonna need my end," Bull said.

Terry could see Jer shake his head, no.

"No can do, Bull. You know the drill. Five years we said."

"Fuck five years, man. I bit the bullet. I did my bit and I never said a fucking word, not even in my fucking sleep."

"You stood up, Bull. We all know it. It was the honourable thing and you're an honourable man. I'd like to think that any one of us would have done the same thing, but you're the man who did it."

"And now I want my end. That's all."

"Not a good idea, Bull," the other one said. "They'll be watching you."

"They won't fucking know where I went. I'm going to disappear."

"They'll know," Jer said. "You're going to need a vehicle. You'll pay cash."

"Bullshit!" Bull said. "What's this thing Billy's cruising around in? New fucking Sierra."

"I get the employee discount," Billy said. "I make monthly payments, just like everybody else."

"You're a solid citizen. What about you, Jerome? What are you driving these days?"

"Nobody's done anything to draw attention to themselves, Bull."

"Yeah, yeah, who gives a fuck? You all got jobs and cars and houses because I ate shit for twenty-eight months."

"Sooner or later they'll pull you over," Jer said. "And they'll want to know where you got five hundred thousand dollars in cash."

"Five hundred and eighty-seven thousand, five hundred dollars," Bull said. "And I know exactly how to carry it, hide it, spend it."

"Can't take that chance," Jer said.

"Hey, Jer," Billy said. "What's the big deal? It's just a year or so early. You know Bull. He won't say anything."

"We made a pact," Jer said, "like a blood oath. It's unbreakable."

"Fuck you, Jerome," Bull said. "Nobody elected you God and this isn't the fucking army. I'm the one put this deal together. I'm the one went to jail to keep it together. I want my end. You want to watch me count it out that's okay by me. Just stay the fuck out of my way."

Bull walked around to the rear of the Sierra and pulled out a short-handled shovel. When he turned to face them, Kramer shot him through the heart from eight feet away. The arrow went clean through Bull's chest and hit the rear driver's side quarter panel of Billy's new vehicle leaving a long silver scar in the fresh black paint.

They buried Bull in the bottomland. Sank him deep in the mud. Terry watched them do it. There was a big argument. Billy almost went crazy. He kept saying that he couldn't believe it.

"What else could I do?" Jer said.

Billy cried, and after a while he left, and Jer and the other man dug a hole and buried the body.

Terry was shaking and didn't trust himself to move quietly. He had seen a murder. Bull had dropped like a veal calf at the packers. The arrow must have cut his heart in half. He stayed where he was while Jer and the other man retraced their steps up and over the ridge, sweeping leaves over the trail they'd made dragging the body down the hill. Terry could hear his brother's pickup heading down the logging road and then Jer and the bearded man came back down the hill, still tidying up after themselves. When they got to the spot where Bull was buried they spread more leaves and rolled a big rock over the spot and moved some underbrush. Then they talked about the money.

"What about Billy?" the other one said.

"I can handle Billy. Don't worry about Billy Warren. He'll do what he's told."

"You sure about that? He fucking freaked. What if he comes back, tries to dig it up, then what?"

"He doesn't have the guts. He knows what would happen."

Terry thought to himself that they would all be very surprised if they went looking for the money. It wasn't where they put it the first time, and it wasn't where Jer thought he'd moved it later on, and it wasn't anywhere they could find it. Bull Hollyer had died for something they no longer possessed.

The cops down on 17 were packing up, driving away. Terry came down from the ridge and began searching for things they might have missed, things he might have overlooked. He needed to check Coughlan's section of the woods. The police might never make it over there, and it wasn't part of the Warren property, but it was all the same bush, and there were messes over there that needed to be tidied. So many loose ends, so many things to remember. A full month's worth of complications. He should have stayed away. He knew that now. He should have said no at the first invitation. He didn't have to be part of it. He could have remained invisible until all the damage was done. And he would have, except for Trina.

SEPTEMBER — One Month Ago

If Beverly hadn't asked him he would never have been invited to The Big Sex Weekend. They had bumped into each other at the Mac's Milk out on the highway. He was picking up some Tylenol for his father and Salada tea for his mother and, as long as he was there, a pack of Juicy Fruit for himself, when Beverly showed up to buy cigarettes and cans of Dr. Ballard's for her dog Bruno. It was raining hard. Terry looked up just as Beverly's little truck came out of the rooster tail of a big rig heading north up 35 and pulled into the parking space in front of the glass door. Bruno had his head sticking out of the window in the rain and Beverly kept walking back and forth between the door and the dog saying, get inside you silly bugger, well, pull your head in you dumb animal, then she went back to the glass door but didn't come in because she looked back and the dog still had his big shaggy head hanging out in the rain and she had to walk back and say it over again: get your head inside. Meanwhile she was holding a seat cushion over her head for an umbrella.

"Terry? Hi," she said, like she was really glad to see him. Big smile. She was wearing a purple sweatshirt and it was wet across the top shelf of her bosom. Beverly's boobs were legendary.

Every high school needs a king and queen, and the year Terry started at Dockerty High, his brother Billy and Beverly Jannis were the royal couple. B&B they were called. Billy Warren was the quarterback on the football team; Beverly was the head cheerleader. They wore orange and blue at Dockerty High.

"Haven't seen you in a while," she said.

"Hello," he said.

"I'm soaked," she said. "Look at me. Have you ever seen this much rain?"

Terry grabbed a stack of napkins from the coffee counter and handed them to her. "Here," he said, "have some. On the house." And they laughed.

She was Beverly Hollyer now. The local gossip was that her husband, "Bull" Hollyer, had run off on her again.

"God, I hope it's nice next weekend," she said, dabbing at her face with the pad of napkins. "Look at that stupid dog," she said. "You've never smelled anything until you've smelled wet Bruno."

"How about a barn full of wet goats?" Terry said.

"You got me there," she said. "What are you doing next weekend?"

That's how she got him to go to the Labour Day party at the Kramer's cottage. She told him that Billy and Trina were going to be there and that Trina had invited her and told her she could bring a date and would he like to come? As her date. And all Terry could think was, Trina's going to be there.

Terry had fallen in love with Beverly's kid sister, Trina, when they were assigned to the same homeroom that first day at Dockerty High. Trina Jannis was a flower. She wore white and pink and sometimes daffodil yellow. Her hair was blonde, and she wore it, when he first saw her, in a ponytail tied with a ribbon, and forevermore that was his preferred way for blonde girls to wear their hair. Trina wasn't anything like her sister. She had dainty breasts, boyish hips, and she always smelled pretty, clothes and hair, not musky like Beverly's scent, more like lilacs. Terry never thought of it as perfume from a bottle but as the way someone like Trina would naturally smell. Once he held her coat for almost an hour while she went back inside the school to see somebody about something and didn't come back right away. He sat on the wall by the bicycle racks with her coat folded over his arms. It was a beige duffel coat. When no one was looking he buried his face in the collar and inhaled her scent, her flower smell, her shampoo smell, the smell of her neck above the label. He could have sat there forever, holding her coat, pressing it down onto the front of his pants, making himself hard inside his jeans. He found that if he rocked back and forth just a little, with his head bent over to let him inhale the smell of her, and his arms inside the folded coat, pressing down and gently rubbing back and forth across the swelling in his pants, he could get to the part where his eyes would flutter, and the strong taste, the way electricity might taste, rose behind his throat and his nose. He was almost all the way there when she came back and took her coat away. She was angry at something, or someone; she was snapping, and her eyes shooting sparks almost, and she snatched her coat away from him, and, as she put it on she did a little twirl that slapped his shin with the horn toggle button near the hem of her coat and then marched away, and as he bent forward to rub the sharp sting below his knee, he shuddered and gushed inside his pant leg.

She hadn't been mad at him, she was angry about something that happened inside the school, but her anger and the slap of that button against his leg were forever connected to what he'd done. After that, whenever he saw Trina wearing that coat, he felt a stab of fear that she would suddenly turn on him and tell him that she knew, could tell by the way it was wrinkled, that he'd used it to play with himself. Later that autumn he stole the coat from the school cloakroom while Trina was trying out for the choir.

Most days they rode home from school in Billy's Pontiac, sitting side by side, schoolbooks between them, in the back seat, while Billy and Beverly sat up front and talked about what to do on a Saturday night. When Billy would pull Beverly close to him, Terry would steal a glance at Trina. She was always staring out the side window. Twice, while they were waiting for the Pontiac to drive up, they'd had a conversation, of a sort, Terry listening, Trina angry about something. She had a temper. She once told him that she hated Beverly's boobs.

Everything changed in the February of that year. Dockerty High rustled with whispering. The royal couple had broken up. B&B was over. Billy Warren had asked Beverly's kid sister Trina to the dance, and when Trina said yes, the whole school knew that something really romantic and scandalous and exciting had just happened. That was the end of Terry's spending time close to Trina. She was Billy's girl now; they did their homework together, they went everywhere together, and they were in love — their world revolved around that one fact.

And Terry began to shadow them.

The very first time his brother kissed Trina, Terry was there.

The first time Billy had touched her breast and asked her to touch the front of his jeans, Terry was nearby. They only caught him once.

It was a Saturday night in March, bitter cold, basketball season going badly, the scandal of Billy and Trina's romance still very much alive. Almost everyone in school wondering if they were doing it, they danced so close in the gym under the spinning mirror balls after the games, plastered to each other, in a private world. Billy was playing poorly but nobody on the team could talk to him about it. Trina was like a new religion to him.

St. Francis Xavier 63, Dockerty High 44. Billy held to 6 points, fouled out in the third quarter, heard boos from his own schoolmates for the first time. His teammates left him alone in the locker room and went to a dance at the Civic Arena across town, and Billy met Trina on the third floor in the Teacher's Lounge.

"Not here," Trina said.

Billy was clearing newspapers off the couch.

"Where?"

"Not here," she said.

"Not here," Terry's lips formed the words but made no sound. There was dust in his mouth and he could touch the floor of the cloakroom with his tongue. He could see Trina's feet and halfway up her calves. When Billy pulled her onto the couch he could see her knees and the top of her blonde head above the couch arm.

"I'm too nervous here," she said.

Terry would remember every word, would store every image of her, every scent, the clothes she wore, hoard it in the secret part of his mind marked "Trina." The first time she had said, "Do you love me, Billy?" he heard his own name spoken, whispered, cried. "Terry, oh Terry, touch it, you may, you may touch it." That's what he heard. And in his mind he touched her.

"You little shit!"

Billy was dragging him out of the cloakroom by his sweater, dragging him across the floor with one hand and slapping him across the back of the head.

"How long have you been in there? How long?" Hit, hit, slap, slap. "Sneaky little prick bastard!" Slap, slap.

"I knew there was someone in there," Trina said. She was kneeling on the couch. Terry caught a glimpse of her fingers buttoning the front of her blouse and he filed away the image even as the blows were falling.

"I came to warn you," Terry said. "The janitor is looking in the rooms."

"You were spying!" Billy wouldn't stop hitting him. Terry's right ear rang from the slapping, his right eye blurred, his windpipe was being crushed as Billy shook him back and forth like a sack, strangling him with his own sweater.

"If I ever catch you again I'll kill you, you little shit-prick! I'll beat your head in with an axe. I swear to Jesus Christ, Terry, I'll kill you. I'll fucking kill you!"

And Billy dragged him across the floor of the Teacher's Lounge and shoved him into the hall. "Get out of here! Just get the hell out of here. Go on, get. Get. I'll kill you, Terry; I promise, I'll fucking kill you."

And Terry looked back with his clear left eye and had one last glimpse of Trina, kneeling on the couch, her bare knees showing, the tail of her blouse hanging outside the waistband of her plaid skirt, her hands across her mouth, her blue eyes looking directly at him as the door slammed. Terry stood in the dark echoing hallway on the third floor of Dockerty High and didn't move for a long time, until he heard their voices again, whispering to each other in the dark, and then he very carefully, silently, knelt, lowered himself to the door and looked through the keyhole.

They never caught him again. Over the next five years he was the silent witness to a hundred of their meetings. He was there the first time they made love. And the second.

Billy never spoke of the incident and Trina never spoke to Terry again. Ever. Not a word. Not at the wedding, not at Christmas, never again. To Trina, Terry was invisible. And Terry came to believe that the power of invisibility was something she had bestowed on him.

Trina and Billy got married and moved to Oshawa and Billy went to work at "The Motors" on the assembly line, installing electrics. Trina went back to school for a while, and after that she started a business of her own, something to do with fashion. Terry was never sure exactly what she did. When he shadowed her in the city he had to stay far back. She met people, she had lunches, sometimes she would go to a movie and then he would sit in the dark, many rows above her, and watch the back of her blonde head as she nibbled popcorn or sipped a Coke. Trina never laughed at comedies or gasped at violence. Her head was mostly still, her pale hair easy to focus on in the reflected light from the screen. Terry sat far away from her, high and above her, hooded and hunched, the toggle buttons from her duffel coat in his pocket like dull bear claws softly raking back and forth across the tight erection trapped inside his pant leg.

Terry had been there the afternoon she met someone at the movies, a man he'd seen at one of the department stores — the same man who met her twice for lunch. And after the movie he watched them check into the Sunset Motel. And after that man, there were other men. Billy never knew.

Terry had to limit his trips to Oshawa to one day a week. He usually went on a Wednesday. Those were the days Trina was most likely to go to a movie, and meet a man, and go to a motel. One time the motel was perfect and he watched it all through the blinds. He saw all of Trina, her whiteness, her legs raised high, her madness when she came. That time Terry broke into the man's car and stole his briefcase. After that there was a different man.

"You can bring a bathing suit. Or not."

Beverly had a husky voice and there was invariably a suggestion in it, the way she said things so you could always come back with something if you wanted to. Her conversation left the door ever open for further discussion. She was giving him the details about the next weekend.

"For sure, sounds good. Real good."

He followed her down the aisle as she got canned dog food.

"This stuff is terrible," she said, dismissing a popular brand. "I feed him this he shits red turds."

"Billy going to be okay about this?" he asked her.

"Hey," she said, "we're invited. Don't worry about it." She paid for the dog food and the smokes and immediately tore the cellophane off the cigarette package. "Besides, it's not as if it's any of Billy-boy's business. It's not his cottage." She headed for the door. "You should maybe get a haircut, though. If you want to make a good impression. This Kramer guy has money."

The rain had stopped and they stepped outside so Beverly could light up. Bruno stuck his head out the truck window again and made a coaxing noise in her direction, half strangled bark, half petulant whine.

"Relax," she said. "Most spoiled dog in the universe." She blew smoke into the cool night air, then turned to Terry and looked him over appraisingly as if wondering how to fix him up for the coming engagement.

Seven

At the steady clip Adele Moen was holding, it would take them forty minutes to get to Haldane, and if the interview didn't take more than an hour, Orwell figured he could be back in plenty of time to clear his desk and reassure his Staff Sergeant about tomorrow's funeral. Formal interments were important to Rawluck. He probably had his own planned right down to the last chorus of "Bringing in the Sheaves."

"Dang, I forgot my cellphone," said Orwell. "I'm always doing that."

Adele laughed. "Stop looking over your shoulder," she said. "He's not chasing us."

"Followed me to the parking lot."

"I had an Uncle Jake used to wax his moustache," she said. "Drove me nuts he could never get both ends the same. One side drooped."

"Roy would never stand for that."

They passed the Dockerty limits heading down 35. Once past the South Mall the scenery changed abruptly to fields and farmhouses.

"I am officially out of my jurisdiction," he said.

"This case is like the United Nations anyway."

That was true enough, Orwell thought, although it was something of a stretch to involve the Dockerty Police Department in anything beyond office space and perhaps a handy interview room. The corpse was headed down to Toronto, Newry County was being combed by Ontario Provincial Police teams under Sergeant Dean, Durham Region had already professed their "personal interest" in the matter, and Metro Homicide was officially in charge of the investigation. That the detective in charge had specifically invited Dockerty's Chief of Police to accompany her on the first interview wasn't an altogether gross breach of protocol, but it was highly irregular. She probably misses her partner, Orwell reckoned, or maybe she likes talking things through out loud.

"Macklehenny and a guy I don't know, loaners from Durham, went around to give her the news," Adele said. "Said she acted like she was expecting something like this, like her husband was away a lot doing macho stuff — moose-hunting, like that. Maybe he came close to getting killed other times."

The highway rose and fell and from time to time Orwell caught a glimpse of Lake Ontario. Or maybe it was reflected light off the low cloud cover.

"Make a right here, 7A," he said. "We'll go west through Port Perry and head down 12. Used to be a quaint little town years ago, Haldane. Now it's mostly developments."

"Bedroom community."

Boxter Crescent had an unfinished look; newly planted scrawny trees, driveways unpaved. The lots were narrow and the lawns were stingy. The houses all shoved two-car garages at the street in lieu of porches and verandas.

Francine Kramer opened the door for them and Orwell noted that she didn't look at all bereaved. She was almost pretty. She was wearing a skirt and sweater and a string of pink pearls as if anticipating a visit from the church ladies.

"Good afternoon, Mrs. Kramer. I'm Detective Moen, Metro Homicide; this is Chief Brennan of the Dockerty Police Force. You up to talking with us for a few minutes?"

"Of course," said Francine Kramer. "The water's hot for coffee, or you could have some juice."

"No thanks, ma'am," said Adele.

"Oh, no trouble," she said. "It's all ready."

They followed Mrs. Kramer down a narrow hall toward the kitchen. Orwell had a quick look around. All very proper yet somehow vacant. The broadloom was vacuumed; the hall table had a white vase with fake flowers in it. There was a bad painting over the couch in the living room, a Parisian street scene painted in a factory by someone who had never been to Paris. There were no books in evidence except for a Toronto phonebook open on the coffee table.

In the kitchen the major appliances were all the same colour. Three stools faced a counter that was part of a miniscule food preparation island in the middle of the floor. Not enough room to chop an onion, Orwell thought.

"We could sit in the living room, if you'd rather," Francine said.

"This will be fine," said Adele.

Francine Kramer gave them cups of instant decaf in three matching teacups with saucers. She presented them with the cups, tiny spoons and six cookies on a pink plate.

Adele dutifully tasted the coffee and smiled or grimaced. "I know this is a bad time for you, Mrs. Kramer. We want to make this as easy as we can so that you can get back to the important things, like making arrangements, things like that."

"When *can* I make arrangements? Do I have to send someone to get Jer's body or will they deliver it?"

"They'll let you know when the body will be released. It shouldn't be too much longer. Your funeral director will know what to do then."

"Oh. Okay. Because I have so many people to call. I was on the phone since those other detectives left. Everybody wants to know about the funeral, of course."

Orwell saw Adele push her teacup, still half-full, delicately away. She took out her notebook and uncapped her pen.

"Okay, first, you knew your husband was going hunting last weekend, did you?"

"Oh yes. He went a couple times a year. Skiing, fishing trips, hunting."

Orwell had a question: "Did you ever go with him?"

"I'm not much for the outdoors," she said. "Jer went with the guys. You know. Men friends. They were always off on some activity."

"About the men friends," said Adele, "I wonder if you could help us make a list of men he would go on these trips with. For instance, last year he went deer hunting about this time with another man. Who would that have been?"

"Let me think. I'm not sure I know. It might have been Tony. Or Ted. No, Ted's his skiing buddy."

"Was there anyone who was a bowhunter specifically?"

"That would be Tony, I think. Jerry and Tony both belonged to the archery club. They joined together a couple of years ago."

"Could you give me Tony's last name?"

"Tony . . . Tony . . . Tony Italian-something. Isn't that awful?"

"It's all right, take your time."

"He didn't come here, Tony. I only met him once or twice. Scapini? Something like that."

"Would your husband have anything like an address book we could check?"

"Oh certainly. It'll be in there. Jer has everything organized down to the last detail. Would you like to see it?"

"Please."

Francine led them back into the hallway and opened a door with stairs leading down.

Half of the basement held the furnace and the laundry room and storage. Orwell was struck by how neat it all was. Where were the boxes and cans and broken tools?

"This is Jer's den," said Francine.

The basement was divided down the centreline by a cinder block wall. The door was locked.

"Oh dear," Francine said. "He always keeps it locked. I don't have a key."

"I have his keys," Adele said. She had an envelope in her bag. "We'll return all his personal effects as soon as possible."

"Are those Jer's?" For a moment Francine looked as if she were about to confront the fact of her husband's death, but she shook it off. "I don't know which key it is."

"This one looks about right," said Adele, and unlocked the door.

The room was paneled in wood. There was no window to the outside. Orwell flicked a light switch and stepped back to let Adele and Francine enter. Francine seemed to hesitate in the doorway as if about to break a long-standing rule. It was a man's room. A man who spent a lot of money reminding himself of his maleness. There was an exercise area with a Bowflex, a Nordic-Track, a Stairmaster, a rack of stainless steel dumbbells, and a full-length mirror. A year's worth of Playmates of the Month, framed under glass, hung above a wet bar well stocked with brand-name liquor — Canadian Club, Chivas, Stolichnaya, Jack Daniels. A pair of leather recliners faced a large flat-screen HD Sony with separate speakers.

"Do you mind if I go back upstairs while you look around? I still have a bunch of calls to make."

"You go right ahead, Mrs. Kramer," Adele said. "We'll lock up when we're finished."

Adele listened to the footsteps hurrying up the stairs. She turned to Orwell. "What do you think?"

"I think she's glad to be rid of him," Orwell said. "Maybe that's not exactly right, but she doesn't seem sad. A little nervous. As if he's going to show up any minute and spoil things."

"What do you think of this place?"

"Spent money on himself, that's for sure. The rest of the house feels vacant, down here it's all extras."

"Wouldn't you like a room like this, Chief?"

"I've got a room," said Orwell. "More of a cubbyhole, smaller than a jail cell. I measured."

"Got a locked drawer here."

"There's general lack of respect for seniority in my house," Orwell said.

Adele unlocked the drawer in the bookshelf-desk unit.

"Finally," Adele said, "something personal."

Jerome Kramer's DayMinder was dead centre. She began paging through it.

There was a double-door cabinet under the drawer and Orwell unlocked it. Adele took a step back to let both doors swing open. On the bottom shelf was a neat stack of *Hustler* magazines. Above that was a full shelf of pornographic DVDs and videotapes.

"This was a very private man," said Orwell.

"I've seen creepier," Adele said. "But this is pretty anal. Room locked, sex tapes, address book and he had the only set of keys." She resumed paging. "Got a Saracini, Antony Saracini. Whitby address."

"Could be the one," Orwell said. He unlocked the tall mahogany cabinet and looked at Kramer's collection: three shotguns, four rifles, five handguns, a compound bow and a generous supply of shafts. "Mercy," he said. "That's a Weatherby."

".357. Nice," said Adele.

Orwell hefted a pretty double-barreled bird gun. "Italian," he said. "Worth a small fortune."

"He treated himself pretty well," she said. "I wonder how he treated the missus."

As they came back up the basement stairs they could hear Francine's voice in the living room. Adele put her hand on Orwell's sleeve to slow him for a moment. Francine sounded bright and conversational, as if she were making vacation plans.

"Oh, I think I'll be fine, I think so. Jer always carried lots of insurance. I called Mr. Beane, the lawyer, and he said everything was in real good shape. Life insurance, and life insurance on the mortgage, RRSP, some bonds and things. I'm going over there tomorrow and he's going to explain it all. You don't have to worry about me, really." There was a longish pause while Francine listened and Orwell fidgeted. Adele held him back a bit longer. "Maybe I will, Angela. After the funeral and everything. Maybe I'll stay with you a little while until I decide what to do. I'm not sure I want to stay in this neighbourhood, you know. I don't mind if they know that Jer got himself killed, but the wives around here, you know how they'll be since I'm single and all. I don't want the aggravation."

Orwell looked at Adele. She shrugged. They moved down the hallway toward the living room.

"What'd you think about Mrs. Francine Kramer? She seem genuine to you?"

"More like she was playing a part," Orwell said climbing into the car and buckling up. "Wearing pearls and a skirt, serving coffee in teacups. The rug had just been vacuumed."

"The whole house was spick and span."

"Maybe she just had it done. Visitors coming."

"This Saracini sells mirrors. I think we'll just drop by his store unannounced, what d'you say?"

Adele made two neat passes on the inside of a slow moving RV and the outside of a delivery van and beat three lights in succession, all on amber. Orwell was impressed. She made a left onto St. John street just as the light went red, spotted a Corvette pulling out of a parking spot half a block ahead and was into the space like a rabbit down a hole. An old guy in a Volvo beeped at her angrily. He'd been fussing with signal lights and positioning his rear end. "You snooze . . ." she said, and shut off the motor. The Volvo went looking elsewhere. They were three doors down from Saracini's mirror store.

Saracini's display window held a selection of ornate gilt-framed mirrors. Some were beveled glass, some were etched with flamingos or sailing ships. The store itself was carpeted in grey broadloom. The ceiling was festooned with chandeliers and mirrored balls.

Antony Saracini had a black mustache and a full head of black hair. He wore a grey raw silk jacket over a peach silk shirt open to reveal a selection of gold chains and amulets — a cross, a Saint Christopher medal, a Star of David.

"Can't believe it," he said. "You get the guys with guns out there and they're always knocking each other off. Bowhunters? No way. Jesus. Jer Kramer. Woulda thought it'd be the other way around."

"What do you mean, sir?" Adele asked. "Was he looking for trouble?"

"No. Just, he's the kind of guy — *was* I guess, the kind of guy, knew how to look after himself."

"You done much bowhunting, Mr. Saracini?" asked Adele.

"Not so much anymore. Few years ago I was into it big time."

"When was the last time you went hunting with Jerome Kramer?"

"Oh shit, three years ago. Up near Bancroft."

"I understand he went hunting with someone else last year. Wasn't you, was it?"

"Last year this time I was in divorce court getting my gold fillings removed."

"And this year? He didn't ask you to go along?"

"I haven't seen much of him for a while. I couldn't have gone anyway. Business has been so shitty. I had to let two people go. Wait, do I need an alibi or something?"

"I don't think that's a problem," she said. "You can account for your whereabouts last weekend?"

"You're looking at it," he said, with a grand gesture at his emporium. "Seven days a week. I'll be all over the security tapes. Me and about three customers."

"One less thing for us to worry about," she said.

"But it was an accident, right?"

"We have no way of knowing exactly what happened until we can find whoever it was in the bush with your friend. Is there anyone else he went hunting with?"

"Could've been. Could've been somebody he met up with at the club."

"What club is that?" Orwell asked.

"Haldane Rod and Gun," he said. "I haven't been going much lately. Jesus. How's Francine taking it?"

"Very well," Adele said. She noted that Orwell was checking his reflection in a huge mirror and reflexively throwing back his shoulders. "You know Mrs. Kramer?" she asked.

"Well, you know, a couple of do's at the club. Barbecues. Like that. She's a terrific dancer."

"Really."

"Oh yeah, once she lets her hair down she can really rumba. Tango. Samba."

"You like to dance?"

"Oh sure." He did a little samba step on the broadloom.

"How about Mr. Kramer?"

"Jer? Not so much."

"You ever dance with Mrs. Kramer?"

"Couple of times. She was always looking for somebody to dance with. She spread her attention around, you know."

"Lots of different partners?"

He paused then to consider where the conversation had led. "I don't want to say stuff that would be gossip. I don't know anything for a fact. I never saw her with anybody in particular. I know my ex-wife once said that Francine was looking for trouble. Even accused me of sniffing around, but she wasn't my type. Maybe there's something in it. Jer didn't seem to be worried."

"He wasn't the jealous type?"

"Jer? He acted like he owned everything anyway, so how could he get jealous? When he crooked his finger, Francine came running."

"So he didn't mind if she danced with a lot of men as long as she came running back when he whistled?"

"That's about it."

Orwell was wondering if it might be time to have his hat steamed and blocked. He turned from his reflection. "How many times had you and Kramer gone hunting together?" he asked.

"That was it. One time."

"Any idea how he found this place to hunt way up near Dockerty? Did he know the farmer?"

"I don't know. Could have. Or maybe somebody up at the club told him about it."

The Haldane Rod and Gun Club secretary was Hartlan Cornish. Mr. Cornish favoured cavalry twill and tweed. He found them the guest book for the previous year. On the first page they opened, they found a familiar name. Billy Warren. Guest of Jerome Kramer. Billy Warren had written his name Billy rather than William. He'd given his address as 3374 Euclid Street, Oshawa.

"Knew it," said Adele. "Had to be."

Euclid Street was part of a new development near the lake and east of the General Motors plant. There was a white BMW parked in the driveway, and a woman carrying a bag of groceries and a dry cleaning bag was climbing the porch steps as they drove up.

"Mrs. William Warren?" Adele was out of the car and walking up the front walk.

"Yes?"

Orwell stood by the car, flexing his knee.

"How do you do, ma'am. I'm Detective Moen. This is Chief . . ."

"Chief Brennan," Trina said. "I think I went to school with one of your daughters."

"Diana," Orwell said.

"That's right. That was a while ago. How is Diana?"

"Studying for her bar exams," Orwell said.

"My," Trina said, "you must be very proud."

"Could we have a word with you please?" Adele asked.

"Is something wrong?"

"Actually, we'd like to talk to your husband. Is he at home?"

"No, he's not. What happened?"

"Nothing to worry about. We're trying to trace the movements of a person your husband might know. May we come in for a moment?"

"Yes, of course. Let me open the door."

Orwell took the bag of groceries, mostly vegetables and fruit, he noted, and he held the garment bag for her, high so the bottom wouldn't trail on the porch. Trina unlocked her front door and they went in. It was a new house. The broadloom was still shedding an occasional thread. The dining area boasted a copy of a Tiffany lamp swagged over an arrangement of dried flowers on the table. A modest step up in taste from the Kramer house. Orwell figured Trina was in charge of such things.

Trina took the bag of groceries from Orwell and plunked it down on the dining table along with her keys and gloves. She relieved him of the dry cleaning. "I'll be just a moment," she said. "Please sit down." She went up the carpeted stairs quickly and Orwell could hear a closet door sliding open and then footsteps down a hallway and another door closing.

Adele stepped into the living room and looked around. "Smells new," she said. "The leather couch. Like a Mercedes."

"She doesn't drive a GM product," said Orwell.

"Is that significant?"

"Employees get a big discount."

"Maybe she doesn't need it."

"My husband's not here." They hadn't heard her come down the stairs. She had changed into soft slippers.

"Would you have an idea when we could expect him?" Adele asked.

"I mean he's not living here at present."

"Oh," she said.

"We've separated."

"I'm sorry to hear that, Mrs. Warren. Is this a recent development?"

"He moved out some time ago. About a month."

"Would you know where he's staying?"

"He's been staying with somebody he works with. I can give you the name and address."

"Have you or your husband seen Mr. Jerome Kramer recently?"

"Jer? Is something wrong?"

"I'm sorry if this comes as a shock, Mrs. Warren, Mr. Kramer was found dead early this morning. It looks like it might have been a hunting accident."

Orwell watched Trina sway and then grab hold of the newel post at the bottom of the stairs.

"Oh Christ," she said. "A hunting accident?"

"Yes, ma'am," Adele said.

"Oh Jesus Christ," she said again. She went into the living room and sat down on the new leather couch. "But I just saw him."

"When was that, Mrs. Warren?" Adele asked.

"What? Oh. Just . . . ah . . . Labour Day Weekend. Jer. And his wife. Francine. We were at their cottage."

"I am sorry we had to bring you the bad news, Mrs. Warren. Is there anyone we could call for you?"

"What? No. No. That's all right. I'm all right. I suppose I should call Francine. She knows?"

"Yes."

"Oh God. A hunting accident. I hate guns."

According to Trina, her husband was staying with a man named Brent Styles, recently divorced and living in an apartment on Simcoe Street in Whitby, just a few minutes down the highway. Mr. Styles was not at home, but an accommodating neighbour, who seemed thrilled to see their badges and positively delighted to learn whom they were seeking, had, with some ceremony, pointed out Johnny O's Sports Lounge across the street, where, she said, they might find him.

The bartender pointed to a stubby, sullen man watching muscular women in skimpy bikinis parading on the big-screen TV.

"Mr. Styles? Hi. I'm Detective Moen. We're looking for your new roommate, William Warren."

"Why don't you get off his back? He's paying fucking support. That's all that bitch thinks about. Show me the money."

"We're not after him for support payments, sir. Do you know where Mr. Warren is right now?"

"He went back up to the farm, up in Hooterville," Brent said. "Somebody got hurt up there, I don't know. Said he was going back to see if they needed him."

"Okay," Adele said. "As long as I've got you here, did you see Mr. Warren this past weekend?"

"Are you kidding? We just got back last night."

"Oh really? From where, sir?"

"We went to Buffalo. Went down for the Bills game. Bills-Raiders."

"Just you and Billy?"

"Four of us went. We all work at the Motors. Darryl, Glen, Billy and me."

"Bills game was it?"

"Yeah. We do that a couple of times a year."

"You all go in the same car?"

"Two cars. Me and Billy in my car."

"Where did you stay?"

"At the Maple Court Motel. It's a couple of miles from Ralph Wilson Stadium. Not bad. We've stayed there before."

"What'd you get, two rooms, four rooms?"

"Darryl and Glen stayed at another place. I forget the name."

"So it was just you and Billy at the Maple Court?"

"Yeah. We all went out together, the four of us, Friday night. Got a little blasted, you know, nothing too hairy."

"So, you stuck together Friday night. What did you do Saturday?"

"We had tickets for the hockey game."

"You all went together to the game?"

"Yeah. Leafs and Sabres."

"And Sunday you went to a football game?"

"Bills-Raiders. Right."

"You and Billy and Darryl and Glen?"

"Glen and Darryl had seats on the other side. We were in Section 204. We had way better seats."

"You and Billy?"

"Right." Brent Styles looked back at the big screen where a woman with white-blonde hair and a Jamaican tan was flexing her back.

"So you didn't see the other two during the game?"

"I could see them on the other side of the field. Darryl had a red blanket with him."

"You all get together after the game?"

"Billy and me headed back."

"So Saturday, at the hockey game, was the last time you hung out with Darryl and Glen. From then on it was just you and Billy until you drove back here?"

"Well, I could see Darryl across the field with his red blanket."

"But could he see you? Did you and Billy have a red blanket?"

"No. We didn't have one. It was just Darryl's car blanket."

"All right," Adele said. "Let me wrap this up and you can get back to the bodybuilders. You and Billy Warren drove to Buffalo after work on Friday. You checked into the Maple Court Motel, and later that Friday evening you went out with the other two men, Darryl and Glen, and had some laughs. Saturday, the four of you were together again for a hockey game. Is that right?"

"Yeah. Leafs got hammered."

"And on Sunday you all went to a football game. Except you were seated on different sides of the stadium so it was just you and Billy at the game. Is that right? You were together?"

"Yeah. Right."

"Together. Sunday. And you saw your friends on the other side of the field, but you don't know if they saw you. Then after the game, you and Billy drove back from Buffalo to Oshawa, again together. Is that right?"

"Right. Me and Billy. In my 'Vette. Together."

"Getting back here about what time?"

"About 10:30 last night."

"What time did Darryl and Glen get back?"

"I don't know. I haven't seen them yet."

"All right," Adele said, putting away her pen, "that'll be all for now. Looks like the one in the yellow got first place."

"You think those women are on steroids?" Orwell wondered.

"Oh sure," Adele said, starting the car. "Women don't get muscle mass like that without some kind of help. Plus boob jobs, otherwise your hooters shrink from the steroids. Then they *really* look weird."

"Heavy price to pay," he said.

"So's putting on five hundred pounds to wrestle sumo." She got them headed back up 35/115. "Not too late to drop in on Billy Warren, is it?"

"Styles was nervous the whole time," Orwell said. "He was tearing up pieces of paper under the edge of the table. Matchbook covers. He went through three of them. Every time Billy's name came up he looked away at the TV screen."

It was getting dark by the time they got to Dan Warren's place. The outdoor lights were turned on and the three Warren men were standing beside a green John Deere tractor parked near the barn. Billy Warren had a large frame, handsome face, weak mouth.

He pouts, thought Adele. He said something to Dan and Terry and came to meet them in the lane.

"You want to talk to me?"

Adele showed her badge. "William Warren?"

"Yep."

"Hi. I'm Detective Moen, Metro Homicide, you probably know Chief Brennan. We'd like to ask you a few things if we may."

"About Jer, right?"

"That's right, sir. Is there someplace we can talk?"

"There's a bench over there in the orchard, that okay? My mother's lying down."

"That'll be fine, sir. Lead the way."

He led them off the driveway through a hedgerow of sour cherry trees and into an orchard. The trees were mostly bare and hadn't been pruned in a long time. They found the bench in the middle of the orchard. It was an old church pew, warped and damp. There were windfalls on the bench and William swept them to the ground. All three declined to sit. Orwell recognized the apples underfoot as russets.

"Used to get bushels out of this orchard," said Billy. "Pears, plums, sour cherries. Not this year."

Orwell said, "It was a bad year for everything, just about."

Adele uncapped her pen.

"Now then, Mr. Warren, just for the record, you knew the deceased, Jerome Kramer?"

"Jer. Jerome. Yes."

"When did you meet?"

"Few years ago, I guess. I don't remember exactly. We were both getting a runaround from the same insurance company. We went and had a few beers and pissed and moaned about what rip-offs they were. I guess we started a friendship then."

"And the friendship continued?"

"We stayed friends, yeah. I mean we didn't hang out."

"You did socialize?"

"Yeah. We went to a party at their house, and we went out for an evening a few times."

"On those occasions, did your wives go along? These parties and nights out just for the guys were they?"

"No, we went out as couples. I mean Francine and Jer, me and Trina."

"You were pretty close friends then, the four of you?"

"For a while there. And then we sort of started tapering off."

"Why was that?"

"Lots of reasons."

"I understand you aren't living at home at present? You and your wife are separated?"

"It's not a legal separation. Not yet, anyway. It might come to that. If she decides. I'm tired of being the only one who gives a shit, you know what I mean?"

"Mind if I ask what you were doing this past weekend? Say from Friday the 8th until Sunday the 10th?"

"I was in Buffalo with a friend, the guy I'm staying with right now. We went to a football game."

"Just the two of you?"

"There were four of us but we stayed at different motels."

"You were in Buffalo all weekend?"

"Left after we ate, after the game, Sunday night. Got back before midnight, I don't know exactly. Traffic was messed up."

"Would you mind giving me the names of the other men who were on the trip? Just for the record."

Terry spelled out the names — Brent Styles, Glen Hoebel, Darryl Demarchuk.

"Now sir," Adele nodded, flipped a page. "That takes care of what you were doing at the time Mr. Kramer was killed. I'm always happy when people's whereabouts can be substantiated that much. It makes my job a lot easier. We're still pretty confused about what Mr. Kramer was doing that weekend. According to his wife, he left Friday afternoon from their home in Haldane. You know the place I'm talking about, 21 Boxter Crescent?"

"I've been there."

"Recently, sir?"

"Not for months. Summertime, sometime."

"Okay, fine. So there we are, Jerome Kramer departs 21 Boxter Crescent at about 2:30 Friday afternoon, and heads off for a weekend of bowhunting. By the way, did you know he was coming up here to hunt, Mr. Warren?"

"No. We'd talked about it. He was up here last year, with a friend of his, but he didn't say anything definite, last time I talked to him."

"And when would that have been?" she asked. "The last time you talked to Jerome Kramer?"

"I could figure it out. On the phone. Maybe three weeks ago."

"That would be about the time you moved out of your home and went to stay with Mr. Styles, am I right?"

"Somewhere around then, I guess."

"So when you talked to him, I suppose you told him about the change in your personal situation."

"I might have mentioned it. Probably. I didn't talk about it like I talk to Brent about it. Brent's been through that shit himself. Jer, I probably said something, but I sure as shit wasn't looking for sympathy."

"Not a particularly sympathetic man, was he?"

"Wouldn't piss on you if you were on fire. Excuse me."

"Okay, to get back to last weekend," Adele placed a neat period and flipped to a clean page. "He takes off Friday afternoon and he shows up here, at your father's farm, Saturday afternoon. You got any idea what he was doing for what, twenty-four hours?"

"No idea."

"Last year, when he came up here, he was with a friend. Would you know the name of his friend? Where we could reach him?"

"I don't know him," Billy said. "Jer had lots of friends. I never met most of them. I wasn't much into some of the things he was into."

"Like what?"

"Like skiing. I'm not much into skiing. And I couldn't get into the archery thing. I mean, I tried it. I went a couple of times to the club he belonged to. Got the gear, you know."

"You own a bow, Mr. Warren?"

"Yeah, I bought one. Couldn't shoot worth shit."

"Where is it now?"

"It's still at the house. I haven't moved out. I just took some clothes and stuff."

"What kind of bow is it?"

"It's a . . . wait . . . a Fred Bear. What they call a recurve. I could never get the hang of it, kept slapping myself on the arm, you know? I was going to get the other kind, a compound, with the two wheels and crossover strings."

"Kind of like a pulley arrangement?"

"That's it. But I never bothered. Stopped going."

"Didn't enjoy it?"

"I was never much into hunting or fishing. My sports are like basketball at the Y."

"Would you say that your interest in bowhunting tapered off about the time your friendship with Mr. Kramer started tapering off?"

"Well, not exactly. I'd say it came first."

"Which?"

"The hunting thing. I kind of gave up on the hunting, well I never went hunting anyway, but the practising part up at the club, before we stopped hanging out together."

"You and your wife and Mr. Kramer and his wife would still be going out on the town once in a while?"

"Yeah, we went out a couple of times after that I guess."

"Did the breakup of your friendship with the Kramers have anything to do with the breakup of your marriage?"

"I'm not ready to break up. I just want to see some evidence that Trina gives a shit about what happens to it. I can't be the only one who's trying to make it work. She has to make some moves in that direction too."

"Okay," said Adele, flipping her book shut. "I think that's enough for right now, Mr. Warren. Will you be spending the night here, or going back to Mr. Styles's place?"

"I'll be here for another day or so I guess. Help out a bit."

"Good. I may need to talk to you again, but with this trip to Buffalo and three friends to corroborate your whereabouts that weekend, I think we're in pretty good shape. Thank you for your co-operation. I wish everybody I talked to made things this easy."

Billy looked as if he wanted to shake hands with Adele, as if they'd made an agreement or something, but she was already picking her way out of the orchard. Billy looked up to see Orwell watching him from the other side of the tree.

"Jeez, forgot you were there, Chief," he said.

"Still got your ticket stub from the Bills game?" Orwell asked him.

"I don't know," Billy said. "Probably."

"Hang onto it," said Orwell.

"What'd you think?" Adele asked. "About that interview?"

"He avoided a couple of questions."

"He surely did," she agreed.

"Like the last one. When you asked him did the breakup of his marriage have anything to do with the Kramers, he deflected that one, didn't give an answer. He did that a couple of times."

"Right. Something happened between the four of them somewhere along the line. Bet money on it. Francine liked to dance. And flirt."

"Can't see Billy straying too much. Doesn't sound like he's happy with this separation business."

"Well, then," said Adele, "maybe he wasn't the one who was straying."

Orwell had missed supper hour, which was nigh on blasphemy at Erika's table. Nonetheless she gave him a bowl of excellent goulash and proceeded to collect the items necessary to the proper polishing of the brass buttons and gold insignia on his dress uniform.

"You eat your breakfast before you put this on tomorrow," she told him. "One of your ties had maple syrup down the front."

"I thought it was a stripe," he said. "It's right down the centre."

"Don't be flippant," she said.

"Patty in the stable?"

"She thinks Belinda might go into labour," Erika said. "I told her not tonight."

"Leda's in the attic listening to Edith Piaf."

"And Lotte Lenya. She wants to move to Paris and meet Van Gogh."

Orwell concentrated on his food for a while. "Why don't you come?" he invited. "Show the flag. Wear that lovely black shawl."

"Ha!" she said, and there was no laughter in it. "I have things to do more important than wasting half a day on someone I never met, wouldn't recognize, and probably wouldn't have liked."

"Now you know how I feel."

"It doesn't matter how you feel. It's your job." She finished the buttons and moved to the insignia with a clean cloth and a different can of polish.

"Is there dessert?" he asked.

"I saved a piece of strudel."

Orwell carried his dishes to the sink and wondered where it was hiding.

"It's in the oven," she said. "Staying warm."

"Of course it is," he said.

She looked up from her work. The gold bars on the lapel were gleaming, the buttons glowed. Orwell hadn't moved from the sink.

"Well?" she said.

"In a minute," he said.

"You saw a dead man today."

"Hanging in a tree. With arrows in him."

"You didn't know him?"

"No. But it happened on Dan Warren's place. Back in that big bush."

"Breithaupt," she said. "Means 'big head,' like you."

"Sam Abrams says there was a murder in there a hundred years ago."

"Not that long," she said. "After the first war."

"What's the story?"

"Who knows anymore? The one I like is where Breithaupt was a spy for the Kaiser and couldn't go home. You should ask some of those snoots on the Knoll. Before they all die off." She smiled at the thought, or perhaps it was the gleam of Orwell's buttons.

"Is there ice cream?"

"No, real cream," she said. "In the refrigerator."

Eight

September

The Kramers' cottage was big for a summer place, two stories, stone fireplace, cedar paneling. It smelled of summer. Billy was drunk when they got there. He was sitting on the couch. The drapes were closed, the TV was silent, the fireplace was an ash pit. Billy looked neither happy nor unhappy to see his brother. Beverly went to sit beside Billy and pat him on the shoulder and Terry stood around for a few minutes until the two of them started whispering about something, and then he backed away, wondering what he was supposed to do, reluctant to meet Trina without Beverly nearby to make it permissible. There were voices from upstairs, muffled, inarticulate. On the couch, Beverly was making soothing sounds; *I know I know I know*, she was saying. Someone in a bathing suit was on the deck, someone with her hair in a ponytail, slim legs and painted toenails. Terry drifted to a position behind the sliding screen door. The lake was visible through the trees. The woman on the chaise wasn't Trina. Terry let out his breath. The woman turned and took off her sunglasses.

"Well, hello," she said. "Come on out and take your shirt off."

She said she was Francine Kramer, and he told her he was Terry Warren, Billy's brother. She asked him to please get her a spritzer, and then explained what it was, and how to fix it just the way she liked it. He went back inside and looked around the kitchen for what he needed. Billy and Beverly were still on the couch. He thought that Billy might be crying because his head was hanging and he was snuffling, tearing the label off his beer bottle with both thumbs. Beverly was sliding closer so she could offer him her boobs to cry on if he wanted.

Francine had a big sip of her spritzer and told him it was just right; then she told him again to take off his shirt. "I believe in getting comfortable," she said. "Pull up the other chair. Look at my legs. It's September and I'm still pale as a pillowcase. Oh, you've got a bit of a tan, working outdoors I guess."

"We had some sunny days last month," he said, "I had my shirt off when I was drawing bales."

She ran her fingernails down his arm and left faint white lines on his skin. His arm was instantly covered with goosebumps.

"Oooo," she said, "the sensitive type." She smiled at him. She was a nice shape. She was wearing a two-piece bathing suit and her belly button was like a winking eye.

They sat together for half an hour or more, long enough for him to get her another spritzer and a Coke for himself. Francine talked quietly, like it was private between them and not for anyone else to overhear, and she waited for him to say something back. She looked at him like she was interested in what he had to say, and she smiled each time he responded, and every so often she would stab his arm or his chest with a long red fingernail, just sharply enough to bring back the goosebumps.

After a while Trina and Jer came downstairs. Trina was wearing a white terrycloth robe. She barely acknowledged Terry's presence with a hooded glance before she made him disappear. Jer had on a pair of shorts and his feet were bare. He was a mastiff. Broad, aggressive brow, a thick pelt on his belly and chest. He walked and stood like a sea captain, legs apart, turning his thick body to meet the wind, or the newcomer, head on. Jer came straight for Terry and his grip was a declaration. He looked Terry over, measuring his shoulders, staring him down, dismissing him as not a threat. He told Terry to make himself at home and said he remembered him from when they hunted on the farm the previous year and how he hoped it was it okay if they hunted there again this year. Terry's face gave nothing away.

Trina announced that she was going to have a bath and that she'd be back in time to eat. Billy and Beverly were still inside. Jer fired up the barbecue.

Francine leaned closer. "As you have probably noticed," she whispered, "my husband and your sister-in-law are currently sharing a bed."

Terry said nothing.

"Your brother was supposed to be in love with me by now, if my husband's grand scheme had worked, except that I like to choose my own friends, thank you very much, and besides, your brother is simply devastated by his wife's falling for another man."

"What about you?" Terry said.

"Aren't you sweet to even give a damn how I feel about this?" she said. She stretched her arms above her head showing her nude armpits dotted with droplets of sweat catching the last of the sun. The bra part of her bathing suit lifted as she stretched, and Terry could see a rounded bottom of one of her breasts. She smiled a lazy smile and leaned a few inches closer and traced a wavy line across his belly with her fingernail. "I'm handling it pretty well I think . . ." She poked right into his navel with her fingernail, stabbing him with a little red dagger. ". . . since you showed up." He felt the shock of it through to his backbone and he grabbed her finger with his right hand to keep her from wounding him, impaling him. He felt her finger in his hand, her living finger, crooking in his hand to squeeze his thumb and when she looked at him her eyes fluttered and he felt the numbness behind his mouth, tasted the electricity. "I'm having a nice time," she said. "Studying my options." She handed him her empty spritzer glass.

Francine Kramer wore engagement and wedding rings, and on her other hand, a long, black stone surrounded by diamonds.

She wore earrings, silver dangling ones with black stones like the one on her finger, and she wore a silver chain around her neck that had long silver strands with black stones at the ends, the strands fanned out across the tops of her breasts. Her lipstick was an even deeper cherry red than her fingernails and toenails. Her hair was streaked with almost-blonde. She was languid in her movements and softly suggestive in her talk and she made him feel that he was the only person in the world that she wanted to spend time with. When he made a little joke she would laugh appreciatively. Not a big braying laugh like Beverly's, nor Trina's dismissive little snort, but a purring chuckle, deep in her throat, and a nod that said, "Oh, isn't that the truth," and she would touch him, all the time — little pokes, little strokes, never lingering long enough to force him to respond or even acknowledge that there was physical contact, but every few seconds, for emphasis or reassurance, the most natural thing in the world — until by the time the sun went down she had gentled him like a quivering colt and he was used to her touch. She asked him to get her a jacket, she was getting chilled — his would be just fine — and when he brought it she leaned forward on the chaise to let him help her put it on. When she pushed her arm through the sleeve she sniffed his scent on the blue leather and made the purring noise.

After a while, Billy and Beverly came out onto the deck. Billy was pretty drunk and his eyes were red but Jer grabbed him in a headlock and rubbed his skull with his knuckles and made him laugh. "Hey now, big fella," he said to Billy, "don't be so hard on yourself. Learn to go with the flow. Bev will tuck you in, won't you, Dolly Parton? She'll ease your troubled mind. You getting enough to drink there, Gordy?"

"His name is Terry," Francine said.

"Ooops, sorry," said Jer and then he turned as if just now noticing his wife sitting close to Terry. "So that's how it is, eh?" he said. "Didn't that work out okay?"

"You'd be surprised," said Francine, and then she gave Terry a reassuring look as if to say, *don't pay any attention to him, Terry, this is between you and me.*

It wasn't much of a party. Jer and Trina ate steak off the same plate, Billy wasn't hungry and passed out on the couch. Beverly sat in front of the TV and ate her steak off a tray while she watched a movie and watched Billy at the same time. There was some kind of whispered conversation in the kitchen between Beverly and Trina shortly before Trina went upstairs with Jer but Terry couldn't hear much except that Billy's name was mentioned more than once.

After a while it got quiet, and very dark, and Terry asked Francine, "You know where I'm supposed to sleep?"

"Oh, do we have to think about that now?" She stretched. "It's so nice here in the dark. No mosquitoes." She turned to look at him. The light from the kitchen was soft on her face. The chaise was wide enough for two. "Are you getting sleepy?" She shifted sideways. "Stretch out, why don't you?"

"It's getting cool," he said.

"Tell you what you do, when you come in the front door there's a bathroom on the left and a bedroom on the right. In the bedroom there's a duvet on the bed and a couple of pillows. Why don't you go and get them?"

He got up. "What's a duvet?" he said.

The lights were low in the living room. Beverly had put an afghan over Billy and had shifted her chair closer to the couch so she could touch his shoulder from time to time. She was watching a Clint Eastwood movie with the sound turned down low, sipping a beer, drinking from the bottle, sipping and smoking and patting Billy's shoulder while he snuffled in his sleep.

Terry came back with the duvet and the pillows and Francine lowered the back of the chaise and put the two pillows side by side. Terry took off his shoes and lay down beside her and she pulled the down comforter over them so they were private in the same warm dark space. And she finally touched the part of him that had been aching for hours. She did it smoothly and quietly, privately. No one heard a thing, not the clink of his belt buckle nor the rustle of her bathing suit, nor the soft purring in her throat. He heard the murmurs and explosions from the television in the living room and once he thought he heard Trina coughing upstairs, but after a little while he forgot about everyone else, forgot about everything except the feel of her hands and her mouth. When she rolled on top of him, she covered them completely with the duvet so that they were in a tent. She straddled him and squeezed him deep inside her. She kissed him, soothed him and rode him gently like the new-broke pony he was.

Nine

DAY TWO — Tuesday, October 12

Orwell could feel the eyes of his Staff Sergeant checking him up and down as he walked toward the front doors of St. Bartholomew's.

"Pass muster, Staff?"

"Very nice, Chief."

"Erika pressed my handkerchief. You can't see it, but it's perfect."

He removed his cap and entered the church. It was to be an Anglican service. Orwell opined that Church of England ceremonies were closer in style and protocol to the Catholic services of his youth than were the new-fangled Masses. He wasn't sure what had happened to the church he'd grown up with, they'd deliberately thrown out all the stuff he liked.

The casket was flag-draped with the old Ensign. Groton was obviously a traditionalist. Or a die-hard Diefenbaker Conservative. The family sat in the front row with their stiff backs to him. He identified the widow by her pride of place and severe black-veiled bonnet and was happy he wouldn't have to face her pursed lips for at least an hour. No sooner had he located his assigned space than the matriarch swiveled her head like a scrawny screech owl and favoured him with a look of utter disdain. Spoke too soon, he muttered, flashing her an insincere smile. I should at least get points for the buttons.

The Reverend Horace Gilchrist, a man whose plummy tones were so cultivated as to be unintelligible to all but the gentry, and, presumably, their loyal servants, conducted the service. The eulogy, delivered by a former Cabinet Minister, the Right Honourable Garnett McRae, was interminable, but at least in a language with which Orwell had a passing familiarity. He was doing his best not to nod off when he felt his sleeve sharply tugged by Roy Rawluck who motioned with his head to the back of the church where Stacy Crean, in uniform this morning, was signaling as discreetly as she could. Short of a nuclear attack, Orwell was certain it couldn't be as bad as the unending list of accomplishments and examples of ponderous wit that were the legacy of the recently departed. He whispered to Rawluck, "If I'm not back in time, please make my apologies."

"Try to get back."

"With all my might," said Orwell. He avoided eye contact with Mayor Donna Lee Bricknell as he made his departure.

Adele Moen was waiting for him on the church steps. She looked him up and down. "Looking sharp, Chief."

"These things eat up most of a day. How can I help you, Detective?"

"We've got second interviews to do," she said. "Can't crap out on me now."

Orwell did a quick mental calculation of how much backlash he'd have to deal with and decided he could live with it. "Bless you," he said. "Tell Roy I've been called away," he said to Stacy. "The murder investigation."

"You'll miss the pipers," she said. Wicked smile.

"I'm sorry Dean didn't grab you."

"Appreciate you putting in the word, Chief."

"Let's get the Haldane trip out of the way first," Adele said. "We won't be able to talk to those friends of Billy's until after work probably."

"Don't suppose I can get out of this outfit?" he said.

"You kidding?" she said. "All that brass will put the fear of God into them."

Jerome Kramer's body hadn't been released, but there appeared to be a wake of some kind at 21 Boxter Crescent. There was coffee and cake. There were shrimp puffs. There was a green moulded Jell-O salad with canned fruit and miniature marshmallows trapped inside. The men, no more than four of them, were relegated to the back porch where they drank rye and ginger ale and talked about snow tires. The women were in the front room with Francine and the minister. A few kids appeared — a teenage girl looking after someone's toddler, a trio of rambunctious boys in the backyard kicking a soccer ball.

The woman who let them in said that she was Francine's sister, Ronnie, who lived just a few blocks away. She wondered if they couldn't come back some other time.

"I realize it's a bad time," Adele said, "but when is it going to be a good time? Wouldn't it be just as well now, while she has the support of her friends around her?"

Francine was only too happy to talk to them. She greeted them like honoured guests at her party. First she had to introduce them to the minister, Rev. Bruce Claymore, and to her other sister, Estelle, who had driven up from Utica, New York.

"I was thinking, for some privacy," Adele said, "we could go down to Jer's den for our little talk. Would that be okay? It shouldn't take very long."

"I don't have the key," Francine said.

"I do," said Adele.

Orwell flicked on the lights as he came through the door. Francine followed Adele, who closed it behind them. Francine didn't sit until Adele indicated one of the recliners and took the other for herself. Orwell sat on the bench end of the Bowflex machine.

"I'm sorry you haven't been able to make arrangements yet," Adele began.

"It was so confused. Not knowing when we can have the body. I thought we could at least have a reception since everybody's here, more or less."

"We managed to get in touch with Mr. Saracini," Adele said, and the pen came out, and the notebook flopped open. "And through him we heard about the Haldane Rod and Gun Club, and there we found out that Billy Warren had been a guest of his. It was Mr. Warren's father's farm where your husband was killed. Did you ever meet this Billy Warren?"

Orwell watched Francine cross her legs and lean back a bit in the La-Z-Boy. Her thoughts turned inward.

"For sure. Billy and Trina. Our very best friends in the whole wide world."

"Were they?" Adele looked up.

"You see either of them upstairs?"

"But you were friends for a while?" Orwell kept it on track.

"For a while. We did everything together."

Adele looked over at Orwell.

"When was all this?" was the best he could come up with.

"Oh, last year, up to a month or so ago."

"You didn't mention their names when we were here the first time," Orwell said.

"Why should I have? I didn't know Jer was up on Billy's father's farm. I would've thought that would be the last place for him to go."

"Why is that?"

"Oh, you don't know about that part yet, do you?"

"What part?"

"The part about Jer and Trina."

"No," said Orwell calmly, "what about Jer and Trina?"

"Have you talked to her?"

"Yes we did," said Adele.

"She didn't tell you, huh?" Francine leaned farther back and the leg-rest came up and she suddenly looked much more at home in Jer's private den.

"She didn't mention that she and my husband were having a very passionate affair? They were quite open and obvious about it. They didn't care who knew."

"Billy knew about it?"

"Well, of course. He was there when it started."

"And when was that, Mrs. Kramer?"

"Oh Jesus," she said, leaning forward abruptly to collapse the leg-rest and get to her feet. "I'm going to need a drink for this one. You two want anything?"

"No thank you," said Adele. "You go right ahead."

Francine sauntered over to the bar and made herself a rum and Diet Coke with lots of rum and lots of ice. Orwell and Adele waited quietly. Francine had a big sip of her drink, topped it up again and came back to her seat. She took a deep breath.

"Okay. Here's what happened," she said. "One day Jer shows up here with this guy, nice-looking guy, Billy Warren. He's having trouble with his insurance broker or something and Jer's helping him, or I don't know. They show up here and they're like half in the bag, and we order in a pizza and Jer brings us down here and plays some of his nudie movies, which he thinks is really choice entertainment. I'm having a few drinks, and I'm getting the feeling that Jer wants me and Billy to do it. He's making hints, you know, like 'I married her for that ass' — classy stuff like that, like they've discussed it before they got here, right? At first I'm a little flattered but then after a while I got pissed off. I'm not prudish, but it wasn't as if they were being sexy about it. It was like Jer was saying, 'Here, you want her? Help yourself,' and I'm like, 'Whoa, hey, wait up here, nobody's consulted me about this deal,' you know? So, I don't know, I got mad. I left. They stayed down here, got pissed, watched movies, whacked off for all I care."

She went back to the bar and replenished her drink. She rummaged in a drawer and found a package of cigarettes and a Bic lighter and lit one for herself. She took a drag and a sip of rum and Diet Coke and surveyed the room and the two cops.

Orwell felt a need to fill the silence. "So that was the first time you met Billy Warren?"

Francine waved off the question, her mind elsewhere, gathering her thoughts. "Yeah. So. It didn't end there. Couple of weeks later Jer says we're going out, yearly dance up at the club. I don't mind. Get out of here at least. So up we go some hall up in Uxbridge, and there's Billy and Trina. They're our guests. Surprise, surprise. You've met Trina? She's snooty. 'Doesn't really enjoy this kind of thing,' she says, like who does? It's just a dance. It's not like she has to meet the queen or anything. Anyway, I like to dance. Jer's not big into it. So I dance with Billy. He's not a great dancer, but hey, it's nice dancing with somebody. Meanwhile, Jer and Trina are all over each other at the table. It got embarrassing. So after that we all came back here and they're spending the night 'cause Billy's too bagged to drive, yada yada, and we're all feeling pretty good, and we put music on and Billy and I danced some more and Jer and Trina kept fooling around and one thing led to another and we sort of switched for the night."

"Switched? Switched partners?"

"Switched," Francine said. "Trina and Jer in the guest room and Billy and me in our bedroom. And that's when it started with Jer and Trina. The big love affair. That night." She shook her head at a memory of something sour and put out the cigarette.

"And at the same time, you were having an affair with Billy Warren?" Adele wanted to keep going.

"No. No," Francine said. She came back to sit with them. "That didn't go anywhere. Jer kept trying to get us together again but I wasn't interested. We all went up to the cottage for Labour Day and Jer wanted us to get together then, but it was just an excuse for him and Trina to carry on. He figured if I slept with Billy it was okay for him to carry on with Trina. But Billy wasn't interested in me. He was listening at the walls all the time, listening to what was going on in the other bedroom. It was tearing him up. What they were doing."

"How were you handling this?" Adele asked.

Francine laughed. "I was ready to split up with Jer four years ago when he was screwing somebody from his office, some secretary, Caroline or Carolyn somebody. He said he'd never do it again and I, shit, I didn't want to start all over anyway. Carolyn Drewer. I wasn't ready for a new life, I don't know, I sort of forgave him, but not all the way. I never felt close to him after that. He wasn't easy to be close to anyway."

"In what way, Francine?" Adele asked.

"Being so secretive all the time. Locking away his stuff, not ever really saying where he was, or where he was going to be, or when he'd be back, or what he was doing. Keeping everything separate, like his stuff and my stuff shouldn't get mixed together. He wasn't a real intimate person, you know?"

"So you weren't all that happy in your marriage the last few years?" Orwell again.

"Who's happy? I just didn't see any future in it. He didn't want children. He had a vasectomy. He didn't even give me the chance to have kids. What was in it for me? Sit around here in Nowheresville and wait for him to come home from wherever he was? I was getting ready to do something about it before Trina came onto the scene. I just wasn't exactly sure how to go about it."

"And after that weekend at the cottage, your husband and Trina Warren continued their affair?"

"Boy, did they. And he kept telling Billy to call me because I really wanted to see him again, when I definitely didn't. Billy did, a bunch of times, but just to talk about what was going on with Jer and Trina. I felt sorry for him. It's one thing if you don't really care a lot about a person, like I didn't much care what Jer did by this time. I wasn't jealous because he was screwing somebody, but they were taking weekend trips, he was buying her stuff. It was a big deal for him to take me out for Chinese food, and they were drinking champagne. That's the part that pissed me off. The other part, tell the truth — Jer and I hadn't had sex for over a year before this happened and I didn't care of we ever screwed again. I was hoping he'd ask for a divorce,"

"But Billy didn't feel that way about his marriage?" Adele again.

"One time on the phone, he started crying, like really blubbering, like a kid. I said to him, 'Shit, if you feel that way, go get her back. Punch the shit out of Jer! That, or face the fact that your marriage is wrecked and split up with her,' I told him. And, I mean, what's so special about her anyway? She's skinny, snooty, walks like she has a pickle between her cheeks. I don't see the big attraction, myself."

"Now who the hell was *that*?" Adele was shaking her head.

"Big change from the perfect wife of the first interview," said Orwell.

"I almost believe this version," she said. "Never really bought the pearls-and-sweater-set look."

"She seemed to know her way around hubby's private den too."

"Probably the only fun room in the joint."

Trina Warren got out of her white BMW and turned to watch the two cops getting out of their car and coming toward her.

"Hello, Mrs. Warren. Detective Moen. And you know Chief Brennan. How are you today?"

"I'm tired, Detective. And I need some lunch." She unlocked the door and flicked the hall light on inside. She didn't invite them in.

"She left the door open," Adele said.

"Very gracious," said Orwell.

Trina walked ahead, leaving them in the hallway "I'm going to have a drink. You want one? Chief?"

"Wish we could," said Orwell. "You go right ahead. This is probably a rough time for you."

Trina ignored the comment, went into the kitchen.

Adele followed her. "I suppose you know that there was a wake for Mr. Kramer today? I guess you didn't feel like going to that."

"No, I was unaware of it." Trina poured herself a glass of white wine. She looked over her shoulder at the two cops standing in the kitchen doorway, shook her head. "I suppose we'd better sit down."

They sat on one of the leather couches, Trina sat facing them across the chrome and smoked glass coffee table.

Adele started briskly, flipping the notebook, uncapping the pen. "Mrs. Warren, you gave us kind of the wrong impression when we were here yesterday."

"In what way, Detective?"

"Well, remember we asked you if you knew Jerome Kramer and you said . . . you . . . said . . ." She flipped to the appropriate page in her notebook. ". . . 'Yes, he was a friend of my husband's' . . ."

"That was true."

"True as far as it went, I suppose. But in fact, you were closer to Mr. Kramer than you let on. Isn't that so?"

"I thought it would get out eventually. I didn't want to talk about it just then. I was upset. And I didn't want to complicate things for my husband."

"In what way, Mrs. Warren? Complicate things for your husband how?"

"Well." She reached into her pocket as if looking for a package of cigarettes and then left her hand inside the pocket when she realized that it was empty. "It's just that with Billy moving out, and being so jealous, and I didn't know what you knew about the two of them, that they weren't really friends anymore, that they were more like enemies lately. I didn't want to raise any suspicions."

Orwell spoke up. "Did you think that your husband might have done something?"

"I didn't know, did I?" She seemed exasperated with the two of them. "He might have. All right. It was my first thought, when I heard about Jer being killed, my first thought was that maybe Billy had done it. Then I found out that he was in Buffalo for that weekend and I stopped worrying. But right at the beginning, I wondered if maybe Billy had done something stupid."

"Did you believe that your husband was capable of doing something stupid?"

"I hoped not." This time she got up and left the room and returned with a pack of cigarettes and a lighter from somewhere in the hallway. "Billy was in a bad state these last few months. Because of Jer and me." She unwrapped the package and held onto the crumpled cellophane and tinfoil while she pulled out a cigarette.

"When was the last time you saw Mr. Kramer?"

She sat down and dropped the wrappings onto the smoked glass. "Friday night and Saturday morning."

"That would be Friday the 8th and Saturday the 9th of October? Here?"

"No, not here. We stayed at a motel. I didn't like being here with him. There was always a chance that Billy would come barging in. He did that once and it was most uncomfortable for all concerned." She lit her cigarette and took a deep drag. "We stayed at a motel Friday night. Jer was going to come back Sunday after he got his deer, or even if he didn't."

"May I ask you what you did after he left, Saturday noon? What did you do for the rest of the weekend?"

"I came back here. Saturday I didn't do much. Sunday I went to church."

"Church?"

"Yes, Detective, I went to church. That okay with you?"

"Certainly, Mrs. Warren. Church. Okay." Adele nodded to herself as though everything made perfect sense. "Listen, one other thing — your husband told us he had some archery equipment in this house. Would you mind if we had a look at it?"

"Help yourself. It's all in the garage."

Trina showed them how to get into the garage through the kitchen. She told them she'd be available if they needed anything else and went upstairs to run a bath for herself. Orwell followed Adele into the garage. It was bigger than the living room. The floor was concrete. The sports equipment was in one corner. Billy's archery equipment was next to the tennis racquets. He had two bows. One, a Fred Bear recurve of polished Osage Orange wood, the other a metal compound bow, a complicated arrangements of pulleys and wheels — a short, brutal tool. There was a metal clip attached to the bow. It held four arrows. There was space for six. The arrow shafts were mottled black and green; the plastic feathers were the same, two black and one green on each shaft. Adele stood in front of the archery gear for a long moment.

"My my," she said.

"The arrows are the same colours," Orwell said. "Maybe they're all like that, I don't know, but these look the same as the ones they pulled out of Kramer."

"One of these arrows is missing a blade," she said. "It's supposed to have four."

"Can't match arrows like bullets though, can they?"

"Be surprised what they can do these days."

Trina Warren was waiting for them in the front hallway.

"We're going to take these along with us, Mrs. Warren."

"Of course. Did you want anything more from me today?"

"That will be all for now, I think," said Orwell. "You've been very helpful."

"Have I?" she said. "I don't see how."

They found a small Italian place and had bowls of black bean soup with sausage and shared a loaf of crusty bread. Orwell would have enjoyed a cold beer but as he was conspicuously wearing every decoration he was entitled to, as well as being, however unofficially, "on the job," he kept their bottle of San Pellegrino water in plain sight.

"Get good service with you decked out," Adele said.

"I especially hate this hat," Orwell said. "I like my felt hat."

"It's all bent," she said.

"Yeah, but it never blows off in the wind," he said.

Adele ordered biscotti and espresso, which sounded like a great idea to the Chief as well. His Sam Brown harness creaked agreeably as he sat back.

"Not looking too great for your boy Billy," she said.

"Turning into a domestic drama," he agreed.

"I bet we wrap it up today," she said. "You ever do a murder?"

"Do drunk drivers count?" he asked.

"They should."

Orwell sipped his coffee. "My first wife, Laura, was killed by a drunk driver," he said. "Twenty-six years ago." He looked at her. "He was back on the road inside two years, drinking, driving, looking for another victim." His biscotti was a pile of crumbs on his plate. "If that wasn't a murder, I don't know what is."

"I'm sorry about your wife," Adele said.

"Got so I hated three-lane highways. Personally. Isn't that weird? Started giving them names — Shithead, Bastard — other names I'd rather not say out loud." He laughed at his own childishness.

"You were OPP?" she asked.

"Long time," he said. "They're a good outfit, mostly."

"You just don't want them taking over your town."

"They'd do a good job. They just wouldn't do the job we do. Foot patrols, real beat cops on the street, downtown, all night, checking locks, looking in windows. My guys do crossing guard duty at the high school, give you a ride home if you've had too many, keep the dope dealers hopping and the bar fights brief."

"How many?"

"Thirty uniforms, six investigators," he said.

"They'll be out of a job?"

"Some of them. The older ones have a decent pension set-up; I've got a few good ones who could go anywhere. I've got some who'll have to look harder."

"Hope it doesn't come to that," she said.

"Can't fight the tide coming in," he said. "Sooner or later all the small town police forces will be gone."

They got lucky. When Orwell and Adele arrived, all three men on their list were together at the sports bar, engaged in a heated discussion about something other than sports. Brent Styles saw them first and sighed as if his life was turning out badly. Orwell and Adele sat without being invited.

"Darryl Demarchuk and Glen Hoebel? Is that right?"

Darryl was a short strong man with thick dark hair. He wore a muscle shirt to show off his biceps and he had tattoos on both arms — a Harley Davidson eagle on his right arm and a naked woman with her hands behind her head on the left. Glen was tall and rangy. He had spiky blond hair and a short, unfinished beard. He had on a jacket with leather sleeves and crests from a junior hockey team.

"We need to clear up a few things about this Buffalo trip, fellas." Adele got out her note-keeping equipment. "We've talked to Brent here, he probably told you, and we just need to get some information from the two of you, okay?"

Darryl shrugged, Glen raised his eyebrows and Brent Styles turned his back on them and concentrated on a televised drag race.

Adele flipped to a new page in her notebook, numbered it, and then looked across the table at the two men facing her and at the back of the one who was not. "It is my understanding that the four of you went down to Buffalo together. You three and Billy Warren. In two cars. Stayed at two different motels. We've got all this from Brent there. What was the name of the one you two stayed at?"

"Sneaky Pete's," said Darryl. "It's a dump, but it's cheap."

"Sneaky Pete's. Okay. And Friday night, after you checked in, the four of you, you three and Billy Warren, went out and had a good time, had a bit to drink, a few laughs, like that, right?"

"Right," said Glen, looking at the back of Brent's head. Brent was watching a Motomaster commercial as if it were sudden death overtime.

"Next morning, Saturday morning, the four of you met up again for breakfast, is that right too?"

"Wasn't that early," Darryl said. "Wasn't breakfast. Was more beers."

"Okay. You had a liquid breakfast. Brunch, rather. Then what did you do?"

Darryl looked at Glen and then at the back of Brent's head. "Right. Okay. We took off. Me and Glen. Went back to the motel. I flaked out for a while. Then later we had something to eat and went to the game."

"The game. You mean the Bills game, Sunday?"

"No, we had tickets for the Sabres-Leafs. Big sports weekend. Hockey and football."

"Okay." said Adele. "Sounds like a great weekend. So you all went to a hockey game Saturday night. Billy too?"

Orwell could see the tension in the back of Brent's neck, could almost see the hairs standing up.

"Billy didn't show up. He was sick or hungover or something," Darryl said.

"He didn't go to the hockey game? Oh my. But he was okay for the football game the next afternoon?"

Darryl looked at Glen. "We were on the other side."

Adele flipped back a dozen or so pages in her notebook. "Brent there says he could see you two on the other side of the stadium because of your red blanket."

"Yeah, well he's full of shit, because I didn't have my fucking red blanket, as I just told him before you got here — he must've been looking at some other asshole."

"And you couldn't see them either?"

"How the fuck are we supposed to see them? Seventy thousand people. I didn't even know what section they were in."

"How about after the game? Did the four of you get together after?"

"We were supposed to, but when we showed up at their motel they'd already checked out. I didn't know what was going on. We stayed Sunday night like we planned. Fuck 'em."

Adele sighed. "Let me see if I have this. The last time you saw Billy was Saturday, noonish, when you had your liquid brunch. Is that right?"

"That's right," said Glen Hoebel with finality and glared at the back of Brent's head. "He's trying to get us to say we could see them at the stadium, but we couldn't."

Orwell spoke up. His voice had the sharp crack of command. "Mr. Styles? Could we have your attention here, please? The program's been over for quite a while now."

Brent turned reluctantly.

"Could you tell us why Billy didn't go to the hockey game Saturday night? Was he sick?"

"I don't know. I guess."

"Did you talk to him before the game? After the game?"

"I guess. I don't remember."

"Do you remember seeing him before the game? After the game?"

"I don't know."

"Okay," Adele said, looking vexed. "I'll go through it, minute by minute. Did you see Billy Warren Friday night?"

"Yes."

"Did you see him Saturday morning?"

"Yes."

"Saturday afternoon?"

"Partly."

"Partly what?"

Brent suddenly looked tired and fed up with it all. "He took off. Borrowed my 'Vette, goes somewhere. I didn't see him until after the game on Sunday. When I got back from the game he was back at the motel."

"You're now telling us that he was gone from Saturday afternoon until Sunday evening?"

"Yeah, right. You happy now?"

"No, I'm not happy, Mr. Styles. You could have saved us a great deal of trouble if you had told the truth the first time. It's entirely possible that you may be charged with obstruction. Does that make *you* happy?"

Sergeant Dean had been instructed to bring Billy Warren into the Dockerty Station. He was there when Adele and Orwell arrived. Sergeant Dean asked to be present at the interview. Adele said he could watch on a monitor in the next room but that she would rather handle the interview herself. Sergeant Dean, Officer Rush and two other OPP uniforms stayed in the observation room.

Detective Moen informed William Maxim Warren of his rights and asked him if he would like to have a lawyer present at his interview. Billy said not. But he said he would like to have Chief Brennan present if that was okay. Adele said it was.

Billy was wearing a leather jacket and Orwell could hear it stretching, could hear the oak chair creaking. Billy had his feet wide apart, flat on the floor, prepared to spring. His thigh muscles were tight and his heels made rapid, barely audible thumping noises on the grey carpet.

"Look here, Mr. Warren," Adele started, "why don't you just tell us what really happened? We know you didn't go to any football game. We know you borrowed Brent Styles' Corvette and that you were gone from Buffalo for at least twenty-eight hours. We've got your bows and arrows and the arrows match the ones we took out of Jerome Kramer's body."

"I didn't do it," said Billy Warren.

"Okay," said Adele, "who did?"

"I don't know."

"You've got to admit it looks kind of bad here. You had a pretty good motive for killing Mr. Kramer, don't you think? He was having an affair with your wife, breaking up your marriage. We know that you weren't happy about the situation."

Billy looked for a moment as though he wanted to say something to the Chief, but then shook his head and dropped his eyes.

Adele continued. "You knew where Jerome Kramer was going to be, knew where to find him in the middle of the night. You had the motive and the weapon and the opportunity. You lied about your whereabouts and tried to get your friend Brent to provide you with an alibi. Am I leaving anything out?"

"Just I didn't do it."

"Mr. Warren," Adele began quietly, almost gently, "this isn't going to disappear. We have a blade from one of your arrows that we found near the murder scene. It looks like it has a fingerprint on it. If that print belongs to you, it's going to be impossible to convince anyone that you weren't in the bush that night."

Billy stifled a sob.

"You sure you don't want a lawyer, Billy?" Orwell asked. Adele gave him a sharp look. He persisted. "I could call Georgie Rhem for you. He could be over here pretty quick."

"You think I need that?"

"I think Detective Moen here has a pretty solid case. I mean if it was me, I'd be feeling pretty secure that I'm getting to the end of this business. I'd be thinking that it's almost time to have a talk with the Crown Prosecutor. Unless you've got some really good explanation for what went on that weekend, why yes, I'd call Georgie Rhem or maybe Don Lauk if you want to spend the money, and get some legal advice."

Billy thought over his options for a long minute. "Okay then," he said, "I'll talk to Georgie."

"I'll get you a phone," Orwell said.

"You going to arrest me?"

Adele delivered a brief glare at Orwell before turning to Billy. "Yes, Mr. Warren, I am," she said.

Sergeant Dean, Officer Rush, and the other OPP visitors didn't bother thanking anyone for their hospitality. Sergeant Dean went out of his way to snub Orwell as he passed him on the stairs.

"Wrapping it up, Sergeant Dean?" Orwell disliked speaking

to a man's back. Dean didn't deign to answer, but a voice from the other direction caught his ear.

"It's my stupid partner's fault," Adele said. She was at the front desk, checking paperwork for the transfer of Billy Warren down to Metro. "Breaking his fucking leg when I needed him."

Orwell descended the three steps to stand near her. "You did splendidly," he said. "That was a good arrest."

"At least Paul knows the basics," she said. "Shit! I could've had a statement. Now we've got to go over all this shit again and again." She turned to glare at him. She was nearly as tall. "Where do you get off butting in at a crucial moment? I asked him if he wanted a lawyer, didn't I? Right off the top. He said no. It's on tape, it's on a fucking video."

"Yes, you did."

"Why in Christ would you do that, right when I was this close to getting a written statement?" She was holding up two pinched fingers.

"You don't know that."

"Don't tell me what I know. I've been doing this for a while."

"He was starting to lose it."

"Duh. What do you think I was shooting for? Jee-zuss H. Fucking Christ! Talk about sticking your nose in."

"It won't be the last time, Detective."

"It will if I have anything to say about it."

"I expect you'll have a great deal to say about it," said Orwell. "I don't think you got the right guy."

Orwell, for all his size, usually took stairs two at a time but he stopped on the landing to catch his breath before the last flight to his office. A hundred chores, attendances and annoyances were waiting and he really didn't feel like climbing the last eleven risers. There was a sour acid burn in the back of his throat. Probably the bean soup repeating, he thought.

Staff Sergeant Rawluck was casting a baleful eye over the

recently abandoned command centre and complaining about how the OPP guys had scratched the desk and wrecked the map he'd provided. Dorrie, as always, had anticipated her boss's arrival and was holding out a sheaf of messages.

"Hang onto them, Dorrie. I'm going home to change out of this outfit, and then I'm going to have a meal with my family."

"You don't want to issue a statement about Billy Warren?"

"I do not. Billy was arrested by Metro Homicide, and he is on his way to Toronto, well out of our jurisdiction. We'll let them make the announcement."

"I should have something I can say when the phone starts ringing."

"You can say that his first court appearance will be early next week and it is likely that he will be charged with First Degree murder. Georgie Rhem has been retained as his lawyer and will be arranging a bail hearing."

"That's it?"

"That's it from me," he said. "You can refer them to OPP Region if you like. Sergeant Dean may have a statement." Orwell raised his voice for Rawluck's benefit. "You may now restore Sergeant Dean's work area to its former glory, the OPP will no longer be needing space in our house. At least until we're evicted," he added under his breath.

Roy Rawluck crossed the floor, still resplendent in his best uniform.

"Her Honour was wondering where you took off to," he said with just a hint of censure.

"Her Honour the Mayor should know better than to wear a pink hat to an Anglican funeral," Orwell said, entering his office. "And frankly, it's none of Her Majesty's bloody concern where I went on official police business. Those bluenoses up on the hill think the world comes to a halt every time one of the anointed hands in his dinner pail."

"It was a fine service."

"I'm sure it was, and it only cost twenty-four man-hours which might have been spent doing actual police work. Her Ladyship's going to miss that kind of attention when the OPP comes to town."

"You don't think we should take a little credit?" Dorrie wanted to know. "For the arrest? You were part of the investigation."

"Might do us some good," Roy said.

"Truth is, I just went along for the ride," said Orwell. "Second truth is, I don't feel like patting myself on the back just yet."

Orwell was sitting in his little home office under the stairs, a room barely big enough for himself and his desk and his chair. He had a muddy aquarium in there to make up for the lack of a window. But he hadn't been looking after the fish all that well since the novelty had worn off. The aquarium stank like a little swamp when he lifted the canopy to feed whatever fish were left. He suspected that the Oscar had eliminated most of them. The algae on the sides of the glass made it hard for him to keep track of exactly who was in there.

Erika came around the staircase and knocked on the open door. "You were in Oshawa?" She was holding a receipt from the Italian restaurant. "Fourteen dollars for a bowl of soup?"

"Good soup," he said.

"I hope so," she said.

"It's deductible," he said. "Maybe. I'm not sure how official it was. Although I must say, I looked pretty darn impressive playing detective in my Admiral's outfit."

"Didn't you have dessert?" she asked. "Like maybe a twenty-dollar piece of pie?"

"I guess Adele must've paid for that one."

"Adele?"

"Detective Adele Moen. She was in charge."

"Aha. This gets even more interesting. You get all dressed up, say you're going to a funeral and then run off to the city with 'Adele' to eat fancy soup."

“Oh, and we might have had coffee, too, along the way.”

“Along the way.”

“Yes, we were on the road a lot.”

“How cozy,” she said. “I’m going to bed now.”

“I’m waiting for a call. I’ll be up soon.”

“Who’s calling at this time?”

“I’ve left messages for Detective Moen.”

“This would be the Adele woman?”

“Yes, I have a strong need to speak to her.”

“What’s so important?”

“Billy Warren doesn’t smoke.”

“That’s it?”

“That’s enough,” he said.

“Diana is coming up for the weekend. It would be nice if we could all have a meal together.”

“Yes, that would be nice,” he said.

She squeezed into the room and bent over to kiss him. “When you come to bed will you rub my back? It helps me sleep.”

“What if you’re already asleep?”

“Rub my back anyway. Maybe I’ll wake up.” She made a face at him and went upstairs. The two dogs and the two cats trotted upstairs behind her, the cats with their tails straight up, the dogs with dutiful smiles. They followed wherever she went.

He leaned back again, more carefully, and found the fitting angle in the slanted ceiling where it met the wall. His pleasure at being able to stretch out only slightly diminished by the whiff he got off his green-water aquarium close by his left elbow.

A few hours of reflection had persuaded Orwell that he had overstepped his place during the interview. And why had he done it? He knew better; any rookie would have known better. Not that interviewing murder suspects was one of his fields of expertise, but he had interviewed a few thousand bad-asses in his day and he certainly knew that interrupting a partner’s closing was a serious breach of protocol, not to mention very bad manners. Still, there were "things" nagging at the back of his mind. Things. That's as far as his definition went. Must make a list, he thought. There were inconsistencies. There were . . . things.

His cell phone sang in his pocket. Leda had programmed "I Heard It Through the Grapevine" as his ring tone. Sometimes it embarrassed him but he was touched that his daughter had taken note of his fondness for old Motown. And that she didn't hold it against him.

"Brennan," he said.

"Chief? It's Adele Moen. Sorry to call this late at night."

"That's fine, Detective, I was hoping you'd get back to me. I have a few questions about the Billy Warren business."

"They can wait, Chief."

"Just a few things to straighten out in my mind. Otherwise they'll keep nagging at me all night."

"This isn't a social call, Chief."

"Look, I'm sorry, truly. I was out of line."

"Something else has come up," she said. "I wanted to tell you before you heard it from somewhere else."

"What?"

"Billy Warren hanged himself in his cell tonight."

"Oh sweet Jesus," said Orwell.

"He wet his shirt in the toilet, tied one sleeve to the grate and the other around his neck, and just let his feet go out from under him. Didn't make a sound."

"Lord have mercy," said Orwell. "The poor sad sonofabitch."

Ten

September

Terry drove Francine home from The Great Sex Weekend a day early. Sunday afternoon. The sun was shining again, not much traffic on the highway. You wouldn't think a little truck like that would be so much fun to drive but it just skimmed along, humming like a sewing machine. Francine paid for a full tank of gas.

"Probably make it to Winnipeg on four tankfuls," Terry said.

"But why would you want to go?" Francine said. She made a sour face. "Only direction I want to go is south. Florida, Mexico, Costa Rica, some island, I don't care which one as long as there's a beach and sunshine every day and somebody who can bring me a cold drink once an hour. I don't want to hear the words overcoat, antifreeze, cold front, wind chill, you get the picture, ever again." She swung around in her seat so that she could watch his face. "You ever been to a place like that?"

"Which, Florida or Winnipeg?"

She gave him an appreciative chuckle and smacked his arm lightly. "Doesn't have to be Florida. I think maybe one of those Caribbean islands if we can find one that isn't full of drug lords and revolutions and that kind of thing. They can really screw up a good vacation."

"You've took vacations there?"

"*Taken*, sweetie, I've *taken* vacations. The answer is yes and no.

Jer took me. To Nassau. It was okay except for Jer. He was doing things with dollars and back and forth and who knows what, and he brought along another couple and they were fighting and then Jer and the husband were fighting about dollars and bank rates and that kind of thing and the wife flew home early and I had a rotten time." She smiled at him and waited with the smile in place until he glanced her way and smiled back.

"I could have had a nice time with you."

Terry took a deep breath. She was touching him again. Walking the fingernails of her left hand up his right leg and dragging them back toward his knee.

"We could swim naked in our own little swimming pool. There are places you can get like that. They have a privacy fence around the patio and a private pool. You can walk around with no clothes on and get brown all over. I think it's good for a person to get their butt brown once in a while. Poor bum-bums, always covered, never getting any sunshine."

There were times when she talked to him in baby talk, or like she was the baby, or they were both babies. Sometimes she was a little stern with him, correcting his grammar and commenting on his table manners and then she spoke like a schoolteacher. And sometimes, most of the time, her voice was softly seductive, praising him and telling him he was strong, or big, or too big. Telling him he made her feel all soft inside, made her wet. Saturday, when they were having breakfast, all six of them, sitting around the table on the patio, Billy hung over like a poisoned dog and Beverly shoveling pancakes and sausages into her face and Trina and Jer feeding each other pieces of toast and jam, she whispered to him that he was making her wet again and she took his hand under the edge of the table and touched herself with his fingers to show him.

"I could never take you any place like that," he said. "Probably costs thousands of dollars for a trip like that."

"It's only money, silly," she said. She slapped him lightly on the front of his jeans. "Money isn't the problem," she said and touched him again. Stroking this time, lightly up and down the inside of his leg petting his penis almost as though she didn't know it was there, like it was her pet.

"Would you take me there?" she asked him. "If there was enough money? Someplace warm. You could rub oil on my ass and my tits and watch them get brown?"

Terry had to concentrate on his driving; he had almost drifted into the wrong lane. He was hard again and there wasn't room in his pants. She stroked and stroked and gently scratched the underside and after a while she tugged his zipper down and freed him.

"Now you drive very carefully," she said, "because I'm going to undo my seat belt for a while."

She turned on the radio, it was a country station, Country 105. Pam Tillis was singing "Maybe It Was Memphis."

She made him park at the new mall two blocks from her house and then told him carefully and in detail how to come up a back lane and through a back gate and down some steps to a basement door. She told him to keep his head down and she made him wear the Blue Jays cap she found between the seats.

"People don't have to know our private business," she said.

Jerry wouldn't be back until Monday night at the earliest. They had lots of time. Time to do things without having to be careful. All he had to do was walk quickly and quietly up the lane like he was a repairman going somewhere definite, find the green gate with the white posts and the blue recycle bins, come to the basement door below the deck. The door would be open. She got out of the truck and walked across the parking lot to the corner where her street began, and halfway there she swung around to look back at him and put her finger to her lips like she was saying shhhh, and then she sucked her finger into her mouth and gave him a wicked smile like she was having such fun on their great adventure, and it wasn't over yet.

Terry closed the basement door behind him and took off the Blue Jays cap. There was a rec room to the left and the door was open, the lights were warm and low inside. She wasn't there. He heard the shower running in the bathroom at the end of the rec room, heard her voice singing along with the music, singing along with some old romantic song, Frank Sinatra maybe, one of those. He could see her shape through the fog on the sliding glass doors.

"What are you waiting for?" He heard her say. "Nothing like a nice hot shower after a long trip."

He took off his clothes and she slid the shower door open and invited him into the steam and the bubbles and the heat and the stinging water. She washed him from head to toe using a big sponge and soap that she squeezed out of a tube.

"There now, doesn't that feel good?"

He said yeah or he thought he said yeah, it didn't matter. She just kept on talking and washing him, every inch of him, like he was a baby.

"This is Jer's private bathroom," she said. "I'm not allowed to be in here. Not allowed to use this sponge, not allowed to touch this soap or this shampoo or this razor. This is Jer's private place and he thinks he has the only key." She hummed and purred and washed between his legs. "You know what he would do to me if he found out I was using his private bathroom?"

"What?"

"He would hit me." Then she sang "Come Fly with Me" for a few bars while she washed his legs and feet.

"Has he hit you before?" he wanted to know.

"He hits me all the time. He likes hitting me. That's all he likes doing to me anymore. He likes hitting women. Now, you wash me."

She gave him the sponge and the tube of soap and stood under the showerhead with her eyes closed and let the water pour down over her head and let him wash her all over. It was the first female body Terry had ever known up close. He could see where she had got some sun, her belly was pink gold, not burned, she had been very careful with sunscreen and rolling over and covering up, but she had the beginnings of a tan on her belly and back, and her breasts were white, and the triangle of skin below her belly was white, and the fur between her legs was trimmed short. He washed her the way he used to wash Billy's Pontiac, scrupulously, every inch, washed in circles. She purred and sang as he scrubbed her back and he knelt on the shower floor to wash her bottom and her legs.

"Did he do this?" he asked.

"Do what, sweetie?"

"This bruise on the back of your leg."

"Is that still there? That was months ago. Is there one on the other leg?"

"Not as much."

"Lord, that was a bad one. I don't know what got him started that time. I think I bought myself a pair of shoes without checking with him. Right, he wanted to teach me something about shoes. He beat me with them."

He gently washed the backs of her thighs and felt her slide down inside his embrace, slippery as an otter.

That night, in bed, when they were snuggled together in the dark, she began to cry.

"What's the matter?"

"I just hate the thought that we can't be together always," she said.

"I hate that too," he said. He didn't know what else to say.

"You are just so good for me, so strong. I feel like you would protect me, if you could."

"I would."

"But it would be too dangerous."

"I'm not afraid of him," he said. "He's getting a gut on him and he drinks too much. I don't think he's in such good shape."

"Oh, I'm not worried about how you would handle yourself,

sweetie. I've felt your muscles. I know you could take care of yourself. But what about me? When you're not around. He'd probably kill me."

Terry felt an obligation to respond. "I wouldn't let him."

"You won't be there to stop him, sweetie."

She rolled away and he rolled over to hold her from behind and she snuggled back into him.

"Let's not worry about what we can't have," she said. "Let's just enjoy this little time we have together."

"Why should he care, anyway?" he said. "He's got Trina. He carries on with her in front of you and Billy. Why should he care what you do?"

"He'd be upset if he knew that you were a much better lover than he ever was." She laughed like a sneaky little kid, "If he knew that your cock was bigger than his." Snicker. "And stayed harder than his. But I would never say that to him. It wouldn't be worth it. He might lose it. He'd beat me black and blue if I ever said that." She twisted around so that she could look at his face over her shoulder lit by a streetlight through a gap in the bedroom drapes. "It's much more complicated than that, sweetie. It's money. He'll never let me go because it would cost him too much money. He wouldn't let me divorce him because he would have to show a judge where all his money is, and I know where all his money is."

Terry knew that wasn't true. "Is he real rich?"

"Pretty rich. But to tell the truth, he's worth more dead than he is alive." And she giggled again and hid her mouth with her hand and wiggled her bum against him like a bad little girl.

"Is he going to marry Trina?" he said after a while.

This time her laugh was very grown up. "He'll be tired of her in a month or so," she said. "She'll start to get on his nerves. Pretty soon she'll tick him off so he hits her. Then he'll apologize and buy her something and maybe they'll make up. But he'll hit her again. Maybe next time she won't want to make up. Depends on how much she likes getting knocked around."

Terry rolled away and stared at the ceiling. "I don't think she'd like it," he said. His hands had balled into fists and his muscles were tensing.

Francine sensed the change immediately — had been preparing for it without knowing exactly what she'd been probing for. She connected it with the hundred little signs she had observed over the weekend; how his body stiffened each time Trina's name came up, whenever she appeared, the way his mouth seemed to dry up when he tried to talk to her, the way he rarely looked her straight in the eye. Francine didn't touch him now; she pulled herself up against the headboard and tested the waters carefully, gauging his reaction to each carefully measured phrase.

"Poor Trina," she said. She could feel the tension in him through the bedsprings. "She doesn't know what she's let herself in for."

"I hope he doesn't hit her in the face too much. He's usually pretty good about that but accidents happen. He gave me a black eye once. I had to wear dark glasses for a month. In February."

Terry was holding his fists off the bed now.

"You love her, don't you?"

He made a sound like something tearing.

"Shhh, little one. It's okay. It won't hurt my feelings. You can tell me."

"Mmmmmm." His throat was constricted and his eyes were stinging.

"There, there. I know what it's like to love someone when they don't love you back. You and Trina never made love, did you?"

"No."

"She doesn't know what she's missing." She began to stroke him lightly on the shoulder with two fingers, softly, like petting a budgie. So softly. "If she only knew I bet she'd drop Jer like an old shoe." He rolled away and she moved to stay in contact with him, stroking his shoulder and his back while he sobbed into the pillow. "My, my, my," she said wonderingly, "who would have thought my new man was so passionate? You're really on fire, baby, I can feel the heat rising off you."

After a while he found his voice and spoke into the hot, damp depression in his pillow. "I don't expect her to love me. That's not what I want."

"You like to worship her. From afar."

Francine leaned back against the headboard again and continued to stroke him as he cried softly. After a while she got up and left the room.

When he went looking for her half an hour later he found her sitting in the kitchen, drinking a glass of wine and smoking a cigarette. When she saw him standing there she smiled sweetly. It was a motherly smile, all-forgiving, all understanding.

"Hi, sweetie. You want a Coke?"

He nodded and she indicated the fridge with a tilt of her head. When he passed her to get it she grabbed his cock and gave it a friendly squeeze.

"How are you feeling, baby? You all cried out?"

He popped open the Coke and had a long drink.

"Close the fridge, sweetie."

He closed the fridge door and burped, long and loud.

"Oh dear," she said, "and cover your mouth at least."

"Sorry." He sat on a stool on the other side of the counter. "I didn't know you smoked."

"Sometimes I do. When I have serious thinking to do."

"About what?"

"Guess." She smiled a lazy pussycat smile.

"How to get a divorce, right?"

She shook her head. "No. I told you. He won't give me a divorce. He'd kill me first."

"You could go to the police. Tell them he beats you up. They could protect you."

"They can't protect anybody from anybody, sweetie. Don't

you read the papers?" She butted the cigarette in a saucer and went to the fridge for more white wine and soda water. "Nope. Divorce won't work. It has to be something else."

"You could run away."

"With what? A borrowed truck and a credit card? How far could we get on that, do you think?"

He had another gulp of Coke and this time he covered his mouth when he burped.

"I don't know if I should tell you this," she said, sitting down again with her fresh spritzer. She looked at him for a moment, making up her mind, deciding. "What if I told you he's already hit Trina? More than once."

"Did she tell you?"

"I saw him do it. I went to the bathroom upstairs at the cottage and I saw him smack her against the wall. Remember how she had those sunglasses on all the time? Remember how puffy her face was?" Terry crushed the can slowly in his right hand. She reached across the counter to pat the back of his wrist. "He's not a nice man," she said.

"He better not hit her anymore," Terry said.

"There's really only one way to stop him, sweetie." And she looked deep into his eyes, forced him to look directly at her, held his wrist tightly. "Only one way." Then suddenly she smiled sweetly as though all her troubles had vanished. "That's enough doom and gloom for one night," she said. "Let's go back to bed and get some sleep."

She led him back into the bedroom by his penis. "Good boy," she said. "Come along now, that's a good boy."

"What's the only way to stop him?" he said.

"We'll talk about it in the morning," she said. "We'll talk about our options in the morning. For the rest of the night we'll just snuggle like two bugs in a rug and dream about warm sandy beaches far from here."

Terry woke up in a king-sized bed in an unfamiliar bedroom late that Labour Day Monday morning, almost 10:00, half the day gone. He had stomach cramps and gas in his bowels and he spent a long time in the bathroom with the door locked before he got some relief. He didn't know where his clothes were.

He put on the robe he found hanging behind the bathroom door and went looking for Francine, moving quietly and pausing at the top of the stairs. He heard the sound of a washing machine coming from the basement and started down in his bare feet, lifting the hem of Jerry's robe, dark blue terrycloth with stitching on the chest. The door to Jerry's private room was open.

Francine was scrubbing Jerry's bathroom. She was on her knees, wearing cutoffs and a T-shirt and yellow rubber gloves.

"Need any help?"

She looked over her shoulder at him.

"Your clothes can go in the dryer now," she said. "Just turn the dial to forty-five minutes, that should do it."

He went out into the basement and located the washer and dryer behind the stairs. His clothes had been flattened against the sides of the tub by the spinning. He put them into the dryer and closed the lid and studied the dials and knobs trying to figure out how it worked. Her yellow-gloved hand reached around him from behind and turned the dial expertly. He felt her firm body pressed against his back.

"You look nice in that robe," she said. "Blue suits you."

"It's long."

"It's made that way. Full length. Turn around, let me look at you."

She looked him up and down and smiled approvingly. "Such a handsome young man," she said. "Lovely blue eyes. Did you sleep well?"

"A long time."

"Not so long," she said. "We didn't close our eyes until after three." She grinned and headed back to Jerry's room. "I slept like a baby. I'm almost finished; keep me company for a minute, then I'll make us some breakfast."

He stood in the doorway to Jerry's private room while she finished wiping down the bathroom floor.

"It would never do for him to come home and find evidence of what we did in here. He'd go crazy if he knew we were making love in his shower."

She finished the bathroom floor with a final swipe of a J-Cloth and collected her cleaning supplies: Mr. Clean, Vim, Windex. She carried them past him into the basement area and stacked them on a shelf near the drier along with the yellow gloves.

"Final check," she said, and brushed past him into the room again for a last look around. "Just the way he left it." She crossed the room to a tall mahogany cabinet. "Want to see some stuff?"

She had a set of keys in her cutoff pocket and one of them fit the lock. Inside was Jerry's hunting gear. Terry went to stand beside her and look at the equipment. Three hunting bows, four rifles, two shotguns and four handguns.

"He's got a lot of stuff."

"Oh, he treats himself very well," she said. "I have to practically submit a requisition form if I want new shoes, but Jerry . . . of course he never pays full price. All this stuff is either hot, or sold under-the-table, or a bonus for something he did for somebody, like that makes it okay for him to have it and for me not to have anything nice of my own."

Terry looked at the dark green and brown Hytex compound bow. He had seen it before. He wondered for a moment which shaft in the quiver had passed through Bull Hollyer's heart.

He left by the basement door, his clothes still soft and warm from the drier. She met him in the mall parking lot and directed him to another mall some miles away where they wouldn't see anyone she knew. They had lunch together in a Greek restaurant called Omega, near the lake, a view of water and boats and gulls wheeling near a jetty.

He was hungry and had souvlaki, both his and hers. She didn't eat, picked at a Greek salad and drank two glasses of white wine that smelled like pine trees. She stared out the window at the grey water of the lake.

"You okay?"

"Don't mind me, sweetie," she said. "There's nothing you can do." She patted his hand absently. "I'm just feeling a bit sorry that our little weekend is over. It went by so fast." She had a sip of wine. "I'm sorry I didn't meet you years ago."

He didn't know how to cheer her up, had no experience dealing with a woman's moods, felt helpless and clumsy.

"I could maybe visit you sometimes, if he goes away or something."

She turned from the window and looked directly at him, her eyes searching for something. "I don't know what I'm going to do, sweetie. I have to get away from him somehow but I don't know how. I'm afraid of him. He gets so angry sometimes, he loses control. He can lose it so badly he doesn't know what he's doing and then who knows what could happen."

She took his hand squeezed it tightly. "Jer's got your brother pretty much under his thumb. He took his wife away from him and what does Billy do? He hangs around like a whipped dog and lets Jer do whatever he wants. If Trina was your wife you wouldn't let some man come in and take her away without a fight, would you?"

"I'd probably have to kill him," he said at last.

She looked at him proudly. "I know you would. That's because you're a man. Not to say anything bad about your brother but," here she leaned forward, "it takes a man to do something like that. Somebody who isn't afraid to do what's right." She shook her head sharply as if denying tears. "He's ruining so many lives. And there isn't anyone with guts enough to stop him."

Terry looked out at two sailboats tacking rail to rail away from the marina, a match race with no prize but air. "Somebody should kill him," he said.

She looked at him with an expression of hope, fleeting, then gone. "It would be dangerous."

"He deserves it."

Eleven

DAY THREE — Wednesday, October 13

Patty had decided to call the new foal Wichita.

"Witch, for short," she said, looking over the stall door with that soft and smug look women get when they've been up all night making miracles. "Look at her, isn't she something?"

The newborn was buckskin, like her mother Belinda, with black trimmings, mane, tail and four knee-high black stockings. Purebred Quarter Horse. Patty was unswerving in her dedication to preserving the true American Quarter Horse, untainted by Thoroughbred blood which, she contended, was refining the breed past recognition.

"Just like laying an egg. No fuss, no hitches, just plop, there she was. Perfect. Her little black hooves. Looked like she'd been to a manicurist before she came."

"Was Barry here when it started?"

Patty laughed happily. "No, he had an emergency call in Little Britain. Poor darling. I'm glad I didn't have to drag him back, but it was easy peasy. And it's *Gary*, Dad."

"Sorry, Gary. Right. I suppose I should commit that to memory."

Orwell was leaning heavily, his arms hanging over the stall door. He was freshly shaved. Patty could smell the Williams shaving soap smell. Once or twice she'd bought him expensive shaving soap, once a mahogany bowl of Winston Churchill's favourite that had set her back a hundred and fifty bucks. Orwell maintained that he was saving it for best.

"Yeah, Dad, commit it to memory."

"It's serious then?"

"Well, you know, we're . . . close. We get along. I'm not in a blinding rush, not after Richie, but neither is he. We both kind of like it the way it is. For now."

Orwell straightened up and leaned back to crack a few vertebrae. He didn't look fully awake, despite the close shave and the fresh shirt.

"You were prowling last night, weren't you, Dad? Every time I looked up at the house, the light was on in a different room."

"It wasn't a good night for sleeping."

"Why didn't you come down to the stable? I was awake."

"I didn't want to disturb you."

"You thought Gary and I might be making out. Right?"

"Everyone needs some privacy."

She hugged his heavy arm and pushed her face up against the fresh shirt and felt the smooth coldness of the gold pin in his collar brush against her nose.

Her freckled nose, like her late mother's nose, Orwell thought, looking down at her coarse sandy hair and broad brow. He felt her snuggle as she always had, as she did when she needed his strength. Not often, he thought, not often enough for him perhaps, but sufficient to her needs.

"Yeah, you've always been pretty good that way, Daddy. You're not very nosy, for a cop."

"I know. Probably makes me a bad cop."

"No, that's not true. People want to do things for you, they want your approval, they move heaven and earth to do a job for you. They're all trying to make you remember their names."

"Billy Warren killed himself last night. In jail."

"Aw, shit," said Patty with deep disgust. Patty no longer had any time for the Billy Warrens of the world. "What a dumb, stupid thing to do." Belinda shook her head and blew through her nostrils and Patty led her father away from the stall to keep the bad energy from the newborn. They stood near the doorway to her tack room and Orwell looked inside admiringly. Brass and leather and Indian blankets. Everything in order. Everything polished or oiled.

"You want some coffee? It's almost fresh."

"No. Thanks, sweetie, I've gotta go. I just came down because Erika said you had a new arrival and I should have a look."

Patty shook her head. "How does she know? I haven't been up to the house yet."

Orwell smiled. "What doesn't she know? About time for you to take off too, isn't it?"

"Doris Heffernan is driving the morning run for me today. I'm going to lie down, soon as she sucks one more time. I just like looking at her."

"She's a beauty," said Orwell. "Just beautiful. So are you, sweetie. You've perked me up."

"You don't look too perky."

Orwell turned at the stable doorway and looked back at his daughter. She looks like she should have five kids by now, he thought. Almost six feet tall. A bosom that could nourish a tribe. A pelvis made for procreation. "Well, we're both short a few hours sleep," he said. "But we ain't dead yet."

He blew her a kiss.

She caught it and slapped it onto her cheek.

That Blomquist, Gary, should get his act together, thought Orwell as he headed back up the lane towards the house. Making baby horses is fine. Couple of grandkids before they stick me in the ground wouldn't be bad, either.

Orwell spent most of the morning attending to things that should have been taken care of earlier in the week. He concentrated on administration, morale, evaluation and facilitation. Any nagging questions about the murder of Jerome Kramer were relegated to the back of his mind. He was diligent, patient and suitably apologetic about his procrastination, treating the various demands on his time and attention with a measure of deference appropriate to his derelictions. He sat through an interminable budget conference without once threatening the town comptroller, met individually with his lieutenants and sergeants for decisions on rosters, assignments, holidays and fitness reports, and distributed a lavish allotment of approbation around the station to the point where some veterans wondered if the Chief were about to resign, be fired or enter politics. By noon, with his desk just about clear, he began to ponder what pies might be available at the Kountry Kitchen. There was the distinctive sharp rap on his half-open office door.

"Chief?"

"Yes, Staff Sergeant?"

"Region just faxed us Kramer's postmortem." Roy Rawluck was holding out a sheet of fax paper.

"Hey, we're right in the loop, aren't we?" Orwell said with just the merest trace of sarcasm.

"Did you want to look at it?"

"Might as well, since they went to all that trouble."

"But the case is closed, right, Chief?"

"I don't think it's officially closed as far as they're concerned, Roy. There'll be a hearing probably, maybe an inquest."

"But as far as *we're* concerned it's all over."

Orwell looked up from the fax. "Sit down for a minute, Staff. Got a question for you. You think if I resigned it would derail this OPP plan of Donna Lee's?"

"Would you do that, Chief?"

"Hell no! I'm just wondering if you think it would do any good."

Roy took the chair across from his boss and automatically

straightened his jacket front. "Probably not, Chief," he said after judicious consideration. "General thinking is, she was floating the idea before you came to town."

"Argyle knew about it?"

"If he hadn't died he was due to retire in a year or two. She was going to wait him out."

"Messed up her timetable, did he?" Orwell barked like a sea lion, a laugh he reserved for special revelations. "Now I know why her first two choices turned down the job. They knew they'd be jetsam in a couple of years." He wiped his eyes. "Tell you one thing, Roy. I don't plan on making it easy for her."

"If I make speak frankly, sir, the Department in general is hoping you can make her life a living hell for a long time to come."

"I'll do my best, Roy," Orwell said. "Grateful for the solidarity."

"Still speaking frankly, sir, you're our only hope."

Orwell's new laugh was genuine, but carried the rueful cognizance that his Staff Sergeant might have preferred a more polished standard-bearer. "Point taken," he said. "I won't let you down." He rose abruptly and rubbed his big hands together as if preparing to eat a plate of ribs. "Okay," he said. "Here's our next move. We figure out how much they'll save, on paper, versus how much the town will lose by having a smaller police presence. This isn't some bend in the highway with three bikers and two guys growing their own weed. Dockerty's got burglars, cocaine dealers, car thieves, vandalism; hell, read the paper, we even helped catch a murderer this week."

"We should have taken more credit for it."

"It would have been premature, Roy. Trust me." The Chief was staring at the aerial photograph of his portion of the world. He could trace the two main branches of the Snipe River through the hills of green and brown to the darker green that was the forest. He ran his finger over the aerial photograph, searching for Road 17. "Roy?"

"Still here, Chief."

"Breithaupt's Bush."

"What about it, Chief?"

"You know who this Breithaupt guy was?"

"That's our famous old missing persons case, Chief. Chief Argyle had a file on that one. It was his little hobby for a while."

"Any arrests, people questioned?"

"Chief Argyle had a theory that it was it was a scam. The guy was taking down payments for farm machinery that never got delivered. Argyle was pretty sure this Breithaupt took the money and ran. There were some disgruntled locals."

Orwell stood by the window looking out at Armoury Park. He liked the trees across the street; some of the maples were ancient.

"Anything else, Chief?" Roy was waiting to be formally dismissed.

"An answer to your original question, Roy. No. The case is *not* closed. Not as far as I'm concerned, and that means as far as *we* are concerned. Solving murders may not be part of our mandate, but if the other organizations aren't following through, I think we have an obligation."

"You have any leads, Chief?"

"Not a one. Just a bunch of questions."

The Staff Sergeant considered the situation. "We have a couple of qualified investigators of our own."

"I know we have. Truth is, Roy, I've been told to stay away from the whole Kramer business by about ten different people, any one of whom could, if they had a mind to, impede, or even harm, the careers of investigators too stupid to know when they've been profoundly warned to bugger off. You wouldn't want me to jeopardize the futures of investigators who may very well have their sights set on career advancement in other branches of Provincial law enforcement, would you?"

Roy stood up and squared away his jacket again. "For the record, Chief," he said, "if Region or Metro hassles you about this, well, you've got about thirty people be proud to go to bat for you."

Orwell nodded modestly. "Good to know, Roy. Thank you."

"Anything else, Chief?"

"Roy? Thirty?"

"You've got to allow for one or two sour apples, Chief."

"I s'pose," Orwell said. He made an immediate resolve not to wonder who the sour apples might be.

Orwell located his $18.95, +2.50 diopter, Shoppers Drug Mart reading glasses, and put on a serious face appropriate to the reading of a Medical Examiner's report. Reduced to its essentials, the report told him what he already knew. Jerome Kramer had died twenty-four to thirty-six hours before his body had been discovered, of massive internal bleeding generated by having his liver and lights cut to shreds by two four-bladed broadhead hunting arrows. Jerome Kramer had not died instantly. The ME's best guess was that it would have taken at least fifteen minutes for him to bleed out, although there wouldn't have been much chance of saving him even if he'd been shot right in front of a hospital. The damage inflicted by a hunting arrow made Orwell's stomach sour as he read. He had dealt with death before. For brutality, he didn't think much could top some of the mangled highway corpses he'd had to look after, but the Kramer killing was cold. It felt like an execution.

Rhem, Swain & Treganza — Barristers, Solicitors & Notaries, had offices on the second floor of a three-storey brick building on Hawksbury Street, just around the corner from the Bank of Commerce. Wicks' Trophies, Engraving and Novelty occupied the street-level space. The third floor was vacant now that Murray Alberg had retired to Florida after thirty-eight years filling out tax forms for the citizens of Dockerty.

Georgie Rhem was a dapper ex-jockey who rarely wore anything plain. He fancied bright bow ties, argyle socks, red suspenders, feathers in his hats and tassels on his shoes. At seventy-four, he still moved like a bowlegged bantamweight. Most of the people who knew him, including the Chief, called him Georgie, and he, for some reason known only to the two of them, called the Chief "Stonewall." The Chief was barely at the office door when Georgie was shooing him into the street. He liked to be on the move.

"Damned stupid thing to do," Georgie said as they walked toward the park. "They never would've got a conviction. The Crown had a pokey little case, full of holes. Full of holes. All circumstantial."

"They thought it was pretty solid."

"You sure that's what they thought, Stonewall? Gord Blumberg was going to prosecute. He's a guy who likes all his ducks lined up. Some of his ducks were missing on this one. No witness, no murder weapon."

"They had a weapon."

"Right. *A* weapon. Not *the* weapon. No way they could prove it was *the* weapon. A bow's a bow. An arrow's an arrow. I would've brought ten bows and arrows into court and made them prove that any one of them wasn't the murder weapon. They couldn't have done it. I went to Jensen's yesterday. They had, in stock, eighty-six Easton Gamegetter arrows just like the ones they took out of that poor schnook. Eighty-six. One store. Most popular shaft they sell. And bows, hell, you can fire an arrow out of anything. Piece of wood and a sash-cord. Hell, you can walk up to somebody and jab them. Who's to say what bow was used to shoot him with? I'd have had the, quote, murder weapon, close quote, trashed so fast it would've made Gord Blumberg's eyes water. Murder weapon, my Aunt Fanny."

"What about his alibi?"

"What? What? Anybody see him up here in that yellow Corvette? That's not exactly a low profile vehicle. Yellow Stingray. Vanity plate says 'VROOM.' Kind of thing people notice, don't you think? Where'd he park it while he was off doing the deed? Only tracks they had belonged to some import. Yeah, yeah, I know about that. Some little car or truck. Word gets around. Weren't the tracks from a Corvette, I know that much. Weren't big fat Goodyear radials. Nosiree."

"So where was he that weekend?"

"Immaterial. He could've been anywhere. The Crown's job would've been to place him up *here*, and unless they came up with somebody who saw him, or the car, up here, on or about the ninth or tenth, they couldn't place him at the scene. If he'd said, 'Hey, I drove up to Kapuskasing and back,' who's going to prove otherwise? They couldn't prove he was here on that weekend. And there was no way they could prove that his bow was the murder weapon."

"He had a motive."

"Motive. Fine. Bring that up and what's the jury going to say? I'll tell you. They're going to say 'prick had it coming,' that's what. Jury would've been on Billy's side on that one. Would've been looking for a way to let him walk." He paused for a moment and looked around, seemed surprised to notice that they'd walked as far as the locks. "Never would've got a conviction. I told him too. I said, listen Billy, I can do this for you. Just take it easy, breathe in and out like a good kid and let me do my thing. I'll make them look like the putzes they are." He seemed to sag then, as if realizing that the fight had been cancelled before he'd had a chance to dazzle them with his footwork. He sighed and leaned on his cane. "I was looking forward to it too, Stonewall. Haven't done a murder trial in eighteen years. I was primed for this one. Poor sad sonofabitch robbed me of my comeback." He sat on a bench, leaned over his walking stick, hands folded over the silver handle. Orwell sat beside him and wrapped himself deeper in his coat.

"That's exactly what I said when I heard about it," Orwell said. "Poor sad sonofabitch. Why'd we think of him that way, Georgie?"

"That's what he was. One of those big guys you know doesn't

have a clue how to make it in the world. Time he was a kid everybody telling him he was destined for big things because he looked like the kind of person was destined for big things and nobody explained to him what they meant by that, how he was supposed to go about moving on to bigger things. Beautiful woman sets her cap for him. She probably thought, 'Hey, this big handsome guy is destined for bigger things.' Then, eight, ten years later, she says to herself, 'So when are the bigger things going to show up?' He wasn't going on to bigger things. He didn't have it."

"The guts you mean?"

"Other parts too," Georgie said. "Character, sense, ambition, drive. Didn't have any of that. Just a big handsome schmo without much brainpower."

"He didn't have any record," Orwell said. "Not a speeding ticket, not a domestic disturbance, clean as a whip."

Georgie poked the wet grass with the tip of his walking stick. "His wife, she was the force in that marriage. Wouldn't you say, Stonewall?"

"Trina is a cool customer."

"Always got what she wanted. She wanted Billy. Swiped him right out from under her own sister."

"Does that a lot," Orwell said.

"Sister wound up marrying that badass biker. Piece of work he was. Maybe she though he was destined for bigger things too."

"I've met her sister. What's her name again?"

"Bev. Beverly. She's famous."

"How so?"

"She is, as they say, 'amply endowed.'"

"Oh yes," said Orwell. "Beverly Jannis."

"Hollyer. Married that thug, Bull Hollyer. Meth dealer. I think he's still doing time in Kingston. Millhaven."

"Serious incarceration."

They started back across the bridge.

"Georgie," Orwell said, "you think Billy did it?"

"What does it matter now?"

"Matters to me. No reason they'll reopen it just because I have doubts, now he's gone and killed himself."

"That's going to close it for them," said Georgie. "Saved the courts some money. Better than a signed confession."

"So I'm asking; you think he did it? Can't hurt now."

They both looked up at the same moment to watch a V-formation of Canada honkers, high above, heading south.

"Truth? I don't know. Schmo wouldn't tell me anything. Only talked to him two times, both times he sat there staring at his shoes, like he didn't give a damn about anything anymore. So I don't know if he did it or not. But I didn't have to know. Not my job. My job would be making Gord Blumberg sweat. Come up against me a case full of holes you could drive a bus through. He'd have had a hard time getting a conviction with what he had." Georgie paused in the middle of the bridge and looked down at the water. "I'll tell you exactly what he said to me, okay? 'Just keep Trina away from it. Don't make her come to court.' That's what he said."

"Buy you a lunch, Georgie? Piece of pie?"

"I'll take a rain check, Stonewall. I've gotta see a guy who's suing somebody because the Siamese cat they sold him had one eye that turned brown. Siamese cats' eyes are supposed to be blue."

"I'm sticking my nose in where it isn't wanted," Orwell said. "I'll keep you posted."

"Do that, Stonewall. I'd appreciate it." Georgie resettled his fedora and gave his stick an artful twirl through his fingers and over his thumb until it touched his hat brim neatly in a dapper salute. "Would have got him off, you know. Poor, sad etcetera, etcetera."

Twelve

September

It took Terry almost an hour to get up the courage to drive the last klick back to the cottage. He sat in the Sunys diner on Highway 12 nursing a Coke and blankly turning the pages of someone's day-old Sunday *Sun*, not reading anything beyond the headlines, forgetting them before the next page settled. He didn't want to see any of them. He didn't want to explain what he'd been doing. He didn't want to see it in their faces that they already knew. He still had stomach cramps. He felt dirty and shaky. And he felt exposed. He'd been lured out of the shadows and he was visible. Francine left tracks. She was too smug, too brazen, too pleased with herself. She thought she was smarter than he was, but she didn't really know anything. He decided he wasn't going to see her again if he could help it.

When he drove by the cottage it was dark and empty. No cars, no lights, no sounds from inside. He parked in the driveway and climbed onto the back deck. Through the glass doors he could see the kitchen dishes stacked haphazardly in the sink, and the empty beer bottles on the coffee table in the living room. After a while he left the deck and climbed into Beverly's little truck and drove away.

It was getting dark when he got to Beverly's house. Bruno barked at him from the fenced backyard. The front door of the house opened and there was Beverly, wearing a pale purple robe, holding a tall glass and smiling at him with a knowing glint in her eyes.

"Well, there he is, " she said, "Finally. The wandering trucker. Where have you been?"

"Took her home to Mississauga," Terry said.

"That was yesterday, said Beverly. "Tsk tsk. You took the long way, didn't you?"

Terry couldn't think of anything to say. "Truck runs good" was the best he could come up with.

"Come on in," said Beverly. "I'm making some supper. You must be hungry, all that driving."

She held the door open for him and Terry came up the porch steps and into the hall, brushing past her, handing her the keys to her little truck and feeling her breasts bump his arm. There was country music coming from the radio in the kitchen. He hesitated in the living room doorway. Trina was sitting on the couch. She was smoking a cigarette and holding a tall drink like the one her sister had. She was wearing dark glasses. Beverly came up behind him and bumped him into the room with her hip.

"Siddown," she said. "Want something to drink? Beer? We're drinking rum and Coke."

"Just a Coke," he said. "No rum."

He sat across from Trina and stole a quick look at her. She still hadn't said a word.

"I stopped by the cottage," he said. "Everybody was gone."

Trina looked at him finally. She looked tired.

"Here," Beverly said, handing him a glass filled with Coke and ice. She sat in the armchair at the end of the coffee table and lit a smoke. "So," she said, "How'd you like The Great Sex Weekend? Lotsa laughs, wasn't it?"

"Give it a rest, Bev," Trina said.

"Lotsa laughs for me anyway. How about you Terry? You got your ashes hauled, didn't you?"

Terry stared deep into his glass.

"Sure you did. That Francine. She's built like a snake isn't she? Crawled inside your pants before you knew what's what. So what'd you do last night, stay at her place? How was it?"

"Leave him alone," Trina said. "It's all too damn tiresome listening to this crap."

"I want some details. I want to hear what her house is like. Did you do it on Jer's bed?"

"You are so common."

"Oh, really? And you are so refined. Running around in a bath towel and getting your ass slapped every five minutes." She took a deep drag. "Anyway, I've got to get my jollies where I can. God knows I wasn't getting laid this weekend. Spent all my time cleaning up after your husband. Just so pathetic."

"Nobody asked you to."

"Well, what would you do, just leave him lying there, wouldn't you? You rub his nose in it and you don't care that it's making him crazy. You like it that he can't stand it."

"Don't tell me you weren't happy to step in and take care of him. Must have been a dream come true for you."

"Oh yeah, it's been a dream of mine for years to wipe Billy's ass."

"Maybe you'll have better luck when he wakes up."

"When he wakes up you can take him home."

"Billy's here?" Terry said.

"In my room," said Beverly. "Sleeping it off. It was a job getting him upstairs."

"He won't wake up 'til tomorrow," Trina said. "I'm going home,"

"Take your husband with you when you go. If you don't mind. He's yours, not mine. My husband is on the other side of the country."

"Your husband ran out on you. Why don't you just get used to it?"

"You don't know anything about Bull and me," Beverly said. "We have an understanding."

"Would he understand about you hanging around Billy all weekend?"

"He'd understand that I have to get out of here once in a while. He would understand when I told him nothing happened."

"Not because you didn't want it to."

"Jesus, Trina, what is it with you? You want it both ways. You want to act like a slut when you feel like it, and then come on all Miss Prim when it looks like other people might enjoy life. You're a hypocrite."

Beverly got up and walked into the kitchen. Terry could hear the sound of pots and pans being moved around without care. He sipped his Coke and allowed himself a glimpse of Trina over the rim. He was surprised to see the tears on her cheek. She was staring at a spot on the coffee table and silently crying.

"Trina?" He had a difficulty with her name. Rarely had he said it aloud. "You okay?"

"What?"

"You all right?"

"Oh," she said, wiping her cheek with the back of her hand. "It's okay. I'm just a little fried." She took off her dark glasses to dab at her eyes with a napkin. Her left eye and cheekbone were discoloured, bruised.

"You've got a black eye."

"Oh, that," she said. She put the glasses back on. "Jer and I had a little fight after you and Francine took off. Things weren't very pleasant for a while."

"Where is he?"

"I don't know. He left. Maybe he went home. He has places he goes. Maybe he has other women too."

"I don't think he's a very nice man," Terry said.

She looked up at him. Almost smiled. "No. You're right about that."

"Then why . . . ?"

"It just happened," she said. "Who knows how these things get started? One minute life is going along in one direction, and the next minute you've turned a corner and you're on a different road and you don't know where it's going. That's how it happened."

"You going to keep doing it?"

"It's . . . it's complicated," she said.

Beverly came back into the room.

"Anybody hungry? There's some baked beans and bacon and toast."

"I could eat," said Terry.

"Trina?"

"I'll just stay here for a while," Trina said.

"Suit yourself," Beverly said. She looked at Terry. "In the kitchen."

Terry had another look at Trina sitting on the couch. Her cheeks were shining again. He didn't want to leave her. She'd been talking to him almost like a person. After a moment he followed Beverly into the kitchen.

"Siddown," she said. She put a plate of beans and bacon in front of him. There was buttered toast on a plate in the middle of the table. "You want a fried egg with that?"

"No, this is good, this is fine," Terry said.

"It's no trouble," Beverly said. "I'm having one myself."

"Well, okay then. I'll have a fried egg, if it's okay."

"Just take a minute," she said. "You start on that."

Terry had a forkful of beans. They were homemade, tasting of molasses and onion and salt pork.

"These are good," he said.

"Just like my aunt Grace used to make."

Beverly cracked a pair of brown eggs into a pan of sizzling butter and shook the pan gently to keep the eggs from sticking. She sprinkled a little salt and black pepper over them and then used a spoon to baste the eggs with the hot butter.

"What was the fight about?" Terry wanted to know.

"What fight?"

"There was a fight after me and Francine took off?"

"Gawd," Beverly said. "There were fights all afternoon. If it wasn't one thing it was another. Fuck and fight, fuck and fight, that's all those two know how to do. And Billy puking and crying all over the place. It was a crazy house. If you hadn't taken my truck I'd've been out of there so fast. I mean, that's it. I have had it with Jerome fucking Kramer. He is such a bullshit artist."

She carried the pan over to the table and slid a perfectly fried, sunny side up egg onto Terry's plate. She went back to the counter and put the other egg on her plate, then picked up a strip of bacon and took a bite as she carried her plate to the table.

"I only went because Bull told me to talk to him," she said.

Terry looked up. "Bull did?"

"Last time I saw him," she said. "In Kingston. A couple of months before he got out."

"Oh."

She looked across at him, her eyes searching for something. "You haven't seen him, have you?"

"Me?" Terry's egg yolk dribbled off his fork.

"Heard from him?"

"Why would I?"

"I don't know," she said. "Because you know things," she said. "You have secrets, Terry. You hang around looking like you don't belong and all the time you're listening, watching."

Terry concentrated on the food. He thought it would be a good time to keep his mouth shut.

Beverly pushed her plate away, no longer hungry, lit a cigarette and leaned back on the wooden chair. She hadn't taken her eyes off him.

"You know what's going on, don't you?"

"What?"

"You know. Billy and Jer, and Bull. You know about what they did, don't you?"

"What they did?"

"I think you know. I think you know what they did. *I* know what they did. Trina knows what they did. Bull told me everything. And Billy's no good at keeping secrets. Not like you." She had a sip of her rum and Coke, made a face and got up to pour the dregs into the sink and fix herself a fresh one. "Were you in on it?"

"Me?" he said.

"Yeah, you," she said, mocking him. "Were you part of the big plan?"

"No," he said.

"But you know about it." It wasn't a question.

"I . . . I might've heard some stuff," he said.

"You might've, eh? Yeah, I bet you might've. Does anybody else know?"

"The other guy."

She closed the refrigerator door and looked at him.

"Who's the other guy?"

"I don't know," he said. "I only saw him one time, when him and Jer went deer hunting."

"When was that?"

"About a year ago," Terry said.

"How do you know he's a part of it?"

There was no more food on Terry's plate. His glass was empty. He had nothing else to occupy his hands and face. She was still looking at him.

"Well?" She wasn't going to leave it alone. "Jer and the other guy went hunting together on your daddy's farm. Did you hear them talking?"

"Sort of."

"Did you hear them talking about what they did?"

"Sort of."

"Jeez, it's like pulling teeth." She took his empty glass and fixed him a drink. This time she put rum in it. "Drink that," she said, putting it down in front of him.

Terry had a sip. He felt the heat of the rum down his gullet.

"Good boy," she said. "So what did you hear?"

"Just . . ." he had another sip. "You know . . ."

"No, I don't know."

"They were just talking."

"Where were they talking?"

"In the bush."

"So you went hunting with them."

"No."

"But you were in the bush."

"It's my bush," he said.

"Five hundred and eighty-seven thousand, five hundred dollars," she said. "Have you heard that number before?"

He looked at her. She wasn't staring at him anymore. She seemed to be somewhere else, with Bull. Terry realized that she was probably drunk.

"Bull made me memorize that number. Made me say it over and over and over. I went to see him before they sent him to Millhaven. He was okay, it was a bullshit drug beef, he wasn't happy, he knew they were going to make him do the full bit and he was prepared." She turned to look at him and her eyes moved across him and settled on Trina who was standing in the kitchen doorway. Beverly looked at Terry. "Drink your drink," she said. "I'm telling you stuff because you're going to tell *me* stuff, so drink it up."

Terry had another swallow. It was tasting better. Trina was sitting at the table now. Beverly looked at her audience. She gave a little snort of derision. "It's cards-on-the-table time," she said. "Bull said to me, 'Listen up, Bebber,' that's what he calls me, he said, 'I can do this standing on my head, but in case something we can't predict happens, I want you to know that you've got something going for you.'" She looked at Trina. "Billy ever say anything like that to you?"

Trina helped herself to one of Beverly's cigarettes. "Billy hasn't been living at home for a while."

"Really," Beverly said. "My oh my. And why is that do you suppose?"

"It's just life, Bev, that's all. So we both married assholes, big deal."

Beverly stood up violently, banging the table, slopping drinks, spilling ashtrays. "Bully is not an asshole!" she yelled at her sister.

Terry was righting glasses and sopping up spills with both hands. Beverly went to the refrigerator for fresh ice, fresh Coke, another drink. She was lurching just a little, not mindful of where things were. "You may be married to an asshole. And the prick you are currently fucking is definitely an asshole. But not Bully. Bully is loyal and strong and honourable. They tried to get him to rat everybody out for the other thing. You know that? They promised him a walk if he'd give it up and he laughed in their faces. Billy Warren would have folded like a pup tent. Jerry Kramer would have sold them his mother. Not my Bully. He laughed. He laughed in their stupid faces. He knew they didn't have jack shit." She leaned against the sink counter, holding her fresh drink in one hand, her arms folded under her breasts. "He told me to just be patient and don't say anything to anybody, no matter what happens, you'll still get your end. I've made sure of that. All you have to do is talk to Jer when the time comes. And don't let him shave anything off the top. It comes to five hundred and eighty-seven thousand, five hundred dollars. Say that to yourself. Five hundred and eighty-seven thousand, five hundred dollars."

"So where is it?" Trina said.

"Well that's the five hundred and whatever thousand dollar question, now isn't it, Trina? Do you know?"

"I don't even know what you're talking about," Trina said.

Beverly laughed. "The fuck you don't. You're in bed with the one person who does know. Don't tell me you haven't been able to fuck it out of him. That's what you're there for, isn't it? Well? Isn't it?"

Trina took off her glasses and lifted her chin with some defiance. "No, he hasn't told me anything about any specific money, or where it is, or how much it is, and when I tried to bring it up, very carefully bring it up, this is what I got. And he told me to mind my own business. That'd I'd be taken care of when the time came."

Beverly laughed. "Yeah, that's the same bullshit I got." She came back toward the table, moving carefully, aware now that the booze was affecting her. She lowered herself into the chair and went searching for a dry cigarette. Her voice was quieter now, filled with disgust. "I was going to drive down to Kingston to pick up Bull when he got out, but he called me from the pen, said Billy was coming to get him. Then, later on, that asshole Jer calls me up and says Bull asked him to tell me goodbye, and he'd let me know as soon as he got a place for us out on the West Coast and then I'd go and join him. Jer said it was going to be safer if Bull went alone." She lit another smoke and had a sip of her drink and sniffed. "I believed him. I wanted to believe him. But I didn't say anything about the money. I could have used some, but something told me not to say anything. I said thank you, Jer, and I hung up and started to wait. I waited a year. Then I called and asked him has he heard from Bull and he says not to worry, Bull's fine, and I say how do you know that, did Bully call you? And he says Bull called him from someplace on Vancouver Island. And I say why would he call you and not me, and he says because they might be checking my phone bills to see where he was,, and I say why would they be looking for him that hard, is it because of the money? And he says what money? And I say the five hundred and eighty-seven thousand, five hundred dollars. And he says don't worry about it. It's all safe. And then he invited me to the Labour Day weekend. Tells me he'll explain things."

"So what happened?" Trina said. "Did you ask him?"

"Sure, I asked," Beverly said. "Sure I did. When I could find a free minute between you two putting your things together, and Billy banging his head on the wall, and Francine the Anaconda Woman trying to swallow Terry in one big gulp. Sure I asked him. And he says, you know how he talks, Trina, like he's giving you a secret deal on a used car, he says the time isn't exactly right and I should ask him in six months. That's the deal they made, him and Bull. In six months they'll be getting the money."

"That's not right," Terry said.

"It sucks," Beverly said.

"It's not the deal they made," Terry said.

"What do you know about it?" Trina said.

"I know it's not six months from now. It's like four weeks from now. In October."

"What is?" Trina was insistent. She was reaching across the table, gripping his arm. He felt her touch as an electric shock. He felt the rum working on him, Trina's naked, bruised face confronting him, her red-rimmed eyes compelling him.

"When they dig up the money. In October. There's a full moon on a weekend in deer season. They're going to go hunting, and then at night, they're going to dig it up."

"Who is?" Trina wanted to know.

"Jerry and the other guy, and Billy I guess."

"You guess."

"I don't know. I only heard Jer and the other guy talking, after Billy left."

"When was that?"

"The day Bull got out," Terry said. Then he looked up. He'd said too much.

"Was Bully there?" Beverly was gripping his other arm. He felt Trina's thin fingers around his left wrist, Beverly's stronger hand on his right forearm, a pair of leg-hold traps holding him in place, pulling him open. "Was Bull there?"

"Yeah," he said at last. "He was there,"

"This is the day he got out? Last year? Where did you see him?"

"In the bush. With Billy. Billy brought him."

"Billy brought him," Beverly said. "Right. Then says he took Bull to the bus station."

Trina said, "He told me that Jer took Bull to the bus station."

"Well *somebody* took Bull to the bus station. Didn't they? Terry?"

"No," Terry said. "Bull never went to the bus station."

Beverly couldn't speak.

"Why not?" Trina said.

"Because he's dead," Terry said.

He heard Beverly sob. She let go of his arm and covered her mouth with both hands and her wide eyes filled with tears. "What happened?" she said. Her voice was muffled.

"I let Jer and the other guy in the front gate and they headed back to the bush and I followed them. They never saw me."

"Where was Bully?"

"He came in the back way. Billy drove them up the logging road."

Beverly sat with open mouth and silent tears as Terry told it all. When she heard of Bull's plan to run with her to the West Coast, she held herself as if to cradle an invisible child. There was a sudden intake of breath when she heard how Jer shot Bull without warning, and a quiet moan when she listened to the story of her husband's interment in a hole in the ground. Her voice was a whisper when she finally spoke.

"Do you know where he is?" she asked.

"What? His body?"

"Yes, his body!"

"I saw them bury it. I know where."

"His body. His body. Bully's . . ." she began rocking in her chair.

"Now what?" Trina said. "You want to give him a decent funeral?"

"He's just in a hole!"

"That's where everybody winds up, isn't it?" Trina said.

"Did they wrap him up in anything?" Beverly grabbed Terry's shoulders and her mouth was close enough that he could smell the rum and cigarettes and the food and feel the heat pouring off her face. Her eyes were red and puffy and there was mucus unattended on her nose and lips. Terry tried to wrench himself away but she had his shirtsleeves twisted in her fists and was shaking him. "Did they wrap him up in anything for Jesus sake? Terry? Jesus, Terry. Fuck."

"Just his coat," Terry said.

Bruno started barking and scratching at the back door. Beverly let go of Terry's shirt and covered her wet face with both hands. "Just his coat. His coat. His blue coat? Was it his blue . . . ?"

"What difference does it make?" Trina said.

"I think it was blue," Terry said.

"Get hold of yourself, Bev," Trina said. "We don't have time for this."

"It's not your husband lying in the mud, in the swamp, like some pitiful animal. No. Not yours. Your murdering husband is upstairs puking on my sheets. Your murdering husband is sucking Jer's cock."

Beverly got up and went to the back door. Bruno barged in, woofing with agitation, whimpering with concern, his claws skittering across the tile floor.

"Jesus, Bev," Trina said, "would you get that monster out of here. You know I'm allergic."

"You're not allergic. You just don't like dogs. And they don't like you." She grabbed Bruno's furry jowls and rubbed her forehead against his. "That's right, isn't it, Broonzie? You don't like Trina, because she's really a cat in disguise."

"Just put him outside where he belongs."

"He belongs wherever I fucking well say he belongs Miss High and fucking Mighty. This is my house, my kitchen, my dog, and if you don't like it you can just get the fuck out of here!"

"Oh Jesus, he's licking your snot," Trina said.

"Here Bruno, here's a treat for you," Beverly said. She opened a box of Milk Bones and gave one to her dog. Then she opened the back door and led him out to the sun porch, threw a few more treats into his bowl. "Just eat your treats and go to sleep. It's okay. Mommy's okay. Mommy's okay. There's a good boy. Mommy's okay."

"Mommy," Trina said under her breath. "Jesus!"

Beverly came back inside and closed the door. "There. You happy now?" She went to the kitchen sink, shifted dirty dishes, ran cold water into her cupped hands, buried her face, scrubbed hard, blew bubbles like a horse at a trough.

Terry turned to look across the table. Trina was staring directly at him, studying him, her head tilted enough to suggest that he was an object worthy of careful scrutiny.

"Well, now," she said, "aren't you the surprise package of all time?"

"I am?"

"Years and years. All this time I had you pegged as a little sneakyboy. Turns out, you are the champion king sneakyboy."

Terry felt a need to defend himself. "It's my bush," he said.

"It's your bush." She smiled.

"It's mine," he said again. "It's not me sneaking. They're the ones sneaking, hiding money, shooting people. They're the ones kept messing it up, digging holes, and I have to clean up after them."

"And nobody knew you were there," Trina said.

"Nobody ever knows," he said.

"You saw them bury the body?" she said.

He nodded.

"You saw them bury the other thing too? The money?"

He nodded again.

She shook her head. "You've got a lot better since that time Billy caught you in the teacher's lounge."

This time he didn't nod, but he looked at her, met her eyes without flinching. "Yes," he said.

"Did you tell Francine where the money is?"

He shook his head. "She thinks Jer's rich. But she didn't say anything about the robbery thing. She says he has bank accounts and insurance. I don't know if she even knows about the bag. It doesn't matter anyway. He doesn't have it. He has the bag they buried it in. The money isn't in it."

"What's in it?"

"Surprises."

Trina studied him for a long moment. Her sunglasses were on the table beside her empty glass. "So he came back? Jer? Back to the bush where they had it buried?"

"After Bull got arrested. Four years ago. Jer came back on his own and dug it up."

"And you were there again."

"I heard him coming."

"I guess he hasn't opened it yet."

"I guess not."

"So where is it, Terry?"

"It's safe."

"On the farm?"

"It's safe."

"What are you going to do with it?"

That was the part that Terry had never been able to figure out to his satisfaction. He had counted it, divided it into brick-size bundles, wrapped each brick in plastic and foil and duct tape and clay from the deposit on Coughland's farm, and used the bricks to build a floor for his treasure room. He had treated the money as if it were worth something, and yet to him it had no real value. He knew that it was something everyone else wanted. They wanted to buy things with it, go places, make their lives better, but the only worth that he could see in it was the value everyone else placed on it.

"There's about five thousand missing. Mice got into it."

"Ha!"

"Do you want it?"

"What?"

"The money. Do you want it?"

"I want it!" Beverly said. "I want Bully's five hundred, fuck! Five hundred and eighty-seven thousand, five hundred fucking dollars. I want every penny. And I want Bully to have a decent burial. In his suit. And I want Jerome fucking Kramer dead. Absolutely. Deader than Bully is dead. My poor Bull."

"You can't have everything," Trina said. "You can't have a funeral."

"I can't just leave him there."

"Why not? You know what a big deal it would be to dig him up? You want the police poking around? What are you going to carry him in? Where are you going to put him?"

Beverly sat on the floor with her back to the sink. She looked all cried out. Her face was naked and vacant and she was looking at her kitchen ceiling. "I want that murdering fucking bullshit lying bastard dead in a hole. A hole smaller and uglier than the one my poor Bully is in. Can I have that at least?"

"And the five hundred and whatever?" said Trina.

"That too. I want Bully's share. He said it was for me. He left it to me."

"So how many shares are we talking about?" Trina said. "There's you and me and . . . Terry, you'll be taking a share, right?"

"What about Billy?"

"Yes," Trina said. "What about Billy?"

"And there's the other guy," Terry said.

"What other guy?"

"There were four guys. Billy and Jer, Bull and the other guy."

"What other guy?" Beverly wanted to know.

"I don't know his name."

"What does he look like?" Trina said.

"Red beard. Long hair, sandy red hair, in a ponytail."

"Didn't anybody say his name?"

"It's Doug," said Billy Warren. "Doug Maloney." Billy was standing in the kitchen doorway. His shirttail was out and the front of his red shirt was caked with yellow and white.

"Who is he?"

"I need some water," Billy said.

"Murderer!" Beverly hauled herself off the floor and lurched toward the refrigerator. There was a yellow tin breadbox sitting on top. "Evil, cocksucking . . ." She fumbled inside the breadbox and turned with a small bundle wrapped in a grey washcloth. "You killed my husband!" There was a pistol inside the cloth, a small automatic with mother-of-pearl grips and a nickel finish. She pointed the gun directly at Billy's face. Her hand wasn't shaking. "I knew you were an asshole, Billy. Even back when I used to give you handjobs at the drive-in. You were a lousy fuck, and an asshole, and now you're a lousy, cocksucking, murdering asshole."

"I didn't do it. I didn't do anything," Billy said.

Bruno started howling again, scratching at the back door.

"I was just there. Jesus, Beverly. Can I have a glass of water? Can you put the gun down please? I need to get a drink of water."

"You were just there," she said, her voice a taunting, sing-song, "I was just there. I couldn't do anything. Because I'm just a drunken fucking asshole."

Trina got up and crossed the kitchen to her sister. She reached out and carefully took the pistol from Beverly's hand. "Where did you get this little monster?" she said.

Beverly sagged, held onto the wall. "Bully gave it to me," she said. "In case I came up against any assholes!"

Trina opened a cupboard and got a glass, ran cold water and carried the glass back to Billy.

"You want some Aspirin?" Trina said.

"Yeah," Billy said, "and more water. Please."

"Bev? Where do you keep the Aspirins?"

"In the fucking bathroom. Where do you think? In the medicine . . . the medicine . . . Bruno, be quiet." She started to cry again.

"Sit at the table, Bev," Trina said. She helped her sister to the table and sat her down, then went to get Aspirins and more water for Billy.

Terry watched it all without moving a muscle, his physical presence in the room dissolving into the shadow of the pantry door. He watched as his brother looked around for some place to sit, afraid to take one of the kitchen chairs near the table, near Beverly who was making dry, heaving noises, tears all used up, nothing left but rasping throat and scalded cheeks.

Trina came back with tablets for Billy and another glass of water. She pulled one of the chairs away from the table and put it nearer the doorway for Billy to sit on. Then she fixed fresh drinks for Beverly, and herself, and for Terry. When she put Terry's rum and Coke in front of him, she let her fingers touch the back of his hand for the briefest instant, a jolt of direct current that stopped and restarted his heart like a punch in the chest.

"Well, I hope you're all just fucking happy," Beverly whispered. "All you smarty smart bank robbers. I should just call the fucking police and let them lock you up. You and Jer and Doug the mystery man. You should all go to jail for killing my husband. You should all go to Hell for what you did."

"I swear," Billy said, "Beverly, I swear to Christ I didn't do anything to Bull."

"Didn't do anything to stop it either."

"I didn't know it was going to happen. I was on Bull's side. I said he should get his share, Jer should give him his share. I was trying to smooth things over. I didn't expect Jer to do that."

"He couldn't let Bull have his share," Terry said. "It wasn't where you guys buried it."

"Where is it?"

"Terry has it," said Trina. She looked at him and lifted her glass in his direction. "Don't you, Terry?"

Thirteen

DAY THREE — Wednesday, October 13

"Detective Moen for you, Chief."

"Thank you, Dorrie," Orwell said. He leaned back in his chair and allowed himself a moment of anticipation before picking up the phone. "Hello, Detective, how're you doing?"

"What is this shit?"

About what he'd been expecting. "What shit would that be, Detective?"

"This formal request. There's no way you get a copy of the case file."

"Why not? I was part of the investigation."

"Bad judgment on my part," she said. "Last time I do something that stupid."

"Sorry you feel that way. I had a splendid time," Orwell said. He was enjoying the exchange. "I'm ready to carry on to the conclusion."

"It *is* concluded," she said. "It's over. Caught the bad guy, he took the slimy way out. Now I've got six different assholes I have to explain myself to."

"You were by the book, Detective. Most professional. I'll be happy to put that in writing, in fact I'm drafting such a report right now."

"Piss off! I'm not in trouble. He was in good shape when I

booked him. After that he was transferred, fed, saw his lawyer. No problems."

"Good, good, happy to hear it. Now, if it's not too much trouble I'd appreciate getting a copy of the case file."

"It is too much trouble, and it's none of your business, and when Hell freezes, and also over my dead body. How's that?"

"I've made a formal request. Your Captain has a copy."

"My Captain thinks I stepped on my dick letting you come along in the first place, and he thinks you're a bush-league shmuck, and he has no intention of giving you the time of day."

"Nonetheless, I'll keep asking."

"You do that."

"By the way, when you have a chance to check your notes, look back at the first Billy Warren interview. Check out what bows Billy said he owned. I think you'll find that he only mentioned one."

"So what?"

"As I recall, we found two."

The day had turned blustery again. A thin whippy rain, sharp, fine as sand. Joe and Orwell sat in the Ramcharger with the doors open, parked off to the side of County Road 17 where it crossed a humpbacked bridge over the Little Snipe River. Behind them the dark wall of trees climbed the first rise of Breithaupt's Bush.

"River's all riled up," Joe said.

"I never liked fishing this end of the Snipe," said Orwell. "I'm not saying it's a bad river, but it's kind of all over the place you know."

The slope of the forest curved away from the road as the Snipe angled north and east, cutting its way through the hills toward the lake. The river was high up its banks, moving like a lava flow, opaque, the colour of wet cement. There were branches and roots heading downstream, clawing at the banks as they swept by.

Joe reached for his tobacco and peeled a paper off the pack.

"You're a trout snob," he said. Joe was a muskie fisherman. He had long ago given up the pursuit of anything else. Truth be told, his friend Orwell wasn't really much of a fisherman of any kind. Joe managed to get the Chief out on the water once or twice a year, but that was about all.

Orwell got out of the Ramcharger, walked to the bridge, and stood there looking down at the swirling water.

Joe leaned against the fender and lit his smoke. "So, what's your problem?"

"Billy doesn't smoke," said Orwell.

"So?"

"Those cigarettes you found up the hill weren't his."

"Never said they were."

"No, but you said they were put there that night."

"Likely were. Not an exact science."

"Okay, for the sake of argument, let's say they were put there that night."

"Okay."

"And if they were put there that night . . ."

"Okay . . ."

"Billy wasn't alone."

"Maybe the victim put them there."

"He didn't smoke either. No smokes, no lighter among his personals. You remember what kind they were?"

"I didn't look that closely," Joe said. "They weren't cork tips, they were white. Maybe a gold band. Can't you get a look at the butts yourself?"

"Well, yeah, maybe I can, if I want to make the trip into Toronto to see them, if I can make it through all the people who'll want to know what the hell I want to see them for, if they haven't been lost, destroyed, misfiled, thrown out. Sure, I can see them. Mostly I just wanted to know what kind they were if that's not too taxing for everybody."

"Wouldn't that be in a report?"

"Maybe. But I don't have a copy of the damn report yet, do I? Officially, I'll get a copy when someone at OPP Region decides I should have a copy. Which is probably never, although I have been invited to send in another request." He walked back to join his friend. "Trina Warren smokes," he said.

"And?"

"And the widow Kramer smokes."

"You going down to talk to them?"

"Officially it's way the hell and gone outside my jurisdiction. The best I can do is suggest to Detective Moen that she should check it out."

"Think she will?"

"It's not unreasonable is it?" Orwell's voice was getting louder. "To want to know who exactly was puffing away out there while somebody was getting themselves murdered. Billy Warren never smoked a cigarette in his life. And . . ."

"And?"

"Billy's got big feet," Orwell said.

"Whoever I was tracking didn't have big feet. And they smoked."

"Ergo," said Orwell, "they weren't Billy Warren."

"Ergo," said Joe.

"So who were you tracking? The killer?"

"Or somebody before or after the killer."

"And if it wasn't the killer, and if Billy Warren *was* the killer, then how in the name of Jesus did *he* get in?"

"Big bush," said Joe. "Shared by three farms. Altogether there's a few hundred acres of hardwood. We only checked the path up from the hill and down to the swamp."

"Where the shooter came in."

"That's what it looked like."

"But there are other ways?" The Chief was insistent.

Joe sighed and explained with care. "That was the way that

someone came in. That person climbed the hill and sat under a tree and smoked cigarettes and then went down the hill toward where the man was shot in the tree. We found the evidence. A blade from an arrow, footprints, cigarette butts."

"And it wasn't Billy Warren."

"I could have missed something. Won't carry a lot of weight in a courtroom, but my opinion whoever smoked those smokes and left those footprints had a bow and was headed in the direction of the man in the tree with two arrows through his belly."

"And then there's the business of the small car parked over there. Probably an import Dean said."

"What does that tell you?" Joe asked.

"Billy's a General Motors man. He wouldn't be caught dead in an mini from anywhere."

"Could be a clever ruse."

"Yeah, well the real cleverness would be stashing the Corvette he was supposed to be driving that weekend." Orwell turned at the sound of an approaching vehicle. A yellow bus was heading their way, coming over the bridge, bringing kids home from school. "Lord, is it that time already?"

The bus pulled up alongside and the driver slid open her window and waved.

Orwell had three daughters, and whenever he saw one of them in public, he got a goofy look for a minute. Joe had noted this before. The bus driver was Patty, Orwell's oldest, a big, good-looking woman with a hint of sadness in the tiny crease between her eyes.

"Hi, kiddo," said Orwell. "Thought you were taking the day off."

"Just the morning," she said. "Hi, Joe."

Orwell walked around to the doors and Patty opened them. Orwell climbed aboard, touched her hand on top of the lever and looked back down the length of the bus. He waved at seven children who were on their way home, carrying pumpkin paintings.

Some of their paintings had been caught in the rain and the jack-o-lantern faces were here and there smeared, making them both sinister and brave.

"Hi, kids," said the Chief, "you all have a good day at school?"

The kids weren't overly enthusiastic about their day, but a few held up their pumpkin paintings for inspection.

"Jack-o-lanterns," said the Chief. "Real nice work."

"Gotta go, Dad," Patty said. "I'll see you at home."

"Okay, darlin'. Bye-bye, kids."

The kids dutifully said bye-bye and Orwell stepped back to let Patty close the door.

"Wait a minute!" Orwell stuck his hand out and caught the closing door. He climbed back aboard. "I just want to ask these kids something." He held onto the overhead rail and looked down at the children. "Got a question for you guys, maybe you can give me a hand," he said. "Were any of you on this road last Saturday? Did any of you see a car parked along here? It was right over there probably, somewhere in the weeds. Might have been there last Friday too."

Most of the kids looked blank. One or two tried to look like they were thinking hard. The littlest girl just kept shaking her head in an emphatic no, never, not me.

"Saturday. Maybe you were driving into town with your folks? Help me out here, Patty. Anything unusual happen Saturday, might stand out for these guys?"

Patty swung around to face the kids. "It was the Omemee Fair," she said. "I went to look at some horses. Anybody go to Omemee for the fair?"

"Some of you guys went to the fair, right?" said Orwell. "And you would've been coming this way, right? And right over there, parked off to the side, might've been a car. Almost in the ditch. Anybody remember that?"

"I do," said the littlest girl who was still shaking her head no. She had the neatest pumpkin painting on the bus. The rain couldn't touch it because it was protected by Saran Wrap.

Orwell took the vacant seat ahead of her and sat sideways with his legs in the aisle.

"You do? What's your name?"

"Marjorie."

"Marjorie, do you remember anything about it? How big it was, what colour it was?"

"It wasn't a car," she said. "It was a little truck."

"I saw it too," the boy behind her. "I remember. It was a red Nissan pickup with a camper-back. My uncle has one like it only his is blue."

"Nissan? You think?"

"It had Nissan on the back. My uncle says it's a gutless wonder, but it's good on gas."

"I've got to get these kids home, Dad. You'll have to continue this on your own time."

"Yep. Okay, sweetie, I'm on my way." Orwell stood up and beamed at the seven children. "You've all been a big help and I'm really happy I bumped into you out here. I'll be seeing you."

The kids all said goodbye and a few of them giggled as the Chief of Police gave their bus driver a big kiss on the face. Orwell waved as he stepped off. The door closed and the bus headed down the road under a darkening sky.

Orwell walked back to the Ramcharger.

"Patty cheered you up, did she?" Joe said. "You've got a smile on your face for the first time today."

Orwell reached for Joe's tobacco. "The kids all had pumpkin paintings."

"I guess Halloween's coming up pretty soon."

"It was a little truck, Joe. A little red Nissan pickup with a camper-back." Orwell rolled himself a small cigar. "I got it from an expert."

Orwell placed another diplomatic call to detective Moen knowing it was unlikely to be answered any time soon. In truth he got the distinct impression that the detective on the other end would likely pigeonhole the message in the circular file under his desk, but at least he'd made the effort.

"I need to track down a red Nissan truck, Roy. Don't have a plate number. Probably local."

"Why are we looking for it, Chief?"

"That's what was parked on County Road 17 the weekend of the murder. A little red Nissan trucklet with a camper-back. I want to know who it belongs to."

"Region could track it down faster than we can, Chief."

"I'd rather keep this in-house, Roy, if you get my meaning. It'll just upset people who are already a bit pissed at me."

"Might take a while."

"Give the patrols a heads up, and get me a list as soon as you can."

"Puslinch can work the system."

"Remind me, Dorrie."

"Graham Puslinch. Records."

Graham was the station's acknowledged computer maven. There was little nerdiness in his aspect. He played left wing on the police hockey team where he was known as "Elbows."

"Graham. Got it. Okay, let me know what he finds. Right away."

"This a stolen vehicle, Chief?"

"Hope not, Roy. Hope it's somewhere within my purview." Orwell headed back to his office, stopped at the doorway. "Roy?"

"Still here, Chief."

"Detective Crean? What's her caseload?"

"She was in court most of the day. Just got back. "

"Like to see her."

"Right away."

"Metro's not the only outfit with detectives," Orwell said.

Twenty minutes later Stacy Crean showed up wearing her "court outfit," a dark pantsuit and a plain blue shirt.

"Wanted to see me, Chief?"

"Come on in, Stacy," Orwell said. "How'd it go?"

"The usual. His lawyer says it was for 'personal use,' I told him two kilos of bud was excessive even if he was having chemo, which he wasn't."

"Too bad you had to bust him before you found the grow-op."

"Oh, I'll find it, Chief."

"Know you will, Stacy. Know you will."

"Something else, Chief?"

"Yeah, bear with me, I don't really know what in hell I want. Come in, close the door for a minute, sit down."

"Yes, sir."

"The Billy Warren case."

"I heard," she said.

"Rotten development," Orwell said. "Just rotten."

"What's left to do?"

"That's just it. I've already stuck my nose in more than I should. I've been trying to get a copy of the case file, get a look at some evidence, and evidently I'm not entitled. I just had a call from a very nice man named Hammond who is the Deputy Chief of OPP District who told me very politely that I should keep my big nose out of things that were really none of my business. He told me that my continued attempts to involve myself in an investigation outside my jurisdiction could only lead to resentment and criticism."

"You tell him to piss off, Chief?"

Orwell smiled as he swung around to look out the window at the bare trees. "It was, as they say, a full and frank exchange."

"Are you continuing to involve yourself, sir?"

"Cold hard truth is, Stacy, I don't know where the hell to go with this thing. We've got two couples who swapped partners. The two husbands are currently dead, and the two wives are off-limits, being decidedly outside my dominion."

"All I know is from talk around here," Stacy said. "This swapping went on for a while?"

"First time was at the Kramer house," Orwell said. "Second time we know about was at a cottage where the two couples went for a weekend."

Stacy frowned. "That's it?"

"The only ones where all four were together. Mr. Kramer and Mrs. Warren evidently had other, private assignations."

"We ever find out where that cottage was, Chief?"

Orwell turned as if the sun was coming up. "Well now," he said. "Mayhap that cottage is somewhere within our reach. More or less." He frowned. "Can we find it without setting off any alarm bells?"

"Anything you want, Chief. I'll give it a shot."

"Whatever we do we'd better do it outside District's peripheral vision. I'm afraid we can't ask Francine Kramer."

"We know what lake it's on?"

"Wait a minute," Orwell said. "She has a sister in Haldane. Lives two blocks away. Wait a minute, Rhonda, Ron . . . Ronnie. That's it. Last name Cooke."

"Why don't I call her sister? Just for the hell of it?" said Stacy.

Stacy called Francine's sister with a lie that she'd been having trouble getting hold of Francine and wondered if she was there.

"She must be out shopping or something," said Ronnie.

"Oh," Stacy said. "I was hoping she could give me directions to the cottage she owned with her late husband."

"Oh, that's easy," Ronnie said. "I can tell you how to get there."

Stacy took detailed directions and managed to extract tacit permission to visit the cottage. It didn't come up that permission was not necessarily Ronnie's to give, nor that the person to whom she had given it wasn't necessarily authorized to ask for it.

"A bit outside our town line, isn't it?" Orwell asked.

"It's on Farrelton Lake, on the way up to Fenelon Falls, not *that* far out of our jurisdiction. I pass the road on my way in."

Orwell thought about it for a moment. "Well now, suppose I were to ask you to just drop by there tomorrow morning. As a favour to me. Would you have any problem with that?"

"Not at all, Chief."

"Now why would I have asked you to do that, do you think?"

Stacy flashed her wicked grin. She was way ahead of him. "Because you've been wondering where Billy Warren parked that yellow Corvette last weekend and you wondered if . . ."

"Yeah, that'll do," he said, pleased with her powers of invention. "You're trying to get a line on that yellow Corvette. Make sure you ask around at the gas station, whatever."

"There's a country store right by the turnoff."

"If they can point you toward the cottage, so much the better." He looked at her approvingly. "You planning on going inside?"

"Ronnie told me where they hide the key."

"Watch out for an alarm system. The place may be wired into Region. I doubt it, but you never know."

"I'll be fine, Chief. If I get busted, I can handle it."

"And I'll be sure to give you a stern talking to when you get back. All the same, it would be better if nobody caught you in there."

Fourteen

September

The four of them spent the night at the kitchen table discussing the situation, making and discarding plans of action. The first plan floated was for Terry to get the money from wherever he'd hidden it, divide it four ways and they all go about their business.

"What do you think Jer's gonna do," Billy said, "just forget about it? When he opens the bag and the money's not there he's gonna come after us. As far as he knows the only people who could have taken the money would be me or Doug. Doug's Jer's friend, shit, they probably worked this out together. That leaves me. They figure I took it they'll come down on me like a ton of shit."

"Not if you take off," Trina said.

"Yeah, right," said Billy. "What do I do, I quit my job and blow town? We *all* blow town? Because if I'm not around you can bet your ass they'll come down on you. All of you. Jer won't fuck around. Doug won't fuck around."

"He has to go down," Beverly said. She had cried herself coherent and almost sober. She was eating again, toasted tomato sandwiches with Miracle Whip. No one else wanted one. "Jer has to pay for what he did. The other asshole I don't care about so much, but he should be gone too."

"We're talking about two very nasty guys here," Billy said. "You don't want to mess around with them."

"You think Doug knows that Jer pulled a fast one?" Trina said. "You think they were in it together?"

"Probably. I don't know. I never met Doug Maloney until Jer brought him around."

"Jer dug it up by himself," Terry said. "The bag. He dug it up and covered the hole like it was before, like nobody could see what a crappy job he did of camouflage, and he took the bag away. I don't know what he did with it."

"But the money wasn't in the bag," said Trina.

"No. I put something else in the bag that weighed about the same. It looked exactly the same. I fixed it up perfect."

"I'll bet you did," Trina said. She'd been looking at him more and more. He was no longer invisible to her. Each time her eyes touched him he felt it.

"What about Francine?" Trina said. "Does she know about the money? Terry? You've spent time with her." And Trina smiled at Terry and it crossed Terry's mind that he had risen in her estimation, that she now saw him as a man. "What's your assessment, Terry?"

"She wants Jer to be dead," he said. "That's what she was getting at all the time I was with her. She kept trying to get me to say I'd kill Jer for her. She said that he was beating her, and that he'd beat you." And he looked at Trina and she touched her discoloured eye. "And she said that if he was dead she'd have lots of money and we could go away together."

"Everyfuckingbody wants that asshole dead," said Beverly. "I say it's unanimous."

"How did that sound to you, Terry?" Trina said. She was using his name more and more and he was becoming familiar with the way it sounded in her mouth. "Did you consider that option?"

"What?"

"Getting rid of her husband for her?"

"Why would I?"

"Why would you?" Trina said. "You already have the money."

"I already have the money."

"Still," Trina said, "even if you won't do it for Francine, we still have to do something about Jerome."

"This the same Jerome Kramer you've been fucking for a month?" Beverly said. She laughed. Her mouth was full and there was dressing dribbling down her chin. "Jesus, Trina, you are one cold bitch and that's a stone fact."

Trina picked up a napkin and wiped her sister's chin. "That's the same Jerome Kramer who gave me this black eye yesterday, and who told me that if you mentioned Bull's money to him one more time he'd have to kill you. Yes, that Jerome Kramer."

"Prick, fucker," Beverly said. "Kill me? Fucking kill me? That'll be the fucking day, mister. You don't kill me. You're the one gets to die this time, asshole."

"So we're agreed, then," Trina said. "We have to get rid of Jer."

"And Doug," Billy said. "Don't forget Doug."

"We'll have to do them both," Trina said.

Billy went back up to bed after a few hours. He hadn't made much of a contribution to the plan, spending most of the time sitting like a kid in the principal's office listening to one end of a telephone conversation that was all about his failings and about which he could offer no real defence. Beverly stayed for another hour, finished off the bottle of rum, then announced that she too needed some sleep. It was the first time Beverly had shared a bed with Billy Warren. Neither was aware.

Trina stayed in the kitchen with Terry, sitting across from him. The ice in his forgotten drink had melted.

"Looks like it's just you and me, Terry," she said. "Looks like we'll be the ones who have to figure this out. Billy won't be much help. He's been the next thing to a basket case for a long time." Trina started cleaning up. She worked efficiently and without much clatter, clearing the table, scraping the scraps, wiping the surfaces. "I knew something really bad had happened. A year or so ago. He started drinking more and more. He'd start crying for no reason that I could see." She started a pot of coffee and ran a sinkful of hot soapy water for the dishes. All the while she kept talking, speaking to Terry as an equal, as a confederate, a confidant. "Now I know what was bothering him. I thought it might be something else."

She stopped scrubbing dishes for a moment to look at him, to see how he was taking all this confidence.

"Jer wanted to keep Billy in line," Terry said. "Doug, the other guy, said that Billy could be a problem, and Jer said that he could handle Billy, that he'd keep him in line."

"That's what he did all right. Kept him in line by starting up with me."

"Why'd you let him?"

She brought the fresh coffee to the table along with sugar and cream and clean mugs. She drank her coffee black. Terry had two sugars in his. And cream.

"I was flattered for a while, I guess, all that raging attention, it was exciting, I'll admit it. I needed some excitement in my life."

Terry didn't say anything. There were secrets he still wouldn't share. His image of Trina and the strange man through the motel window hadn't faded. "How about you, Terry? What keeps the excitement in your life?"

"I like my life to be pretty quiet," he said.

"Hmmm," she said. "Maybe, but I bet it has some excitement in it anyway. Doesn't it? Somebody like you has so many secrets, you must spend a fair amount of time . . . learning things."

"I know some things," he said.

"I bet," she said. She sipped her coffee, glanced up at the kitchen clock. "My my," she said, "it's morning. You'd better drive me home. Billy will need his car to get to work." And she smiled again. "You know where I live, don't you, Terry?"

Terry drove Trina home to Oshawa in Beverly's little Nissan truck as the eastern horizon was beginning to blush. It was Tuesday morning, the day after Labour Day, Trina had a job. Billy had a job too, but he was working the three to eleven shift at the Motors and could afford a few more hours' sleep. Beverly had decided to call in sick to her job. She felt she was entitled. She would claim she had the flu but it was her widowhood that justified the day off. Terry drove straight down 35 to the 401 and turned west toward Oshawa. Early morning traffic was picking up on the 401. Long-range commuters heading for Toronto, forty klicks over the one hundred kph limit, convoys of big rigs as long as freight trains weaving down the centre lane.

Trina sat apart from Terry, with her back to the door, twisted slightly in her seat to lift her left knee into the space between them, not touching him, her body as far removed as it could be in the narrow cab, and yet her position was inviting, she was facing him, looking at him, turned to him, shoulders and hips, leaning against the passenger door, her head tilted on the glass. The window was lowered by an inch and there was road noise and windsong and Trina's blonde hair was ruffling on top, glinting gold in the light of the sun rising behind them.

"It would be good if we knew," she said, "whether this Doug guy was in on the doublecross with Jer or not."

"Maybe Billy could find out," Terry said.

"Maybe Billy could find out," she repeated. "How would he do that?"

"He could ask him."

"He could ask him," she repeated again. "That might work. And if he was in on it, he'll be defensive, he'll tell Billy not to worry, everything is okay, something like that, then he'll get hold of Jer and tell him they have a problem." Trina straightened in her seat and went looking in her bag for a pack of smokes and a lighter. Her movements were brisk, no fumbling, she knew where to look. She was energized, her mind sharp, her receptors tuned, her goal clear. "And," she went on, "if he wasn't in on it, he's going to be seriously pissed off. He'll want to go after Jer."

"He'll want Billy in it with him," Terry said.

"And he'll want Billy in it with him. Yeah. May-be." She lit her smoke and thought for a while. "We'd have to tell Billy exactly what to say," she said at last. "We need him to handle this carefully."

Terry crossed two lanes of traffic and merged neatly onto the ramp into Oshawa.

"Should have taken the next one," Trina said.

"No," Terry said, "this one's better in the mornings."

Trina had a puff and nodded to herself.

"He should say," Terry began, "he should say that he was in the bush cutting some firewood for the old man, and he looked at the spot where the money was hid, and it didn't look right to him. He didn't want to dig it up before he talked to Doug and Jer, and he was calling Doug first to find out if anybody had been near the place lately."

"That's good," she said. "That's very good. He didn't dig it up because he wants to confer with his partners first, but he's worried."

"Hunters could be roaming around," Terry said, "or maybe a wild animal, like a bear could have been digging around, smelled something."

"Right. So he's not accusing anybody. He's just concerned."

"And then we know where Doug stands," Terry said. "And we can go on from there."

"And we can go on from there," Trina said.

They stopped at the Big X Diner for gas and breakfast. The parking lot was crowded with big rigs, arriving and departing. The huge diner was packed with truckers bitching about the price of diesel and trading stories of bad drivers, shithead dispatchers, lineups at the border. Trina and Terry grabbed a table and were immediately served coffee and menus. They ordered eggs over, toast and sausages. The previous customers had left a *Sun* more or less intact on the bench seat beside Terry and he picked it up and looked at a front-page photograph of Labour Day carnage on the highway.

"You want to look at the paper?" he said.

"Not that rag," Trina said. "Fifty pages of car-stereo ads and the Sunshine Girl."

"They moved her to the back page," Terry said. "She used to be on page three."

"You like the Sunshine Girl?"

"Sometimes," he said. "It's a different one every day."

"What about today's?"

"Not so much," he said. Today's Sunshine Girl was a brunette with dark eyes and a deep tan.

"Not your type."

"I guess."

"What is your type, Terry?"

"I don't know."

"Sure you do," she said.

Breakfast arrived. Terry was hungry. He put ketchup on his home fries, dipped toast in his yolks, ate his sausages whole. Trina was less motivated. She nibbled toast, checked the jam and marmalade selection, looked around the room to assure herself that they were anonymous, inaudible in the general din, leaned forward across the table.

"This isn't an easy thing we're planning," she said.

"I know," he said.

"Who, exactly, is supposed to do it?" And she giggled at the sheer ridiculousness of the situation. "You? Me? Billy? Ha! Yeah, right. At least Beverly's motivated. Or she was last night. When she wakes up she'll be all depressed and she'll spend the day eating Doritos and watching soaps." She decided on the honey and peeled open the little vacuum pack, drizzled some on her toast. "I wish we could just get the money, you and me, and run off. I don't mean together, necessarily. You run your way, I run my way.

Just disappear." She had a bite of her honeyed toast. "Where would you run to, Terry? If you ran away?"

"I don't want to run anywhere," he said.

"You never wanted to see the world? Live someplace warm and beautiful? Like Hawaii, or Spain, or Rio? Someplace with beautiful women walking on beaches, sipping tall drinks under big umbrellas."

"That's what everybody talks about," Terry said. "Francine. That's all she could talk about. Warm beaches. Getting a tan with no clothes on." He finished his eggs, wiped his face with a paper napkin, spilled sugar into his coffee. "Is that what Jer talks about?"

"He says he wants a boat. A sailboat. He wants to live on it and sail the Caribbean."

"Someplace warm."

"Someplace warm."

"I'm not . . ." He struggled a bit to find his thought, ". . . I'm not one of those people. People who want to leave here. I don't think about other places. I have a place."

"You like things the way they are."

"Pretty much."

She shook her head. "But you've been getting around a bit lately," she said. "Coming out of your shell."

"I guess."

"So? Think about it for a minute. What do you want out of life?"

He thought about it for a minute. But he couldn't say it. She was sitting right in front of him and he couldn't say the words. What he wanted. All he had ever wanted.

"I'm pretty okay," he said at last.

"No, you're not," she said. "You're just . . . settled. You've got yourself into a situation that feels secure, feels like it will last. But nothing lasts, Terry. Trust me on this one. Nothing lasts forever." She leaned forward again. Whispered. "Think about it for a minute. If any of this gets out, there'll be police all over your little woods, digging up Bull Hollyer, looking for the money, asking questions about all of us. Think about it."

"I don't want that to happen," he said.

"Then we'd better be careful," she said. "We'd better be very damn careful. We'd better figure this thing out." She reached across the table and took his hand. "And it's just you and me that have to figure it out. Terry? Look at me. We're the ones who have to do it. Can you do this? Can you be really careful, and really discreet, and keep a really really big secret?"

And Terry looked into her eyes. "I can keep a secret," he said.

She nodded. "Yes. That's good. But we can't keep secrets from each other, can we? We have to know what we're both doing all the time. We have to trust each other."

"I don't think it would be a good idea for you to drive right to the house. We should start being discreet right now. You can drop me at the 7-Eleven, it's only a block away."

Terry knew where the 7-Eleven was, a block from Trina's front door. He had been there many times, pretending to browse the magazine rack, purchasing a pack of gum he didn't really want, respectable loitering, waiting for Trina to leave for work on a Wednesday morning, his mind filled with possibilities, where she might go, who she might see, what they might do.

"Are you going to talk to Billy and tell him what to do?" he said.

"I'll have it written down," she said, "what he should say, how he should say it. I'll be right with him."

"You should be listening too."

"I'll be on the other phone," she said.

"You should record it," Terry said. "Then we can hear how his voice sounds."

She undid her seatbelt. "How would I record it? Could I use the answering service? No, that wouldn't work."

"Radio Shack," Terry said. "Tell them you've been getting dirty phone calls and you want to tape the guy."

She smiled. "Okay."

"And pay cash," he said. "And when they ask for your address and stuff, for their files, tell them no thanks, just pay cash. Don't use a Radio Shack where people might know you. Go out to the mall near the Sunset Motel. It's safe."

"Now you're beginning to scare me," she said.

"I'm just being discreet, like you said. I don't want anything bad to happen." He almost said "to you" but he didn't. He stopped himself in time. Still, the unspoken words hung in the air. She could hear them as clearly as if they had slipped out. "You said we have to trust each other," he said. "That means we shouldn't do anything that the other person doesn't know about."

"Yes," she said. Her voice was quiet,

"When Jer calls again, record him too. We need to know what he's talking about, where he's going."

"Yes."

"Beverly can't do anything stupid. Or Billy."

"I'll handle Billy," she said. "He'll do what I tell him."

"I'll talk to Beverly," Terry said. "I want to, anyway. I'm thinking of buying this truck. I'll need a vehicle, and nobody knows it around here."

"Do they know your other vehicle?" she said. "Around here?"

"And I should have your phone number too," he said, "so we can work stuff out."

"Don't you already have my number, Terry?"

"Someplace, probably," he said. "I'll phone you tomorrow. We should get Billy to talk to Doug pretty soon. The full moon is on the 11th of October. That's a Monday. They probably figure to come up Friday or Saturday to dig up the money, but it could happen before that. We have to know when."

"If Jer thinks he already has the money, why would he come?"

"That's why we have to know what Doug Maloney knows. As far as Jer's concerned it's Billy who wants to dig up the money. Maybe Doug is expecting to dig it up too. Jerry will have to do something."

"Maybe he plans on killing Billy too."

"Or Doug Maloney."

"What did you put in the bag, Terry?"

"Just some old bones," he said.

Fifteen

DAY FOUR — Thursday, October 14

"Got sixteen Nissan pickups, Chief," said his Staff Sergeant.

Orwell was engrossed in his thesis defending the Dockerty department's existence. It was going to need some serious editing. "That all?"

"Thought you just wanted the red ones."

"Could be worse," he said. He scratched out an impolite paragraph. "Could be looking for a blue Chevy."

"Puslinch here says he's got something might shorten the list."

Orwell looked up from his scribbling. Roy stood aside to usher in a tall young man with a pleasant face who had probably had his nose broken once or twice. "You have my complete attention, Corporal."

"One of the Nissan's is registered to J. B. Hollyer," Graham said.

"Hollyer," Orwell said.

"Jersey Bernard Hollyer," Graham read off the top sheet. "a.k.a. 'Bull' Hollyer,"

"Not the baddest outlaw we ever had in town," said Roy. "But close."

"Bull Hollyer's wife, Beverly Hollyer, formerly Beverly Jannis, William Warren's sister-in-law."

"My my my," said Orwell, sitting back in his squeaky chair,

"that's the second time in two days that connection's cropped up. And where is this Bull Hollyer at present?"

"I think he's in Kingston, Chief," Roy said. "He went up for a methamphetamine beef."

"When was this?"

"About five years ago. Busted right here in town."

"By us?"

"No. Looks like Durham Region was invading our bailiwick that time," said Roy.

"They do like to take liberties, don't they?" Orwell said. "Okay, track down his file for me, would you? Nice work, Corporal. Puslinch," he added as an afterthought.

The young man nodded modestly as if he'd been awarded another stripe.

The store at the corner of Highway 36 and Lakeview Way wasn't open. Stacy drove up the tar and gravel road until she saw the red roof Francine's sister had mentioned. The driveway curved downhill to the lake. The cottage wasn't yet buttoned up for winter; it still had that between-weekends look. The barbecue was against the wall under the overhanging deck. Oars and fishing rods, life vests and a dip net were scattered in the bottom of a fiberglass canoe left on the lawn and half-filled with water. The key was where she had been told to look, under a flat rock in a half-barrel planter covered in wet yellow leaves from the birch tree beside the porch. She wiped her feet carefully then decided to slip out of her shoes altogether, leaving them beside the front door.

Pretty much what she had expected. A bit messy. Empties by the back door. A view of the lake, not a great view. Glossy prints of Lamborghinis and Ferraris, a cork board with Polaroids of dead fish held high and people eating hamburgers. Two bedrooms upstairs, both beds unmade. The larger bedroom had a television and a VCR and a selection of X-rated tapes.

Stacy checked the drawers in the matching side tables. The

one closer to the door held two broken cigarettes. On the other side of the bed, Stacy stubbed her stockinged toe on an old Polaroid camera. In the drawer she found the pictures. Billy Warren fellating a man she took to be Jerome Kramer, a slim blonde woman masturbating both men. Who took the Polaroids, she wondered? Francine? She searched the backgrounds of the pictures looking for reflections. There was a photograph of Billy sitting on the downstairs couch, naked, drunk and red-faced. He was weeping. Through the window behind his head she could see a Nissan pickup truck parked outside.

"Bull Hollyer's sheet, Chief."

"Thank you, Roy. Give me the short version."

"Short version is he was released from Millhaven 13 months ago and hasn't been seen since. OPP has been trying to ascertain his whereabouts."

"Were we advised to keep an eye out for him?"

"I can't find notification."

"Odd, isn't it?"

"He's not wanted for anything, they'd just like to know where he is."

"Well," Orwell said, standing up and nodding his head, "so would I. I'd like very much to know where Mr. Hollyer is at present. In for meth, you say?"

"Did the full bit. Model prisoner."

"Chief?"

Graham Puslinch was standing in the doorway.

"What have you got?

"You remember a big armoured truck robbery down in Oshawa about five years back?"

"This is the Securex job?"

"In Oshawa. Five years ago."

"I'm sketchy on the details."

"Daylight robbery, three men wearing ski masks, automatic

weapons. There may have been a fourth man, driving the getaway car, which was found abandoned at a mall in Ajax. Durham was looking at a Quebec connection but nothing came of it. I just talked to a detective in Oshawa. A guy named Trowbridge."

"I know him to see him," the Chief said.

"He's been working the Securex job since the beginning. He was sure Bull Hollyer was involved, but he couldn't come up with anything that would stick."

"Never anything that pointed up here?"

"He said it all pointed toward Montreal, at least that's the angle they were concentrating on. The getaway car was traced to Montreal where it had been stolen two days before."

"How did Hollyer fit in?"

"He used to ride with some guy named Reggie Sombrero, if you can believe it, and Reggie Sombrero was the brother-in-law of an ex-Securex employee they had their eye on. They suspected these guys of supplying the getaway car. Anyway, Sombrero was heavy into the Montreal meth and cocaine business, and about a month after the Securex job, Bull Hollyer was arrested for possession with intent to distribute. They knew where it came from. Trowbridge made the connection between Bull Hollyer and Sombrero and the ex-Securex guy. They couldn't get anything that would stick about the car, but Trowbridge had a feeling there was something there. He tried to get Bull to roll over on his partners for the Securex robbery, offering him a deal. Bull told them he didn't know what they were talking about, so they made it as tough on him as they could for the drug bust. He got four years. Did twenty-eight months."

"And hasn't been seen since."

"No, sir."

"Well somebody's driving his car."

"Most likely the wife," said Roy.

"Most likely," Orwell agreed.

"I though you weren't supposed to talk to Mrs. Kramer."

"There's off-limits, and then there's sort of off-limits," Orwell said.

"I'm just driving the car, Chief," said Stacy.

"That's right. Can't fault you there."

"What do you expect her to tell us?"

"Well, for starters, I wouldn't mind knowing if she ever saw her husband and Bull Hollyer together. I wouldn't mind knowing if Bull Hollyer showed up at the famous cottage weekend, or if the name Hollyer appears anywhere in her husband's DayMinder."

"You think they knew each other?"

"I have no idea," he said. "But I know one thing, Detective, someone knows a helluva lot more about this than I do, and the only way I'm going to get any answers is to question people I'm not supposed to talk to."

Stacy rang the bell and peered through the diamond window in the front door. "Bell works," she said. "Doesn't look like anyone's moving around inside."

Orwell said, "Still shopping? Maybe at her sister's."

"What do you want to do, sir? Want to wait?"

"Let's check the backyard," he said. "Maybe she's gardening or something."

Gardening would have been difficult. The back yard was three-quarters concrete. The basement door was open.

"I see it," Orwell said.

"I usually take one of those as an invitation," said Stacy.

"Got a pair of gloves with you?"

"Certainly, sir."

"Then go right ahead, Detective," Orwell said generously.

Stacy ducked under the overhanging deck and pulled on a glove before pushing the lower door fully open. "Mrs. Kramer?" she called out. "Dockerty Police paying a house call. You home? Anybody home?"

"You see a light switch?" Orwell asked.

"Right inside the door here, Chief." She turned on lights, called again. "Mrs. Kramer?"

"After you, Detective."

"What's in there?"

"Kramer's personal space," Orwell said. "It's usually locked."

"Not this time," Stacy said. She swung the door wide. "Hello? Anyone in here?" She found the light switch. "Got a body, Chief."

Francine Kramer was sprawled in one of the recliners.

"Shot twice, chest and head," said Stacy. "Lots of blood."

"Watch your step," said Orwell. "We'll call the local cops first, it's their house, let them call whoever else needs to know." He stepped aside to let Stacy out of the room and stood in the doorway for a long moment. "Used to be a big TV set in here, speakers, DVD player. This place is a lot emptier than when I first came here. Maybe she was selling off her husband's things. Or giving them away."

"Or robbed," Stacy said.

"Don't know if Metro took them into custody, but that cabinet held some serious ordinance."

"Want me to check?"

"No, we're on thin ice as it is. Let's back out nice and slow and make the proper phone call. Maybe they'll let us have another look after they secure they place."

They didn't, of course. Within twenty minutes the crime scene was under the absolute control of a Durham Region Homicide team, a medical examiner, crime scene specialists, and a dozen uniforms. Stacy and Orwell were shoved outside the perimeter, just short of the gawkers gallery, where they gave statements. Their admittedly lame (and mutually agreed upon) reason for being there, was concern for the security of the Kramer's cottage, considering the raft of burglaries that had recently occurred in the neighbourhood. They were told to head back to Hooterville and keep themselves available for further inquiries.

"Instead of going back the way we came, maybe we could swing west, head home by way of Uxbridge, would that be a big deal?"

"No, sir, no problem at all."

"We can go up 48 and come back through Goodwood."

"We never did mention the little truck, Chief."

"No, we did not. And I must say I have misgivings about that omission. I didn't want to deal with the question of how we came by that photograph, which was obtained, you will admit, under somewhat dubious aegis, and I really didn't want to have to explain why we're still sticking our noses where they aren't wanted. Anyway they will have neither the time nor inclination to deal with who might own the little truck barely visible in the background of a bad photograph." He laughed. "Besides, very shortly someone from OPP Region, or Durham, or Metro Homicide will be pounding on my door demanding a full explanation of what we were up to."

"We likely to get reamed out, Chief?"

"Not you. You're merely indulging your meddling superior. But they might decide to chastise me to some extent." He smiled smugly, and settled back in the passenger seat. "I look forward to it."

"Did you want to go right through Uxbridge, sir?"

"Just like tourists," Orwell said after a moment. "I won't know which way to go unless we go through the town. It's a left turn on the other side of the railway tracks but I don't know what it's called. Been years since I've been through there."

"Mind telling me where we're going, Chief?"

"Going home, Stacy. I just want to drive by a place, remind myself what it looks like. It's not too much out of our way."

Stacy turned off Highway 48 and headed back east. It was dark now. She tuned the radio to a soft rock golden-oldies FM station and kept the volume low. The Chief didn't comment one way or another. She vaguely heard news weather and sports but the scores and temperatures didn't register. Music resumed. She felt the Chief move in his seat and saw him reach forward for the volume control. The car was suddenly filled with "Sally Go 'Round the Roses." The Jaynetts. A haunting, churchy, organ riff, the girls sounding as if they were at the bottom of an elevator shaft. The Chief listened all the way through. She could feel the car rocking ever so slightly as he moved to the beat of Detroit City. She could hear him softly singing a harmony in a clear, light baritone.

The women were singing about how sad it was to see her baby with another girl.

As the Jaynetts faded out and the DJ segued into "Rocky Mountain High" the Chief reached forward again and turned the volume down. There was a sad smile on his face.

"That was Motown a-borning, Constable."

"It was nice," she said.

"1962, '63, somewhere in there. Used to get the Detroit stations late at night. Rhythm and blues. Sometimes we listened all night long."

The Uxbridge sign appeared on their right as they swept down the hill through Goodwood in the night.

"Sir?" she said. "This will open the whole Billy Warren thing up again, won't it?"

"Confuses the hell out of me, Stacy, is what it does. That's the truth. Make a left at the next one up please. That's it," he said as they passed the street sign. "Logan. Turns into Durham Road 28. There's the 28 sign. This is the right road."

"How far up, sir?"

"Oh, let's see, maybe five minutes. This'd be about twenty years ago I used to come through here. I was OPP back then, working the highways. Erika had a little place up near Sunderland. I'd be coming up from the city on weekends and such. This was before we were married. The Jannis family lived just down the road from her place. Diana, that's Erika's daughter, used to go to school with the Jannis girls. There was Beverly and Katrina, Trina. Slow down now," he said. "It's up here on the right. Around this bend. There's the nursery on the left where Erika had some dandy fights over substandard shrub roses. There it is. Slow right down."

He was rolling down the window as she cut the speed and they cruised past a red brick house set back from the road. There was a thick stand of firs hiding most of the front yard, but the driveway was wide and they could see the little Nissan truck parked just inside the gate. It was red. It had a camper-back.

"You want to stop, sir?"

"No, Stacy," he said. He rolled the window back up and turned up the volume on the radio. Marvin Gaye was singing "I'll Be Doggone." He closed his eyes. "You can get us home now."

Sixteen

September/October

Beverly's house was the accepted meeting place. It was private, comfortable, neutral ground. They sat at the kitchen table to drink coffee, refine the plan, listen to recorded phone conversations.

"Hey, Doug, it's me, Billy Warren."

"Oh, yeah? How's it goin'?"

"Pretty good."

"Pretty good? Good. What's up?"

"Nothing. Just. Hey, getting pretty close to the time, you know."

"Yeah."

"Well, I'm just saying, been a long time."

"Look, I got stuff to do here."

"Okay, sure, but here's the thing, I was out there, in the bush, cutting firewood, and I checked on the place, you know, and it looked different."

"Different how?"

"Like, ah, somebody had been messing with it, or an animal was rooting around or something, I don't know, so I figured I'd give you and Jer a call, you know. I didn't touch anything, because I wanted to check with you guys first, you know, make sure you knew what was going on. You guys haven't been out there, have you?"

"Have you called Jer?"

"No, I called you first."

"I don't want to talk on the phone. Come up here."

"Okay, but I've got a job. Like Saturday, Sunday?"

"Sunday. Come up on Sunday."

"Should I call Jer?"

"Let me talk to him."

"Maybe he should come up too. We should have a meeting."

"That's not maybe a good idea. I'll mention it to him. You come up here to the store on Sunday and we'll figure out what's what."

"Okay."

"It didn't look like the thing was missing, did it?"

"No, it just looked kind of messed up. Not the way we left it."

"Probably just some animals or something."

"Yeah, well they can do a lot of damage. Maybe it's time to get it out of there."

"No more on the phone, okay?"

"Okay. I'll see you Sunday."

Trina switched off the recorder. She patted Billy on the arm. "You did fine," she said.

"Shit!" said Beverly. "That doesn't tell us squat."

"Sure it does," Terry said.

"Yeah, what?" Beverly said.

"It tells us that Doug doesn't want Billy talking to Jer."

"So? What does that mean?"

"I don't know yet," Terry said. When he looked up he saw that all eyes were on him, they were waiting for him to clarify matters. "It might mean Doug and Jer have something cooking, or maybe Doug thinks they have something cooking and now it's falling apart. We don't know yet, but we know that Billy isn't supposed to be a part of it."

"He sounded funny," Billy said. "He wasn't happy to hear it was me."

"When you see him on Sunday you should have this recorder in your pocket," Terry said. "Put the microphone where it can pick up what he says. This one's okay. Can anybody sew?"

"Sew what?" said Beverly.

"Sew the microphone into a jacket. Into the collar, so it's like hidden in a buttonhole or something, with the wire coming out inside the pocket."

"I can do that," Beverly said. "I can fix it so nobody can see it."

"Fix it so it doesn't move around," Terry said. "Otherwise you get noise from the rubbing and you can't hear anything."

Billy Warren was staying with Brent Styles in his apartment in Oshawa. Brent was divorced from Myrna, and estranged from his seven-year-old son whose arm he had accidentally slightly broken while showing the little whiner a wrestling hold. This account of what had happened was part of the official Children's Aid, Family Court and police records, along with Myrna's countering version, which maintained that Brent had been drunk and abusive to both her and the boy. That Myrna had been drinking as well wasn't mentioned. Brent was currently proscribed from getting within fifty meters of his wife or his son without supervision, a stricture that, in his morosely self-righteous view, granted Brent the license to declare a moratorium on the entire sad affair. "Fuck 'em all!" he said.

Terry had never been inside Johnny O's Sports Bar but he had cased the place more than once, checking for parking spaces, rear exits. He knew it was where Billy would be when his shift was over. It was a Friday evening, the first day of October. Billy had an important visit to make on Sunday. He was going to face Doug Maloney on his home ground. Brent Styles would spend the weekend drinking and Terry didn't want his brother falling into the same pit. He wanted to get him up to Beverly's so they could go over the plan, work on what he was going to say.

"Fuck me, this'll be fucking great!" Brent Styles was in the ebullient early stages of his Friday night drunk. "Way better seats. Those clowns will be getting nosebleeds."

Billy didn't see his brother arrive. He rarely did. He was used to it. Terry was just there, or just gone, that's how he was.

"Fuckarama! It's Farmer Joe," said Brent. "Hey, Farmer Joe, how's things in the cornfield?"

"What are you doing here?" Billy said.

"Thought maybe we could go up together."

"Just in time to buy a round." Brent signaled three fingers to a young woman with a tattooed thigh and cutoffs short enough to show it off. The tattoo was a twist of barbed wire and lightning bolts circling her upper left leg. There was a suggestion of further embellishment under her clothes.

"When? Tomorrow?"

"Go up tonight," said Terry. "Have a couple and I'll drive us up to Bev's for the weekend."

"Shit, not tonight," said Billy. "I just did a day's work, man. In a factory. Like real work. I want to kick back. I'll come up tomorrow."

"You'll be hung over."

"Jeezus Kee-rist, leave the poor fucker alone," Brent said. "Doesn't feel like hoeing sugar beets on his days off. Is that a crime? Give. This one's on you."

Terry handed a twenty-dollar bill to Brent who passed it on to the illustrated girl bringing their three beers. When she bent over the table, roses and thorns were observable between her breasts.

"How far down do the roses grow?" Brent inquired.

"Roses don't grow down," she said. "They grow up."

Terry leaned closer to his brother. "This weekend is kind of important you know? And we've got a lot of things to figure out."

"What's the big deal?" Billy said. "I'm just going to talk to the asshole."

"Shht!" Terry whispered. "Nothing public. Not anything. Ever."

Billy hung his head, picked up his fresh beer. "You gonna drive?"

"I'll drive."

"Then can I have a few? Is that okay? You just sit there and do whatever it is you do, and don't lecture me, and let me kick back for a while. In fact, why don't you like fuck off and come back in a couple hours. Then I can enjoy myself."

"You'll stay here?"

"We'll be here," Brent said. "We got stuff to figure out. What's that motel called? The one we stayed in last time?"

"I didn't like that place. It wasn't near anything."

"What the fuck do we care? We got the 'Vette, baby. Vroom vroom!"

"Aren't you taking the Sierra?" Terry said.

"No freakin' way," said Brent. "It's a race, man. You gonna drink that beer?"

"No," Terry said. "Was there any change?"

"What can I say? You're a big tipper."

"I'll come back later."

"You do that, Farmer Joe. Much later."

Terry drove to Trina's house. He parked two blocks away and approached the house from the opposite direction. The garage door was open, the door to the kitchen was locked. He tapped on the glass.

"Terry?"

"Yeah."

She opened the door. She was wearing her hair in a ponytail.

"Billy's not taking the Sierra," he said.

"Why, is he drinking?"

"To the football game. He's going down in Brent's Corvette."

"What does that do?"

"I don't know."

"I can change his mind," she said.

"Maybe it's not a bad thing," Terry said. He'd been thinking it through on the drive to Trina's, sorting possibilities. "Maybe if it was in getting serviced or something. He could use Brent's car.

It would help his alibi. He just has to be here for an hour maybe and then he goes back in time for the football game. When they ask him where he was, he was in Buffalo, he didn't have his car, he was there for the weekend."

"What if they question Brent?"

"He'll say Billy was with him in Buffalo at the football game. If Billy borrowed the car and went out for a couple of hours, so what? Maybe he went to a strip club."

She was wearing faded denims and a cotton shirt, freshly washed, still smelling faintly of Bounce. Her feet were bare, and from behind she looked fourteen. Music coming from the living room, an FM station pledged to soft rock and easy listening.

"Do you want anything?" Trina said. "I opened some white wine."

"Got a Coke?"

"I don't know what's in there. Have a look."

No Coke. Club soda, Diet Sprite. 2% Milk. He sniffed the milk. It was okay. He found a glass.

"You want a cookie with that?"

"Got any?"

"I was joking. I don't keep any around," she said. She refilled her wineglass and brushed by him to put the bottle back in the refrigerator. "Where is he right now?"

"Johnny O's. With Brent."

"Is he drunk yet?"

"I'll go get him in a while. I'll drive him up."

"What about Bev's truck?"

"I'll have to leave it here."

"Where? Right here?"

"I'll stick it in the lot by the GO station. Pick it up Sunday night or something."

She moved away from him, padding to the sink and along the counter. Her bare feet made tiny sucking sounds as she moved over the tiles. "This is too complicated," she said. "This is way too complicated. You're just making this up as you go along. Half the time I can't figure out what happens next."

"We don't have to go through with it," he said. "I can divide the money myself." He drained the entire glass of milk in one long draught, and wiped his mouth on the back of his hand. "Four shares. Jerry, and Doug, and Billy, and Beverly gets Bull's share."

She stopped and turned to him. "You wouldn't get anything that way."

"I don't care."

She stared at him. "You have milk on your lip," she said. She moved toward him with fingers outstretched and he backed away. "What?" she said.

He wiped his milk moustache on his shirtsleeve and ran his hand over his mouth and chin. "I got it," he said.

"I wasn't going to hurt you."

"It's okay," he said.

"Give me the glass," she said. She collected it at arm's length and rinsed it at the sink under running water. "Think I was going to poke you in the eye."

"You wouldn't get anything either."

She set the glass on the drainboard and retrieved her wine from the counter top. "I'd get a share of Billy's."

"I guess," he said. "None of my business."

She had a sip of wine, watching him over the rim of her glass. "And if we do it your way, how does it work?"

"If we do it my way, we cut Doug and Jer out of the deal."

"Still four shares?" she said. "Billy, Beverly, me and you, right?"

"That would be fair," he said.

She had another drink. "He won't be able to handle Doug Maloney. Sunday? He can't do it."

"He just has to say a couple of things."

"He'll let himself get pushed around."

"Doesn't matter," Terry said. "As long as he says what he has to say. He's been doing real well."

"He's trying, I guess. I'll give him that." She went back to the refrigerator to refill her wineglass, smirked and waggled the milk at him before closing the door. "Do you really know what you're doing, Terry? You sound like you know what you're doing."

"I know a few things," he said.

"Like what?"

"Like Jer and Doug don't a hundred percent trust each other. And if they thought the other one pulled a fast one, they'd do something about it."

"What is it? Like sort of a game with you? You say you don't care about the money. What do you care about?"

He had to pause and sift words and choose his lies with care. "They shouldn't get away with what they did. Killing Bull like that."

"Is that it?" She smiled at him. "I didn't think you knew Bull all that well."

"They did it in my bush."

"Oh. So it's a housekeeping problem."

"I better get Billy. I have to find a place to park."

"You been in touch with Francine lately?" she said.

"No."

"Tsk tsk. Very ungentlemanly. Spend a weekend in someone's bed and then not even phone."

"I'll phone her," he said.

"You will?"

"Tell her I'm going away for a while or something. Just in case she comes up looking for me or something."

"Really turned her on, did you?" She moved toward him slowly, tiny toe noises on the tiles, her voice softened by wine, her eyes grown sleepy, her mouth like velvet.

"It's just a precaution," he said.

"Did you like it?"

"What?" He gauged his distance from the door as she came closer.

"Being with her. Fucking her." She was close now. He could smell the sharpness of the wine on her breath, the trace of fabric softener. "She liked it, I bet. I bet she liked it a lot."

The door to the garage was two steps away. Locked. He fumbled with the bolt, wrenched the door open, looked back to see her watching him, to hear her laughing.

He walked to Johnny O's from the GO station parking lot. He had sequestered Beverly's Nissan in a crowded corner where it was unlikely to invite attention — unattractive as a joyride, unprofitable as plunder and undriveable without the distributor he'd removed and stashed under the seat.

Billy had reached the maudlin stage; Brent was denigrating the institution of marriage.

"Fuck 'em!" Brent was in full voice. "But don't marry 'em! Am I right? Eh? Am I right?"

"Just don't trust them," Billy said.

"Where you been, Farmer Joe? We were getting worried. Figured you might of fell into the old combine harvester."

"You ready?" Terry said to his brother.

"Shit! The night is young," Brent said. "Billy's only puked once. Doesn't count as a full-service drunk yet."

"Did you eat anything?"

"No."

"I'll stop at a drive-through on the way up," Terry said.

"Let me finish my beer," said Billy.

"I'm going to the washroom," Terry said. "You finish up."

The men's room was in the basement. Steep, constricted stairs, broom closet, narrow corridor, the bathrooms identified by pictures of Maria Sharapova bending over to pick up a tennis ball, and Joe Carter sending one over the left field wall to win the 1993 World Series for the Blue Jays. Terry opted for the Joe Carter door and went in to relieve himself. He stared at the sports page that was tacked to a corkboard on the wall above the urinal. It was from the morning paper. The World Series was in progress. Toronto wasn't involved. Terry wouldn't have cared if they had been. The door banged open behind him as he was zipping up.

"What are you, his fucking mother? Why'n't you just piss off and leave us men to conduct our fucking business."

Brent blocked his way to the door, leaned in close and breathed beer fumes and garlic and tobacco at him. "Why'n't you just fuck off back to Dinkytown. In case you haven't fucking noticed, shithead, in case you haven't fucking noticed, your brother is getting fucked over by his cunt wife who never met a dick she wouldn't suck . . ."

Brent was hit so hard in the solar plexus that he began puking before his knees buckled and he landed in his own spew with a splat that Terry managed to avoid by stepping around him. Brent was on his knees, facing the half-open cubicle door, retching deeply. Terry put his foot on Brent's rump and shoved him into the stall.

"Do it in the toilet," Terry said.

Terry drove Billy's big GMC Sierra up 35/115, rising and falling with the hills and curves. North of Kirby, before the highway forked, Terry stopped at a Burger King and got food for his brother. Billy didn't move from the passenger seat, didn't comment on Terry's driving, ate the burger without comment, without enjoyment.

"I'm gonna be sick again."

"Can you wait 'til I find a place?"

"Find someplace."

When the highway forked, Terry stuck with 35 as 115 angled toward Peterborough. The traffic on 35 was less concentrated, room to maneuver, wide shoulder to ease onto. Billy opened his door and leaned out to get rid of his food and beer.

"Aw, Jesus, fuck it, all over the armrest."

"Undo your seat belt. You can lean out further."

"You got the four-ways on?"

"Can you get out?"

"No, fuck, I'm done. There's nothing left."

"Here." Terry handed him a wad of paper napkins.

Billy wiped his face and dabbed at the armrest and threw the wad of paper onto the shoulder. Terry didn't like it that they had left garbage behind to mark their trail. He signaled left and pulled back onto the highway. The big V8 had them back up to cruising speed before there were lights in the rearview mirror.

"Aw, shit," Billy said. "I dropped my fucking wallet."

"Back there?"

"Fuck. When I was leaning out."

Terry grabbed the first crossover they came to and swung them back south, trying to identify the place they'd stopped. When they were clearly south of the spot Terry pulled into another crossover and started them north again.

"Keep your eye open for the spot," Terry said.

"How should I know what the fuck it looks like? I had my head hanging out the door."

"Where was it? The wallet?"

"In my shirt"

"In your shirt pocket?"

"You rushing me to get out of there. I just stuffed it in,"

Terry spotted the wad of wet napkins beside the road and recognized the hydro towers nearby. He pulled over a second time.

"Give me that Burger King bag," he said.

"What for?"

"Pick up some garbage," he said.

The wallet was wet and speckled but not hard to find. Terry wiped it off on a corner of napkin that was still untouched. He crammed the wet wad into the paper bag and rolled it tightly. He felt better that he'd picked up the garbage. There was a trash barrel nearby. He walked it over, prodded it under the top layer of Pizza Pizza boxes and Styrofoam cups. He stepped back from the can, wiping his hands on the seat of his pants.

"You find it?"

"Here." He handed Billy the wallet as he climbed in. "Put it in your pants."

"I know where to keep my wallet. I don't need you telling me where I should keep my wallet. You rushing me to finish my beer."

"You bought another one while I was in the washroom."

"So? What's it to you? I earned the right, I earned the right to have some beers after work, after a day's fucking hard work, which you don't know shit about."

"You can sleep at Beverly's."

"I hate it at Beverly's. Sticks me in the sunroom. Stupid dog snores all night. Farts in his sleep."

"Not much longer. Two weeks, then it'll be done."

"Why don't we just give them the fucking money and be done with it? The four of us can split the other half. Or maybe we can say there's six people in it now, and we divide it six ways instead of four. That's reasonable. It's still a lot of money."

"Won't work anymore," Terry said.

"Why not?"

"It just won't," he said. "Those guys did a murder. You were there. You're a witness. You're also an accessory. What happens if one of them gets arrested? Then you get arrested, and Beverly gets dragged into it. Trina gets dragged into it."

Billy was silent for a while, staring out at the darkness and far-off lights. They stopped in Dockerty for gas at a self-serve Sunys. Billy went off to visit the bathroom. Terry shook his head as the gas tank sucked back sixty-three dollars worth of high-test. As he paid for the gas, in cash, Billy came in looking cleaner and more awake.

"Got any Bromo?" he said.

"Aisle 3," said the kid behind the counter.

Billy chose a bottle of Pepto Bismol instead of Bromo, a package of Juicy Fruit and some chocolate milk. He had a deep gulp of the pink stomach medicine, then opened the carton of milk. When he saw the kid behind the counter staring at him, he reached for his wallet.

"I got it," Terry said.

"Aren't you Mister Moneybags?" Billy said.

Terry shot him a look as sharp as a slap to the face. "I'll see you out there," he said.

Beverly was watching a movie when they arrived. Terry didn't recognize it. There were aliens in it and explosions. The Statue of Liberty blew up.

"Got anything to eat?" Billy said.

"You know where the kitchen is," she said.

Billy went into the kitchen to forage. Beverly raised an eyebrow to Terry.

"He's not too bad," Terry said. "He had maybe six or eight on an empty stomach. He threw up most of it."

"Is this soup?" Billy's voice.

"What does it look like?" Beverly shook her head.

"Looks like soup."

"Probably soup then. Eat some. It'll settle your stomach."

"I don't like soup."

"Eat some anyway."

They heard Billy rattling crockery and cutlery, heard scratching and whining at the back door.

"Let Broonzie in for a while, but don't give him any soup. Makes him fart."

"No shit," Billy said.

Terry sat on the couch and looked at the television screen. Brave men were battling impossible odds with the future of earth at stake.

"When's Trina coming up?"

"I don't know," Terry said. "She didn't say. Sunday morning I guess."

Beverly was watching him closely. He avoided her eyes.

"Didn't she now? What's she doing Saturday night?"

"I don't know."

"Didn't she say?"

"I didn't ask her."

Beverly reached for her smokes and lighter. She tapped him on the knee as she collected the ashtray. "You see her tonight?"

"Just for a couple of minutes. Before I picked up Billy."

"You two are spending a lot of time together."

"There's stuff to work out."

"Oh, I know there is." Beverly lit a cigarette, arched her back when she blew smoke at the television. She lowered her voice. "You fucked her yet?"

Terry snapped his head around and looked at her. She flinched.

"Okay, relax, it was just a question. No skin off my ass one way or the other. Be nice to hear that *somebody's* getting laid around here."

Billy came into the room with Bruno following close behind, his eyes never leaving Billy's tray. Billy had soup and bread and cold cuts laid out.

"He can have a slice of salami," Beverly said. "He likes salami, don't you, Broonzie?"

"Get his own damn salami," Billy said. He gave Bruno a slice anyway.

"He likes you," Beverly said.

"He's a mooch," Billy said.

"I'm taking off," Terry said. "I'll be back in the morning, breakfast time."

"Not too early," Beverly said.

"Don't scratch my paint," said Billy.

Terry looked back at them when he got to the door. They were patting Bruno and watching explosions and sharing salami.

Seventeen

DAY FIVE — Friday, October 15

The Nissan truck was in the driveway. A black dog watched them arrive from behind the fence. When Orwell got out of the 4x4, the black dog stood on hind legs and asked to be let out.

"How're you doing, pal?" said Orwell.

The dog explained his situation.

"I would if I could, but I can't do it," Orwell apologized. "You hear what this dog is saying, Detective?"

Stacy said, "He sounds pathetic."

"Doesn't he?" Orwell started for the front door. "Dogs are such liars. I count two bones and three chew toys in that backyard, plus a hole deep enough to bury a flagpole. That dog's got it made and don't let him try to tell you otherwise." He rapped on the aluminum storm door and the inner door was opened almost immediately.

Beverly Hollyer avoided the impression of being simply overweight by virtue of a splendid bosom and a belt four inches wide and cinched with double rings. Stacy figured the brassiere would have six hooks in back, minimum. Beverly was either letting her natural hair colour grow out or had skipped her regular visit to the salon. There was a mass of it, tousled bed-head, most of it reddish, the roots darkish.

"Beverly Hollyer?"

"That's me."

"Hello. I'm Orwell Brennan."

"I know who you are."

"You do?" The Chief beamed as if he'd been asked to sign an autograph. "This is Detective Crean."

Beverly opened the aluminum door and leaned out to speak to the black dog in the back yard. "You settle down," she said, "we'll go later." Then she looked at her visitors. "This about Billy or something?"

"Is this a convenient time?" Orwell asked.

"Good as any," Beverly said. "Come on in."

Beverly led them into the front room and offered them a blanketed couch to sit on.

"You want coffee?"

"Had breakfast, thanks," said Orwell, "Detective?"

"I'm fine," Stacy said.

Beverly retrieved her own cup from the coffee table and a smoldering cigarette from a glass ashtray, and, Stacy thought, did a little bump and grind before settling into the armchair opposite them. Maybe it was just the physics of shifting masses above and below the wide belt that made the motion provocative, but Stacy suspected that Beverly knew exactly what she was doing when a man was nearby.

"So go ahead," Beverly said, "you ask, I answer."

The Chief held his hat in both hands between his knees and leaned forward just a little. He was looking directly at her with appreciation.

"Mrs. Hollyer . . ." he began.

"Call me Beverly. I'd shitcan the Hollyer part except it takes so damn long to change all my ID, driver's license, credit cards. I'll get around to it, but it's a pain in the ass."

"Are you divorced?"

"Will be, if I can ever track the sonofabitch down. He took off for the West Coast over a year ago and hasn't been in touch since."

"Sorry to hear that."

"Ahh." She was dismissive. "He was in jail more than he was home. I'm used to living alone."

The Chief put his hat flat on the coffee table and arranged his fingers comfortably. "Beverly, I can see you're a straight-ahead kind of person and I'd like to be straight-ahead with you. I'm butting into an investigation that really isn't in my jurisdiction and you don't have to talk to me if you don't want to, except as a favour. The only reason I'm sticking my nose in is because I know, or knew, so many of the people involved — Billy, your sister, you, for that matter, although you probably don't remember me too well."

"Oh, I remember you, Chief. You married Erika Daily who used to live down the road. Diana used to be over here all the time."

"So there you are, people I know are involved here," Orwell continued, "and now there's this third unfortunate death."

"Now who died, Chief?"

"Jerome Kramer's wife Francine, was murdered yesterday. In her home in Haldane. No arrest yet."

Beverly hadn't known. Stacy was sure. The woman's face had paled under the pancake makeup and her eyes had shown a brief flutter of pure fear.

"Francine. Oh Jesus. Oh Jesus."

"Did you know her?"

She got up and moved around the room as if looking for something to do with her hands. Her voice was very quiet. "What a fucking nightmare."

"I'm sure it was on the news."

"Oh shit, Chief, I don't watch the news, I watch the Nashville Network."

Orwell said, "And one of the weird things about this whole situation is that your little truck out there keeps popping up in this situation."

Stacy felt it was her turn. "I visited at the Kramer cottage," she said, "and I came across some photographs of a party. Polaroids of Billy and Trina and Jerry. And in one of the pictures I could see your truck parked outside the cottage. Had your sister borrowed the truck that weekend?"

Beverly sat down with less sway than previously.

"The Big Sex Weekend?"

"Is that what it was?"

"That's what Jer Kramer called it." Beverly made a noise of disgust, spitting out a bad taste. "The Big Sex Weekend. The Social Event of the Season. It was mostly a big excuse for him to screw Trina for a few days. He certainly wasn't interested in screwing his wife, and he turned me right off."

"You?"

"Who do you think took the pictures?"

The Chief got interested again. "This is all new information you're giving us here, Beverly, and we're grateful for it, I can tell you. This big weekend, we got the impression that there were only four people there. Now it turns out there were five."

Beverly looked genuinely offended. "Hey now, I brought a date."

"Oh," said the Chief with a note of apology in his voice. "Of course. Who would that have been?"

Beverly laughed bitterly and shook her head. "Big Sex Weekend. What a joke. It was mostly Jer and Trina humping away up in the bedroom except for Sunday when we all got a little fried and Billy did something he pretended didn't happen."

"Except you took his picture doing it." Stacy was looking at her.

Beverly shook her head reflexively as if erasing the image. "I was so pissed off at him. I've had a thing, I used to have a thing for Billy Warren, years ago, only Trina got him. So she says for me to come along to, like, The Big Sex Weekend, because he didn't really go for Francine all that much. So I went, but it was a big dud. The only thing going on was Trina and Jer, with Billy hanging around trying to be part of a threesome and it got gruesome. I had a shitty time."

"Francine told the Toronto detective she left early, Saturday morning."

"No. She left Sunday. She had a shitfit after breakfast over Jer being such a sleazebag and she took off. Maybe she was pissed off because Billy Warren didn't find her attractive. Maybe she felt like a fifth wheel. I know I sure did."

"Did she leave before or after you took that Polaroid?" Stacy wanted to know.

"I guess after, if the truck's still in the picture, that's what she went home in. Like I say, we all got a little fried. Started with a certain person deciding she wanted an all-over suntan."

"Your sister?"

"Who else? She's got the body for it. I look better with a scarf over the lamp if you know what I mean." Beverly managed a semi-flirtatious blink in the Chief's direction, but Orwell was preoccupied with his hatband.

"So that started freeing things up a little?" he said.

"You might say. Francine decided, finally, that she was shocked or something, don't ask me why she got so huffy."

"Could it have been because she saw her husband in a homosexual situation, do you think?" Stacy wondered.

"That was maybe it. It was kind of unappetizing. Not sexy, just sad, like Billy didn't care anymore, like he just wanted to be part of whatever was going on between Jer and Trina, whatever it took, even if he looked pathetic."

"So, Francine left. And you stayed?"

Beverly leaned back a bit in her chair and looked up at the ceiling, arching her back and elevating her breasts as if to reassure herself they still obeyed. "Yeah, I stayed. I was too fried to drive. Don't drink and drive, right, Chief?"

"Always the best policy," said Orwell to his hat. "Was Francine sober enough to drive?"

"Couldn't tell you," said Beverly. "She'd had a few drinks, I'm sure of that. She liked wine." She slumped and let gravity win a round. "She had a designated driver."

"She didn't leave alone?" Stacy asked.

"No. She went. With my date. " Beverly helped herself to another cigarette.

"Your date?" Orwell prompted.

"Terry," she said.

"Okay, we're going in a minute," Beverly called to the black dog as she let Orwell and Stacy out onto the porch.

"Nice looking dog," said Orwell, "got some Newfoundland in him, or what?"

"You might be right, Chief," said Beverly. "He's a bear. Aren't you, Bruno? You're a big bear."

Stacy was looking at the Nissan truck. She knew without any doubt that the treads would match the casts of the tire prints taken from below Breithaupt's Bush. She wanted to ask the Chief to impound the truck, but she wasn't sure it was their place to do that. In any event, the Chief was going into the backyard with Beverly and saying hello to her shaggy black dog who seemed eager to make his acquaintance. They looked like they were dancing, the dog on hind legs, big feet like muddy bedroom slippers, his tongue hanging out and his toothy grin dementedly jolly. The Chief was ruffling the floppy ears and scratching the thick mane while Beverly stood to one side, arms folded below her breasts looking at once proprietary and absurd.

I've been to a few bad parties in my day, Stacy thought, but that must have been a really dismal. Poor Beverly, complete washout at The Great Sex Weekend, the man she'd hoped to seduce wasn't interested in her, and her date had departed with another woman. Gruesome for you, but very interesting for us.

They were back in the Chief's vehicle, the Chief driving sedately.

"Should we be doing something about the truck, sir?"

"Oh yes," said Orwell, "the truck. I was halfway out the door when I saw the darn truck sitting in the driveway and remembered what the heck it was we went there to ask about."

"Well," Stacy began, carefully, "it was a pretty interesting story. Terry being there, leaving with Francine."

"I'm kind of sorry we now have to turn this all, right over, immediately over, to Metro Homicide and let them do the work. Moen should've been up here already. Do I sound like I'm justifying myself, Stacy?"

"I'm positive those tire prints will match, Chief," she said. "We can put that little truck near the scene of the crime on the day of the murder."

"That's right," said Orwell, making another left turn, "we can do that. We can also put someone, or a couple of someones in that truck the week of the murder."

"We can?"

"Because when I finally woke up and remembered the reason for our little visit, I engaged Mrs. Hollyer in conversation about her hairy, part-Newfoundland, gorilla-dog, whose muddy footprints I bear down my front, and managed, finally, to ask a few relevant questions about trucks and things. She informed me that she and Terry Warren arrived together in the little truck on the Friday evening of The Big Sex Weekend, and that on Sunday, Terry drove Francine Kramer home to Haldane in that same Nissan truck. And the following Tuesday, Terry put a down payment of four hundred dollars in cash on the aforementioned Nissan truck and said he wanted to buy it. Then, a month later, three days *after* Jerry Kramer's murder, Terry returned the truck and said he had decided to buy something else. Beverly kept the four hundred dollars."

"Terry had the truck when it was parked on Road 17," she said.

"Oh hell," Orwell said. "We'll be going down Road 18 anyway. Surely I can drop in on a neighbour, see how he's holding up."

There was a pall of mourning over the house and Orwell could feel it pressing on his shoulders like an unwelcome stranger. Never was a really welcoming house, he thought, with the main entrance off to the side like it was snubbing the world. Irene Warren was coming toward them from the direction of the barn, wearing rubber boots and carrying a hayfork. She unlatched the gate and let it swing inward.

"Is that an invitation, Chief?"

"Almost," said Orwell. He got out of the cruiser.

"Hello, Irene," he said. "How are you holding up? Your sister still coming up from, where was it? Wisconsin?"

"Michigan, Chief. She said she'd try. I know what that means." Irene leaned the hayfork against the gatepost and stripped off her work gloves. "You looking for Dan? He's gone to the Co-op for rat poison." She sounded tired, dispirited.

"I was hoping to talk to Terry. He at home?"

"He's in the barn. You'll have to get him yourself."

"I don't want to stop him doing what he's doing."

"I never know what he's doing," she said flatly. "They're going to let us bury William tomorrow. Finally." She turned to the house. "Dan will want his lunch when he gets back."

"You go ahead, Irene. I'll see you tomorrow. Where is it going to be?"

"Just the cemetery. Not bothering with a church funeral." She started away. "Just the cemetery."

The barn was the biggest building on the place by far. The upper level was accessible from the driveway through giant double doors. The interior was as lofty as a church, framed in massive posts and beams. Some of the rafters were still holding onto bark after a hundred years of service. The open timber roof was clear-span its entire length, from the thick crossbeams where the roof pitch began, to a peak high overhead. A pigeon fluttered and resettled on the hayfork track which ran west to east the full length of the barn just below the peak. The eastern half of the barn was half-filled with bales of hay and straw. At the far end of the barn a single round bale stood flat against the wall.

"Terry? It's Orwell Brennan. You in here?"

Terry's voice came up through the floorboards. "Down in the stables, Chief. You can come down the ladder or walk around, or should I come up?"

"That's okay," said Orwell. "We'll come around."

The lower level of the barn was below grade from the north and open on the south side and Orwell and Stacy walked around by the west end and down a steep narrow path to stables and cattle pens behind the barn. Manure piles stood near a barnyard where a trio of caked and muddy Holsteins gathered around an open bale of hay.

One of the stable doors was open and Terry stepped out and watched them approach. He shook his head.

"Should've brought your rubbers."

"You've got me there," said Orwell. "You remember Detective Crean?"

"Hello, Mr. Warren."

Terry was standing half in and half outside the open stable door and he wavered, Stacy thought, flickered like a flame, in and out of shadow, his expression hard to read, his eyes difficult to see.

"Terry, I noticed when I checked the report, that you said you didn't know the name of the man in the tree."

"I guess I was upset about the dead body being there."

"I'm sure you were," Orwell went on, "but see the thing of it is that we've since learned that you knew all along exactly who the man in the tree was, that you had spent some time in his company, that you knew the man's wife, and you knew the man was having an affair with your brother's wife. You knew all of that, and yet you pretended that you didn't know the man at all."

"I shouldn't have done that, I guess."

"You'd be right, guessing that, Terry," Orwell said. "You lied to the police, and that's not a good thing to do. I wonder if you can tell me why you would lie about knowing the man."

"Because of Billy," he said. "I didn't want it getting out about what was going on between Billy and Trina."

"And why is that, Terry? Did you think your brother might have done something?"

"Well, you arrested him," Terry said.

"Yes, we did," said Orwell.

"I didn't think he'd go and kill himself over it," Terry said, "but I knew he was going to be in trouble."

"But you did know the man, Jerome Kramer."

"Yeah. I knew him."

"And where he came from?"

"I knew the man's name and where he came from."

"And where was that, Terry? Where did he come from?"

"Down in Haldane."

"You know the address?"

Stacy saw the flicker across his pupils.

"Sure, Chief. I know the street but I don't remember the number. I was only there the one time when I drove his wife back home when she wanted to leave."

"That was when she wanted to leave the weekend party early?"

"I wanted to get out of there too, Chief. I think her husband had the idea that everybody wanted to be in some kind of an orgy or something, only not everybody thinks that way, you know? I could put up with . . . certain things as long as they were done in private, but when they brought them down to the living room and out into the yard it was too much for Mrs. Kramer and too much for me. She needed a lift and I took her home."

"Took her home in Beverly Hollyer's Nissan truck."

"That's right. I'd come with Beverly."

"So you drove Francine home."

Orwell looked around for a place to settle his bulk but there wasn't a suitable perch. He scraped his boots ineffectually against the edge of a stack of barn boards. Stacy kept her position, slightly to the side and two steps back with a clear view of Terry and his hands and his eyes. Orwell rubbed his face.

"Did you get to know her at all when you took her home, Terry?" Stacy asked. "Did you have a chance to talk about her husband and your brother's wife and what was going on there?"

Terry said, "She didn't talk much. She was pretty upset. She cried part of the way."

"Did you feel sorry for her?"

"She was pretty mad about Trina. You know, how she'd stolen Jer from her and wrecked her marriage."

"And you sympathized with her."

"Well, yeah," Terry said. "She had a right. What Trina and Jer did was wrong."

"Did she say what she was going to do about it?" Orwell asked.

"No, Chief," he said. "She was just upset, you know."

Orwell let his eyes sweep south across the two nearest fields. Where all else was grey and brown, the fields were a fine pale green with winter wheat showing; a small wager placed on spring.

"You know she's dead now, don't you, Terry?"

"I heard it on the news this morning."

"Did you? Probably happened day before yesterday. During the night they think. You weren't anywhere around Haldane Wednesday night, Thursday morning, were you?"

"No, sir, Chief."

"Where were you?"

"Heck, right here, I guess."

Orwell gave up on his shoes. "Awful set of coincidences don't you think, Terry? Six people went to that weekend party and half of them are dead now. Kramer is murdered, and Billy killed himself, and now Francine is murdered."

"It's almost like a punishment," Terry said. "For what happened that weekend."

"Did you see her again?" Stacy asked. She caught another flicker in his eyes and she didn't quite buy his headshake, a shade too vehement, a shake too long.

"Just dropped her off and you know, said goodbye. She said she wanted to have a shower."

"So you only saw Francine Kramer that one time? When you met her that weekend and drove her home in Beverly's little truck?"

"That's right," Terry was firm. "Just that one time. I was just doing the neighbourly thing, is all."

"How'd you like that little truck?" There it was again, Stacy thought, a fleeting glimpse at the quick machinery of his mind.

"Liked it fine for a while."

"Liked it enough to want to buy it?"

"Was going to buy it. Had it for three, four weeks. 'Til it died on me."

"Just up and died?" Orwell looked surprised.

"Other side of the bush. Road 17. Coming back from town. I had to park it by the side of the road for two days until I could get a new water pump."

"How'd you get home that day, when you had to park it?"

"I just cut up through the bush, Chief. Came across the fields."

"This was all about the same few days as the murder, wasn't it?"

"More or less. I believe I got it up and running the day before Jerry Kramer showed up to go hunting. Maybe the day after."

"Any way you can pin it down for me?" Orwell was trying to be helpful. "It might clear up a few small details."

"Lemme see," he said, "I believe it was the day before, Chief."

"The day before you found the body?"

"Pretty sure."

Orwell nodded. "I think you're right. I think it must have been the day before, Terry, or maybe the night before, because we checked out Road 17 the day you found the body and there wasn't any truck there then. Just the tracks where it had been parked."

"Believe you're right, Chief. I got it up and running some time before Jerry Kramer showed up at our place to go hunting. Got a water pump at Canadian Tire, put it in myself and then I took it back to Beverly. Asked for half of my down payment back, but she said I couldn't have it cause I'd been driving it for three weeks."

"I talked to Beverly this morning and she said you brought it back two days after Jerry Kramer was killed. Is that about right?"

"She'd probably know, Chief. She'd spent the down payment by then."

"What I'm wondering is where the truck was from the time you got it running again to when you brought it back to Beverly?"

"Oh, it was down at Gary's Service Centre. On 35. I wanted him to check it over, see if there was anything else that might go wrong with it."

"Ah," Orwell said, as if it all made sense to him. "Okay, so you parked it on Road 17 and walked home through the bush and across the fields. Then two days later you got it running again with parts from Canadian Tire, that the one at the mall or the one down 35?"

"35."

"Right. So now it's running again and you took it down to Gary's to have it checked over. Have I got this all straight, about the truck?"

"That's about it, Chief."

"Gary give you a lift home?"

"Caught a ride with some guy coming this way."

"Wouldn't happen to remember his name, would you?" Stacy asked.

"Gord something. Lives up in Fenelon Falls. Drives a Dodge Dakota."

Stacy watched Orwell grimace as if his stomach was bothering him. He turned away from Terry and looked out at the green fields again. Stacy saw Terry's eyes follow the Chief.

"You smoke, Terry?" Stacy wanted to know.

"Smoke?"

"Cigarettes. You smoke cigarettes?"

"No, ma'am. Never believed in it."

"Just wondered. Somebody was smoking cigarettes back in that bush the night Kramer was killed."

"That so?"

Stacy followed Orwell back up the path and they wiped their shoes as best they could in the tall grass growing alongside the barn. As they drove through the gate, Dan was waiting to turn in. Orwell rolled down his window.

"Be 11:00 tomorrow morning, at the Avalon cemetery, Chief. If you wanted to be there."

"I'll be there, Dan," Orwell said. "I'm really sorry for your loss."

"It's a hard one to handle. I won't try to pretend any different. God forgive me, it crossed my mind once or twice that I didn't want to be around much anymore myself. Except I know it's even harder on the wife. Just as hard, anyway."

"Terry didn't put a foot wrong, did he?" Orwell said. He was driving faster than he usually did, almost reaching the posted limit. "Explained about the tire prints. Explained why his footprints might be in the bush. Covered just about everything."

"There are a few things we can check, Chief. The new water pump on the truck, see if he really did have one installed. Gary's Service Centre, see if the truck was there for two days."

"Yes," Orwell said, "and some guy named Gord from Fenelon Falls driving a Dodge Dakota. We can do that. But, just for the sake of argument, let's say Gary's Service Centre never heard of the truck, Canadian Tire never sold a water pump for the truck and the guy in Fenelon Falls is a figment of Terry's imagination, so what? We still don't have anything that ties him to Kramer's murder or Francine's murder. Nothing substantial."

"What about Trina?"

Orwell was circumspect. "She does not, on the surface at least," he qualified carefully, "have a motive for killing Jerry Kramer. They had just spent part of two days in a motel and were discussing plans for a future together."

"Maybe the plans didn't sound too great to Trina. Maybe he dumped her."

"Parted as friends, according to the motel manager's statement," Orwell said. "She and Jerry had a big smooch before getting into their separate cars."

"Maybe it was an act. Maybe she followed him."

"Drove off in opposite directions," said Orwell. "The motel manager again."

"That's a very observant motel manager," said Stacy.

Eighteen

September

They listened to the second recording on Sunday evening with wind blowing outside, porch windows rattling, Bruno howling in the backyard, the little recorder in the middle of the table.

"Have you listened to it yet?" Trina asked.

"Shit, all I know is how to turn it on," Billy said.

"Hey, Doug, how's it going?"

"How's it going?"

"Looks busy."

"Time of year. Where'd you park?"

"Out by the arrow."

"Let's go have a look at that Sierra of yours. Hey, Cecil? Take over back here for a few minutes I gotta see a man about a truck."

(The sound of boots on a wood floor, the sound of a door, the crunch of boots on gravel.)

"You talk to Jer?" (Billy's voice.)

"I can't get ahold of the sonofabitch."(Doug's voice, a clear note of irritation.) "Francine says she doesn't know where the fuck he is. You haven't seen him?"

"Nope."

"Fuck. You know what he's like, always got some fucking deal cooking." (More crunching, crunching stops.) "Issat true about the four of you? You and Francine and him and . . . none of my fucking business, I don't

give a shit, I just heard a rumour that you were getting friendly with Jer's wife is all."

"No. That's bullshit," (Billy's voice.) "I don't even like her."

"None of my fucking business." (Doug again. Sounds of feet on gravel circling the Sierra.) "Pop the hood." (Sound of door opening, hood released, lifted. When voices are heard again they have an echo, and an intimacy, as of heads leaning together over a V8 engine.)

"Where'd you hear that anyway?" (Billy.)

"I don't fucking know; Jer, I guess. I mean it isn't common knowledge. He said you and Francine were hanging out, and him and you know, your ah missus, were . . . none of my fucking business what you guys get up to in your spare time."

"When did he tell you this?"

"What? Jer? I don't know. Sometime."

"Like it must've been pretty recent. Did he come up here?"

"I don't know, like maybe on the phone or something."

"You talked to him since, you know, since, like what happened, you know, last year?"

"Yeah, sure, fuck. We've talked a couple of times."

"What else?"

"What, what else?"

"What else you talk about? Besides him screwing my wife."

Billy shot an embarassed look at Trina who had a smile on her face as if she were listening to a particularly entertaining radio program.

"Is that all the conversation was about or were you talking about other stuff?"

"It was just conversation."

"Not about the thing?"

"The thing. No. We didn't talk about the thing."

"Because I saw him last week, Labour Day weekend, and I said it's getting close to the time we said, five years, like we said. October is five years exactly."

"What'd he say?"

"He said he knew it was five years."

"Right."

"And I said we should pick a day, you know, start making some kind of arrangement, pick a day, agree on how we're going to do this thing, because I'm telling you, Doug, I don't want to get into one of those situations like we got into last time with Bull."

"Shut the fuck up!"

"No, you shut the fuck up. I'm telling you. We make some kind of arrangement and we stick to it, because I'm not going into the bush with you two guys with my fly open and my weenie hanging out. I'm going to bring along a damn shotgun just to make sure there aren't any arguments about who's got the right to what share and when it gets dug up and all that shit."

"Keep it down. You got nothing to worry about."

"I've got a lot to worry about. Beverly's asking questions about where's Bull and when is she getting her end, and you and Jer are having meetings I don't know about."

"What about you? I wasn't invited for any fucking Labour Day. I guess I don't have a wife to throw into the pot."

"I told you what Jer said Labour Day. What'd I'd like to know is what you guys talked about?"

"We're just shooting the shit, keeping in touch, you know how it is."

"No, I don't know how it is. All I know is the place looks like somebody's been dicking around out there and I get a feeling that you and Jer have been talking about stuff, maybe doing stuff and not telling me about it. And that thing better still be where we put it or the shit's gonna hit the fan big time. Big time."

"Just calm the fuck down, Billy. Fuck, take it easy man, what are you getting so worked up about?"

"What are you talking about? Worked up, why wouldn't I be worked up? I'm going to go do some damn digging on my own, that's what. Reassure myself things are where they're supposed to be."

"Don't do it, Billy."

"Who's going to stop me? You? What are you going to do? It's on my

damn property. My old man's damn farm. Private frickin' property. Why shouldn't I check it out?"

"Because that's not what we said. We made a pact."

"Yeah, right, we made a pact, and then you and Jer decide the pact is worth doing a guy over . . ."

"Keep it fucking down!"

"Nobody's out here. We're all alone here Doug. You and me. Aren't you worried about the thing? Are you sure it's okay? You aren't a little bit worried about the thing? Because I'm telling you, that thing better be where it's supposed to be. And I'm not gonna be caught like you-know-who. I'm going to be prepared. You guys come on my property with your frickin' bows and arrows and figure you're going to screw me over you got another think coming. I'll be coming into the bush with my 12 gauge."

(No talking for a full minute or more, the sound of boots, Doug Maloney's boots, walking away some distance, the sound of the truck hood slammed shut, very loud and sharp.)

Terry stopped the recorder. Beverly and Trina both lit cigarettes. Billy seemed embarrassed by his performance; Trina gave him a gentle punch on the shoulder. "Look at *you*," she said. "Mister actor guy. I'm impressed."

"He pissed me off," Billy said.

"Doug and Jer are in it together," Terry said.

"Or Doug thinks they are," said Trina.

Beverly got and went to the refrigerator. "Who's ready for a beer?"

Billy put his hand up. Trina looked at Terry. He turned the recorder on.

(Doug's voice, faint, at the far edge of the microphone's range.) "Come over here a minute." (Billy's footsteps, and then Doug's voice, closer.) "Look, Jer didn't want to say anything until the right time, but, the thing isn't there anymore."

"What do you mean?"

"I mean, Jer moved it."

"See?" said Terry.

"Moved it when?"

"Couple years ago. Before that other thing happened."

"Moved it where?"

"It's safe."

"Yeah, right, sure. Safe from me. When was I supposed to hear about it?"

"When the time was right."

"What are you talking about, when the time was right? What's that supposed to mean?"

"Jer got worried, after Bull got scooped for the meth. He thought Bull might crack, tell where it was, so Jer moved it."

"Bully would never crack," said Beverly. She handed Billy a beer. "Bully was a rock."

Trina waved her hand. "Shhh."

"And I want to know where he moved it."

"Someplace safe."

"Yeah, yeah, I heard that, but I didn't hear any specifics. You know where it is, don't you?"

"Yeah. I know."

"So?"

"So, I want to talk to Jer, figure out when's the best time to do the thing."

"Screw the best time! I want to know where it is. A quarter of it is mine."

"A third. Bull's not in it anymore."

"What about Beverly?"

"What about her? Jer figures he'll give her some money, we'll all kick in, she'll be cool."

"So where is it?"

"It's in the bear."

"It's just a black bear," Billy said. "Pretty big for a black bear. It's in the bow shop, standing in the corner. They sewed the bag inside the bear. He says they didn't open it."

"If they had they'd have been surprised," Trina said.

"Wouldn't they, Terry?"

"Prick thinks he'll give me a few bucks and I'll be cool, does he?" Beverly had a deep pull at her beer, burped. "Big surprise coming, asshole."

"Doesn't matter," Terry said. "We already have it."

"Pisses me right off," Beverly said.

Terry's mind was working. "Time to give Jer a call," he said. "Get them thinking about each other. Get them worried."

Tina put her arm on Billy shoulder. "You up for this?"

"I've been doing okay."

"You've been doing great."

Terry put a sheet of paper in front of his brother. "You know what to say?"

Billy pushed it away. "I got it," he said. "Give me another beer."

"Jer? Hey, where you been? I've been trying to get hold of you."

"I went out of town for a few days."

"Yeah. Well, I'm thinking we should maybe have a talk."

"What about?"

"You know what about. The thing. It's time to do what we said."

"I'm waiting for the right time."

"Yeah, well the thing of it is, I went over to Omemee and had a talk with Doug."

(Long pause, careful response.) "Oh yeah?"

"And he says you guys stuck the thing inside that thing in the store."

(Longer pause.) "Yeah."

"Well, that thing you stuck inside the thing in the store isn't what you thought it was."

"What're you talking about?"

"I'm saying I had a feeling you might pull something, and I was right."

"Wasn't expecting that," Beverly snorted. "That woke him up."

"Shhh." Terry turned up the volume.

"What did you do, Billy?"

Billy laughed. "Got your attention now eh, big man? Now all of a sudden you don't have all the cards."

"Okay. You've got my attention. You going to tell me what you did?"

"About a week after we stuck it there, I went back up and moved it to a better place. That thing you dug up isn't what you think it is."

"What the fuck are you talking about?"

"I'm saying you don't have what you think you have. I have it."

"Where?"

"It's there. Not far from where we put it, only in a different hole."

"Don't fuck around, Billy!"

"You think I'm . . . screwing around? Been a lot of that happening hasn't there? Looks to me like you and Doug been trying to screw me around."

"What do you want, Billy?"

"For starters I don't want to be . . . screwed around by my so-called partners 'cause they're stone killers trying to screw me, so I don't give much of a shit about my so-called fucking partners."

"Nobody's trying to screw you, Billy. I was just being careful. I figured Bull might blow the whole thing."

"Didn't get around to telling me, did you?"

"No. Maybe I should have. But, I was going to tell you."

"When?"

"When the time was right. You know, like around now, when we said, five years."

"Right. Five years. And when I asked you about it last weekend you told me to dummy up. And when Beverly tried to talk to you about it, you told her to piss off. So when, exactly, were you going to mention it? After you and Trina ran off to Hawaii or someplace?"

"I'm not taking Trina anywhere. That thing's over. It maybe wasn't such a good idea."

"It was your idea."

"I'm just saying, maybe it wasn't a good idea. Got everybody all worked up, got my good buddy all pissed off, bent outta shape, now he's threatening to cut me out of the deal. Gotta hand it to you, Billy, you

outplayed me this time. But I wasn't out to screw you. You've gotta believe that. I was just doing what I thought was best for everybody."

"Sure you were."

"So, what do you want, Billy?"

"I want half."

"Half?"

"It's fair. I'll make sure Beverly gets her full share. Bull's full share. You and Doug can split the rest."

"Have you told Doug?"

"No. I'm not going near him again. You and him can work it out between you. I'll give you half, you can split it with him."

"When do you want to do it?"

"Exactly when we said. Five years. October 9. Full moon weekend."

"Good," Terry said. "And now the other one."

"Doug?"

"Yeah?"

"It's me, Billy."

"Yeah? What?"

"You might want to have a look inside that bear. That thing in there isn't what you think it is. I think Jer's screwed us both."

"What are you talking about?"

"Trina and me, my wife Trina, we had a kind of a reconciliation. She's not with Jer anymore."

"So? That's not any of my business."

"Well it is, 'cause she says he got drunk one night and started running his mouth about how he'd screwed everybody over and how he was the only one who knew where the thing really was."

"Where is it?"

"Why don't you just check that thing you have and make sure I'm not shitting you. But if you come up empty, maybe you'll call me back and we can talk about what we're going to do about it."

"Wait a minute. What the fuck's going on here?"

"Just check. See what you find. Or don't find."

Two hours later Doug Maloney called back.

"Okay. It isn't there."

"Right. Did you talk to Jer?"

"No."

"Good. 'Cause I think he figures to take it all and blow the country."

"He better not be thinking that."

"He says he wants to come up and shoot a deer next weekend. I'm going down to Buffalo with some guys from work, see the Bills-Miami game. We planned it months ago."

"You're not going to be there?"

"I'll be there. I can make it back in time to catch up with Jer in the bush when he digs up the thing. You want in?"

"Fuckin' A. I want in. I want my end."

"Maybe we should give Jer a call, give him a chance to explain things, organize this thing so we're not stumbling all over each other in the dark."

"What? Oh yeah, that'd be a great plan. You really are a dumb fuck."

"You figure we just meet up on the road, on 17?"

"Yeah, sure. Park all the cars in a line and have a picnic. Fuck. Use your fucking brains for a minute. We get there, wait until he digs it up, and then we say hello."

"I don't want another scene like the last time. I don't want to be digging graves in the middle of the night."

"Shut the fuck up! Just make sure I know when he's coming up. I want to be there when he gets there. I don't want to have to go looking for him."

"Yeah, you're probably right, about not saying anything."

"You got any idea where he moved the thing?"

"He told Trina it was real close to the first place, just in a different hole."

"You been out looking for it, Billy?"

"I got a good idea where it is, but I'm not going near it. I don't want him getting suspicious of me. He's already killed one guy . . ."

"Shut the fuck up! Shit!"

". . . I'm just saying, he's a dangerous man."

"He's not the only one."

Nineteen

DAY FIVE — Friday, October 15

They parked the Ramcharger in Orwell's space and transferred to Stacy's unit. Orwell said he didn't feel like driving for a while. It suited Stacy, the Chief drove like a farmer. The Family Inn was straight down Highway 35 past Pontypool, almost to the 401, a line of contiguous red units with windows facing a parking lot. There were two big rigs parked across the highway near a gas station and six cars parked in front of the motel units. A larger structure, detached from the accommodations, housed a cramped lobby and a small coffee shop/café with a magazine and gift shop crowded into the passage between the two. Two men lifted their heads in unison as Orwell and Stacy entered but went back to eating their hamburgers after noticing that the big man had a badge on his hat. Both men were wearing baseball caps. One cap said *Mack*, one cap said *Peterbilt*. The truckers, Stacy figured, heading north, decided to jump the median and run across the highway for eats.

The manager was named Willhemina Provine and had already spoken to the police on two previous occasions about the guests in unit 9 but would be quite happy to tell the story again. A square-shouldered, bustling, bowlegged fussbudget in a Dynel wig — the Carol Channing model — which failed to hide grey stubble on the back of her neck, she had on a house dress and a cardigan, support stockings and a pair of Adidas cross-trainers — about a hundred and eighty dollars at Foot Locker, thought Stacy, who had priced a similar pair not long ago and decided she couldn't afford them.

She sat them at a table by the window and told them to call her Willi, Willhemina being so long and formal sounding. She turned to check on her other customers. "How are you guys doing?" Her voice was harsh and raspy and she stood with her elbows out and her bony fists on her narrow rib cage. "Those burgers suit ya? You gonna have room for pie? Coconut cream. Homemade."

Orwell heard the words coconut cream pie and reminded himself that he'd only eaten a small bowl of bran flakes for breakfast prior to spending a long and dismal morn being pawed by a gorilla and standing up to his fetlocks in cow dung. "You getting hungry, Detective?"

"No, sir. Are you?"

Willi was delivering to the truckers generous wedges of a white and gold pie as high as a four egg cake.

"I suppose I could wait till we get back up to town. No sense spoiling my appetite at 2:30 in the afternoon when my wife will be setting the table for supper in . . ." he checked his watch ". . . oh, about three hours I guess."

"That pie looks awfully good, sir. I'd be tempted to have a piece, if you were going to."

Orwell nodded graciously and gratefully. He was transparent, but she was tactful, insightful and quick on her feet. And he was getting a slice of pie out of the deal.

Willi brought cups of coffee to go with the pie, which turned out to be entirely too rich for Stacy's taste but appeared to have the Chief's complete consideration. Willi was settling herself like a hen ready to hatch another egg and Stacy thought that she was enjoying this just a bit too much.

"I'm sorry you have to go over this again, Mrs. Provine," she smiled charmingly, "I mean Willi."

"Oh I don't mind," said Willi. "I'm happy to help. I helped catch a bank robber six years ago. His picture was in the paper the morning he checked in here. I called 911 and they arrested him right out there in the parking lot. He had a stolen car and over fifty thousand dollars on him. My picture was in the paper the next day. It was a picture of me holding the newspaper with his picture in it. I had it framed. It's in the lobby."

"That's great," said Stacy. "You're extremely observant."

"Boy, you have to be observant in this business," she said with fervour.

"I'm sure you do," Stacy agreed and reached out her fork to take a diplomatic taste of pie only to find that the Chief's fork was already mining the claim. "So what was it about the guests that weekend that caught your attention?"

"Well, to begin with," she lowered her voice a few notches, "they weren't married. The man signed them in as Mr. and Mrs. but they came in separate cars and anyways married people don't act like that."

"How did they act?" Stacy asked, still holding her fork. It appeared that the Chief was absolving her of all responsibility for the pie.

"Well, you know, they smooched quite a bit, in public I mean, like right where youse two are sitting." She looked approvingly at the two clean plates. "That pie suit ya, Chief?"

"Quite acceptable," said Orwell, who had reservations about the quality of the undercrust and the browning of the coconut topping, but was otherwise inclined to give it a passing grade. "Very toothsome. Generous servings as well."

"It's not a big menu," said Willi, "but we get a lot of people come here for the food if you can believe that."

"I can believe it," said Orwell. "That true, fellas, you come here for the eats?"

Stacy saw that the two truckers were saddling up and counting out bills on the paper tablecloth.

"Sure is, Chief," said Peterbilt. "Will's pies are famous along here."

"Worth the risk, you figure?"

"What risk?" asked Mack. "Why you haven't had any salmonella here for what, Will, three years?"

Mack laughed and Peterbilt laughed but Stacy noted Willhemina did not. "Will-eee," she said. "Not Will. Will is a man's name."

"I meant the risk you take getting over here," said Orwell. "You've got to dodge across two lanes of high-speed, northbound traffic, climb over a concrete median, then dodge two lanes of high-speed, southbound traffic just to get a piece of pie."

"It's getting back across with a full belly that's the tricky part, Chief," said Peterbilt.

"Well, you two be careful," said Orwell. "Jaywalking a major highway is dangerous. In fact, I believe the practice is discouraged in the Transportation Code and might — I could look it up — might carry a monetary penalty. I don't have the darn book with me just now or I'd check for you, but I seem to recall something to that effect."

"We'll watch our step, Chief," said Peterbilt, looking sullen. Cops never stop being cops. Even for lunch.

"Have to start lobbying for a pedestrian overpass for you, Will," said Mack. "Your pies being so alluring and all."

"Will-ee," she said as they trooped out the door and started across the parking lot. "Will-ee."

The Chief seemed intent on the progress of the two truckers who were stranded in the middle of the highway, straddling the median while they waited for a gap in the northbound traffic to make a run for the far side.

"How far to the next turnaround?" said Orwell. "How far would they have to go to drive around to this side?"

"Oh, they'd never do that, Chief." Willi was amused. "Truckers have been coming across the highway like that for years, since it was built."

"But say they did want to get around, park on this side, how far would they have to go?"

"They made it," said Stacy, with a measure of relief. The truckers were getting ready to hit the road. Peterbilt was climbing into a red Mack Titan and Mack was opening the door of a chrome and blue Peterbilt. Isn't that sweet, she thought. They traded caps.

Orwell turned away from the window and looked at Willhemina Provine for what, in Stacy's judgment, was the first time.

"Well, you certainly are a magnet here, Willhemina. They come from far and wide. Truckers, bank-robbers, honeymooners, murder victims. Must make you feel downright irresistible."

Willi wasn't exactly sure how to take that. She thought there might be a put-down hidden in there somewhere. "Those two sure weren't honeymooners," she said firmly. "They were married, but not to each other. They were here for a rendezvous."

"And the rendezvous ended at what time?" asked Orwell politely.

"Saturday after breakfast."

"Did they check out?"

"He checked, she went to get her bags."

"And in your previous two statements you said that they had a big smooch, in the parking lot."

"They did, too."

"And then they got into separate cars?"

"That's right."

"And drove off in opposite directions."

"Right."

"Neat trick, with that median in the middle of the highway," said Orwell.

Stacy blinked.

Willi looked confused. "But they did. They did."

"If you would just think back for a minute, maybe you can tell me how they did it."

Willi thought long and hard. Stacy kept staring at the concrete median in the middle of the highway and wondering why it hadn't registered. Then Willi's face lit up with pride and vindication.

"He wasn't parked on this side," she said, chin up, eyes bright, mouth pursed, grace restored. "He was parked over there. By the gas station."

Stacy drove south to the Bolton turnoff then under the overpass and back into a northbound lane.

"He probably made the turnaround while she was packing. Came over to this side to gas up and get pointed in the right direction," Orwell said, glumly. He was quite sure that his brilliant observation would prove ultimately worthless, had merely been an exercise in self-importance and as such, unworthy of him. Playing at Charlie Chan. "But, Madame, you have perhaps forgotten cat's footprints in snow." He granted himself a rueful, absolving chuckle at his own pomposity. "Probably means nothing."

"Who knows?" Stacy said. "New information. Can't beat new information for keeping us hounds on the scent, can you, sir?"

Orwell snorted. "Yeah, that's us, Stacy," he said after a moment, wiping his left eye, "a couple of bloodhounds chasing our tails."

"I don't think we're chasing our tails, sir. I think we're looking for answers and so far the answers don't make a whole lot of sense and until they do, we can't stop." She glanced over to see how he was taking this. He was listening. "At least that's the way I see it, sir."

"No, we can't stop. That's the pitiful truth. There it is, Detective; got its own off ramp. Orono Fuels."

Stacy pulled them off the highway.

"And Taxidermy," added Orwell. "Did you see that one? Off to the side. Orono Fuels. And Taxidermy."

Jerome Kramer had indeed filled his gas tank at Orono Fuels on the morning of October 9th. Good old charge slips. Full disclosure, no holding back, right there in blurry purple and blue: forty-six dollars worth of premium gas and a jug of Bug Off windshield cleaner at 09:35.

"Thank you for your trouble, Mr. Zelnicker; we appreciate your help," said Stacy.

"No problemo, officers."

Mr. Zelnicker stank strongly of petroleum products and could produce clear, black fingerprints on any surface without resorting to an inkpad. He had already contributed a good set of left-hand partials to the fender of their unit and was ineffectually smearing at his spoor with a once-red rag. Stacy wished he'd stop wiping the fender, he wasn't making it any better.

The Chief climbed out of the passenger's seat and spoke to Mr. Zelnicker across the roof. "Tell me something," Orwell said, "would the taxidermy office have been open that morning, at about that time, 9:30 on a Saturday morning?"

"Oh, sure," said Zelnicker. "Hunting season? You bet. Sid Maloney. He takes all his winter orders, all his winter work right here in September, October."

"Then he closes up the office?"

"Well it's not really an office," said Mr. Zelnicker who had just discovered six rusty lug nuts hiding in the folds of his wipe rag. "Just that little camper over there. Usually he's got the camper outta here by this time. His nephew Doug is usually there on the weekends. Hunters pull in, sometimes they got a deer, sometimes they just want to make sure he'll mount one if they get one. He's one of the best. He's always booked up full."

"So he'd be where, now, Mr. Zelnicker, home stuffing deer?"

"That's it," said Zelnicker who was wondering if he was responsible for the scratch near the headlight. "He'll be home stuffing."

The Chief was staring out the passenger window, drawing a line with his knuckle in the condensation on the glass.

"Damn," he said. "Just keeps getting murkier and murkier."

"I could talk to Mr. Maloney tomorrow, Chief," Stacy said. "It's Saturday. I could just drop in."

Orwell sniffed loudly and shook his head as if foiling a fly. "There's likely to be a whole lot more of this, chasing around after nuggets of useless information, such as why does the trucker cross the road, and how many lug nuts can you hide in an oily rag." He wiped with the back of his big hand at the knuckle design he'd been making. "And I can no longer invest this much time in what may well turn out to be a wild goose chase. Much as it pains me, I must forego my Charlie Chan impersonation for a while and concentrate on doing what the town pays me to do." He turned in his seat. "You see the sense in all this, I'm sure."

"We're not closing down the investigation, are we, sir?"

"That's just it, Detective. It's not our investigation, except by default. And like a good team-player I am obliged to spend the weekend waving flags at our brothers and sisters at the OPP and Metro Homicide, and perhaps even Durham Region — although I'm somewhat miffed that they haven't been returning my phone calls. And I will attempt with all my might to entice one or more of their representatives to pay us a visit. I can do no more, now can I?"

"No, sir."

"Anything germane to Francine Kramer's murder gets handed over to Durham, anything connected to Jerome Kramer's murder goes directly to Detective Moen, and Sergeant Dean of the OPP must be kept in the picture re: Nissan trucks and such, and that way we can say we did our best. And, should they decide to pay us a visit and listen to our story, I will of course let them take over. Understood?"

"Of course, Chief," she said. "What if none of them show up?"

He lost his frown momentarily and laughed out loud. "Well, since this whole business is simply an indulgence on my part, I will indulge myself further by keeping you on the trail. Over the weekend if you felt inclined to visit a taxidermist or a service centre or a Canadian Tire outlet just to satisfy some curiosity, I certainly would have to support your effort and applaud your tenacity without giving more than tacit approval."

"That'd be fine with me, sir."

"One more thing," he said. "I'm going to call Joe Greenway and see if he can visit the taxidermist with you. He knows a fair amount about hunters, game, equipment, that sort of thing. If there is anything to be learned relative to those matters he'll be the one to spot it. That okay with you?"

"Yes. I'd be happy to partner up with Mr. Greenway for the day."

"Good." Orwell seemed mildly surprised to see Argyle's bronze visage staring at him as they arrived at the station. "Just drop me in the parking lot, I don't feel like explaining myself to the office watchdogs." He shook his head. "Hell, we may all be out of work if I can't slow down Donna Lee's steamroller." He checked his watch again. "Look at that. I'll be home in time for supper for the first time in days. Won't be able to eat, of course, that little bit of pie gave me an awful bellyache."

Stacy pulled around to where Orwell's Ramcharger was parked in its customary spot under the chestnut tree. No one else wanted to park there, too many things dropping from above. Orwell maintained that he enjoyed wiping leaves or blossoms off his windshield.

"Okay," he said, climbing out, "keep receipts, anything good pops up give a call."

"Yes, Chief. And thanks. I'm enjoying myself."

"We're both in so much trouble."

"That's part of the fun," she said.

"Good hunting," he said.

"Can't figure out how I missed that median," she said, with a laugh. "I was looking right at the whole time and it didn't register."

"I was looking at the median, Detective," he said. "You were looking at Willhemina Provine."

"Yes, I was."

"Of course, the fact that you never did notice that Willhemina Provine was a man, might suggest another line of work. But I have faith in you, Detective. I have faith."

And with that he waved goodbye and sauntered over to his vehicle and proceeded to sweep brown leaves off his hood.

Twenty

October

"Hello?"

"Hi, ah, Francine? Hi, it's Terry. Terry Warren."

"We-ell, hello stranger. What happened to you?"

"I had things to do. Farm work. Up here."

"Plowing fields, milking cows . . ."

"Is this a bad time to call?"

"What? No-o, I'm all by my lonesome, very lonely out here on the wrong side of everything. You ever going to come see me?"

"Where's Jer?"

"Who knows? Probably screwing Little Miss Perfect this weekend."

"Oh. Do you know that for sure?"

"Might be somebody I don't know about yet. Wherever he is, he's either screwing something or shooting something."

"But you don't know for sure?"

"What's the difference?"

"Wouldn't be smart for me to come down for a visit unless I knew where he was for sure."

"Do you want to come down? I thought we were getting along pretty well, and then you disappear for a month."

"Not that long."

"Almost that long. Tell you the truth I didn't expect to hear from you. I thought maybe I'd scared you off."

"It did make me a little nervous, what you were talking about."

"Forget all that. It was just a fantasy. A little fantasy of mine."

"It kept going around in my mind."

"Really?"

"I thought maybe we could talk about it again some time."

He could hear her moving around on the other end of the line, something clinking, a murmur, perhaps the television, a thump, a door closing, a room tone different from when they began.

"What have you been thinking about?" she said.

"You know, what you said. Doing it."

"For me?"

"I guess. Partly. Then, you said there was a lot of money involved." He heard soft seductive laughter. "Is there? Because if I was going to think anymore about it, I'd need a better idea of what I was getting myself into."

"And what you'd be getting out of it."

"I don't think it's a good idea to talk about this stuff on the phone."

"Remember where we went that time? That Greek place by the marina?"

"I remember how to get there."

"Good," she said. "Let's do lunch."

Terry left the phone booth and walked to the Nissan truck parked near the exit on the far side of the lot. He was less than two blocks from 21 Boxter Crescent. There had been someone else in the house with Francine, he was almost certain. Not Jer. Someone she spoke freely in front of, someone who kept their mouth shut when necessary, someone whose company she could leave without explanation, someone who was very quiet. Almost quiet enough. Terry got his blue leather jacket from behind the passenger seat. In the pocket was a knitted watch cap. He turned up the collar and pulled the cap low on his forehead, then crossed the road and walked past the intersection where the eastern terminus of the crescent met the main thoroughfare. He held a pocket street atlas open to a wrong page. Should he be forced to explain his presence in the neighbourhood (highly unlikely, even Terry would admit) he could prove that he was quite obviously lost.

21 Boxter Crescent was hidden by the curve of the street, ten steps along the sidewalk before Terry could see the front door. To his right was the entrance to the lane that curved behind the houses at his end of the crescent. He heard the footsteps behind him and moved forward, out of the way, not looking up from his map. When he heard the steps receding he turned to see a young man in a red baseball cap and a hooded sweatshirt walking to the intersection and waiting for the light to change. Terry crossed to the other sidewalk and moved parallel to the young man, crossing the intersection, slowing down as the young man paused to unlock his bike from a rack. Terry watched as the young man rode away, then he got into the pickup and drove out of the lot.

Terry stayed in a motel that night. He paid cash. Twenty-dollar bills. Random serial numbers. Part of the brick he determined was safe to use for expenses. He paid cash for a new jacket the next morning. A sport jacket, dark blue, not cheap. He thought Trina would like him in it.

Francine was wearing gypsy clothes, Terry thought, red hoop earrings, a fringed shawl and red leather boots with stiletto heels. Her hair was different, wavier, more dramatic, her eyes were accentuated by lashes and shadow and arching brows. Terry was wearing his new jacket and polo shirt.

"Don't you look nice?" Francine said.

"You look good too," he said.

"Why thank you."

She kissed him on the cheek and he inhaled her scent — it reminded him of cinnamon and young cedars.

"Don't kiss me back? Oh dear."

"It's public."

"Nobody cares."

"Somebody you know could see."

"I don't know anyone, sweetie. I live in Haldane. It's like being in Witness Protection."

They sat by a window that gave Terry a view of the city skyline to the west and Francine a view of Terry's face.

"Let's have some calamari," she said.

"What is it?"

"Squid. It's delicious. And some white wine, but not retsina this time, something clean, a Chardonnay."

Terry let Francine order, kept his face turned toward the window, watched a gaff-rigged ketch change directions through the server's transparent reflection, watched the server walk away.

"So? What have you been up to?" Francine said.

"Getting ready for winter, you know. Got some second cut hay but it got rained on before we baled it."

Terry looked out the window again as the server arrived with the wine.

"Terry? Would you like to taste the wine?"

"Could I get a Coke?"

Francine tried the wine, pronounced it tolerable, accepted a full glass, dismissed the server to search out a Coke, had a sip, then a swallow, all the while watching Terry watch the skyline.

"Afraid she'll remember your face?"

"You never know what could trip you up. Some little mistake, something you forgot to do, something you should have done."

"You've been thinking about this a lot."

"It's just common sense."

"I'm not sure murder qualifies as sensible."

He grabbed her wrist and stared hard at her.

"I was *whispering*," she said.

"Doesn't matter. It's a bad habit. Pretend everybody is your enemy."

Terry's Coke arrived with a basket of hot crispy calamari. He tried one.

"Like it?" she said.

"It's okay," he said. "Chewy."

"Okay," she said, "what's this all about?"

"I was just thinking," he said, "wondering if it was something I could do."

"You come to any conclusions?"

"Not yet," he said. "I'd like to know what the results would be."

"You mean the money."

"There'd have to be a pretty good reason for doing it."

"How does over half a million dollars sound?"

"Has he got that much?"

"Once I get my hands on it."

"How do you mean?"

"There's his insurance policy. Bank accounts. The house would clear over three hundred thousand. Maybe more."

"That's it?"

"That's not bad."

"There's no cash?"

"There's cash in the bank. Over fifty thousand. There's an account he doesn't think I know about has thirty thousand in it and his personal account has almost that much."

"And you can get it out?"

"Eventually. After . . . after he's no longer around, it all belongs to me."

"But that takes time doesn't it? I mean, you don't get it until people say you can have it."

"Oh I'll get it," she said. "Don't you worry about that."

"Okay, sure, but it'll take time, and what am I supposed to do? Wait around till you get it? And you wouldn't have to give me anything if you didn't feel like it."

"I wouldn't be like that."

"Because what could I do if you didn't feel like it? I couldn't go to anybody. I'd be the one in the dangerous position, you see what I mean?"

"What you mean is, you'd want some money up front."

"Like a down payment."

She smiled her pussycat smile. "Because this is purely a business relationship, right?" She had a sip of wine and made her lips wet. "There's nothing else involved is there? Nothing personal between you and me?"

"That kind of stuff can get confusing," Terry said. "When it gets mixed up with the other stuff."

"No more doing what we did?"

"I guess you have to figure out which is the most important part."

"Well, when you put it that way . . ."

"I mean, the one thing is kind of nice . . ."

"Kind of nice?"

"Nice."

"Just nice?"

"But it's not real, is it?"

"It was real enough for me," she said. She dipped a red nail in the white wine and licked her finger. "Of course, I'm forgetting how you feel about Trina."

"This wouldn't have anything to do with her," he said.

"Except in a roundabout sort of way."

"Not in any way."

"Except that Jerry wouldn't be bothering her anymore," said Francine. "Wouldn't be hitting her in the face."

He turned away.

"Eat some food," she said, "before it all gets cold."

"She's my brother's wife," he said at last. "It's his responsibility to look after her."

"And this would be purely a business arrangement, between us."

"For now," he said. "Except, I don't think it could work out. I thought the situation was a little different."

"You thought he had money lying around."

"I didn't know it was all so tied up in things."

"It's tied up in a lot of things. I don't know half the things he gets into. There could be more. He's got little companies; he's got different names. I'll probably have to hire someone to track everything down."

"Like a detective?"

"Maybe an accountant."

"See? It could take you a year to get it all straightened out."

When the server dropped by, Francine motioned for her to clear the food away.

"Didn't care for it?" the server said.

"It was fine," said Francine. "We weren't very hungry."

The server poured the last of the wine into Francine's glass then cleared the food dishes. Francine clicked the stem of the wineglass with her red fingernails, like a tiny horse cantering.

"You seem different," she said.

"How?"

"A little more . . . I don't know, mature. Sure of yourself."

"I've had time to think about things. It was all kind of new to me the first time."

She reached across the table and put her hand on top of his. "I remember. Some of it was new to me too."

He didn't take his hand away. He allowed her to run her nails from his wrist to his knuckles, felt the hairs stand on the back of his hand.

"How much of a down payment are we looking at?" she said.

"I should forget the whole thing," he said. "It's a bad idea. I had it going around in my head that maybe I could get away from here or something."

"We could, you know," she said. "We could get away from here. Once it was done, I'd have lots of money. Enough for both of us. I want to get away too."

"I don't know," he said. "It wouldn't be easy to do."

"You could do it. I believe you could do it. In fact you're the only one I know who could."

"Is he going hunting?"

"He's always hunting."

"I mean a specific date. A place."

"I could find out."

"If I had some definite information I could do some more planning. I'm not saying I'd do anything for sure. I have to think it through."

"It's good that you're being so careful."

Terry looked around just as the server was bringing their bill, and she looked directly at him and smiled pleasantly.

"Another Coke?" she said.

Terry shook his head and took the bill from her. "No thanks," he said.

"Let me take care of that," Francine said. "You didn't eat a thing."

"That's okay," Terry said. He put money on the tray. Two twenty dollar bills. "Keep the change," he said.

"Thank you very much," said the server. "Have a nice afternoon."

Terry watched her walk away, then turned to Francine. "We can't ever come here again," he said. "We'll have to meet some other place."

"Are we going to meet again?"

"I'll phone you in a couple of days," Terry said. "Maybe you can find out some things. Maybe you can let me know what he's doing, where he's going."

"There's a motel not far away," she said. "I could get us a room."

"If we need a place."

"I meant right now," she said.

Terry drove Francine most of the way home. He parked at the shopping mall. She put her hand on his thigh.

"Sure I can't talk you into a little relaxation? You look like you could use some."

"If you find out anything, you know, what we talked about — where he's going to be and when, that kind of information — we could meet at that motel you said."

She took her hand away, collected her bag, gathered her fringed shawl about her shoulders and opened the truck door.

"Too bad," she said. "I had all sorts of treats in store for you. I must be losing my charms."

"When's a safe time to call?" Terry said.

"Any time. He's never home. We could go there right now. He wouldn't be there. The chances of him showing up before midnight are a thousand to one."

"It's that one chance that can mess up the whole thing."

"I'll see what I can find out," she said. She climbed out and closed the door, looked in at him through the open side window. "When do you think you'll call?"

"Wednesday," he said.

He watched her walk away. She didn't look back this time.

There were no really good places from which to stake out Francine's house. Boxter Crescent was wide and bare, treeless, picture windows, drapes pulled wide on domestic scenes and TV screens. The lane behind the house was short and dead-ended at a daycare playground. There were eyes everywhere. Terry couldn't understand people living so close to each other, showing everything to their neighbours — this is what we drive, this is our barbecue, this is what we hang on our walls — deliberately, aggressively, hanging signs around their necks, not one lawn unmowed, not one porch light burned out.

Terry cruised the crescent just once, after dark, confirming what he already knew: Boxter Crescent was a kill zone, covered from every angle. He was better off in the mall parking lot, watching both ends of the crescent where they hit the main thoroughfare a long block apart.

Behind him, many of the mall shops began shutting down. The Dairy Queen and the McDonald's would be open for hours. When the lot cleared out the skateboarders would move in. There were already a few of them scraping and flipping and falling down. Terry could see them in the rearview mirror. He saw a young man coming up behind him and passing by, crossing the main road and heading up the crescent. The boy was wearing a red cap. When Terry saw him make an abrupt right turn and enter the lane, he got out of the truck.

Francine's house was on the left, gatepost, recycle bin, concrete patio to the basement door. The young man was rapping quietly, the door was opening. Francine was still wearing the red hoop earrings.

Terry went back to the parking lot, climbed into the little truck and pulled onto the main road, heading east, going home.

"Are you going to see her again?"

"I don't know, maybe not."

"You said you would."

"I said I'd call. I'll call."

They drove in silence for a while. Road 17 was a dark tunnel leading ever downward illuminated only by their headlights.

"How did she look?"

"What do you mean?"

"Did she look nice?"

"I guess. She looked okay."

"I'm sure she looked better than just okay. Did she wear a dress?"

"What? Yeah. She had a dress on, or a skirt; she had boots on."

"Did she make a pass at you?"

"I told her it wasn't a good idea to mix things up."

"How did she take that?"

"She was okay with it."

"Was she? I bet she was surprised she couldn't get you into bed." Trina chuckled. "Or did she get you into bed?"

"She has a boyfriend."

"Has she? How do you know?"

"I saw him."

"What's he look like?"

"Just a guy. He works in the IGA across the street."

"How old is he?"

"I don't know. Not very. He rides a bike."

"Does he now?" Trina laughed. "My my."

"Francine talks too much. She thinks she's being careful, but she likes to play games."

"So? Leave her out of it."

"There's one problem."

"What?"

"After. She's going to think I did it for her."

Terry led her from the bush, across the stream and out into the open bowl. The moon was up, half of it glowing, a week before full.

"Can you see my back?" he said.

"I'm okay," she said. "Right behind you."

"We'll stop when we get to the top of the hill."

"I'm not tired."

"To sit and wait for things to settle."

She sat beside him, below the rim of the bowl, on a patch of long grass near a buckthorn tree. Terry motioned for her to stay put and then snaked a few feet higher to scan the fields beyond. Three long hayfields, each one about twenty-five acres of stubble, a few round bales of late and doubtful hay standing on edge like tombstones. Beyond that, Road 18, headlights moving down the hill from the Little Britain Road, headed for Highway 35. Terry could make out lights still on in the farmhouse, lights moving near the barn. He slid back to where Trina sat. She was smoking. Terry checked the wind to see which way the scent was carrying.

"Things settled down?" she asked him.

"The old man's finishing the milking and the chores. He'll go back in and the two of them will watch the news. They'll go to bed pretty soon. We'll sit here for a little bit."

She lay back against the grassy slope and blew a stream of smoke at the stars. "Nice here," she said.

He lay on the grass beside her, careful not to touch her, leaning on his elbow, looking at the bleached denim tight over her knees, her white sneakers.

"Yeah, it's okay," he said. "It's a little exposed, but you get a good view all the way to the highway."

"I meant how nice it was to be quiet, and just rest a while." The coal of her cigarette glowed and for an instant warmed her face. She was looking at him. "Why don't you lie back? You don't really know how to relax do you? Always watching, always on the move."

"I can be quiet."

She laughed quietly. "Sure you can. Like a cat watching a bird. I mean relaxed. Lie back, it's comfortable with the long grass."

She stubbed her cigarette and he reached for it, pinched it from her fingers, took out his belt knife and made a half-moon, lifted the grass like a scalp.

"Don't you think that's overdoing it?" she said. "Who's going to find that?"

"Nobody, now." He patted the clump back into place, combed a few stray blades and stalks into orderliness

She reached for him, squeezed his upper arm. His muscles jumped, his biceps were hard as India rubber. "Always on the job, aren't you, Terry?"

"I need to make sure things are the way they should be."

"We're really going to do it? Aren't we?" Her voice was throaty, as if aroused. "Can you do it?"

That was the big question, Terry knew. The planning, the organizing, the scheming — these he was good at. But murder? He thought he could kill someone in defense of Trina. It was a scenario he had played in his mind many, many nights. His fantasy was by now refined and embellished. Her assailants, once faceless, appeared now as Jerome Kramer and Doug Maloney; the setting, once a shadowy nowhere, now a grove of paper birches he knew well, and visited often. But fantasies were only that. He understood the difference. The cold, deliberate murder of a man, no matter his sins, made his scalp sweat, made his kidneys cold. He had tried to fit it into his fantasy — Trina in danger, Jer looming over her, Terry advancing — but it wouldn't resolve itself into a climax. He could never pull the trigger, loose the arrow, wield the sword. The man always looked at him, saw him, recognized him, said his name. To do a murder is to expose yourself completely, and he didn't know if he could do it.

"I don't shoot things very much. I used to shoot rabbits with a .22, back when Grandpa Max was still around, but after that I didn't do any. Hunting just upsets the whole bush, so I stopped."

"Can you shoot the new bow yet?" she said.

"I've been practising," he said.

"Is it hard to pull?"

"No, once you get it started it gets easier. When you have it all the way back it feels like nothing."

"Show me," she said.

Terry crawled back up to the rim and had a long look. A few lights along the Little Britain Road, a pickup climbing the hill, no lights at the house and barn.

He reached back for her. "Time to go," he said.

She grabbed his hand and wrist in both her hands and he pulled her up the last of the slope and into the field.

"You're very strong," she said.

"Stay right behind me," he said, and set out, quartering the sharp stubble to the worn track that ran all the way down the middle of the first two fields before angling toward the barn and the drive shed.

"Just stay on this track," he said. "It'll take us all the way."

"All the way it is," said Trina, and she took his hand, and they walked like sweethearts down the dark rutted road.

They came in through the small doorway behind the silo. Terry flicked a switch and a series of low wattage bulbs glowed like street lamps from one end of the barn to the other. She could hear the cows in the stables below, clomping and farting and bedding down, she could hear pigeons cooing in the gloom above them.

"Any bats in here?" she said.

"They won't bother you."

"Snakes?"

"Doubt it," he said. "Some rats probably."

"Rats."

"And barn cats," he said. "To keep them down."

"Where do you shoot?" she said.

"Down this end," he said.

An open space at the eastern end of the barn, covered by a carpet of dusty straw on the plank floor. Terry had a spotlight clamped to the hayloft ladder. When he turned it on, the beam of light illuminated a round bale against the far wall, six feet in diameter, and more than a three feet thick; a massive target butt with a square of white paper pinned dead centre.

"I'll get it," he said.

Terry climbed the ladder. Once out of the light he disappeared into the shadows overhead. No sounds from above. She waited, listening, trying to follow his movements. A whisper of chaff dusted through the floorboards overhead, drifted through the glow of a forty-watt bulb. Now she had him; now she could follow him —

he wasn't a magician. Dust sprinkled down. He was above her. She heard a thump. A black barn cat was staring at her, eyes glowing like empty mirrors.

"Terry?" she called out. "Where are you? There's a big ugly cat staring at me and he looks evil."

No sound.

After a moment, the cat moved into the darkness along the south wall, moved like a predator.

"You okay?" Terry said.

He was right behind her, inches from her shoulder. She jumped. "Jesus Lord!" she said. "Where did you come from?"

"There's another ladder down that end," he said. He held up the bow case. "Want to see it?"

"Yes," she said.

Terry unzipped the leather case and lifted out the compound bow. It had eccentric cams at each forked end, and the string crossed over itself like a cat's cradle. He took out an arrow and fitted it to the string.

"How far away will you be?" she said.

"I can get within ten feet of him."

"Ten. Impossible."

"You didn't hear me."

"Try it from here," she said.

Terry drew and let fly. The arrow buried itself in the hay bale, two feet wide of the white paper.

"Do it again," she said.

His second shot was closer, but not close enough.

"Not very good."

"No," he said. "I'll have to practise more."

"Give," she said.

She lifted the bow, chose an arrow, nocked it neatly, drew the bow smartly, loosed the arrow without effort. The arrow buried itself dead centre in the white paper.

"Like that," she said.

"Ho-ly," he said.

She laughed, delighted to have surprised him. "Ha! What do you think I did at the stupid Haldane Rod and Gun Club? Billy and Jerry talked about cars and hockey scores, Francine was giving tango lessons to anyone in trousers who could count to four, so I took shooting lessons. From a young man named Logan. Logan had big arms. He could reach right around me. Showed me how to draw, aim and release. I took quite a few lessons from Logan."

She shot again. The second arrow hit inches from the first.

"Like that," she said. "When you let go it's supposed to be smooth. Logan said it wasn't like twanging a guitar string, it was like opening your mouth."

She nocked a third arrow, pulled to half-draw. She could see the wondering look in his eyes. He wasn't the only one who had secrets. "It's easy," she said. She pulled to full draw and sighted at the paper. There was a cushioned thump and the black cat was again in the light, staring at her, hissing. Without a second's hesitation she drilled the black cat through the heart at twenty-five paces. The impact pinned the cat to the floor and it lay there, motionless.

"I think we should have it stuffed," she said. "Hang it on the wall like a trophy."

Terry had the dead cat in a plastic bag. They were retracing their steps across the fields, heading for the bowl and the stream and the woods, Terry's woods, where everything was the way he wanted it, where he was at home. She didn't hold his hand this time. He had the bow case slung over one shoulder. He held the plastic bag at arm's length so the cat wouldn't bump his shin with every second step.

"What's the matter?" she said. "You told me you used to shoot rabbits."

"Nothing's the matter."

"I'm sorry. I was showing off."

"It was good shooting," Terry said. "Better than I could ever do."

"You're getting better," she said.

"Not really," he said. "I can shoot a gun okay, a rifle, I'm used to that. That other thing, it feels weird. Like I'm holding an umbrella. It's complicated."

"No, it's not. It's simple."

"For you. You had lessons. Private lessons?"

"Yes."

"Did you like him?"

"Logan? He was nice. Are you jealous?"

He had to shake his head at that. How could she know? His feelings went far beyond jealousy. Her lovers, the ones that he knew about, had all suffered inconvenience once she stopped seeing them — briefcases stolen, cars vandalized, wives alerted — but in each case the retribution he'd inflicted had little to do with the intimacy they'd enjoyed; he had paid them back for turning away from her, for the discourtesy of not pining for her ever after, for the callous way they had resumed their lives as if nothing had happened. He couldn't allow them to forget her. She wasn't like other women. The common rules did not apply. Terry thought he was the one person in the world who knew her truly, understood the secret fires inside her. But as the dead cat bounced off his knee again, he shook his head and admitted that he didn't know her nearly as well as he thought he had.

"When are you going to show me where the money is?" she said. She was walking directly behind him, following the bouncing silver fob on the zipper of the bow case.

"After."

"After you kill him?"

"After it's over. After he's dead. After they go looking for the other one."

"What if they don't go looking for Doug Maloney?"

"We'll make sure they do."

"How?"

"I don't know yet," he said. "I'm thinking about it."

He stopped at the edge of the bowl and looked down at the stream and the edge of his forest. The moon wasn't bright enough to show him more than dark shapes and glints on water, but he could see it all clearly. He could hear the water spilling over the beaver dam, and the sound the poplars made in the wind, like crashing surf on a distant shore. She stood behind him and looked down the slope to the bottomland.

"What?" she said. "You hear something?"

"Nothing that shouldn't be there," he said. "Look right there." He stretched his arm so that she could sight along it. She held his shoulder, leaned close to his arm.

"What am I looking at?"

"The big poplar tree. You can hear it when the wind blows. It makes a sound like the ocean."

"I see a tree."

"Look to the left a little, not much, a few degrees. Can you see the water?"

"No."

"Keep looking. It catches the moonlight. It's moving from right to left. You can see the moon on the water."

"Yes, I can see it now."

"That's where the bridge is, just down from that big tree."

"Okay."

"That big tree is where he's going to be on the night."

"How do you know?"

"His tree stand is still up there. That's where he went last time. That's where he'll be."

"And you have to find it in the dark," she said.

"*You* do," he said.

"I do?"

"You're the only one who can," he said. "I could miss. I could get there without him seeing me, I could get close enough, but I could miss." He turned to look at her face, nebulous in the pale light of the half moon. "I can get you there," he said. "I can get you right in front of him without him knowing."

"I don't know if I can do it," she said.

"Yes," he said. "You can."

He led her through the woods and down the last slope to Road 17 where Beverly's pickup was parked near the bridge. He drove her toward Highway 35 where her car waited behind the lumberyard. She had another smoke as they bumped along the road. They didn't talk. They didn't turn on the radio. They watched the road grow bright before them.

"What are you going to do with the cat?" she said after a while.

"Freeze it."

"What for?"

"Have it mounted, like you said."

"I was joking," she said.

"I know," he said, "but it got me thinking. A trophy cat. Take it to the taxidermist. Drop it off at Sid Maloney's."

"What for?"

"I could put something stuff inside. A pack of money, one that Doug and Jerry handled when they counted it. Something with Bull Hollyer's prints."

"What would that do?"

"Connect Doug Maloney to the robbery," he said. "Like a bear full of money, only smaller."

"That's just weird," she said. She laughed. "That is too weird. Where do you get this stuff?"

"They're going to look for everybody he went hunting with," Terry said. "They'll look for Doug Maloney."

"And?"

"Sid hates Doug," he said.

He parked next to her car in the dark of the lumberyard, turned off the lights, shut down the engine.

"Motor sounds rough," he said. "I better get it serviced before next week. Wouldn't want a breakdown."

"That wouldn't be good."

"You should have yours checked out too."

"Mimi? She's the most pampered little car in the world. Horst loves her at the BMW dealership."

"That's the guy with the bushy sideburns?"

She looked at him.

"How much did you spy on me, Terry?"

"It wasn't spying," he said.

"What was it?"

How could he tell her? He didn't have the words, even if he'd felt sure of her reaction, he didn't have the words. To tell her what was in his heart he would have to testify, proclaim his faith, admit that she was his religion.

"Make sure you didn't get hurt."

"It wasn't any of your business."

"Well it is now," he said sharply. "If you want this to happen, if you want to get away with this, if you want the money . . ."

"Oh, God, how I want the money," she said, and giggled.

". . . and a chance to spend it."

"And I want to get away with it."

"I want you to get away with it too."

She stared at him in wonder. "Do you love me, Terry?" she said. "Is that it? You've been in love with me all this time?"

His voice was tight in his throat, his jaw muscles were moving, his knuckles were white on the steering wheel.

"I wanted to look after you."

"And did you? Did you look after me?"

"When I could."

"How?"

So many times. So many ways. "One time when Billy almost caught you."

"When was that?"

"You and that man from the bank."

"Roger."

"You had lunch at that restaurant by the lake. You were on the deck. Billy and Brent Styles were going fishing in Brent's outboard. They were right below you on the dock, trying to fix the carburetor."

"What did you do? Oh shit, I remember, Roger got a call from the bank, he had to take off. That was you?"

"Billy didn't see you. But he could have."

"I could have handled it. I didn't need you to fix things. I would have handled it."

"You didn't have to."

She unclicked her seat belt, checked her pockets, opened the door but didn't get out. "Makes me feel all spooky," she said. "Like I've been haunted."

"I didn't have to tell you anything," he said. "I could have just stayed quiet until you and Jer and Billy and Doug and everybody else got tired of looking. I didn't have to say anything. Nobody would have seen me, nobody would know about me. I'd still be invisible." There was anger in his voice, an overtone of reproach.

"Why did you?"

"You know," he said. "Don't make me say it all the time."

"For me? That's all? Not the money?"

"I don't care about the money."

"This is all for me?"

He didn't answer. There was no point in answering.

"What do you get out of it?" she said.

More than he ever thought he would get. Her company, her conversation, her proximity, her treatment of him as worthy, worth listening to, worth learning from. "It's enough."

"You don't ask for anything," she said. "You never make a pass at me. You treat me like I'm made out of crystal. It's a little bit creepy, I've got to tell you."

"Only because you know," he said. "I never got in your way."

"I'm glad I know," she said. "I'm glad you told me. You don't have to tell me any more about it. And you don't have to hide from me anymore."

She patted him on the shoulder. He shrugged it off. "What's the matter?" she said.

"That's the way you pat Billy when he does something right. Good boy, Billy. Like he was a loyal old hound dog."

"I'm sorry, I wanted to show you it was all right. That I wasn't angry."

"I don't need to be patted," he said. "You don't have to tell me I'm strong, or I'm smart." He turned to her. "I've seen you handle men. I watched you. You can do anything to them. You just have to smile, pat them on the shoulder, laugh at some stupid joke. They don't stand a chance."

"And it bothers you."

"No," he said. "It's just that I've seen it. I've watched you. I'd make bets with myself how long it would take for you to get what you wanted. But I'm not like them. I'm not like any of them."

"No," she said. "You're not like any of them."

"I don't want to be treated like one of them."

"I won't treat you like one of them," she said. She rummaged in her jacket pocket for her cigarettes and lighter. The flame from the Bic lit her reflection in the windshield for a second. "Don't you hate me for what I am?" she said. "Don't you have a low opinion of me by now? All the men, all the different men. Don't you think I'm evil?"

"No. You're just you. It's how you are."

"Say my name," she said.

"Why?"

"You never say my name. Say it."

"It's Trina," he said.

She chuckled. "Yes, we know it's Trina. I want you to say it. Terry. Like that."

"Trina."

"Yes."

"Trina."

"Good," she said. "And I won't pat you like a good old hound dog."

"Okay."

"Don't you want to kiss me?"

"You don't want me for a boyfriend. I'm not like the ones you go for."

"Maybe you're better. Maybe I never met anyone like you before."

"Don't play with me," he said.

"You don't trust me."

"I trust what I know," he said. "I know you want the money. I know you think I'm your best chance to walk away with the money."

"And then what?" she said. "What happens then?"

"You'll most likely go away after a while," he said. "Someplace warm, someplace away from this place."

"Does that make you sad, Terry?"

"Sometimes I think if you were gone, if you were far away and I didn't know where you were, then maybe I could stop."

"Thinking about me?"

"I could say she's okay, she's safe, it's not my job anymore."

"It never was your job."

"You think I don't know that? You think I don't know it's stupid? Thinking about my brother's wife all the time, driving down to Oshawa to look for you, following you around like some stupid idiot. Wishing you could know how close I was, afraid you were going to see me."

"I had no idea," she said.

"You weren't supposed to."

"No idea you felt that way about me. All this time."

"It doesn't matter."

"And you won't let me even touch you."

"I don't want to be like one of the others."

"You wouldn't be."

"It's all complicated now," he said. "Before, it was private."

"And what did you do in private?" she said.

"What do you think?"

"Just me? Or do you think about other girls?"

"I tried to, sometimes, but it didn't work."

"Poor Terry. You've got a bad case, haven't you?"

"Don't laugh at me."

"I wasn't. I'm not. I'm . . . I don't know what I am. I'm flattered, and surprised, and a little excited. I want to touch you. Not to pat your shoulder. I would like to feel your muscles. Your arms are very hard. I'd like to put my hand on your belly. It's as hard as your arm."

"Don't . . ."

"Shhh," she said. "I don't see why you should get to say what happens all the time. Sometimes you should do what you're told. You need to relax. You need to lean back and close your eyes."

And he let her do what she was going to do. He gave it up and let it go. All the worries and the fears, all the details and anticipations, all the reasons, all reason, he let it go, he surrendered.

And she set him free, and hung above him for a moment like a kestrel hovering, reaching down to hold him straight, to aim him like an arrow, to bury him in fire.

Twenty-One

DAY FIVE — Friday, October 15

Orwell's family was already seated at the table when he came through the door. Erika was asking the Blessing, and his three daughters had their heads bowed. Leda looked up and winked at him. Patty smiled at her plate. Diana, home for the weekend, waggled her fingers at him under the table. Diana was the bonus he got when he married Erika seventeen years ago. He removed his big hat and stood by the kitchen door.

". . . prepared with loving hands. And keep us ever mindful of Thy blessings, in Jesus' name we pray. Amen."

"Amen," said the girls.

"Amen," said Orwell.

Erika reached out and the four joined hands around the table and Orwell stepped closer to cut in. He took his wife's hand in his left and Diana's hand in his right and crouched beside them near the table's edge.

"Guten appetit," said Erika, and they all squeezed hands briefly and then started passing bowls and platters around the table. Tonight there was beef brisket and sauerkraut flavored with juniper berries. Orwell kissed Erika on the cheek as she reached for the potatoes and she wrinkled her nose and said, "Wash your hands and put away your gun and sit down."

"Glad you came home this weekend, kiddo," he said to Diana,

and gave her a quick kiss on the cheek. Orwell went first to his cubbyhole office to put away his sidearm and then to the kitchen sink to wash his hands. "Tell me what's happening in the world please," he said. "What's going in the big city?"

"I know were I'm going to article," Diana said.

"Do you? That's good. So soon?"

"I started hunting months ago, Dad, I told you that."

"He hardly remembers any of it," said Patty. "He likes to hear it but it doesn't penetrate."

"Maybe not the specifics," he admitted. "It's the reassurance I get from the sounds that things are rolling along the way they should."

Orwell selected his dinnertime beer, a Bass Ale, then took his place at the head of the table. There was a moment when he looked up and all three of his daughters were holding out serving dishes with almost identical expressions. Food was serious business in Erika's house.

"Not too many potatoes, you," said Erika. "And not too much butter, the sauerkraut is very juicy, you don't need the calories. Leda, you keep your eye on him."

"Let him eat what he wants," Leda said.

His youngest daughter. The one he and Erika had produced together. Leda always stood up for him. A champion of the downtrodden and the overmatched.

"He's at an age where men drop dead from heart attacks, and he's too heavy, and he's sneaking cigarettes with his friend Greenway because I can smell them when you kiss me, don't deny it."

"Guilty, guilty, guilty. I'm only taking two potatoes and it was just one cigarette last week with Joe."

"I've seen the fat butts from those one cigarettes with Joe because you put them in your pocket like he does and I have to dig them out or they go through the laundry."

"Leave him alone," Leda said. "He's not a criminal."

"Thank you, precious," he said.

"People should be allowed to live without other people making rules all the time." Leda shot her mother a defiant look. "She even hides the butter cookies so he can't find them."

"If I don't hide the butter cookies he'll eat them all, mindlessly, when he roams around the house late at night."

"You found them last week, didn't you, Dad?" Patty had shared them with him in front of the late show.

"You think it's easy being married to a man in the heart attack and stroke years of his life?"

"It's Carey, Michelson and Carey." Diana changed the subject. "They want me as soon as I graduate."

"They're a big outfit, this Carey, Carey and whatshisname?"

"Carey, Michelson and Carey," said Erika. "Pay attention to those names. Your daughter will be working for these people."

"They're not big," Diana said, "but they're selective."

Orwell could tell she was proud of what she'd done. The names meant nothing to him, but the glow in his daughter's face meant that indeed the world was rolling along as it should.

He pushed away his plate. "That was delicious, my darling Erika. Just delicious."

"There's more if you want."

Orwell made the obligatory calls from his cubbyhole to OPP Region, to Metro Homicide, Durham Region. OPP Region told him to pass on any information to Metro. Metro informed him Detective Moen was unavailable. The two Durham guys working the Francine Kramer case were off for the night. He left his home and cell numbers. He decided on a fax. It at least would be on paper. Paper has to be dealt with, filed, passed on to the appropriate people.

No matter how presented, it was going to look rather thin. He tried for a tone that might pique the curiosity of a serious homicide detective like Adele Moen, marshalling his facts, deploying them in what he hoped was a logical ascending order of weight and significance. Terry's possession of the Nissan truck parked on the far side of Breithaupt's Bush the weekend of the murder. Where should that go? That was a new fact, an interesting fact, a fact that raised at least a few interesting questions. Terry's admission that he had come through the bush on foot. That was a feeble sort of fact if one had already dismissed footprints through the bush as immaterial. The collected evidence felt weightless and scanty. Cigarette butts and tire tracks and one brief drive to Haldane. Love to know what you and Francine talked about on your trip, Terry.

Orwell started again. Surely Durham would be interested in the connection between Terry Warren and Francine Kramer. That had to strike them as significant.

It wasn't coming together at all well. He leaned back and studied his fish tank through the algae bloom on the inside of the glass. Oscar looked fat and brooding as he moved between the thick and tangled fronds near the surface. He decided to concentrate on the relationship between Terry and Francine. What relationship? Their mutual departure from The Great Sex Weekend had placed them alone together for a minimum of two hours, the least amount of time it would have taken Terry to drive Francine Kramer home. But who knows? Terry could have spent thirty-six hours with Francine.

He reread his two pages and snorted with disgust. Nothing. Feeble. Adele Moen would think he was a meddling fool. Why was he bothering? Because he didn't believe Billy Warren had done a murder. Why didn't he believe that? Because Billy Warren had been a poor sad sonofabitch and whoever murdered Jerome Kramer was a different animal entirely.

He wrote his report plainly and simply, not trying to colour the material. It wasn't much but it was all fact. He'd let the various agencies sort it out, if they troubled themselves to read it. When it was finished, it was three pages long and there was a lot of white space.

Diana got in just before midnight and found her father dozing at the kitchen table. There was a tall glass with an ounce of milk in the bottom and a plate of butter cookie crumbs and a half-finished crossword puzzle open on the table. Diana ate the last piece of butter cookie and rinsed the plate and the glass.

Orwell woke and flexed his eyebrows a few times to get his eyes open. Diana crossed the floor and sat beside him, putting her purse on the table and checking the crossword to see how badly he'd messed it up this time. He was a supremely unsuccessful puzzle-solver. Tonight he'd made it halfway through the *Dockerty Weekly*. There was a hole clear through the page where he'd corrected himself six or seven times.

"You don't have to wait up for me, you know. Nobody waits up for me in Toronto."

"I was on my way to bed," he said. "I just had a glass of milk. Then I guess I fell asleep."

"Where were they hiding this time?"

"Can't tell you. If it gets out, she'll switch hiding places again. I only took a couple, she'll never notice."

"You certainly messed this up," she said, picking up the newspaper.

"PROSENTMENT?"

"It sounded good. And it fit. Okay, you're home, I'm off to bed."

"Stay a minute."

He sat back down. Took her hand. Waited. "What's on your mind?"

"How can you live with her?"

"Your mother?"

"You're so different."

"I'd hate to live with someone like me."

"I had a fight with Donald tonight."

"Donald. I know Donald. Wait. He a teacher?"

"Donald Underwood. My mother certainly knows his name."

"She knows everybody's name. What'd you fight about?"

"What do you think? He wants to get married. He wants me to live in Peterborough. He wants a family."

"And you don't want that?"

"Not now. Not yet. Maybe not ever." She got up from the table, smoothing her skirt and tucking in her blouse. All her clothes are so city, he thought. She doesn't look like a country girl anymore. "Speaking of romance," she said, "guess whose van is parked beside Patty's pickup down at the barn?"

"I know," he said. "It's whatshisname, the guy from up around Mindon, the travelling whatsit."

Diana nodded. "You get a big B-plus there, Dad. It is indeed whatshisname from up around Mindon somewhere, the travelling whatsit." She gave his arm a squeeze and headed out of the kitchen. "Night, Dad. See you in the morning."

Orwell went to the back door and pulled the curtain aside to look out. There was a light on in the barn.

Orwell had to kick Borgia off the bed before he could get under the covers. The big Rottweiller bitch grumbled at him, but removed herself. He rubbed his wife's back lightly and she grumbled in much the same tone.

"What's his name again, the travelling whatsit from up around Mindon?"

"Is he here?"

"He's down at the barn with Patty. I've got him now. Gary the travelling vet."

"Blomquist is his last name. Try to remember."

Orwell began working on the tight muscles close to her neck. "Donald the professor wants to get married but Diana doesn't want to get tied up just yet."

"Good, I don't like the professor," she said. "Professors live in a tiny world. And he's not smart enough for her."

"Leda's listening to Django Reinhardt."

Erika rolled over to face him. She looked deep in his eyes. "You found the butter cookies, didn't you?"

Twenty-Two

October

Beverly turned off the headlights and drove the last half-klick down County Road 17 by the light of the moon now rising in the east. She pulled the little Nissan off to the side, facing the wrong way.

"Watch it," Billy said. "There's a ditch."

"I know there's a ditch," said Beverly.

Billy was making noises with the shotgun, flattening his palm over the muzzle and pulling his hand away to make a hollow sucking echo.

"You're just going to sit here, right?" he said.

"I'm going to wait right here," she said.

Beverly lit a smoke, cracked her window a few inches. She looked over at Billy. Other than producing a series of mindless muzzle farts with his right hand, he hadn't moved.

"I don't know how long this'll take," he said.

"Well we're right on time, tell you that much. I've got the damn schedule memorized."

"Can't plan for everything."

"No, comes a time you have to actually do something. Come on Billy, go do what you're supposed to."

"I don't see the Cherokee."

"That's good, right? You're supposed to be waiting for him, not the other way round."

Billy looked over at her. "I've just got to say it one time. I'm really sorry about Bull. I want you to know that. I was standing right beside him. I was arguing his side of the conversation. I thought for a minute they were going to kill me too."

"Now you get a chance to make it up." Beverly gave him a shoulder punch. "Go on," she said. "We're all past where we can quit. Go do what's necessary."

Billy got out of the truck and ducked around to the driver's side. He checked his pockets for cartridges.

Beverly rolled the window all the way down. She reached out and grabbed Billy behind his head, pulled him close. "Remember back when we were B&B?" she asked with a smile. "Before a game? I used to give you some tongue?" She pulled him closer and kissed him with an open mouth. "You never lost," she said, "after one of those."

She saw Billy's grin flash. For a brief moment he looked seventeen.

"I'll be back," he said.

Billy jumped the ditch and disappeared into the dark underbrush.

He climbed the first rise to where it met the logging road and then stopped to load the shotgun. The breech snapped shut, a sharp metallic smack. He was aware of moonlight cutting through the sparse foliage. He heard nothing, saw no movement, and after a while he began to climb again.

Near the top of the second ridge there was a depression, a bowl the size of a backyard swimming pool. He skirted the edge of the hollow and walked carefully along the top rim. This is where Terry said they would meet up to wait for Doug. He leaned against a tree and tried to slow his breathing.

"Don't turn around Billy, I've got an AK-47 aimed at the back of your head."

Billy froze. The voice was close behind him, a snake's rattle in the darkness. "Hey, Doug . . ."

"Shut up. Pop the shotgun open, throw the shells away, then drop the gun. What, you think I'm some kind of dipshit city boy, walk into your little trap? What the fuck. Who else is here?"

"Nobody. A private meeting, like we said."

"Throw the piece away."

Billy tossed the open shotgun to the side. It bounced once then slid down the slope.

"What'd you figure, me and Jer'll shoot it out, leave you with the money?"

"It's not like . . ."

"You think I'm stupid? All that shit about who put what where? You think I wouldn't talk to him, say what the fuck, where's the thing? He says you got it."

"And you believe that, right?"

"We go way back. You I don't know from shit. Jer gets here we'll straighten it out."

"Well watch your back. Jer's smarter than both of us, maybe he's the one screwing us around."

"Where's the fucking money?"

"That's what we're here to find out, isn't it? Maybe I've got it, maybe Jer's got it, hell, maybe you've got it."

Doug put a boot between Billy's shoulder blades and sent him face first down the slope to the bottom of the depression.

"Tell you one thing, smart boy, before I leave this fucking bush I'm gonna *have* it, and you can bet the fucking farm on that."

Doug was pacing along the rim of the hollow, looking over his shoulder. Billy pulled himself to his feet, brushed off dirt. He could feel blood running down his face from a cut on his forehead. He had stopped shaking. He smiled up at the man above him. "Jer should be here by now," he said.

Ankle deep in rustling leaves his foot encountered something cold and heavy, the barrel of the shotgun pressing against his ankle. He put his left hand in the pocket with the extra ammunition, his fingertips selected two cartridges, aligned them, thumb across the brass, shells between his fingers like a pair of short cigars.

"Jer's probably coming in the front way," Billy said. "Cross the fields."

"I'll hear him coming," Doug said.

Billy shifted his ankle back and forth along the barrel and stock to determine its orientation. His foot was in the crook of the empty twelve-gauge, the barrel across his instep, the stock at right angles like an open jackknife.

"Hey, Doug? Maybe we should just yell for him."

"Just shut the fuck up!"

"Let him know we're here waiting. He should be pretty close by now."

"You just shut the fuck up, okay, 'cause not much is stopping me from taking you out. One less thing to drag my fucking head."

"How'd you get the money if I was dead?"

"First I'll blow your leg off and then you'll tell me where the fucking money is."

Something was moving down the far slope, the muffled thud of heavy boots negotiating a steep descent, dry branches cracking, the hollow hill resonating like a distant drum.

Doug called out. "That you, Jer?"

The noises stopped. There was no answer.

Doug backed away along the rim of the depression and stood behind the heavy trunk of a big sugar maple. He couldn't see much of Billy from where he was, bracing his weapon against the wrong side of the tree.

Billy hooked the shotgun on his right foot and slowly lifted his knee until it was high enough to grasp. He let it hang at his side and stood quietly for a moment.

Doug yelled out, "Jer? Let's get it on, bro. I ain't got all fucking night."

Billy loaded the empty chambers, left the breech open.

Doug's voice was strained. "If I don't get my end pretty fucking quick I'm going to do some serious fucking damage." He shifted his position further behind the tree. "Jer?! Where the fuck are you man? Enough of this shit!"

Billy took a slow step backward. He could feel the slope start to rise on the far side of the hollow.

A loud snapping sound off to Doug's left, a scurrying in the underbrush. Doug swung his weapon in that direction. "I'm fucking armed, Jer, just so's you know. I'm pissed and I'm armed to the fucking teeth."

Billy turned and climbed hard for the rim of the hollow, digging his boots into the soft earth, gaining the top, falling flat, crawling away from the lip.

"Billy! I told you to stay put! Fuck man, I don't care where you are, I open this fucker up there'll be no place to hide!"

Billy locked the breech with a clear sharp crack.

"That'd be real smart, Doug. Why don't you alert the army while you're at it?"

"Right now, Billy boy, I don't much give a fuck. You move around over there, get a lesson in what an assault weapon does." Billy saw Doug start to turn at a sound behind him, heard him start to form a word. "Wha—"

Four staccato pops were followed by the heavy thud of a body hitting the ground.

"Billy?" It was Terry's voice, behind him, close enough to touch.

"What happened?" Billy said.

"You okay?" Terry said aloud.

"Come on over," Trina said. "Doug's down."

"Jesus," said Billy.

There was a swipe of moonlight across Trina's forehead and right cheek, her eyes were in shadow. She was bending over Doug's body, doing something with one of his hands, folding a piece of paper and pocketing it. Terry crouched near her feet, softly raking the leaves with his fingertips.

"Only found three," Terry said. "Shot four times, right?"

"Four," she said. She was looking at Billy, a mocking smile touched the corners of her mouth.

"Got it," Terry said. He stood up. He had the four brass casings in his hand. He looked at Billy. "What happened to the shotgun shells? The ones he made you throw away?"

It took Billy a moment to connect his brain and his mouth. He was staring at Trina as if he'd never seen her before in his life. "I just dropped them," he said. "They'll be over there."

"He sure got the drop on you, didn't he?" Trina said.

"Isn't that how you wanted it?"

"You're bleeding," Trina said.

"What did you shoot him with?"

Trina held up Beverly's little automatic. "Holds eight," she said. "Got four left."

"Okay," Terry said. "Got them. Give me the shotgun. Billy, give me the shotgun. Billy?" He pried the shotgun from his brother's stiff fingers, checked the safety. "You did all right, Billy," he said. "You stood up, got him talking, got him worried, got the gun back and loaded. That was good."

"That was you on the hill?" Billy wanted to know.

"Yeah. Made him look the wrong way," Terry said.

"He never heard me coming," Trina said.

"I heard you," said Terry.

Terry went through Doug's pockets, found his car keys, handed them to Billy.

"He parked his Cherokee around the bend, near the highway. Just drive it up to where we said, as deep off the road as you can, and leave it. Leave one door open. Leave a few of these hundreds stuck down in the driver's seat."

"I know what to do," Billy said.

"Keep your gloves on all the time."

"We've been over this."

"Just a checklist, sweetie," Trina said. "Don't drive too fast, Beverly has to keep up."

"Where're you going to bury him?"

"Over on Coughlan's end," Terry said. "It's already dug. They'll think he took the money and ran off."

"You'd better go, Billy," Trina said. "Beverly's waiting."

"What about Jer?" Billy asked.

"Jer's already dead, sweetie," Trina said

"Oh Jesus Christ," Billy sat down heavily on the damp earth. One of his legs was touching Doug's boot. "Who did it? When was this?"

"An hour ago," Trina said. "He was just waiting up a tree like he was supposed to. Now he's stuck up there."

"Getting him down won't be easy," said Terry. "We're going to need a ladder. The arrows went right into the tree."

"Which one did it?"

"Well, we kind of both did, sweetie. In a way. Terry kept him busy until I got set." She handed Billy a wad of tissue. "Wipe your face," she said.

Terry and Trina had watched him come over the rim of the bowl and descend into the deep shadows of the bottom field. The sun was below the tree line on the Little Britain Road. The last rays raked the tops of the trees and threw the hedgerows to the west into silhouette. Jer was wearing a camo suit, the wrong colour scheme for the time of year and for the trees. The green and yellow stood out against the browns and tans, and they could follow his every step as he picked his way down the slope and approached the edge of the woods. There he stopped to take a leak, and look around. The poplar tree had been the tree stand of choice for many years. It stood adjacent to a deer highway. Whitetails used to follow it down to the pool below the beaver dam for an evening drink and then bed down in the tall grass by the edge of the woods. Terry knew there would be no deer using that road for a while. A roving pack of coyotes had them skittish and was still in the neighbourhood.

Jer grunted as he climbed the poplar. There was a lot of noise as he established himself. It was a dumb place for a hunter to choose if there had been any real hunting to do.

"Wait a while," Terry whispered. "Let him get comfortable. Make him wait."

"He's going to hear me coming," said Trina.

"No, he won't," Terry said. "Not if you go where I showed you. Go slow. You'll come up behind him." He made her look at him. "I'll keep him occupied."

She backed away into the shadows. Terry was proud of her. She hadn't made a sound.

Terry waited a few minutes until he was sure Trina was deep enough in the woods, then he crossed the stream on the little bridge and moved closer to the tree.

"Jer? It's Terry Warren. I'm not armed."

Jer swung around on the tree stand, looked over his shoulder into the darkness.

"Terry? Where are you, man?"

"I'm right over here."

"I can't see a fucking thing."

"That's good. I don't have a weapon."

"My bow's still in the case for Christ's sake."

"Yeah well, you've got a reputation, okay? I'm not taking any chances."

"What are you doing here, anyway? Where's Billy?"

"He has to drive up from Buffalo. He must've got held up. He wanted me to let you know he's on the way."

"I'm supposed to just sit here?"

"He won't be long."

"You know what we're doing here?"

"Billy told me. You don't have to worry. I don't want any of it. I'm just going to make sure that Beverly gets her share."

"Beverly!? How does she figure into this?"

"Bull Hollyer's share. She says you owe it to her."

"Yeah, well we'll talk about that when Billy gets here."

"And when Doug gets here."

"Yeah, fuck, when the entire fucking farming community gathers here under the full moon. Maybe we can all have a singalong. My way was better. This is shaping up to be one giant clusterfuck."

The sun was down, the moon was rising. Bright enough to stalk by, shadows for concealment. An assassin's moon. A hunter's moon.

Trina listened to Jer talking tough on the far side of the beaver pond. She heard him open his bow case — the tap of carbon fiber against aluminum. An owl beat through a shaft of moonlight, banking up the slope. Trina didn't flinch, she smiled. Another killer off to work.

The place Terry had picked was under a wild apple tree. The branches heavy with unpicked fruit hung almost to the ground. One of the branches had been trimmed away to open a sight line. She could smell rotting apples. Jer was adjusting his bow, stashing the case. He was looking over his shoulder into the darkness.

"Tell you one thing, Terry boy, I don't trust you any more than I trust your brother, or my wife come to that. You sure Francie isn't hiding in the bushes too, waiting for her share?"

Trina's arrow was already on the string, her bow was almost at full draw before she began to raise it. A ray of moonlight caught the razors on the tip. When her fingers disappeared the arrow went exactly where it was meant to go.

Terry heard the first arrow hit. He stepped closer. He could see Jer in the tree, grabbing at the thing that was sticking out of his belly, pinning him to the trunk. He saw Trina step out from under the apple tree. She had another arrow nocked and drawn.

"Hi, Jer," said Trina, and nailed him to the tree a second time.

"You're sure he was dead?" Billy wanted reassurance.

"No doubt about it," said Trina.

"What are you going to do with his car?"

"First I've got to get his keys," Terry said. "You get out of here. You've got to stash Doug's car, then get back to Buffalo. Nothing more you can do around here." He pulled Billy to his feet. "Get out of here now."

Trina patted Billy on the shoulder. "It's all over, Billy. It's done. Take a deep breath."

"You going to kill me too?" he asked her.

"Now why would I do that?"

The full moon was higher in the night sky, changed now from orange to silver, casting shadows of trees and fences across the fields. Beverly was waiting beside the truck. Billy came out of the bush by the logging road entrance and walked toward her.

"Well?" she said. "What happened? Is it over?

"It's over," said Billy. "Jer too. Both of them."

"Holy fuck," she said. "Jer too?"

"They got him first. Before we got here."

"Good," she said. "I wish I'd been there."

"Get in the truck," said Billy. "We've got to move Doug's car. Terry says it's near the highway."

They climbed into the Nissan and Beverly turned the key. "You got some blood on your face," she said. "Is it yours?" She left the headlights off as they started to roll.

"You can turn the lights on," said Billy. "All the bad guys are toast."

"Fuck," she said. "I'd say we're the bad guys. What happened? They say how it happened?"

"I don't know what happened. I was just bait. Terry and Trina had it worked out, I guess."

"Bonnie and Clyde," she said. "Is that it? The blue Cherokee?"

"Yeah, that's Doug's."

"Make sure you can see me in your rearview," she said. "If I get lost you can't get home."

"Home, fuck. Yeah right," he said. "I'll be driving all night."

"Don't speed," she said. "Be a bad night to get pulled over."

Billy climbed out of the Nissan and got into the Cherokee. After a moment the engine turned over and the headlights went on.

Doug Maloney was a big man, wearing heavy boots, all dead weight. The ground was soft, the underbrush thick, the terrain steep and uneven. Terry had Doug across his shoulder in a fireman's lift. He had to stop four times during transport, sagging to his knees and gasping for air.

Coughlan's part of the bush was wild and unkempt and he rarely visited that corner of the woodlot. Terry had calculated that Coughlan's section was about thirty acres more or less, trash trees, bog and beaver wreckage, and one battered hillside facing west by northwest, clear-cut fifteen years ago, now covered with maple saplings and hemlock thickets. Doug's grave was ready on the hillside, grubbed out beneath a thick stand of hemlock sprouts surrounding the rotting stump of a tree that had probably built half a barn a hundred years previous. There would be no reason for anyone to bother with this spot for another hundred years.

By the time Terry was satisfied with Doug's interment the moon was on a downward arc and he was exhausted, dirty, damp, blood on his clothes and hands. He started back toward the beaver pond making only a cursory attempt to cover his tracks. He would have to come back later to do a good job. Now he had to do something about the man up the tree.

Trina was waiting where he had left her, sitting with her back against a big maple. She was smoking a cigarette. Terry didn't like it. He could smell it.

"Don't smoke anymore," he whispered.

"Jesus fuck!" she gasped. "God, Terry. Scared the shit out of me."

"Don't swear anymore."

"What?" She looked at him. "Are you all right? You look awful."

"He was heavy. I need to rest." He buried his face in his hands leaving streaks of dirt down his cheeks. "Why did you shoot him twice?"

"I wasn't sure I hit him," she said.

"It'll be hard getting him down. I'm going to need a ladder."

She massaged the back of his neck. "Get some sleep," she said. "He'll be there in the morning."

"You better go. Don't forget about the cat."

"Don't worry. I even got a thumb print."

"I wish you hadn't shot him twice."

"It'll be all right," she said.

"Bury those cigarette butts," said Terry.

Twenty-Three

DAY SIX — Saturday, October 16

Joe Greenway had shaved closely, Stacy noted, and he was wearing a starched white shirt under his deerskin coat. She wondered if he thought of this outing as a special occasion.

"Morning," he said.

"Good morning, Mr. Greenway," she said. "We all set?"

"Joe," he said, getting in, "then I can call you Stacy." He cracked his window a notch and she could sense him lifting his face a little to inhale the cold air. "Mind?"

She glanced over. "No, go ahead."

"I've been smelling snow for two days but it hasn't shown up yet." He rolled the window back up. "Bit early for Sid Maloney. You got anyone else you need to talk to?"

"Gary's Service Centre."

"They'll be there. They start early, those two."

The two in question were Stan and Norm, Gary's sons, Joe explained, the present workforce and managing partners of a family-run business that had seen them both through school and established their parents comfortably if not lavishly in Naples, Florida. Stan, the elder, looked mournful most of the time, the product of a sour stomach rather than a melancholy nature. Norm would be the short one, Joe said. He ran the refinishing and body end of the business. If she ever saw him it would mean she'd bent her vehicle.

Gary's Service Centre was on the Strip, that section of Highway 36 heading north out of Dockerty. A main building large enough to hold three service bays and an office and a second building where bodywork and painting were done. The front lot held a dozen cars with prices soaped on the windshields and beside the lane,. a line of junkers, wrecks and rusting chassis patiently waited in a queue that rarely advanced.

When they arrived, Stan had his head tilted under the hood of a long, bronze and cream Cadillac and his doleful face had a dreamy expression only slightly marred by the deep creases bracketing his mouth.

Stacy and Joe got out and walked over to stand near the big Coupe de Ville. Stacy tried to hear what the mechanic was listening to. A ping? A chattering valve? Whatever, it was it was beyond her, the engine sounded fine to her ears.

"Sweet motor," Joe said.

"Hi, Joe. Isn't it though?" Stan said. "An '82. Blue motor, see that?" He pointed to the blue manifolds. "That's the one you want. Blue motor. They don't make them like that anymore."

"Stan, this is Detective Stacy Crean, Dockerty."

"Hiya," Stan said. He waved his greasy hand in lieu of offering it.

"Hi," she said. "I'm checking on a Nissan truck that Terry Warren says he had in here for servicing last week. He was thinking of buying it. Would you remember that vehicle?"

"Sure do, Detective," Stan said, "red Nissan D-40 with a Little Chief camper-back. He put the water pump in wrong."

Stacy nodded. "Would you recall when he brought it in here?"

"No problem."

Stan led her through the service area and into an office two steps up from the concrete garage floor. She thought that she might have caught a glimpse of the elusive brother, Norm. Someone was sanding a quarterpanel on a blue Buick in the other building. The garage office was bright and smelled of caramelized coffee and cigar butts. Stan went behind the counter and flipped through a stack of work orders, all of them smudged but clipped together.

"Here we go," he said. "Water pump, oil change, top up fluids."

"Terry said he left the truck here for three days."

"In and out in an hour and twenty minutes, Officer. I didn't waste any time with it. He said he didn't want to buy it after all. He just wanted to get it back to the owner. Didn't even want the oil change, but I talked him into it anyway. Hate to see a motor ruined by neglect."

"The truck was only here for eighty minutes? I wonder how Terry got mixed up. Maybe somebody else picked up the truck?"

"Nope, he stood right here 'til it was done. Drove it away himself."

"So you didn't give him a ride home?"

"We got a couple of loaners if people have to leave a car in for a couple of days. I wouldn't have had to drive him home."

"Have I got a black tie?" Orwell asked.

"What happened," Erika wanted to know, "another of those Knoll trolls decide to go to heaven?"

"Billy Warren," he said. "I promised Dan and Irene I'd show up."

"Good, I don't have to shine any gold buttons."

"Just a tie," he said.

"I Heard It Through the Grapevine" sang out from his jacket pocket across the bed. It was one of the Durham detectives returning Orwell's call. The man's name was Constantine.

"Hi, Chief," he said. The voice was thin and tinny to Orwell's ears. "Got a fax here, and a stack of phone messages."

"Good of you to get back to me, Detective. We've come across a few bits of information up here that might help identify the person who murdered Francine Kramer." Orwell drew breath for what he expected would be a complete verbal report, but Constantine cut him off with an indulgent whinny.

"Appreciate your interest, Chief, but we got our perp last night."

"You've made an arrest?"

"Yowsa," said Constantine. "Seems the Kramer broad was enjoying some teenage dick from the local grocery store. Nineteen years old. Guy's name is Ronnie Leffingwell. He was over there alla time according to the neighbours. Anyway, got a warrant to check out his place and it's full of stuff from the Kramer residence. TV, the whole home entertainment package, Kramer's clothes, sports equipment, hunting rifles, you name it. Also he can't account for his whereabouts on the date in question, and we found a pair of Nikes with Francine Kramer's blood on the soles, so we're pretty solid on this one."

"Have you got a weapon?"

"Not yet." Constantine sounded grudging. "But it won't be long. We like this guy for it a lot. We've got opportunity, we can put him at the scene . . ."

"Motive?"

"Fuck should I know," said Constantine. "Maybe she caught him stealing the StairMaster and the Sony. Maybe he got a new girlfriend."

"Okay," said Orwell, deciding he'd wasted enough time on this. "You wouldn't be interested if there was a connection between her murder and the murder of her husband less than a week previously."

"You got something concrete?"

"It's all in the fax, Detective."

"Yeah, well I read the fax and there's not a fuckofalot in it, pardon my French."

"I'll admit it's a bit sketchy," Orwell said.

"Yeah, that's a word for it," said Constantine. "Tell you what, let me have a little time with our friend Leffingwell, and then I'll get back to you."

"Appreciate it, Detective Constantine," said Orwell. "One

other thing. Next time you speak to young Mr. Leffingwell, ask him if Francine Kramer ever suggested that the two of them should murder her husband."

Sid Maloney ran his custom taxidermy operation out of a log cabin establishment on Highway 7, a few klicks west of Omemee. The place was easy to spot by the sign out front, a twenty foot cedar shaft canted like a falling flagpole, a white and yellow arrow embedded in a bull's eye planting that had been red and blue and gold in late July but was now delineated by concentric circles of brown and brown. Stacy saw the shaft from half a klick away. The words S. Maloney and Taxidermy were on the plywood feathers.

Three buildings on the property, a house, the taxidermy cabin and, fronting the highway, a long white building with the words, RELEASE POINT — Archery.

"Sid's in the cabin," Joe said. "Up the path. His brother Wayne runs the store."

The log building loomed above them, a fort with a porch. Stacy could make out antlers hanging.

"Like to see the store first," she said.

The front window was a mixed bag of posters, announcements, display boxes, product placements. Hoyt, Bear, Gamegetter, Razorback, Snuffer.

"Blood sport," Stacy said.

"Know a Cree man who named his bow Suppertime," Joe said.

There was a fat man behind the display-case counter. Florid face, narrow eyes. A mean drunk, Stacy thought, don't trust his grin, looks like a chainsaw.

"Joe Greenway," the man said, stretching his lips, "long time no see."

"Wayne," said Joe, "say hello to Detective Stacy Crean of the Dockerty Force. Wayne Maloney," he completed the introduction. "We're on our way up to see your brother."

"What's Sid done now?" Wayne said.

"We're checking out a few things for Chief Brennan," Stacy said. "Your brother may have taken a booking from someone down at your mobile office by the Orono service centre on Highway 35. On the 9th of October. Hoping he has some record of that."

"Not my department," Wayne said. "Doug would have done that. Or Cecil would have been down there. This was a weekend, right? Hey, Cecil?"

There were three men at the far end of the shop by the indoor shooting range. Two were customers, trying out a new bow, and the third was a cheerful young man with a nose ring and blue hair.

"Yo," said Cecil.

"You're busted. Cops have come to drag you away."

"Co-ol," said Cecil, and loped over to meet them.

Stacy liked Cecil's open face, his enthusiasm, his loose and easy footwork in the aisles, "Hi, Cecil," said Stacy. "We're interested in any bookings you might have taken down at the Orono station back on October 9th."

"The other Mr. Maloney will have all that. In his desk. I can go and ask him for you."

"That's okay," Stacy said. "We need to talk to him."

"It was probably Doug," Cecil said.

"What was?"

"Took the orders."

"And Doug is . . . ?"

"My son," said Wayne. "He's not here."

"Any idea when he'll be back?"

"Couldn't say. Off hunting somewhere, probably up around Bancroft."

"Bowhunting?" asked Joe. "Season's over."

"When did he leave?" asked Stacy.

"Shit, I don't know. Help me out Cecil, I've been out of town."

"He's been gone since last weekend," Cecil said. "Said him

and another guy were going hunting, wouldn't be back for a while."

"Should've been back by now," Wayne said. "You been running this place by yourself all week?"

"Pretty much," said Cecil. "Hey, Barry, you gonna buy that bow or just wear it out?"

"I'm thinking on it," said a man in a red cap and a camo shirt. "You get any of those daggerpoints in yet?"

"Wait a minute, they're in the back." Cecil smiled at Stacy and headed for the storeroom.

"What happened to the bear?" Joe said. "Used to be a black bear by the window."

"I think the moths were getting to it," Wayne said. "Sid's making it a rug."

One of the customers looked over. "A floor rug?"

"A wig," Wayne said. "Like a hairpiece. Cover up the bald spot."

They made their way up the curving, rising path, climbed the hand-hewn plank steps to a roofed verandah crowded with summer furniture and three freezers.

Inside, the place was all she had feared it would be. The heads of twenty formerly prancing deer, elk and moose stared at her from the windowless side wall. The air was full of dander and dark odours. She tried not to breathe too deeply.

A grumpy troll with snow white hair and bifocals riding low on his nose was muttering to himself in the back of the shop, rummaging through boxes, lifting piles of envelopes and opening drawers in a massive black oak storage unit that once stood in the Omemee Apothecary some hundred-odd years ago. The troll turned and glowered at Stacy.

"I don't do pets and I don't do fish," he said. "Only trophy game."

"Mr. Maloney," she began, "I'm Detective Crean from Dockerty. I wonder if I could talk to you for a few minutes."

Sid Maloney found what he was looking for, but it didn't appear to please him. He snatched the shoebox from a disorganized worktable and poked inside it with a dismissive finger as he started toward her. Whatever was inside the box rolled and clicked.

"Dockerty?" he said. "Thought they disbanded your Mickey Mouse operation."

"We're trying to trace the movements of a man who may have spoken to you. We know that he got gas at Orono Fuels on October 9th and that he might have made arrangements for stuffing a deer."

"Doug probably took the order. You got a ticket?"

"No, sir, I don't. I don't think he got a deer for you to stuff."

"Mount."

"Mount. Okay. His name was Jerome Kramer."

Sid Maloney looked up briefly from his sorting, "He got something," he said.

"He did?" she said. "When would that have been, sir?"

"I didn't throw it out. I treat animals with dignity." He found the glass eye he was looking for and held it up to the light. "He never came around, though. I would've given him a earful. I don't do pets. Never did, never will."

"He sent you a pet?"

Sid put the eye in his shirt pocket and came around the end of the counter heading for the front door.

"Kramer. Right. I think he must be a sick puppy."

On the verandah Sid wended his way through stacks of wicker furniture and opened one of the freezers. She could see a portion of a carcass wrapped in plastic, something with dark eyes and large ears. She looked away. Dead humans she could deal with, had dealt with, but animals, roadkill, dogs run down by indifferent traffic, those crumpled forms always made her wince and turn her head. Sid made another grumpy noise and turned from the open freezer with a black plastic bag hanging heavily from his hand. There was a tag attached to the twisted neck of the bag.

"Would you open that for me, sir?" she asked. She squeezed between an upright picnic table and a wicker rocker and stood beside the old man as he loosened the wire. Stacey reached for the tag and took it from him as the bag sagged open. Dark frozen bundle in the bottom of the bag. She looked at the writing on the tag. It said, "Kramer/Oct. 11/Hold."

"This tag, does this mean he was expected to pick this up on the 11th?"

"No. That'd be the day he delivered."

"That wouldn't be possible. He was killed sometime early morning of the 10th."

Sid looked at her. "Was he now? Well, *somebody* delivered it on the 11th. That's Cecil's writing. He tagged the bag."

"What's in the bag, sir?"

Sid lifted out a carcass. "Cat," he said. He lowered the frozen cadaver gently to the bottom. "I don't do pets."

Dan and Irene were already walking across the grass toward their Sunday car, a Mercury station wagon.

"Did I get the wrong time, Dan?"

"Chief? No. No, it just didn't take long."

Irene wasn't weeping, she looked angry.

"In the ground in ten minutes. That's all he got."

"Terry didn't come?"

Dan shook his head. "I don't know. I don't know anymore, Chief." He sounded tired, tired of it all, tired of life. "After you left yesterday, Terry said he had to go somewhere. Took the pickup. Didn't say where he was off to. Didn't come home."

"Didn't want to be here for his brother," Irene said. "Feeling guilty."

Dan put some distance between them, walked on a few steps toward the car. "She gets these ideas, Chief; it's just grief. That's all."

Orwell held out the flowers. "Would you like me to put them . . . ?"

"I'll show you where," Irene said. "It's over in the corner. There's room for Dan and me over there."

"And Terry?"

"Terry can find his own hole to climb into. I don't want him near me."

The grave was fresh, there was no headstone in place, two men were filling in the hole with efficient measured spadework. They had done this job many times. When they saw Irene and Orwell approaching they backed away a discreet distance, turned shoulders, lit smokes, talked of other things in quiet voices.

Irene stood beside the half-filled hole. Orwell stayed close.

"What would Terry be feeling guilty about, Irene?" said Orwell.

Irene looked back in the direction of the parking lot. Dan was sitting in the car, waiting. "He just won't ever listen. He believes in God, he says, but he can't see a sinner living in his own house twenty-seven years."

"Terry?" Orwell stood as close to her as he dared.

"You know what a sneak is? Somebody you can never trust. Never ever trust. You think you know something about him? No, sir. You don't know. But *I* know. I know he has a secret life. I know he does things people don't know about. I know he steals things and hides them. He has a room but he doesn't live there. He disappears, gone for days. Sometimes he's back for days before I know it."

"What kind of things does he steal?"

"Women's clothes. Her clothes." She shook her head, a sudden shudder as if recoiling from a wasp.

"Whose clothes, Irene?"

"You see who else isn't here today, Chief? You notice anybody else who should be here but isn't? That's how much she loved him. That's how much that . . . person, cared."

"I guess lately, things weren't going very well in their marriage."

"That wasn't a marriage," she said. "That was Billy trying to live up to something he couldn't. Nothing was ever enough for her. There was no way he could give her what she wanted."

"What did she want?"

"That one? More than he could give."

"Did she and Terry get along?"

"Hated him. Give her that. Recognized a snake when she saw one. She never wanted anything to do with him. But Terry . . . he thinks about her. A lot." She took the flowers from Orwell and looked at them apathetically. "Poor, poor Billy. I loved him so much. He wasn't strong. He looked strong, but he was easily used. I loved him. He was the apple of my eye. Would've made a good father too, if he'd had a wife who acted like a wife." She held the flowers against her face for just a moment, and a drawn-out and painful sigh escaped her as she let go of any tattered dreams she might still be holding inside — hopes, grandchildren, resolution. "These are too nice to bury," she said. She threw them into the open grave anyway. "Thank you, Mr. Brennan. You're the only one who bothered to show up."

"You have no idea where Terry went, Irene?"

"Wherever it is, Chief, it smells bad. His clothes always smell when he gets back."

"Smell of what?" he said.

"Dirt," she said.

Dockerty Small Animal Clinic was on Evangeline Street, south of the tracks and north of Borden College's main complex. It was located in a U-shaped mini-mall of professional services and personal indulgences — optometrist, pharmacy, tanning salon, health club, juice bar, palm reader. In the clinic's waiting room, a sad old woman held a cat cage on her lap and rocked back and forth making soothing sounds and patting the top of the cage. On the opposite side of the room, a young man was trying to control an animated terrier puppy eager to explore everything at once. "Rusty. Rusty, come." The cute little monster was attracted to the plastic bag Stacy was carrying. The man tugged on the leash. "Rusty, come," he said. There was no receptionist in sight.

"Let's go this way," said Joe.

He led Stacy outside and along the porticoed arcade, past the tanning salon and down a narrow passage to a service road at the rear. The clinic's back entrance had a clearly posted sign that read "Staff Only" upon which Joe rapped loudly. The door opened and a young woman looked out.

"Yes? Oh, Mr. Greenway. Hi!" she said. Big smile, glad to see him.

"Hi, Barb," Joe said. "Doctor Ronnie in?"

"Sure," said Barb. "Come in."

She held the door open for them and looked at Stacy with frank interest.

"This is Detective Stacy Crean," Joe said. "Meet Barbara . . . Beck? Is that the new name? Beck?" He grinned at her.

"Has been for a month," she said.

"Much happiness," said Joe.

"Thank you," she said.

Doctor Veronica Semple was the Chief Veterinarian. Stacy immediately liked her face. She had short brown hair, good bones, a fine spray of laugh lines around the kindest eyes Stacy had ever seen.

"Usually he brings me wounded owls," Veronica told Stacy, "or orphaned fawns."

"This one I'm afraid, is beyond help," Stacy said. "A frozen cat cadaver. Thought you might be able to give me a quick prelim. Tell me what killed it."

"Let's see what we have."

Veronica pulled on a pair of surgical gloves and handed a pair to Stacy. She laid the bag on an operating table and untwisted the wire around the top. "Lots of baggies right there, if you need to preserve any of this, Detective."

"Thanks," Stacy said. "I'll want that tag on the top, and there may be another piece of paper inside the bag."

"Here you go," said Veronica. She held out a square of lined notepaper. "You can see a clear print on the left side there. Brownish. It might be blood."

"Cat's blood?"

"Most likely. I'll have to wait until it thaws out before I can do any detailed postmortem, but it looks like it was stabbed, or impaled."

"Hunting arrow?" Stacy said.

"Quite possibly," said Veronica. "Went all the way through." She rolled the carcass over on its back, frozen legs pointed straight up. "Someone's already been operating," she said.

"How so?"

"Have a look."

Stacy leaned closer. The fur was softening, water was collecting on the stainless steel, the carcass was beginning to give off a faint odour, the cat's teeth were bared.

"Too weird," said Veronica. "This cat's been split open, then trussed up with string, like a turkey."

"Can you open it up?"

"Sure. Might break something."

"I need to see if anything's in there."

Veronica snipped the string sutures and pried the ribcage open with her fingers. She picked up a pair of long forceps and dragged forth a sausage-shaped bundle wrapped in clear plastic secured with rubber bands. Clearly visible inside was a thin brick of bank-wrapped twenty-dollar bills.

Stacy left the cat with Dr. Semple and took the pack of money, still in the plastic wrapping, now sealed inside a baggie as well. When she and Joe came back up the walkway to the storefronts, they saw the old woman walking toward a waiting taxi, carrying the empty cat cage. The cage door was unlatched, flapping.

"You need me anymore?" Joe said.

Stacy looked surprised. "Don't you want to see what happens next?"

"I know what happens next. It doesn't include me. Your boss knows where to find me if there's any bushwhacking to be done." He favoured her with a courtly bow. "It was a pleasure to be your escort today."

A sudden laugh escaped her. His formality, the bow, the courtesy.

"I enjoyed it too, Joe. You were a big help."

"I'll grab a cab, you have evidence to deliver."

She watched him walk away, saw him catch up to the old woman and take the cage from her, secure the latch. The woman looked up at him with a sad smile. Joe touched the woman's shoulder and helped her into the cab. He carried the empty cage around to the other side of the taxi and got in beside the woman. They drove off together.

Twenty-Four

October

"Slow down!"

"I'm not speeding."

"Yes, you are."

Terry eased his foot off the gas. Forced an inhalation that caught in his throat and hurt his lungs. "I was supposed to talk to her. That's what you said. Talk to her, see what she was going to do."

They were heading east on 7A. The posted limit was eighty klicks. The Blackstock turnoff was coming up.

"She was a loose end," said Trina. She was in the passenger seat, smoking. Her expression was calm, her voice steady. "It wouldn't have mattered what she said. All she had to do was mention the wrong name and it would have been all over. For both of us."

"It's not what we said."

"You missed Blackstock."

"What?" Terry seemed confused by roads he had driven all his life. "I was thinking about . . ."

"Well stop it! Make a left," she said. "To Caesarea. Right there."

The road to Caesarea was winding and empty, the village quiet, few cars, not many people still awake.

"Go down to the water and park," she said. "Find us a private spot."

Terry parked in the shadows near a boat ramp and stared out at the water, both hands still gripping the wheel. Trina reached over and switched off the engine, switched off the headlights.

"Stop thinking about it. It's over. She's not a problem anymore."

"She wasn't part of it."

"She was part of it from the minute she got into your pants," Trina said. "Only you said it yourself, she wasn't as smart as she thought she was."

"She was doing okay. She was happy with what happened."

"And she thought you did it for her." Trina opened the passenger door to let the night air in. "You were the one they'd come looking for, Terry. If she did something stupid."

"What could she do?"

"It doesn't matter anymore. She won't be doing anything."

Trina got out of the truck and walked away to stand closer to the water. Terry could see puffs of smoke rising into the night. He had to force his fingers to release the steering wheel, force himself to lean back, breathe deeply. He was damned. He knew that now. The others, Jer and Doug, there was justice there, justice for Bull, a balancing of the books, he could live with that. And Billy? That wasn't his fault. Billy didn't have to do what he did. He could have been tough, kept his mouth shut, gone to jail if he had to, like Bull Hollyer. He could have been a man. He killed himself because he was weak. Those deaths, all of them, Bull, Jer, Doug, even Billy's, wouldn't damn his soul, they were justifiable, necessary, someone else's sin. He could absolve himself, bury the memories. But this one. In this he was complicit. This time he was a murderer.

"Hel-lo stranger."

"Can you talk?"

"I've been waiting to hear from you. Just waiting and waiting, all alone."

"Are you alone now?"

"And lonely."

"Can I come over?"

"I thought you'd never ask."

"Leave the basement door open."

"How long before you get here?"

"Ten minutes."

"Woo. Can't wait."

Terry came back from the pay phone outside the Petro-Can station and climbed in beside Trina.

"She's there. She's leaving the basement door open."

"Good."

"You going to wait here?"

"Right here."

"What if she . . . ?"

"What? Wants to fuck you?"

"She might. She sounded like she wanted to fool around. The way she sounds."

"So? If you want to fuck her, fuck her, I don't mind. If it'll keep her quiet."

"I don't want to."

"Then don't. Just tell her to keep her mouth shut. Wait for the insurance and the bank accounts to get straightened out. Remind her that if she says anything stupid she'll be charged as an accessory and then she won't get shit."

"I know what to say. I'll tell her."

"Good." Trina rolled down the window and threw her cigarette into the parking lot. "Which one is it?"

"Which what?"

"Which basement door."

"Green gate, blue door, halfway up. It's not far. I won't take long."

"Take as long as you want, just make sure she understands the situation."

Terry got out of the truck, crossed the road, started up the back lane. Somewhere a colicky child was crying, two streets over a yappy dog barked. There was a yellow bug light over the blue door. The door was open. Music was coming from Jerry's den, the kind Francine liked, love songs.

"Francine? You down here?"

"Come on in, sweetie. You know the way."

Francine was in one of the recliners, angled back, her feet up, sipping a drink, wearing something pale blue and see-through. When she saw him in the doorway she smiled and held her arms open.

"There you are," she said. "My brave man."

"Hi," he said. He didn't move from the doorway.

"Come in," she said. "Don't be shy. We're all alone."

"I thought we should talk."

"I couldn't believe it at first," she said. "When I heard, I said to myself, 'Wow. He really did it.' I was so proud of you."

"Billy . . ."

"Billy didn't do it, did he?"

"No, but he got arrested."

"But you were the one, right? I knew Billy didn't have the character." She took a sip of her drink. It wasn't her first. "It's too bad what he did. But it's good too, in a way, don't you think? Wraps things up all neat and tidy." She held out her glass, waggled it side to side. "Freshen my drink for me, won't you, sweetie? Come closer, I won't bite."

He crossed the room, reached for her glass. When he took it she caught him by the wrist and pulled him toward her. "Kiss me," she said. "Like you did down here, in the shower. That was the best." Her grip was strong, insistent. He bent forward and her other hand took him behind the neck, drew him toward her mouth. "I've been planning all kinds of surprises for you," she said, "things to show my appreciation."

Her mouth was hot and tasted of booze and cigarettes.

"I think you need a drink too," she said. "You're as stiff as a plank. Get us a couple of drinks. It's all there on the bar. It'll loosen you up."

There was ice in a bowl and a large bottle of Coca-Cola and a bottle of Bacardi. Terry put ice into her glass and turned to look at her. "How much . . . ?" he began, but Francine was staring at the doorway.

"What the fuck?" she said.

"Hi, there, Francie," Trina said, walking straight toward her.

"What do you want?"

"Not much," Trina said. And then she shot Francine twice with the little automatic. Once in the heart, and once in the head.

"Jesus," Terry said.

"What did you touch?"

"What?"

"The glass? The bottle? Did you touch the bottle?"

"I didn't have time."

"Give it to me."

Trina took the glass. She was wearing gloves. She wiped the glass with a handkerchief and put it on the bar. "Anything else?"

"The doorknob I guess, and the one coming in."

"That's it?"

"I think."

"Don't think, know." She came close to him. "Come on now, you're good at remembering things. What did you touch?"

"That's all."

"Good," she said.

She walked over to the recliner and poked Francine with the barrel of the pistol. Francine was dead.

"Let's go," she said. "You first, nice and quiet. I'll be right behind you."

"Jesus," Terry said. "She was just . . ."

"Just go."

Trina walked back from the water and climbed into the cab. "You okay to drive now?"

"I'm okay."

"I didn't say anything before. I didn't want you to act nervous."

Terry shook his head. "I should have known anyway," he said.

"You don't hate me, do you Terry?"

He couldn't answer. Hate had nothing to do with it. "It's all the bodies," he said. "I didn't think there would be so many bodies." He started the engine but didn't put it in gear. "When it was talk it was just names."

"I think it's time you showed me where the money is," she said. "I think it's time we got out of here."

"Okay," he said. "I'll show you. You can have it."

"Come to my house for the night," she said. "Drive us back down to my place and we'll get some sleep." She squeezed his forearm. "I'll make it all better."

He turned them around and headed back through the sleeping town.

"Maybe I should go with you," he said, "wherever you're going. I don't care. Someplace warm, like you said. Outside the country."

"Now you're talking," she said. "We could live really well. We can take it easy, maybe buy a little place by the sea somewhere, Mexico, Costa Rica, someplace like that, change our names."

"What names?"

"Any names we want," she said. "We'll be brand new people. We'll just disappear."

Twenty-Five

DAY SEVEN — Sunday, October 17

Sunday mornings were complicated in Orwell's house. Patty, a divorced woman, had started life as a Catholic, but after the death of her mother decided there was no God. She modified her stance somewhat when she started seeing the travelling vet and went to the Quaker Meeting House in Uxbridge with him. She didn't yet consider herself a Quaker, but she liked the vet, and she thought Quakers had a nice view of God. Diana stayed away from organized religions and churches, but professed a certain empathy for the Buddhist philosophy, and Leda hadn't quite decided whether she wanted to be a Jew or a Druid, but in either case was out of luck for a Sunday service to attend. Orwell's wife, Erika, was Lutheran. The Lutheran church was in Port Perry and it was a given that whatever else her religiously diffuse family did on Sunday mornings, Erika would be in Port Perry at five minutes to nine. As she didn't drive, it was up to one of the girls, or her husband, to get her there on time, and to pick her up at 10:30. The job lately had fallen to Patty who would drop her mother off, have breakfast at The Nook, read the Sunday *Sun* (saving the crossword for her father) and collect her mother outside the church.

As for Orwell Brennan, he was, as his uncle Edmund, God rest him, would have put it, "a collapsed Catholic." Father Antonio

Zalamea, the latest in a long line of transient priests to occupy the garish Our Lady of Fatima on Evangeline Street, could look forward to seeing Orwell's face no more than twice a year, Easter Sunday and Christmas Eve. Since the death of old Father Haller in 1968, there hadn't been a permanent rector in Dockerty and priests from all over the Catholic world passed through the parish in roughly three-year cycles. With the ranks of homegrown holies sadly depleted by low recruitment and pending court appearances, the surplus of Third World seminarians was a blessing to Archbishop O'Laughlin in his efforts to keep his withering parishes manned. In the time Orwell had been Chief in Dockerty, he had locked horns with a range of consecrated intellects, and picked up smatterings of Kikuyu, Spanish and Tagalog into the bargain. Father Conception had been, by far, Orwell's favourite theological punching bag, and he was genuinely saddened when the apoplectic little man was sent to minister to a sparse flock near Sudbury. This latest one, Father Zalamea, was from the Philippines. He'd been in Dockerty for less than a year and had managed to avoid more than token debate. Orwell thought Zalamea was shifty.

Given that it was neither Easter nor Midnight Mass, Father Zalamea was surprised to see the looming bulk of the town's police chief that Sunday morning. And at the early Mass. Orwell, when he came at all, came to High Mass and glowered from the front row. Today he was in a pew at the back with his head bowed and his face clouded. Zalamea was doubly surprised when Orwell took Communion, something he did only at Easter, and he was almost looking forward to the post-Mass visit. It never came. The Chief genuflected at the back of the church and left quietly the moment Mass was finished.

Orwell needed breakfast. He still fasted before Communion. While he couldn't abide the new version of the Mass — no Latin, no Gregorian chant, no style, no awe, no ceremony — whatever skimpy Catholicism Orwell practised, he followed the old rules as he remembered them, and that meant fasting from midnight before Communion, no butter cookies at 3:00 a.m. He was therefore most pleased to see that his Staff Sergeant had anticipated the needs of those called in for this irregular Sunday conference and was helping himself to a warm doughnut, fresh from the Tim Hortons across the park, when he looked up to see a familiar face.

"Detective Moen, how nice to see you again. Glad you could make it."

Adele gave the room an unhurried 360-degree perusal before returning to face Orwell's outstretched hand. "A beehive of activity," she said.

"Kind of a special Sunday," Orwell said, his hand still extended. "How's your partner's leg?"

"Mending nicely," she said. She took his hand at last and gave it an abbreviated double-pump. "What have you got?"

"I believe this one's called 'honey-glazed' but there's a wide variety in the box. Please help yourself."

Adele was clearly impatient. "I'd like to know what's going on up here."

Orwell motioned Stacy to come closer. "Detective Moen, this is Detective Stacy Crean. I believe I've mentioned her." Orwell turned on his heel and entered his office.

"I recommend the crullers," Stacy said.

Adele muttered something impolite and went after them.

"My Captain . . ." she began.

"The one who thinks I'm a 'bush-league shmuck,'" Orwell confided to Stacy. "Did he by any chance send up a copy of the case file?"

"No. He wants to know why you're still hassling him about DNA tests on cigarette butts."

"Don't suppose he went along with that?"

"Of course not."

"Well then, Detective, perhaps you'll tell me why you accepted my invitation." He smiled.

"He doesn't like loose ends."

"Neither do I."

She shook her head irritably. "I had a nice neat case, motive, weapon, opportunity. Then you stick your big nose in . . ."

"At your invitation."

". . . and now we've got a suicide, an inquest, a Review Board and here you are again, pissing off Metro, OPP Region . . ."

"True, but I'm about to make the Durham contingent very happy."

"About what?"

"I'm just about to give a briefing on those very matters, Detective." Orwell began collecting files.

Adele stood in the doorway. "You're still poking around in my murder investigation."

"Mercy no. Wouldn't hear of it. Besides, you wrapped up your murder."

"What are you doing then?"

"Merely our jobs, my dear. We're trying to locate three vehicles, three Persons-of-Interest to whom we'd like to speak, certain bits of evidence we need to process, and," he made a half-hearted attempt to look modest, "it is within the realm of possibility that the Dockerty Police Force could solve a five-year-old armoured car robbery." He held up the evidence bag with the money inside. "That look like 'Securex' to you, Detective Crean? Stamped on that wrapper?"

"Yes, sir," Stacy said, "Hard to make out, but that's what it looks like."

"How much you figure?"

"Looks like a standard two thousand dollar packet."

Orwell handed to bag to Adele.

"Where'd you get that?" she asked.

"Inside a dead cat," said Stacy. "There was also a note, 'Hold for Kramer.' There's a good-looking bloody thumbprint. Cat's blood or human, Doctor Semple couldn't say right off."

"Inside a cat?" Adele was dubious. "Must be some rural custom I didn't get briefed on."

"The cat was delivered to Sid Maloney's before Kramer's body was found," said Stacy. "No telling the exact time but it was before 08:00 because that's when Cecil checked the freezer. The freezer was known to be empty as of 23:00 the previous night. The dead cat was placed inside the taxidermist's freezer sometime between Sunday night and Monday morning."

"At which time Kramer was in a tree on the Warren farm, dead or dying," said Orwell. "Somebody else put the cat in the taxidermist's freezer." He retrieved the bag from Adele and smiled benignly. "Much as I would like to open this bag and count the money, I think we should be good law enforcement citizens and pass it on to the appropriate unit. Don't you?"

"Who would that be?" Adele wanted to know.

"There's a detective named Trowbridge down in Oshawa who's had the Securex case on his desk for five years. I want him to have the first look at this money. Maybe he can tell us if it came from the armoured car robbery."

Staff Sergeant Rawluck filled the doorway. "In the ready room, Chief."

"That was quick. Thank you, Staff Sergeant." Orwell collected his files and evidence and headed for the door. "Please join us, Detective Moen," he said generously. "I'm sure we can find you a chair. We're not a big outfit."

The ready room was crowded. The Chief made an entrance, striding to the front like Caesar late to the Forum. He turned to face those assembled and granted them a generous grin of appreciation for their attendance.

"Ladies and gentlemen," he began, "I'm sure you all remember Detective Moen from Metro Homicide. She's the one who solved the Warren case for us. Please make her feel welcome." He surveyed his small army. "Those of you who had family outings planned, I appreciate your attendance." He paused for a moment, gathering his thoughts. "You are all well aware that the future of the Dockerty Police Force is somewhat problematic, and, should this force be downsized with extreme prejudice, many of you will no doubt be hoping to find positions elsewhere. Given that I have received numerous warnings, cautions and admonitions from our sister services, I didn't want fallout from my personal fool's errand to adversely affect your future career choices. That's why I haven't wanted to involve too many in this department. After all, it wasn't supposed to be any of our business.

"Nonetheless," Orwell continued, "I feel the time has come to make use of this first-rate workforce, and to mount a more formally structured operation. I give you fair warning that Metro, and/or OPP Region, could, and probably should, show up on our doorstep at any moment, to take charge of the situation." Orwell looked directly at Adele. "I would expect them to do so," he said pointedly. "I have been assiduous in my attempts to pique their curiosity and I still have hopes that some of what we present them with will mobilize their complacent asses."

Another chuckle. Adele didn't appear amused.

"So, here's what I think," he said. "I think we still have a murderer somewhere in the neighbourhood. Quite possibly on the run."

An immediate stillness came over the room. One or two chairs creaked as bodies leaned forward. Nothing like a murder investigation to get a cop's blood flowing. The Dockerty Force, and most especially the detective squad, had felt ignored and underused by the OPP team. The possibility that they might balance the books prompted their complete attention.

Orwell took them step by step, through the Securex robbery of five years previous, the tenuous connection between Bull Hollyer and members of the Montreal biker gang who may have abetted the robbery, the genuine connection of Bull Hollyer to William Warren through their marriages to the Jannis sisters, Trina and Beverly.

"Okay," he said, "Bull Hollyer got out of jail a little over a year ago and vanished into thin air. Any of you figure a guy like Bull Hollyer can vanish into thin air?"

"Unlikely," said Emmett Paynter, the boss of the detective squad.

"Unlikely," Orwell repeated. "So. What's another explanation?"

"Bull Hollyer is no longer walking around."

"And who would want Bull Hollyer dead?"

"You're the one telling the story, Chief," said Corporal Dutch.

This too got a chuckle, brief, and with an edge.

"Bull Hollyer did the full bit for a meth conviction," Orwell said, "even though he was offered a free pass. He was offered the pass if he'd identify his partners in the Securex job. He denied involvement in the Securex job. But . . ."

"But," echoed Dutch.

". . . let's say for the hell of it that he *was* involved in the Securex job. Four men pulled it off. *If* Bull Hollyer was one of them, and *he's* dead, that would leave three of them. And if Jerome Kramer was one of them, and *he's* dead, we're down to two. And if Billy Warren was one of them, and *he's* dead, then there's one left."

"And two wives," said Stacy.

"Two wives," Orwell nodded. "Used to be three but one of the *wives* is dead, Kramer's wife Francine — I'm sure you all made that connection. The other wives, the Jannis sisters, Beverly and Trina, now Hollyer and Warren respectively, aren't dead. At least not yet."

"Lot of bodies," said Emmett.

"Aren't there? And now, we may have identified the fourth man, and his name . . ." Orwell paused and scanned the room. ". . . is Doug Maloney. He runs an archery store near Omemee. Called, Stacy?"

"Release Point Archery," she said. "It's next door to Sid Maloney's Taxidermy. Doug Maloney is his nephew."

"Release Point Archery," the Chief repeated. "Mr. Maloney hasn't been seen since the weekend of the murder."

"Anybody looking for him yet, Chief?"

"So far, he hasn't done anything," Orwell said. "But we now have, I believe, sufficient physical evidence to induce our OPP brothers and sisters to keep an eye out for him."

"What evidence, Chief?" Dutch again.

"I'm glad you asked, Dutch, since you will be the one entrusted with the goods."

Orwell reached into a big envelope and pulled out the baggie containing the cash. He tried not to look like a conjurer producing a rabbit, but he couldn't help the dramatic flourish with which he held it aloft.

"This cash, which may well be connected to the Securex armoured car robbery of five years ago, was collected by Detective Crean. The details are somewhat bizarre, but I'm sure she'll be happy to fill you in." He handed the evidence and the envelope to Dutch. "You walk that down to Oshawa, Corporal Dutch. The detective's name is Trowbridge. I have a call into him as we speak and he should be waiting for you all a-quiver."

"On my way," said Dutch.

"Soon as you know anything."

"ASAP, Chief."

"Okay now," said Orwell, turning back to the room, "here's where we are. We are interested in the whereabouts of three people who may be able to help us with our inquiries. First is Doug Maloney. Sergeant Paynter, we want to know everything there is to know about him. If he's got a sheet, let's see it, look at girlfriends, bars he drinks in, who feeds his gerbil when he's not home. Second is Terry Warren, Billy Warren's younger brother. He hasn't been seen for twenty-four hours at least. Could be with Mr. Maloney for all we know. For now, let's just keep our eyes open. We don't have anything specific connecting him with these people other than family relationships, but he is, at least to us, a

Person-of-Interest. If you spot him, ask him nicely to come in for a chat. Third person is the widow Warren, Katrina Marie Warren, *née* Jannis, known as Trina. These three are all AWOL from their usual haunts."

Orwell took a moment to survey his small army and felt a momentary swelling of pride. They all looked ready to storm a beachhead. Dockerty PD was worth fighting for. "Roy."

"Chief?"

"All yours, Staff. Shifts, routes, assignments. I'll pry loose some overtime money."

"Yes, Chief," Roy said. His moustache quivered with responsibility.

Orwell headed back to his office. Adele right behind him.

"Listen up," said the Staff Sergeant. "We're looking for a dark blue Jeep Cherokee, plate number Nine-One-One-Foxtrot-X-ray-Tango. 911 FXT. The man is forty-one, five-eleven, about two hundred pounds, or, if you prefer, one hundred and seventy five centimeters and ninety-one kilos. He should be easy to make; he's got a red beard, red hair going grey and a ponytail. Last seen wearing jeans, boots and a leather jacket with an archery target painted on the back."

"I was him I'd lose that in a hurry," said Stacy.

That got a laugh.

"The second person of interest, Terry Warren, last seen driving a pea green 1997 Dodge pickup, with farm plates, Whiskey-Whiskey-Romeo-Two-Nine-Seven, WWR-297. He is twenty-nine, white male, medium everything, brown hair, hazel eyes. Also. Keep eyes open for Billy Warren's wife, Trina Warren. Drives a . . . what, Detective?"

"A silver Beemer, Staff Sergeant. "Vanity plate . . ." Stacy made a quick check of her notebook. ". . . Tango-Romeo-One-November-Alpha, TRINA."

"Description?"

"She's blonde, five-eight, slim, blue eyes."

"We want to know if she's anywhere around, visiting her sister, or her husband's grave, or her in-laws. So far we don't stop anybody, we just want to know where they are. If something positive comes back from Oshawa we'll be wanting to arrest Doug Maloney. And, if he's anywhere within our jurisdiction, give or take a county road, Chief says he wants Dockerty PD to be the ones who take him down."

Adele stood in Orwell's open office door.

"Yes, Detective?"

"You *are* working my murder."

"Nonsense, you closed your case. I'm merely looking for vehicles and missing persons."

"One of whom is a murderer."

"Could be. Of course, should that prove to be the case I will immediately turn over everything I find to the proper organization, as I have done from the beginning."

Adele came into the office and sat without invitation. She looked at Orwell and shook her head. "Money inside a dead cat." She laughed.

"Billy said he had one bow," Orwell said. "A Fred Bear recurve. That's the wooden bow we found. He said he was going to buy a compound bow — that's the one with the wheels and the cams — but he never got around to it."

"Maybe he forgot."

"That compound bow lists at three hundred and thirty dollars. You forget purchases of that size, Detective?"

"Not usually. The occasional bar bill."

"Right. I don't think he bought it."

"The wife?"

"The wife was involved, Detective, of that I'm certain. She had it hanging up nicely for us to find, didn't she? If I committed a murder, the first thing I'd do is get rid of the murder weapon. How about you?"

"It's the smart thing to do."

"I will grant you that Billy Warren wasn't the sharpest tool in the workshop, but he had to know he'd be a suspect if Jerry Kramer got murdered. Why else concoct that elaborate alibi?"

She unfolded her arms and looked him in the eye. "Okay, Chief, you have my attention. What do you think is going on?"

"I'm as confused as anyone, Detective, but I know that Billy Warren wasn't the only person involved. I think he was part of an armoured car robbery that took place five years back. I think the money is still lying around somewhere. There was over two million dollars stolen, which is just about enough to bring out the worst in people. I think that his wife knew about the money. Bull Hollyer's wife might know about the money. I wouldn't be surprised to learn that Terry Warren found out about the money. And if the mysterious Mr. Maloney isn't on the run with a suitcase filled with cash, he may have joined his three accomplices in the afterlife."

"I think we'd better start finding some of these people."

"I might suggest that Metro Homicide lend a hand, possibly convince the OPP to join the hunt. It might carry more weight coming from you."

"That's generous," she said. "I'll phone my Captain."

"Give him my regards."

Twenty-Six

October

"Watch out for that soft spot. It's deep."

Terry was taking Trina in by the easiest route, his personal path up from Road 17. She followed him along the narrow path under the bridge and then into the trees, away from the logging road, their ascent steeper, unmarked. Terry moved without effort, without sound, slowly enough for her to follow, and yet every few steps she lost sight of him completely; he dematerialized for an instant in a flicker of shadows and scattered sunlight.

"Over here," he said.

He was above her, standing against the crusty bark of an ancient cedar, shadowed and blending.

"Look up there," he said. "What do you see?"

She looked straight up along the trunk to where the first heavy branches began high above.

"There's a scar," she said. "What was it, lightning?"

"That's what lightning does," he said. "See anything else?"

"It's high," she said. "How do you get up there?"

"The other tree," he said. "This one. It's easy climbing."

"Then you cross over?"

"Mmm hmm." He was watching her.

"Is that where you watched from?"

"No. I have other places."

"Show me."

"They're just places around," he said. "All kinds of places. Bushes, logs, rocks, caves."

"Caves? It doesn't look like the kind of place that would have caves."

"Animals make dens," he said. "Burrows, tunnels. The ground is soft. Lots of roots though."

"I'll bet," she said. "Where's your den?"

"It's around."

"May I see it?"

"It's just a place," he said. "Just a quiet place. You wouldn't like it. It's dark and you'd get your clothes dirty."

"How big is it?"

"Just big enough for me to be in."

"Do you sleep in there?"

"Sometimes. In the summer."

"Do you have a bed in there?"

"Sort of."

"I want to see it."

He wanted her to see it, and he was afraid for her to see it. He wanted her to know his secrets, and he was terrified that she should know his secrets.

"I could just get the money," he said. "You stay here and I'll go get it."

"Is it in your place?"

"Yes."

"Let me see. I want to see how you did it. I want to see how clever you were. I don't mind getting dirty; I'm wearing jeans, same as you."

"It's not that dirty," he said. "It has a floor."

"My God," she said. "Where is the entrance?"

"It has seven ways in," he said with pride. "I can get inside from all over."

"From here?"

"Close."

"Show me," she said.

"Come around here," he said.

She looked down to make sure of her footing on the slope, and she lifted her hand, expecting him to take it and lead her, but when she looked up he was gone. She checked behind the tree, continued around a pile of granite boulders bulldozed generations past into the woods from the open field beyond. There was no sign of Terry.

"Can you see it?" His voice close, muffled, a slight echo.

"No," she said.

"Keep looking."

She knew the general direction now, somewhere near the boulders. She leaned against the biggest of them, pink granite, flecks of glitter, moss creeping from below, lichen crusting across the dome.

"I can't see it," she said.

There was no answer this time.

Between two of the boulders there was a space, a rift no wider than you might expect to see between a refrigerator and a kitchen wall. She had to align her feet, bend her knees, lean back. Her thighs compressed as she forced herself through, the rough surface of the rock scraped across her chest. Her head was still clear but she didn't think she could bear to force her skull into the fissure. And then, abruptly, the way opened and she dropped into darkness so quickly she had no time to cry out and he caught her before she landed, around the knees, lowered her carefully until her feet touched the underground.

"I knew you could find it," he said.

"It's invisible," she said.

"I know."

"It's pitch black."

"No, it isn't," he said. "Wait a minute."

She was in a tunnel. She could see it now. The roof was perforated with hundreds of tiny holes, each the diameter of a bulb planter, each hole permitting a faint, filtered column of light to enter what she could now perceive as a winding shaft that followed the contour of the ridge and curved ever downward, bending into darkness.

"How far does it go?"

"All the way to the water," he said. "A long way."

"Can I see it?"

"There's lights, further down," he said.

He led the way. Where the decline warranted, there were steps, level and regular. The tunnel floor was hard-packed earth, swept and smooth. The walls and ceiling had the look of basketwork, countless roots from the trees above, twisted and woven like wicker. She was in awe. It was a work of art, alive with detail and refinement.

"Stop here a minute," he said.

She felt him bend, heard his hands working in the dark, heard a click and saw the way ahead lit by hundreds of miniature Christmas lights, braided into the overhead rootwork.

"It's beautiful," she said.

"It gets deep for a while," he said. "Too deep for skylights. I tried one once and I had a cave-in, got buried for a while."

"Where's your place?" she said.

"Further down. There's other places along the way."

There were rooms. The tunnel would unexpectedly swell into a resting place, or a storage area, or an observation point with a ladder of polished maple saplings, bound with cord, rising to a shelf.

"It must have taken years."

"I've been fifteen years or so fooling around with it, since I was fourteen I guess. Usually a couple hours a day. Sometimes more."

"It's . . . beautiful," she said.

"Watch out for that post," he said. "It's getting some rot on the bottom. I haven't been keeping after things for a couple of months almost. Since we got started on the other thing. I'll have to replace that." He seemed embarrassed that his secret realm wasn't perfect. "It's hard to keep it looking nice," he said. "There's always some animal gets in, makes a mess. If you leave certain smells around, the big ones won't move in, but mice and like that, they'll get in anywhere, they'll eat anything."

"How much of the money did they eat?"

"Not much," he said. "They were using it to make a nest. I wrapped it up better after that."

He stopped moving forward, blocked her way momentarily. She sensed his reluctance to show her what lay ahead.

"Is this it?"

"Nobody's ever seen this," he said.

"I'm honoured," she said.

"It's my private place," he said. He was almost whispering.

"It's all pretty private in here," she said.

"It's where I keep my stuff."

"It's okay, Terry," she said. "You don't have to be afraid of me. We already share so many secrets. We're bound to each other now."

"I've got a new twelve-volt," he said.

He connected a battery, illuminating his treasure room with the diamond sparkle of a hundred fairy lights. It was far more than she had expected. It was not large, about the size of a second bedroom in a family home, space for a bed and a chair and closets. The ceiling was high enough to stand in comfortably, the floor was planked with pine boards. There was bedding inside plastic bags, rolled and sitting on a mattress, on a bedframe made of braided saplings that seemed to grow out of the curving walls and up from the earth itself. And all around was evidence of her. Photographs, in carved wood frames, her lost boots from three years ago. Her high school coat hung inside a plastic bag. The toggles were missing.

"Oh God," she said, and took a step backward into the tunnel. Terry was standing on the far side of the room, his soul laid bare, hope, fear, pride and shame in equal measures in his body language and on his naked face.

"I'm sorry," he said.

"No, no," she said, "it's all right, it's okay, I'm all right, maybe I could sit down, it's a little bit . . . overwhelm . . ."

"Sit here," he said.

She sat in his bentwood chair on a canvas cushion filled with cedar buds. It was very comfortable, held her like a hand. She concentrated on her breathing.

"It's just stuff," he said. "I've thought about you a lot."

"I can see that," she said. "It's very flattering. I didn't realize I had made this much of an impression. Do you have any water?"

"Oh, sure," he said. "I have some brandy, if you want."

"You do? That would be so great," she said.

"I keep some for during the winter," he said. "Just in case, you know, if it gets real cold and I need something to get me moving."

"Yes," she said.

He brought out a small bottle of brandy, unopened. "I've got a cup," he said.

"This will be fine," she said. She cracked the seal and tipped the bottle to her lips, felt the heat scorch her throat, bloom in her belly, spread outward in her arms and head. She took another nip, then a deep breath. "Well, now," she said, "that's much better." She had another look around the room, cooler, more considered. "I'm everywhere," she said.

"Since high school," he began. "Before you and Billy started. Back when he was with Beverly and we used to ride home in the back seat."

"I remember," she said.

"The first time you walked into Mr. Becker's class. You had your hair in a ponytail, you had a pink sweater."

"I must have made some entrance," she said. She took another sip. She was gaining control now. "Want some?" she said. She held out the bottle.

He shook his head and sat on the edge of the bed, leaned toward her, head bowed like a puppy. "I never . . ." The words were hard to form, the pitch constricted, the rhythm halted. "... in a million years I wouldn't ever let anything bad happen. I would never do anything... I would never want you to be scared or worried."

"I'm not scared now," she said. "I was a little surprised is all. You care about me, very deeply, don't you, Terry? Love me probably, in your own private way." He made a sound and she looked at him. He was hugging himself around the upper arms, his eyes were full and unblinking, heavy teardrops on his upper lids. She had another sip of the brandy. It was sweet and cloying, but it was growing on her. "It's okay," she said, "I'm here now. I'm not upset. Relax. Have a sip."

He took the bottle. When he tilted back, the teardrops lost touch with his eyes and Trina watched them flow over his jawbone and all the way down inside his shirt collar. "There now," she said, taking the bottle from him. "Feel better?"

His cheeks were flushed; he was breathing through his nose.

"I'm okay," he said. "Part of me wanted to show it to you, part of me was really scared."

"It's all right now," she said.

"I'm just, I'm just, well ... you're here, that's all it is. I sometimes wanted real bad to show it to you. Just you. Nobody in the world could ever find this place."

"I know," she said. "It's like the Bat Cave."

"I guess," he said.

She had another sip, a smaller one, she wanted to stay on track. "Is this where you hid the money?"

"It's under the floor," he said. "Your feet are right on top of it."

"Show me," she said.

Terry lifted one of the planks and lifted up one of the bricks. He took out his lockback and slit it delicately down one side. "There's one million seven hundred and fifty thousand, eight hundred dollars," he said.

"The mice must have eaten quite a bit," Trina said. "I thought there was over two million."

"I already gave Beverly Bull's share," he said.

"You did?" she said. "When?"

"I had it separated out," he said. "I had it in a different place. Ever since we started planning stuff. It's fair. She loved Bull and everything."

"What did she say?"

"She doesn't know she has it yet. I didn't want her maybe losing control of herself and giving it away. I wanted you to be able to get away without any worries."

"You think of everything, don't you?"

"I just like to work things out, what could happen, what might happen."

"You are something," she said. She had another quick sip and screwed the cap back on nice and tight. "That's nice what you did for Beverly," she said. "You're really quite sweet in a weird, obsessive kind of way." She rummaged in her purse for a cigarette and a Bic, took a deep drag, dropped the cigarettes, the lighter and the mickey of brandy back into the bag. "And you think of everything. It's so neat the way you did it. The way it all worked out."

"It's too bad about Billy," he said.

"Yes, it's too bad," she said. "But things happen," she said. And then she took out Beverly's pretty nickel-plated Browning automatic and shot him in the chest. "That was a surprise, wasn't it?" she said. And then she shot him again.

Terry had just enough time to say her name before he fell back on the plastic covered mattress.

Trina finished her cigarette.

The planks were tightly fitted, difficult to pry, the money bricks were heavy, securely wrapped in plastic and duct tape, wedged into the earth like paving stones. Freeing one brick required exertion, freeing a hundred left her arms aching, her fingers cramped and bleeding. She gave up on the idea of peeling each block, three layers, tight as drum skins, too much time. What a complete nutbar. Fuck, were they wrapped. She was becoming aware that the afternoon was winding down. Dammit! She should have let him live long enough to dig up the money.

She needed something to hold it. Terry was lying on his back, leaking onto the plastic mattress cover. She had to move his left leg to get at the sleeping bag rolled up at the foot of the bed inside a waterproof sack. Exactly what she needed. She pulled the bedroll out of the bag, and covered the body with it, feeling a spark of annoyance that he was still in the room, and then she loaded the bag with money bricks. When it was full, it was heavy.

Trina had a last look around the room, wondering if there was anything else she wanted to take. It was too sad, too meaningless for her to bother with. Terry could stay here forever, surrounded by his mementos and his secrets, buried deep inside his private hillside crypt. It was probably the resting-place he would have chosen had she given him a choice.

She dragged the sack of money bricks out of the treasure room and up the sloping corridor. The Christmas lights, looping through the roots above her head were growing dim, the tunnel shadows were deeper, the gloom encroaching. No handles on the bag, the thin cord drawstring cut into her palms, strangled her fingers. She dragged her bag upward through the darkening corridor, wrestling with it when it caught on a snag, hauling it up the endless steps, a rebellious child gone slack and sullen. She felt thirsty. There was water back in Terry's bedroom. She had seen it there during her first, cursory rummage. Bottled water, a tin of shortbreads, tools, a sewing kit, a coal oil lamp and a can of fuel. She reproached herself for not thinking to bring the water and the lamp. It looked like the battery was running down for this string of fairy lights. The battery in Terry's place was a fresh one, he had said so. She could go back and get the lamp, get some water, get her strength back. She left the sack of money bricks in the tunnel and wound her way back down toward the faint light. Christ, she thought, this place must be half a mile long. What a crazy fucker her brother-in-law had turned out to be. Smart, she had to give him that, smart like a fox. But foxes lived short and twitchy lives and they weren't much good for anything. Maybe I'll just take a breather, she thought, have a smoke, have a big drink of water, maybe a small drink of brandy, maybe a shortbread if they aren't mouldy. Damp down here.

The fairy lights were bright and twinkling in Terry's treasure room. She found the water, and the lamp, and the can of kerosene, and slumped back against the wall as far as she could get from the mounded sleeping bag upon the bed. A drop of blood was hanging from the hem of the plastic mattress cover. She watched it for a long moment, waiting for it to let go. And then she noticed another blood spot, on the wood planks she had stacked beside her excavation. And there was more blood on the arm of the bentwood chair. And blood smeared across her framed picture on the wall.

She froze.

"Terry?" she whispered.

And then the fairy lights went out.

Twenty-Seven

DAY SEVEN — Sunday, October 17

"People don't disappear," Orwell said with some vehemence. "Disappearing is hard work. We've got three people who might as well have fallen off the earth."

"Four people, if you count Bull Hollyer," said Stacy.

"They might have fallen off together," Adele offered, "grabbed the money and split."

"Maloney's been missing since the night Kramer got shot. The other two, Terry Warren, was seen as late as the day before yesterday, according to Dan, and according to her sister, Trina was at her place last week."

Adele said, "Somebody should talk to the sister again."

"Why don't you and Stacy handle that?" Orwell said. "Stacy's interviewed her once before."

"What have you got, Dutch?"

"It's Securex money, Chief. Trowbridge says no doubt. Two thousand exactly. Drop in the bucket he says, but points all the way up there."

"Thumbprint?"

"He sent it to Metro, see if they can get a match. Gonna try Kramer's and Billy Warren's first. And they think Maloney's prints may be on record because of an assault beef some years back."

"All right, good. Get back up here and join the party. We've got everybody except the Horsemen visiting and who knows, they could show up any minute."

From the beginning, jurisdictional disputes and posturing from OPP, Durham and Metro were kept to a minimum by Staff Sergeant Roy Rawluck, whose firm, non-partisan hand on the tiller brooked no chickenshit. Roy ran his station the way a Regimental Sergeant Major runs a square. Rank carries no weight on parade: Captains, Lieutenants, Sergeants, uniforms and detectives of all stripes were under his direct, tactical supervision and he kept them all pointed in the same direction without traffic jams or trespass.

Roy's control of the complex situation freed the Chief to savour the afternoon, greeting delegates of the sundry services. He knew he was enjoying himself far too much. The newest arrival was a big man with a spiky crewcut. "Detective Constantine?" Orwell rose and stuck out a paw. "Nice to meet you. Good of you to make the trek."

Constantine's squeaky voice didn't match his beefy frame. "Nice to meet you, Chief. This is my partner, Liam Cody."

Cody nodded but didn't speak. Orwell got the impression he was pissed that there were unanswered questions in his previously open-and-shut case.

"I take it young Mr. Leffingwell didn't work out as a suspect," Orwell said with a smile.

"Still got him in custody, Chief. There's the business of all Kramer's stuff. He claims she gave it to him and we might not be able to prove otherwise, but we'll hang onto him a bit longer."

"But you aren't completely satisfied."

"That thing you said on the phone, did she ever suggest to Leffingwell that they should off her husband. He says she did it all the time. Showed him where the guns were locked up. Kept trying out different scenarios. He says he thought she was just playing around, at first, but when Kramer got killed he started wondering."

"I'll bet he did."

"Said he asked her about it, but she said it was a surprise to her. A happy surprise, but she hadn't been expecting it. Anyway, that's what he says."

Orwell directed Constantine and his silent partner to Roy Rawluck's Command Centre just in time to greet the next arrival. "Goodness me," Orwell said, standing and sticking out his hand. "Sergeant Dean, welcome back."

"Hi, yeah, how are you?" Dean said, giving Orwell a half salute "Found that Jeep you're looking for," he said. "Maloney's Cherokee, north of Bancroft, off a logging road in the trees."

"He take off on foot?" Orwell asked.

"Looks like."

"Where to? Algonquin Park?"

"Not the escape route I'd have picked," Dean agreed.

"What do you think? Somebody picked him up . . ."

"Could be."

". . . hoping we'd figure he ran off and got lost or eaten by moose."

"They checked for other tire prints but the road surface was torn up by the bulldozer they used to drag it out of the trees."

"That's too bad."

"Vehicle was full of evidence though. Fourteen hundred dollars in hundreds and twenties, some of it with blood, torn wrappers; an assault rifle, loaded; shovel; green garbage bags. Figure the money might have been buried out there and he was collecting it."

"I take it there's a team out there?"

"Oh yeah. Big one. Plus dogs. If there's anything else there they'll find it."

"Chief?"

"Yes, Staff Sergeant?"

"One of our teams located Trina Warren's BMW parked behind the sawmill off Highway 35."

Orwell was inwardly pleased that it was a DPD unit that found her car. He hid it well. "Tell them not to touch a thing," he said. "OPP will process the vehicle." He nodded at Dean, who acknowledged the nicety with an answering bob of the head. "You might mention that it's okay for them to look through the windows."

"They had a quick look, Chief," Roy said. "Wherever she is now, she was packed for a long trip. Four suitcases."

"Looks like all you folks have your work cut out for you," said Orwell.

Dean shook his head. "Lot of missing persons all of a sudden."

"Odd, very odd," Orwell said. "Weird in fact. Where did they all go?"

"Maybe they didn't go anywhere," said Dean.

"Then they'd all be dead," Orwell acknowledged. "Some of them at least."

"One way to disappear."

"Chief?"

"Yes, Dorrie?"

"I've got a Mr. Sid Maloney, he'd like to speak to you personally."

"And I'd like to speak to him personally. Switch him in here."

"Line two, Chief."

"Thank you, Dorrie. Hello? Mr. Maloney, this is Chief Brennan. You heard from your nephew?"

"Nope. He's took off I guess."

"Oh. What can I do for you?"

"You sent a detective out here, looking into some things."

"Yes, I did. And I want to thank you for being so helpful."

"I'm thinking maybe you should send her out again."

"Find another cat?"

"Not this time."

"Want to give me a hint, Sid?"

"Yeah. Bones. I found a sack of old bones."

"What kind of bones?"

"Judging by the skull, I'd say human."

"Someone will be right out, Sid. Just leave them where you found them."

"They're not going anywhere."

"Where did you find them, by the way?"

"Inside a bear."

Orwell hung up and shook his head.

"You're not going to believe this one," he said to Dean. "Feel like sending one of your units out to collect a sack of bones?"

Twenty-Eight

October

He heard her calling his name but he made no reply. He crawled the rising steps like a broken snake, past the money sack, around a bend to the failing battery, disconnected it, made everything black. He could still hear her far below, calling his name. He could hear the notes of fear and defiance, the coaxing and the concern.

"Water, Terry?"

He had no need for water. He had water stored in many places.

"Turn on the lights."

He had no need for lights. He knew all his tunnels with the intimacy that could only come from digging each one by hand, with a small shovel, over fifteen solitary years. Each sack of earth taken from this place, scattered in the hay fields, each boulder encountered, made part of the structure, each root, handled, twisted, bound. He had no need for light, or water. He had no need for anything anymore. He was a dead man. He knew it in his heart. He was bleeding inside and growing cold. He would die in here. But so would she.

Almost pitch black but Terry knew exactly where he was. He knew that a granite boulder the size of a small car was directly overhead. He could see it in his mind, standing where it had stood for a hundred years since being pushed out of the field beyond. In the ceiling of the tunnel was a cross of heavy beams held in place by a king post of hemlock rising from the dirt floor. The bottom of the post was rotting. Damp rot, insects and mould had eaten up from the footing.

"Terry?" she said. "You aren't going to last very long, you know? You want some water? I have the water here. Turn the lights back on and I'll give you some water." She knew where he was. Around the corner, above the last step. He couldn't be in good shape. Christ he had two bullets in him. Her last two bullets. He should have been dead. By now, at least. Piece of shit, she thought, a popgun.

"Terry," she called out, "what are you doing, sweetie?"

He was digging in the packed earth below the rotted footing of the king post; using his Schrade "Old-Timer" lock-back knife to loosen the dirt. The same knife he'd used to trim a branch from Trina's sightline under the apple tree. The same knife he'd used to prepare the cat. He could feel the post shifting, the rotted wood flaking, could feel it start to slide.

He lay back against the dirt wall and the woven roots and breathed deep the familiar scents of cedar and ancient earth, rocks and humus and mushrooms blooming in the dark. It was all for the best, he thought. I didn't know what was going to happen next. She would have taken her money and run away, but he wouldn't have been able to run with her. This was where he belonged, this place was his. Now it was hers.

Terry felt himself grow cold, felt his face and scalp tingling as the blood drained away, heard a singing in his ears, heard a faint and muffled voice calling him from far below, "Terry?" it called. "Water, Terry?" He smiled to himself. In a way it was perfect, he thought. They were both going to disappear.

And then he heard the crossbeams cracking, letting go, the big boulder shifting above, wood snapping down the length of the tunnel, barn boards, saplings, roots and furnishings, breaking, giving up as the earth fell in.

Twenty-Nine

DAY SEVEN — Sunday, October 17

Beverly could hear Bull Hollyer's voice in the back of her mind, sounding the way he did when he was trying to impress something upon her, like the importance of a number. "Five hundred and eighty-seven thousand, five hundred dollars. Say it over and over." She remembered being shocked by his appearance. He had lost weight and he had a fever in his eyes. She wanted to restore his health. "Now when you get the money," he said, "don't do anything in a hurry. Take time to get organized — take a year, take two. Don't attract attention. You can have a good life with that much money if you're careful. But you have to be careful."

She wanted to count it. She wanted very much to know that it was exactly five hundred and eighty-seven thousand, five hundred dollars. Bully's legacy, exactly as he'd promised. But that would have to wait. She knew that Terry must have put it there. Trina wouldn't have. Not like that, not so cleverly and without any word. If Bruno hadn't run up to her in the back yard with a money brick in his big jaws, stupid grin on his face, look what I found! It was in the doghouse, stacked like duct-taped bricks behind a false wall of scrap lumber.

"Good boy, Broonzie. Good boy. Leave it now. Come inside. Good boy."

Two cops were knocking on the front door, two women. She recognized the dark-haired one.

"Mrs. Hollyer?" the young one did most of the talking. "Remember me? I'm Detective Crean. This is Detective Moen from Metro."

"Sure, I remember you," Beverly said. "What can I do for you?"

"We've been trying to locate your sister, Trina Warren," Stacy said. "Wondering if you've seen her or heard from her in the last few days."

"Not since last weekend," Beverly said.

"Was she here?"

"No, she doesn't come up this way unless she has to."

"So it was on the phone, then?"

"Yeah, we talked on the phone, Saturday or Sunday, I forget which, I've been feeling like crap, I think it's the flu. Anyway, she was packing up Billy's stuff she said. Asked me what I thought she should do with it. I said throw it out, give it Goodwill whatever, just get rid of all the bad memories, you know?"

"I understand," Stacy said. "Did she mention going anywhere?"

"Well, she said she was hating the house. She didn't want to live there anymore. Maybe she's moving. I don't know. She doesn't check with me."

"Can you think of anywhere she might have gone for a visit, or a little vacation — a friend's place, or a spa or something?" asked the other one.

"Not offhand. She sometimes goes to fashion shows. She buys clothes for one of the stores. She goes to New York, for buying trips."

"Have you heard about her coming into some money?" the tall one wanted to know.

"Money? I don't know. The Motors has a good pension deal. Insurance?"

"Insurance doesn't usually pay off in the case of a suicide," Stacy said.

"You've got me," said Beverly. "She'll probably call when she gets back. She usually does. We're sisters. We stay in touch."

"So you aren't concerned that we can't seem to locate her?"

"Hell, no. She's took off for months before. I get a postcard."

"You wouldn't have one of those postcards handy, would you?" Stacy asked.

"Sorry," Beverly said. "I don't hang onto that stuff. I don't need to be reminded of places I'm not likely to see."

"How about you?" asked the tall one. "Have you come into any money recently?"

"I sure hope to," Beverly said. "I'm going to put this place on the market, maybe in the spring, after I get a few things painted, you know, spruce it up."

"Where will you be moving to?"

"Hell, probably nowhere. I just want to see how much it's worth, maybe I can borrow some cash on it. I don't know. I don't want to go far, I've got that big dog that needs room to run, you know."

"All right," said Stacy. "How about Terry Warren? Have you seen him lately?"

"He doesn't come around here. He was going to buy my little truck for a while but then he changed his mind."

"There's one other person we'd like to talk to. Doug Maloney is his name."

"Never heard of him."

"No? He was a close friend of Jerome Kramer."

"Well, y'see now," Beverly said, "there's a big difference right there. I *wasn't* a close friend of Jer's, and I didn't know any of his friends except he was having an affair with my sister and Billy got all weird about it, and . . . well, you know what happened there."

"He never mentioned Doug Maloney?"

"Which? Billy or Kramer? Either one, doesn't matter. Billy never said anything, and I never talked to Jer except when he wanted somebody to get him a beer. Not to speak ill of the dead but he was an asshole."

"I guess that's it, then," Stacy said. "Detective?"

Adele said, "When your sister gets in touch would you let Chief Brennan know? He'd really like to talk to her."

"Sure," Beverly said.

"Oh, excuse me, one other thing. Have you heard from your husband, recently?"

"Ha!" Beverly laughed without mirth. "Bully's probably in jail somewhere and just too fucking embarrassed to let me know. You should be able to track him down. I'd start with Maximum Security. Bully tends get to get segregated a lot."

Beverly thought it was somehow fitting that the cops should go looking for Bull inside their system. Might waste a few days. Big country, lots of jails, Bully had used lots of names — Hollis, Howard, Heyward. It looked like Terry and Trina had made a clean getaway, if there really was such a thing. She hoped there was. She'd be planning a clean getaway of her own for a while. Taking her time. Just the way Bull told her to. Nothing that would attract attention. Making plans. When she left she didn't want even a puff of smoke left behind. She was going to disappear. Maybe the West Coast. That's where Bully always said they should go. Find a spot on one of the islands. Someplace quiet. There was nothing around here holding her now.

Thirty

DAY EIGHT — Monday, October 18

Had the sun shown her face that Monday morning Orwell would have been prepared. He'd been up since 5:00, scrambling an egg with much bustle and clang, brewing too much coffee because he always made a full pot notwithstanding his two-cup restriction, and making enough noise to rouse both Erika and Borgia. The Rottweiller was still groggy, having been disturbed previous to her usual wakeup call. Erika was fully alert.

"This is how you scramble an egg? With a spatula?"

"What's the matter with a spatula?"

"Scratches the pan. Use a wooden spoon, I've told you before."

"I wasn't thinking," Orwell said. "Mark it down as a venial sin."

"Don't be smart with me. Look at this mess."

The testy kitchen gavotte was a continuation of an exchange begun the previous night. Erika charging Orwell with an egregious breach of protocol, he maintaining his innocence.

Orwell had returned home, at the end of that tantalizingly productive Sunday, fully aware that not much of substance had been accomplished, and although it made an impressive list — two vehicles located, a few thousand dollars in loot recovered, bones, blood and a loaded assault weapon — no arrests had been made, no Persons-of-Interest spotted. Orwell wasn't a serious drinker, but he'd been looking forward to pouring himself a few ounces of whiskey. When he arrived, late, they were all in the middle of a splendid Sunday dinner and Gary the horse-doctor had been invited to join them. He was sitting in Orwell's chair.

"Drink some juice with your eggs," Erika said.

"I just wanted an egg," he said.

"Drink it anyway," she said, pouring.

"It was an innocent remark," he said.

All he'd said was that he was looking forward to someday having a grandchild. There had been a suggestion that it might have precipitated the long, whispered discussion Gary and Patty had on the front porch. Erika certainly thought so.

"You're like a clumsy drunk in a china store," she said as they got ready for bed. "You don't think before you speak; you just say whatever pops into your thick head. You could be a snow-plow you're so subtle."

"All I said was I was . . ."

"You think you were being your usual big-fat-jolly self but the young man was sitting in your chair and you glared at him because he wasn't carrying Patty off someplace to make babies for your pleasure."

"First of all," he began indignantly, "I am never big-fat-jolly. I am massive, imposing and regally benign."

She snorted. "How we view ourselves," she said.

"Secondly, I was quite content to sit beside my youngest daughter, the Voice of Oppressed Peoples Everywhere. We were having an intelligent discussion . . ."

"I know your discussions. You talk about holes in noses or worse places. No more mutilations," said Erika.

". . . and finally, the chances of that skinny fellow picking Patty up and carrying her anywhere are remote. He's half her size."

"Are you done now?" she wanted to know. "You have insulted everyone enough, to your satisfaction? Patty is crying in the barn. You have probably ruined her life."

And so Orwell had felt obliged to pull on a pair of pants and head off down the path to the barn where a lamp was flickering and where he thought he could hear his oldest daughter sobbing her eyes out. But when he got to the stable door and started to swing it open, quietly, so as not to upset her further, he realized with a sudden pang that what he had thought was sobbing was in fact something else, a sound akin to sobbing, but two voices, in unison.

He made his way back to the house on tiptoe like a burglar, not sure how he felt about the situation. Happy that they'd made up, of course, it got him off the hook, a tinge of melancholy that his first, darling child, was divorced, living at home and forced to use a tack room for privacy, and something else, a faint guilty thrill that maybe he was getting things his own way after all.

"I think they sorted it out," he said, finishing his breakfast.

"No thanks to you," she said.

"Sometimes all you need is the wrong word at the right moment."

He kissed her. She wrinkled her nose but didn't object.

Joe Greenway made coffee "cowboy-style," an open pot with the grounds on top. Orwell knew it made the best coffee but he'd never mastered the technique.

"Got to keep your eye on it," Joe said. "Can't get lost in a crossword puzzle."

"I'm a notoriously bad puzzle-solver," said Orwell. "Hell of an admission for a cop, wouldn't you say?"

"Secret's safe with me," said Joe.

Joe too was an early riser and Orwell often dropped in for a cup before heading to the station. This morning he didn't appear to be in a particular hurry to get to work.

"You figure the big manhunt can function without you?" Joe asked.

"I don't think they'll find a damn thing," Orwell said.

"Why not?"

Orwell accepted his mug of coffee and inhaled the aroma with appreciation. "Why doesn't Starbucks make it like this?" he asked no one in particular, "I tell you, Timmy Hortons should be taking lessons in the proper way to make coffee."

"Easier to let the machines do it," said Joe.

They were on the deck, looking down the slope. The river was visible through the bare branches. Joe sat beside his friend and Maggie came to sit between them.

"Detective Crean," Joe began, "she a single woman?"

"Far as I know," said Orwell.

"Like the way she handles herself."

"Yeah, she can handle herself."

"Not that I'd want to get in the ring with her."

"Wise move," Orwell agreed.

They sat in silence for a while, as only old friends can sit, listening to the chickadees at the feeder, watching them scatter as a blue jay arrived, Orwell idly carding Maggie's ruff between sips of excellent coffee.

"Why won't they find anything?" Joe asked.

"I talked to a forensics guy last night who was looking at some old bones," Orwell began. "He said whoever it was, they'd been dead for a long time, maybe a hundred years."

"Very old bones."

"Even more interesting," Orwell continued, "he said there was a neat hole in the man's skull, most likely caused by a bullet."

"Plot thickens."

"And so, using my marginal puzzle-solving skills I began to wonder if there were any unsolved hundred-year-old murder cases floating around within my limited jurisdiction."

"Think they're Hermann's bones?"

"We may never know. But just for the hell of it I got to speculating. It doesn't take a big leap to connect them with Doug Maloney. The bones were in a sports bag that had Maloney's prints all over it."

"Well he sure as hell didn't shoot the guy," Joe said. "Refill?"

"Yup," said Orwell, rising to follow Maggie inside. "The bones had been in the ground for a long time. The sports bag had been in the ground for a while too, although not a hundred years. So," he held out his cup, "it would seem that whoever put them in the sports bag dug them up first, then buried them again, then dug them up a second time and put the sports bag inside that mounted black bear in the archery store."

Joe looked at his friend for a long moment before pouring more coffee. "You are dealing with some seriously eccentric people here," he said.

"And in my ponderous way through the labyrinth I put together these facts: hundred-year-old-bones, bullet hole, ergo, 100-year-old murder . . ."

"Ergo," Joe said.

". . . old dirt, young dirt, sports bag, bear, Maloney." Orwell looked down to see Maggie looking up at him with complete attention.

"She wants to know what you came up with," Joe said. He headed back out to the deck.

"Maloney's connected to Kramer, which leads to the Securex armed robbery, which leads to murder . . ."

"Which leads . . . ?" Joe asked.

". . . to that bush," Orwell said with conviction. "If those bones are Hermann's, and the old local legend has any validity, he was murdered in that bush, buried in that bush, and if he *was* buried there, then he was dug up in that bush, and he may very well may have gone into a bag that was also buried in that bush."

"And?"

"And maybe the money was buried there too."

"I see a few leaps of conjecture," Joe said, "but it's a cogent theory."

"Damn right it is," Orwell said. "You said it yourself, it's a strange bush."

"The Warren section is, and that's a fact. Somebody tidies up in there."

"Tidies up *what*, I'd like to know." Orwell said.

Stacy Crean, Adele Moen, Sergeant Dean, Corporal Dutch and a mixed team of Dockerty, OPP and Metro personnel, numbering twenty-plus were waiting by the humpback bridge when Orwell and Joe drove up.

"Ninety minutes," Joe said, getting out of the Ramcharger. "Instant army."

"Roy Rawluck could mobilize a division. Mornin' all," Orwell said grandly. "We're going to take a slow walk through the woods. It'll perk up our appetites for lunch. You know Joe Greenway, he's going to lead the expedition."

"What are we looking for, Chief?" Dutch asked.

"Haven't a clue Dutch, could be anything — money, bodies, bones, cigarette butts, murder weapons, tire tracks, candy wrappers . . ."

Joe climbed up the hill and turned to face the search party. "We'll fan out, say ten feet apart, and climb real slow. At the top it slopes down again, even steeper, then goes up to a second ridge, then it drops down to a beaver pond and a stream. Don't try to find anything in particular, just scan the ground ahead of you, side to side, and if you see anything that doesn't look natural, stop, yell out, I'll come and have a look."

"Should have packed a lunch," Stacy said.

"I've got a sandwich in my pocket," Joe whispered to her. "Don't let it get around." He spread his arms wide. "Okay, folks, let's start climbing."

The line of searchers began to move forward. Joe stayed thirty feet higher, coursing left and right without much of a system it seemed to Stacy. She kept close and moved where he did, trying to see what he was seeing, wondering as she followed why he wasn't looking at the ground so much as listening to it.

Orwell lagged behind, letting the team gain some distance. He sat on a convenient stump and took off his hat, wondering for the second time that month if it wasn't time to have it steamed and blocked. Trouble was, there wasn't a hatter in Dockerty. The hat would travel to Toronto and he wouldn't get it back for weeks, assuming they didn't lose it, and he liked his hat. Maybe Erika could press the brim, get some of the more eccentric kinks out of it.

He inhaled the forest air and looked up. Maple trunks rose high before spreading into a canopy of bare branches and lingering brown leaves through which the sun sent shafts of pale and slanted October light. The forest was picturesque as all get out, Orwell allowed, but definitely hexed. He felt it the second he stepped off the road. Orwell liked cathedrals, the echoes and the faint air of incense, but Gothic cathedrals always felt a tad spooky — they soared, but they squashed too. This place was the same.

"You coming, Chief?" Adele asked. The line was halfway up the first rise.

"I'm the sheepdog at the rear, Detective," said Orwell, "so no one gets lost or left behind."

"Knee bothering you?"

"Not yet. Give it time."

They climbed together, Orwell watching the group's progress, Adele dutifully searching her part of the grid.

"Saw your picture in the paper this morning," she said.

"Did you check out the Mayor's smile?"

"Like she had a dead bird in her mouth."

"A bit much for her to swallow," Orwell agreed, "but she rose to the occasion."

Something had caught Joe's eye and he was wandering away from the line of searchers.

"You seeing something?" Stacy was close behind.

"The ridge," he said. "Over there. Runs along at right angles to these hills, like a wall."

"What about it?"

"I don't know," he said. "Something." He turned to call back to the searchers. "Hold it there a minute," he said, "I want to check something."

Orwell and Adele skirted the end of the line and headed in Joe's direction. Sergeant Dean left the line and came with them.

"What's he looking at?" Dean wanted to know.

"You got me, Sergeant," said Orwell. "I think he has an extra set of eyes."

Joe was motionless, all senses alert, scanning the face of a ridge that rose above him like the upper tiers of an amphitheater. The forested wall curved north south against the natural grain of the rolling terrain. Beyond the treeline at the top was a twenty acre cornfield bound by a broken snake fence of ancient split rails.

"Is the ground supposed to sag like that?" Stacy asked.

Joe turned and grinned at her. "No, it's not," he said. He spotted his friend approaching with Adele and Sergeant Dean, and behind them, as if drawn by a magnet, the entire line of searchers heading in their direction.

"You've got our attention, looks like," said Orwell.

"There's been some kind of cave in," Joe said. "Look, it runs all the way from up there, down the hill, I don't know how far it goes."

"I don't see it," Orwell said.

"Stacy did," said Joe.

"I see it," said Adele. "It's like a long wrinkle."

"That's it," Joe said. He turned to the group, all of whom had come to stare at the wall, some of whom were noticing the unnatural crease in the hillside and explaining it to the less perspicacious of the team.

"Watch your step," said Joe. "I don't think the ground is solid."

"Got some planks sticking up down here, Chief," Dutch called. "Wires and stuff."

Dutch was pulling at a tangle of wires and roots and broken boards.

"What's that on the wires?"

"Looks like Christmas tree lights," Dutch said. "Hundreds."

Thirty-One

December 24 — Christmas Eve

At Christmas, Staff Sergeant Roy Rawluck did his best to accommodate familial obligations, giving priority to officers with young children. Crime, even the local variety, doesn't take vacations, but staggered shifts and a generous attitude allowed him to give most of his force at least a modicum of time off to trim trees and enjoy a spell with loved ones over the holiday. Not everyone was entirely happy with the schedule but the calendar, once posted, was firm. Roy's word was Law.

Stacy Crean, unmarried, childless, and with relatives far removed from the local environs, was down for a double shift on Christmas day. She didn't mind — Joe Greenway had promised her pheasant for Boxing Day. He said it was the best-fed pheasant in the neighbourhood, having gorged on Fern Casteel's corn for months before Joe coaxed him into volunteering for dinner. She was looking forward to it.

The Dockerty station was suitably festooned with swags of Christmas cards. There was a handsome tree in the reception area. The decorations were somewhat overshadowed by numerous front pages — *Dockerty Register*, *Sun*, *Star*, *Globe and Mail* — pinned to every available notice board. Roy's first impulse had been to banish, or at least severely curtail the self-congratulation, but given that the extensive press coverage of the previous two months was serving to quell any immediate urge in the Town Council to disband the force he loved so dearly, he decided to leave them up until the New Year. He was secretly pleased with one colour photograph from the *Toronto Star* that showed him standing at the head of a long table stacked with bricks of money. "$1.5 million recovered" read the headline.

The excavations in Breithaupt's Bush were shut down for the winter but would likely resume in the spring when the ground softened. The place already looked like an archeological dig. The cost of the operation was being shared by the OPP, Metro Homicide and Durham's Robbery division, with negotiations underway to have Securex repay at least some of the expense. Securex held to the position that locating a million and a half of their bucks meant that there was well over half a million still missing. Dockerty Police Department cheerfully took refuge in the fact that all this was happening outside town limits and wasn't costing them a dime.

Terry Warren's body was the first one found. It took four days to dig him out. The autopsy revealed that while he had been crushed by a ton or more of rock, dirt and timber, he was also carrying two .32 calibre bullets in his chest. Whether bullets or granite had ultimately done the job was moot. The slugs were shortly matched to those previously removed from the body of Francine Kramer. This prompted another round of front pages and an article in *Maclean's*.

Trina Warren's body was found a week or so later with the help of an RCMP cadaver dog named Gunther. Trina's body was recovered along with a .32 calibre automatic, unregistered, which proved to be the double murder weapon. This development prompted a visit from the CBC, CTV, Global and CNN. Trina Warren had her news cycle of fame.

It was a super-smart Malinois bitch named Magda who found Bull Hollyer. Magda and Gunther made the cover of *Dogs in Canada*. A producer in Toronto was negotiating for the rights to produce a television series called *Cadaver Dogs*. Magda and Gunther were not being considered for the lead roles. Orwell speculated that the producer probably had bodies buried that he didn't want his stars digging up.

As yet, Doug Maloney's remains, if in fact he was dead, were missing. There was a theory of some currency that Doug Maloney and the departed half-million were on the run. Securex posted a reward. Police forces from Halifax to Boca Raton had Doug Maloney's photograph in plain sight. In the picture he looks like one of Robin Hood's Merry Men, brandishing a longbow and a quiver of arrows. Orwell figured Doug Maloney's body was buried in the bush and it was just a matter of time before Gunther or Magda located "Little John" as Stacy had dubbed him.

There was a second theory that Beverly Hollyer knew where the missing money was. A search warrant was served on Beverly's house and she stood in her backyard smoking and keeping Bruno quiet. The search turned up nothing. Beverly sailed through interrogations by Metro Homicide, OPP Region and an overly large contingent from Durham who had somehow managed to convince themselves, and most of Durham region, that they were personally responsible for solving the Great Securex Robbery, although a certain Detective Trowbridge did acknowledge the Dockerty Police Department had contributed somewhat to the investigation. Beverly answered all questions forthrightly and the interrogators left unsatisfied, although one of the Durham detectives had wondered what Beverly might be doing for fun, once this all settled down.

Beverly was also required to identify her husband's body. They made it as painless as possible — Bull's jacket, watch, prison dental records and a computer-enhanced image of a tattoo which Beverly told them was on his left shoulder were more than sufficient to ascertain the identity of the remains. Bull Hollyer's funeral two weeks later was attended by a brigade of "Righteous Outlaws" on very loud Harley Davidson motorcycles. The presence of such a large gathering of bandits prompted extra patrols by the DPD and OPP but the wake was surprisingly decorous and the bikers left town within thirty-six hours of Bull's interment without a single breach of the peace.

Orwell was almost certain that Beverly knew where the missing half-million was, but as she wasn't a resident of Dockerty, he held no brief to continue investigating. He did mention to Stacy that she might keep her eyes open for any appreciable change in Beverly's financial status.

"She just took out a second mortgage, Chief. She's got money in her bank account."

"Now how would you find that out without a warrant?"

"Same way you did, Chief."

Orwell laughed. "All the same, let's not forget about her."

The bones remained unidentified despite the best work of a forensic anthropologist who would go so far as to say that the man had probably been murdered before his three-score and ten. Whether the bones of Hermann Breithaupt or the bones of Max Warren's father or the bones of someone else entirely, the locals had ample grounds for fresh speculation and the old tales were enjoying fresh currency. Dan had been right; some things are always there.

Detective Adele Moen's partner was off the injured reserved list. She called Orwell to gripe that their latest catch wasn't nearly as much fun as the Kramer case. "How's the digging going?" she wanted to know.

"We've got frozen ground and three feet of snow," he said.

"All we've got is slush and pissed-off traffic."

"I figure they'll have another look come April sometime."

"You still think Maloney's back there."

"Oh yes," Orwell said. "He'll keep until spring."

"Might pay you a visit when the weather improves," she said.

"Look forward to it, Detective. You have a good Christmas."

"You too," she said.

Mayor Donna Lee Bricknell made as much political hay as she could while the sun was shining on *her* police force, a force of which she was "proud and supportive." Sam Abrams was obliged to run her photograph more than once — shaking hands with the managing director of Securex, posing with a stiff-backed Roy Rawluck beside a table covered with bricks of cash, and even standing shoulder-to-shoulder with Orwell Brennan. Sam was happy to print that one. The camera angle and the slanted light conspired to manifest Orwell as a giant of competence and communal regard while swiping the Mayor's face with a crooked shadow (probably from Orwell's hat brim) that made her appear small, mean and devious. Donna Lee wasn't happy with the choice and told Sam so. Sam, riding the crest of an unending wave of developments to which he seemed to have privileged access, was suitably apologetic and promised a photo-op of her choosing. Donna Lee was mollified. Sam had the offending picture enlarged, framed and hung in his office.

And Orwell was filled with Christmas cheer. *Gemutlichkeit*, according to Erika. There was no equivalent English word she said, but his air of regal well-being and generosity toward all was a precise manifestation. He agreed with her. He did feel good. All three of his daughters would be home for Christmas, Gary the travelling vet had promised never to sit in Orwell's chair again, Erika had procured two very fat geese for the feast, and Roy Rawluck had assured him that barring war or natural disaster, his presence would not be required until December 27th. Orwell planned on enjoying all three days.

"I'm off, Roy. I leave the factory in your capable hands. Dorrie, if that sweater doesn't fit, my wife has the receipt."

"Your wife never gets it wrong, Chief, you know that."

"It's a burden sometimes, Dorrie, believe me."

"Don't suppose you're likely to show up for the Christmas service at St. Bart's, are you, Chief?" Roy asked.

"It'll be Midnight Mass at Our Lady of the Rotating Rectors for me, Roy. But if it's any consolation, I'll wear the dress blues."

The southern hem of the Haliburton/Kawartha snowbelt guaranteed that Christmas was always white in and around Dockerty. The snow held off until the middle of the month but by Christmas Eve the drifts on both sides of Vankleek Street were waist-high and the Highway Department's snowplows, sanders and salters were out in force. Orwell was never in a hurry, especially in bad weather. He contentedly followed one of the big highway units down 35 until turning off on Road 17, which wasn't nearly as clear. Orwell put his big beast into four-wheel drive and took it slow and steady over the humpback bridge and along the bottom of Breithaupt's Bush. He'd been taking that route regularly these days, not expecting to find anything or catch sight of Doug Maloney's wandering ghost, just reflexively drawing a line over and over across the bottom of a page in his mind.

He wondered who, if anyone, had been the real victim, or the least culpable. Francine? She was certainly pushing to get her husband killed, but was she in on the larger plan? It must have been complicated. A scheme that ultimately went off the rails. Barring the sudden miraculous resurfacing of Doug Maloney, it was a safe bet that all four of the Securex robbers were dead. Terry, Trina and Francine were dead. Seven bodies. That's a crime spree in any part of the country. How did it all come about? Orwell doubted that he'd ever fully understand, but he suspected that Trina and Terry were at the centre of the mystery. Terry's cave system had given up a multitude of physical evidence, most of which pointed to an obsession with his sister-in-law — photographs, articles of clothing, personal items. One of the rooms could only be described as a shrine. And yet she had killed him. No doubt about that. She had the gun in her hand when she died.

It fascinated him. It was convoluted. Positively Venetian. And, despite his general air of *Gemutlichkeit*, he knew that the questions would be haunting him for a while yet. He resolved to put it aside until after Christmas.

And Beverly? She had a quiet Christmas with her loyal companion Bruno, who got more than his share of salami and ham. Beverly had Bacardi and Diet Coke (she was considering losing a few pounds), a baggie of homegrown bud that made for a very mellow smoke and an uncluttered high, a stack of DVDs from Blockbuster and a photograph of her late husband presented to her at the funeral by a biker historian. In the photograph Bull was astride a Harley Electra Glide, wearing his colours, strong, fearless and vital, the way she promised to remember him. He'd been a handful, and a constant worry, but in the end he'd been what she always maintained, loyal. His legacy was safe. She was in no rush to dig it up from under Bruno's kennel. It could stay there for another year, another two years, another three years, she didn't care. It was enough to know that it was there, all five hundred and eighty-seven thousand, five hundred dollars, just like he said.

Here's a sneak peek at Marc Strange's next

ORWELL BRENNAN MYSTERY

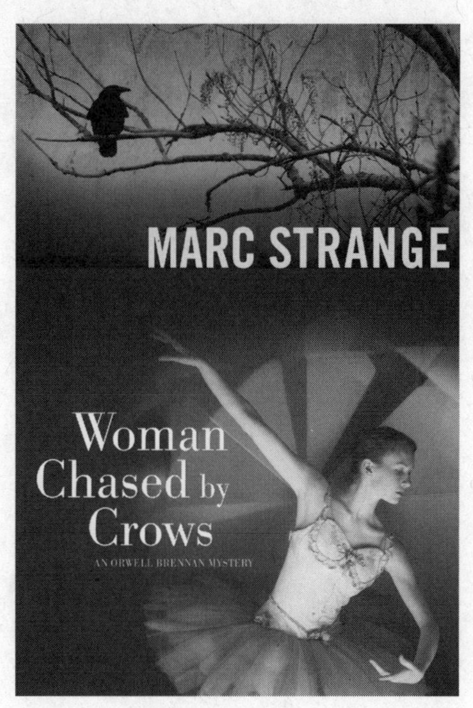

He had almost nothing left.

Only the sapphire and a couple of diamonds, maybe three, he didn't know how many, he hadn't opened the bag in a while. If Louie was still talking to him, maybe he could sell him one. The troll wasn't answering his phone. Probably monitoring his calls. Still pissed off. Couldn't make it over to the Danforth, anyway. No cash. What a ridiculous situation.

He had three stones worth a fortune, maybe five stones — it was time he looked — a nice diamond, not too big, easy to move. One carat, maybe. Louie would give him five for it, surely. No he wouldn't. Louie would know he was desperate. He would take advantage. He was a thief after all, what do you expect? But three hundred at least. *Something.* He needed to eat, he needed to pay for this shitty motel room, he needed to get away. Get away — what a great plan. Look where he was: back where he started, a cab ride from the very place he had jumped the fence. Except that he couldn't afford a cab ride. A fortune in stones, and he was broker than the panhandler on the corner.

It was time he checked the package to see what was left. Please Jesus, there was one small diamond that he could sell in a hurry, without attracting too much attention. He opened the closet and took down the shelf above the clothes rack, dragged over a chair and stood on it, reached up and pushed the cheap cardboard ceiling tile out of the way, felt around in the dust and mouse droppings until he found the cloth bag, climbed off the chair and spilled the contents onto the stained chenille bedspread. Good! Two diamonds. *Two* of them. One of them was small enough, one-and-a-half carats probably, maybe a bit less. Such a waste, selling it for a fraction of what it was worth, but a man has to survive. The sapphire was too big to just give away. He needed to get somewhere. Montreal. If he was careful, he could survive in Montreal. There was someone there who could afford it.

"Been waiting all night for you to come home," said the visitor who came out of the bathroom.

"Oh Christ!" he said. "You scared the shit . . ."

"Is that all of them?"

"That's all that's left."

"You're sure?"

"I swear."

"Put them back in the bag."

"Just leave me one, please, the small diamond. I need some cash so I can pay for this shitty room. I need some cash so I can eat something."

"No, you don't," said his guest, and shot him in the head.

It is always the ruby that takes centre stage in an ornament. The rest — pearls, sapphires, even diamonds — dance attendance upon a great ruby like a corps de ballet.

It is safe to say that Newry County doesn't harbour many rubies, and that whatever red stones are held in the jewellery cases and safety deposit boxes of Dockerty's upper crust, they are neither large, nor legendary, nor, in some cases, genuine. Certain of the dowagers residing on The Knoll are known to have good pieces: Mrs. Avery Douglas is the current custodian of a five-strand natural pearl necklace, a Douglas family heirloom worthy of at least five burglary attempts over the years, including the recent, unprosecuted break-in by their crack-smoking second cousin; Doris Whiffen has a tiara once worn to a reception at Windsor Castle, but not by her; and Edward Urquehart has thirty-odd carats in loose diamonds along with his Krugerrands in a safety deposit box at the Bank of Commerce. None of these are paltry, and some are truly precious, but if all the gems held in all the private safes in Dockerty were heaped upon a table, they would not begin to approach the value of a certain chunk of pigeon's blood corundum. Not in dollars, not in legend, not in human life.

In an early year of the nineteenth century, a man whose name is now lost in the dust of history picked up a loose stone bigger than his fist from a scattering of detritus near a limestone cliff north of Mandalay. Even in the rough, it glowed like a hot coal. It is estimated that it weighed at that time over four hundred carats. A master cutter produced three notable gems from it: an elegant twenty-three-carat cushion cut that is still part of the Iranian National Treasure, a round stone of eighteen carats once stolen by Clive of India, and a masterpiece of ninety-seven carats, one of the largest rubies ever known. Not a garnet, not a spinel like the Black Prince's legendary stone, but a true ruby, a gem of perfect colour. But size was not its most significant characteristic. In its heart there was a star. Star rubies are among the rarest gems on the planet, and most are small. The Sacred Ember, as it came to be known, was peerless, unique, priceless.

One

Monday, March 14

Orwell Brennan's parking space under the chestnut tree offered a generous mix of March's bounty — icy puddles, crunchy slush, broken twigs from last night's blow. He dunked his left foot ankle-deep in scummy water getting out of his vehicle. This made him dance awkwardly onto the dry pavement, at which point he looked heavenward. Mondays always start out bad. Laura used to say that, usually with a laugh. His first wife was killed by a drunk driver late on a Sunday night. That long ago Monday morning had started out very bad. On a scale of one to ten, a soaker didn't register.

Spring was Orwell's second-favourite time of year; a season full of the things he looked forward to all the long Ontario winter — an unselfish angle to the sunrise, spring training in Dunedin, the ospreys circling the big nest near RiverView Lodge. As with most men his age, the arrival of spring signalled a victory of sorts and he routinely breathed more deeply as the vernal equinox drew near. The sodden pant cuff slapping his ankle as he climbed the stairs to his office reminded him that he was a tad previous in his anticipation. It wasn't spring yet. Hitters might be looking for their swings and pitchers working on their stuff in the Florida sunshine, but Newry County was still salted sidewalks and distressed footwear.

"In early, Chief." Sergeant George was a tall, cadaverous man with a face like a basset hound; baggy eyes and dewlaps.

"I am a bit, aren't I?" Orwell said without elaboration. He headed for his office. "Did you leave me any shortbreads, Jidge?"

"Not following, Chief."

The office door clicked shut. Sergeant George saw the Chief's extension light up briefly and then blink out. The Chief was back again almost immediately scanning the outer office.

"Something I can help you with, Chief?"

"Paper towels? Rag? I've got a wet shoe."

"Got Kleenex."

"That'll do." Orwell accepted a wad of tissues, put his left foot on a chair and did what he could to dry his leather. "Beats me how the bag always gets so nicely folded when you work the night desk." He tossed the wet paper into a wastebasket.

"Seen the *Register* this morning, Chief?"

"Why no, Jidge, I haven't."

Sergeant George held up a fresh copy of the paper. "Didn't think you and Donna Lee were that chummy," he said.

The front page featured a shot of Mayor Bricknell and the Chief, both smiling, each holding one handle of a trophy. Dockerty High had won its first basketball tournament in ten years. The award ceremony had taken place Saturday night and evidently nothing sufficiently newsworthy had happened in the intervening thirty-six hours to knock it off page one.

"Didn't think she was going to be there," Orwell said.

"Wouldn't miss a chance like that. Not in an election year."

The flag out front snapped in the brisk and chilly wind, the trailing end of a March gale that had the house moaning all night long. He stood for a moment next to the bronze plaque bearing the likeness of his predecessor, Chief Alastair Argyle, noting that a pigeon had recently saluted the great man. To Orwell's eye, the white stripe across the former chief's cheek wasn't unattractive, rather it gave the dour face a gallant aspect, like a duelling scar, a Bismarck *schmiss*.

As was his custom, Roy Rawluck arrived marching, no other word for it, striding out of the parking lot, heels clicking, arms swinging, sharp left wheel to the entrance. "Bright and early, Chief," Roy said with a nod of approval. It was rare that Orwell arrived before his staff sergeant.

"Sharp breeze this morning, Staff," he said. "*Fresh*, as the farmers put it."

"Coming or going, Chief?" Roy was frowning, just now noticing the desecration of his late boss's memorial.

"Going, Staff. Soon to return."

From the other side of Stella Street, Georgie Rhem was waving his walking stick. Orwell could tell it was Georgie by the feathers on his Tyrolean hat and the distinctive kink in his hawthorn stick. The jockey-tall lawyer was otherwise hidden by the sooty drift lining the curb. "Soon to return," Orwell repeated, heading across the street. Roy marched inside to get his can of Brasso. Argyle's face would be shining again in no time.

"Where to, Stonewall?" Georgie wanted to know. "Timmies? Country Style? The Gypsy Tea Room isn't open yet."

Banked piles of snow followed the concrete walkways on the shaded side of the Armoury, dirty, spotted, stained and slushy, revealing as they melted a winter's worth of litter and unclaimed dog scat. Orwell detected, or thought he did, a tinge of yellow in the willow near the fountain.

"First to leaf, last to leave," he said.

"Say what?"

"It's what Erika says. That willow's yellowing up."

"Jaundice, likely," Georgie said.

"Not the prettiest time of year, I'll admit," said Orwell.

"Think she's had some work done?" Georgie was stopped at a campaign placard planted beside the walkway on spindly wire legs.

"Who? Donna Lee?"

"She looks prettier than usual, don't you think?"

The poster read: "Reelect Mayor Donna Lee Bricknell ~ Experience + Commitment = Consistency."

Orwell tilted his head. The Mayor's photograph was flattering and he suspected some technical process had smoothed her wrinkles a bit, but having spent an unpleasant hour with the woman the previous Friday in her office, he was pretty sure she hadn't undergone any facelifting. "Looks the same to me," he said.

"Don't think this reelection's going to be the simple formality it was in years gone by," said Georgie.

"How many will this make?"

"She's got six terms under her belt." He tapped the placard with his stick and resumed walking. "This would be number seven."

"Think she could lose?"

"Possibility," Georgie said. He pointed at an opposing campaign poster on the other side of the park. A handsome young man with an expensive haircut beamed at the world in general. "Young Mr. Lyman over there has the blood of career politicians in his veins. Son of a sitting MP, grandson of a senator. I smell ambition."

"Wouldn't think a small town mayor's job would be big enough."

"Gotta start somewhere, Stonewall." They waited for the light to change at the intersection. "Hell, he's only twenty-six. Be in Ottawa before he's thirty-five."

"No six terms for him," said Orwell.

Anya was on the couch. "It was gone for almost a year, now it is back." She fidgeted. The psychiatrist wouldn't let her smoke.

In her dream the man has no face and there are shadows

across his eyes. In her dream she is always ready for him, bathed and scented, wearing a white nightgown like a bride, lying on top of the covers, her feet bare, her pale gold hair across the crisp linen pillowcase, her hands tucked under her buttocks, her eyes open as he enters the dark room. When he raises the pistol to kill her, she lifts herself as if to meet her bridegroom's beautiful hands. And when he pulls the trigger she wakes up, lost, missing him.

"Every night?"

"No. Not every night. But often. Enough. Often enough."

"Once a week?"

"More than that. Just not every night. Some nights he does not come." She stood up, rolling her neck and shoulders as if waking from a fretful sleep. "I am going outside to have a cigarette now."

"You can wait a bit longer. We're almost done for today." The psychiatrist drew a square on her notepad and filled in the space with crosshatching. "And you never see his face?"

"It does not matter. It will not matter. It could be anyone. They can send anyone." Anya moved around the room, a restless cat. "They could look like anyone. Young, old, a woman even. In my dream it is a man always, but they could send a woman." She stopped at the window. "But in my dream it is a man."

"Who are *they*?"

"I cannot tell you that. It is probably dangerous for you that I talk at all."

"It's all right."

"You think it is all right because you think I am delusional. You think the assassin is in my mind."

"Isn't the assassin already dead?"

"They will send another one."

After Anya left, the psychiatrist labelled the cassette case and filed the session with the others. There were almost a hundred now. Some of them had red tags. This one didn't rate a red tag.

The case of Anya Daniel was a personal commitment for the

doctor and in a very real sense the only responsibility worthy of her talent. Were it not for Anya and her "special" situation, she wouldn't spend another day in this tiny, empty, backward little town. Some day, if things worked out, she might produce a paper, or even a book (with all the names changed, of course) detailing the bizarre elements of the case. The truly unique aspects would be fascinating, and not only to the psychiatric community.

They walked their coffees back through Armoury Park, Orwell acknowledging the occasional wave or nod of a passerby with his customary magnanimity, Georgie bouncing a few steps ahead, the scrappy flyweight of fifty years back still evident in his step. "Shouldn't be that big a deal, Stonewall," he said. "Not like you're planning a housing development."

"Thin edge of the wedge is how the township views it," Orwell said. "You'd think it'd be a simple matter to build a second house on your own property."

"I'm sure there'll be some leeway if it's for a family member."

"Claim they're merely protecting the farmland."

"Tell you what, my friend," Georgie said. "They're fighting a losing battle. New highway goes in, you're just close enough to be a bedroom community. Won't be too many years."

"That's what they're concerned about, and I sympathize, but hell's bells, a man wants to build his daughter a house on his own land, it should be a right."

"Hey, if they turn you down, we'll sue. Happy to take it to the Supreme Court. That'd be a helluva ride. But I'm not that lucky. My guess, they'll get one look at you in your brass and gold — you *will* remember to wear the dress blues when you make your pitch?"

"I'll bedazzle them."

"— and they'll rubber stamp the application forthwith."

"Forthwith."

"Even so, you're going to want all your ducks in a nice straight line. Everything they could possibly want — pictures, plans, estimates, maps, all the forms filled out."

"Hate forms."

"World's built outta forms. Beats me how you've come so far."

"It's a wonder," said Orwell.

Georgie spun around, planted his feet, grinned, threw a soft left jab at his big friend's chest. "I guess congratulations are in order."

Orwell shrugged. "Not quite. I may be jumping the gun. They haven't exactly set a firm date."

"Dragging their feet, are they?"

"Being prudent, I guess. Patty's had one bad marriage, can't blame her for thinking things through."

"Is there no escaping the man?" Georgie was pointing. Orwell looked over his shoulder to find Gregg Lyman's face smiling at him. Lyman's campaign placards were twice the size of Donna Lee's. His campaign colours were blue and silver, his slogan was "A Breath of Fresh Air," his image had a healthy glow. "There's been money spent," said Georgie.

"His?"

"Well, the family's, I guess."

Sam Abrams, the burly bearded owner and managing editor of *The Dockerty Register*, was heading their way, briefcase bulging, overcoat flapping, delicately stepping around wet spots on dainty feet. Graceful as a dancing bear, thought Orwell.

"*Register* going to endorse anyone, Sam?" Georgie asked.

"It's a one-paper town, Georgie — I can't afford to take sides. Fair and impartial, right down the line."

"Coulda fooled me with that front page this morning."

"Hey, the Kingbirds don't win a championship every year."

"Oh? Is *that* who won? Looked like Donna Lee was getting

the trophy."

"She wasn't scheduled to show up, was she, Chief?"

Orwell shook his head. "There I was, ready to hand the loving cup to the captain, and I find myself in a tug-of-war. Hope that's the last of it."

"Wouldn't count on it, Stonewall."

"I'll make sure Gregg Lyman gets a photo-op real soon," Sam said. "As soon as he does something even vaguely civic."

"Well, you and the Chief here are required to tippy-toe," said Georgie. He gave his walking stick an airy twirl. "Happily, I don't have to be circumspect. I can come right out and say I don't much care for either one of them. Tell you one thing though, young Lyman didn't get that haircut in this town."

"That'll cost him one vote, anyway," Orwell said.

"Doesn't buy his suits here, didn't get his teeth capped here. Doesn't even live here."

"I hear he's shopping for a house," Sam said with a grin. He did a dainty dance around a patch of mud and headed off to work.

"He should sublet first," Georgie called after him.

Georgie and the Chief parted company at a fork in the path; Georgie off to feed cruller crumbs to the birds and squirrels, Orwell heading back to the station. Gregg Lyman's visage confronted Orwell twice more before he reached Stella Street. He doubted the sincerity of the man's smile. He reminded himself that the coming election had nothing to do with him. He maintained as conspicuous a remove from Dockerty politics as was possible for a man in the employ of Dockerty politicians. He kept his dealings with the mayor's office businesslike and his relations with elected officials excessively polite. He refused to be drawn into conversations that might indicate which way he was leaning. In private, and to those close to him, he freely admitted that the Mayor was a thorn in his side, a stone in his shoe and an occasional gumboil, but publicly he was never less than loyal.

And while he had often entertained thoughts of a world without Donna Lee's annoying voice, the prospect of dealing with a new office holder, and one so obviously determined to climb the political ladder, gave him pause. He could do business with Donna Lee, he was accustomed to her, and their differences were clearly defined — she thought he was a sexist pig, and he knew she was a shrew.

Orwell was as convinced that he *wasn't* a misogynist as no doubt Donna Lee was that she didn't have a shrewish bone in her body. How could he be sexist? He lived and thrived in a house of women, his best investigator was a woman, he dealt with women every day — hell, half the storekeepers and waitresses in town smiled and fluttered when he walked in. He was a prince, he was certain of it: fair, respectful, non-patronizing. He had been confident enough of his gender-neutral behaviour to ask his youngest, Leda, Voice of the Oppressed, if she thought he was sexist.

"Well, Dad, you *are* a ma-an." Leda dragged the word out like a schoolyard taunt.

"Can't do anything about that," he said reasonably. He'd been driving the seventeen-year-old home from the Dockerty Little Theatre. She had auditioned, convincingly she thought, for the part of Emily in *Our Town*. Drama was her forte, although she had a tendency to declaim. Orwell worried that she might have picked it up from him.

"It's not your fault," she said kindly. When he started laughing, she gave him a critical look. "But that laugh, the one you're doing now, you don't think it's maybe a bit condescending?"

"How so?"

"Has a sort of 'oh isn't she just the cutest thing' sound to it."

"I was amused."

"In a paternalistic way."

"Right. Me. Father. Laughing."

"Okay, so maybe I can deal with it on those terms, but how

about women who aren't related by blood or marriage? You give them that indulgent chuckle, too?"

"Oh heck, that's just me. I don't patronize — how could I and survive in our house?"

"You indulge us."

"And that's a bad thing?"

"I'll let you know in a few years."

Not the ringing endorsement he'd been fishing for perhaps, but she hadn't exactly reproached him for being an indulgent father. She merely pointed out that he sometimes adopted an air of, oh well, call it *condescension* if you want to be critical. He preferred to see it as the warm and gracious outward manifestation of his need to protect and provide. There were moments of course, late at night usually, when he acknowledged that he could sometimes be a bit . . . what did Erika call it? *Herrisch.* One of those many-layered German words, the simplest definition of which was "manly," but seemed to encompass "imperious," "overbearing," "pompous," "domineering," and a few dozen other concepts that, he had to admit, were clearly implied in his daughter's pronunciation of the word "ma-an."

Anya walked from the psychiatrist's office to her studio. It was a dancer's stride: exaggerated turnout, shoulders back, head high and floating, almost motionless. She changed directions arbitrarily, side streets and lanes, dodging traffic, checking reflections in the store windows, ever watchful, never the same route twice. She was wearing what she wore most days — sweater, tights, a black and grey wraparound skirt, a plain wool coat, flat shoes to nurse her perpetually sore toes. In *Giselle* she wore flowers in her hair. In *Swan Lake* she wore egret feathers and a tiara. She had no use for fashion.

She cut across the parking lot behind Sleep Country. Two

men were loading a huge mattress into a truck. She wondered briefly if a bed like that might help her sleep, but she doubted it. Her problem couldn't be mended by pocket springs and foam padding. She turned into the narrow walkway separating Laurette's Bakery and Home Hardware — Vankleek Street at the far end — but a feathered black lump was lying on a grate, blocking the way.

Dead crow. Very bad omen in a world of bad omens. She sidestepped. For one thing, stay clear of dead birds. Some kind of virus was going around. What was it? West Nile, Avian something, Chinese chicken flu? If you paid attention to all the warnings you heard in one day you would go mad. Diseases, tornadoes, terrorists, escaped criminals — it is amazing any of us gets through a day. But a dead crow carried more than disease. It did not matter if it was killed by a mosquito or a train, it was in her path. On the roof above, other crows were looking down and making crow noises. Blaming me, she thought. Every dead crow is my fault. Go to hell. You get killed, it is your own stupidity, or bad luck, or bad planning, or bad friends. I am not responsible.

On the corner across from the Gusse Building, she lit a cigarette and lifted her eyes to the studio window on the third floor. No movement. No shadows. Three girls were waiting beside the florist shop on the other side, waiting for her to let them in. Just three. Two of them were hopeless, the third one was graceful but too tall. She should tell their parents, but she needed the money. She caught movement behind her.

"*Salut, Mademoiselle.*"

It was the Chinese girl, the one with promise, missed three classes with a sore foot. Get used to it. Anya smiled, the first smile of her day, happy to see her star pupil, the only one who might some day dance, barring the thousand hurdles and pitfalls. "*Salut Christine,*" she said. "How is your foot?"

"Much better, thank you."

"I am happy to hear it." The light turned green. Anya motioned to the crosswalk. *"Continué. J'arriverai bientot."*

"*Oui, Mademoiselle,*" said Christine. She crossed the street to stand with the other three. They were waving at their teacher. Anya nodded graciously and then turned her back to look at the travel brochures in Dawson's window and finish her cigarette. A ship was sailing the blue Caribbean, happy golden couples danced on a beach somewhere, silver planes promised smooth flying to paradise. She blew smoke at the glass and her reflection came into focus. A petite blonde woman with pale, watchful eyes, eyes that missed nothing, took in everything, eyes that immediately saw the dark car drive by and the tall man behind the wheel. That hair: unmistakable.

Georgie said he was preparing a list of what Orwell would need to make his case: plot map, maybe even a survey, photographs, estimate of house size — now how the hell would he know that? That was Patty's decision. He didn't know what kind of house she wanted. Maybe she didn't want a house at all. Maybe he was just being Big Daddy again, throwing his not inconsiderable bulk around. Maybe he should mind his own business.

"Chief? Mayor Bricknell on line one."

"Thank you, Dorrie, just what I need to brighten my day." He knew what that was about. She was trying to wheedle him into an appearance at a conference on civic beautification. "Madam Mayor, I'm sure your presence will be more than enough to persuade the good citizens to tidy up their front yards."

"It's much more than that, Chief Brennan, I want a concerted effort at fixing up some of our more distressed areas."

"I support your vision for a prettier Dockerty and I assure you that the DPD will do what's necessary to facilitate whatever course you and the good ladies of the . . . what is it again?"

"The Dockerty Restoration Society."

"Yes, an admirable organization to be sure."

"You'd only have to put in a brief appearance."

"I know, just long enough for a photo-op."

"I'm sure I don't know what you mean."

"Donna Lee, I truly wish you well in the upcoming election, I mean that, but you already have a picture with me looking supportive. I don't like being co-opted as a tacit backer of your campaign. And I definitely don't want to be trotted out like a prize bull every time you need your picture in the paper."

After he hung up he wondered if he could have handled the exchange with more tact, but he tended to feel that way after most of his encounters with Mayor Bricknell. It was still a month until voting day. A long month.

"Chief?" Dorrie again. "There's a Detective Delisle from Metro Homicide in town. He said he was checking in."

"Well now, that might distract me for a moment from the usual travail." He opened his door and checked the big room. "He here?"

"Just missed him, Chief," Dorrie said. She was wearing a powder blue sweater set. "I didn't want to interrupt your chat with the Mayor."

"Most considerate." Orwell noted, as he often did, how very tidy his secretary looked, not a hair out of place. "Have I seen that sweater before?" he asked.

"Probably. You gave it to me for Christmas."

"Ah," he said.

"Your wife may have helped you pick it out," Dorrie said.

"Yes, as I recall I was going to get you a karaoke machine." Dorrie didn't laugh. It was one of Orwell's missions in life to make her smile. She rarely did. "This detective . . ."

"Delisle," she said. "Paul Delisle, Metro Homicide." She articulated clearly. "Said he was hungry, be back after he had some lunch."

Orwell checked his watch. "Hmm. I'm a mite hungry, too," he

said. "Know where he was planning to eat?"

"I told him to try the Hillside."

"What's he look like?"

"Can't miss him, Chief: redhead, taller than you even, looks like a basketball player."

"That colour suits you," he said.

"Thank you," she said. "And may I say that green tie suits you."

Orwell thought he detected the briefest flicker of a smile on his secretary's face, but he could have been mistaken.

Paul Delisle *had* been a helluva basketball player. Good ball-handler for all his size, decent outside shot, not afraid to stick his face in there. Went all the way through college on his rebounding and his outlet pass. He still had a floating grace in the way he moved, his head was always up, expressive wrists, wide square shoulders. He was sitting by the corner window with an angle on the bridge to his right and a long view of Vankleek for three blocks west.

"Detective? I'm Orwell Brennan, understand you were looking for me. Don't get up."

"Chief. Pleasure. Paul Delisle."

Delisle put down his hamburger, wiped his hand and extended it across the table. The two hands together were the size of a picnic ham.

"Mind if I sit down?"

"Oh yeah, please. You don't mind me eating?"

"Hell, I'm here to eat, too," Orwell said. "Doreen, sweetie, give me a small steak, tell Leo it's for me — he knows how I like it."

"Anything to drink, Chief?"

"Canada Dry, lots of ice. Thanks. Cut your hair. Looks nice."

"Thanks," Doreen said. She fluffed her new look as she headed for the kitchen.

"You know everybody in town, don't you? I watched you walking this way."

"Small town. I'm easy to spot."

"Me too," Delisle said, "but I'm more anonymous."

"That's the big city for you. So. How can I help you? You looking for somebody?"

"It's sort of complicated." He looked out the window at the Little Snipe flowing past. "There's a ballet teacher in town. Calls herself Anna Daniel these days."

"She a witness? Suspect?"

"Tell you the truth, I don't know what the hell she is." Delisle stared out at the river. "It's probably a waste of time."

"Something personal with you?" Orwell asked.

"Anna Daniel used to be with the Kirov or the Bolshoi or one of those, twenty-five, maybe thirty years ago," Delisle began.

"Anya."

"Say again?"

"Her name. Not Anna, An-ya. I've met her," Orwell said. "My youngest daughter, Leda, took some classes before deciding she'd rather save the world than do pliés." Orwell's steak arrived, charred on the outside, red in the middle, salad on the side. He had foregone the excellent baked potato and sour cream he would have liked. He was trying to lose a few kilos. Again. "Where's your partner?"

"I had some vacation time coming."

"So this is personal."

"What'd you think of *Anya*?"

"Can't say we talked much. She was forthright. Said Leda was too tall, uncoordinated and had an attitude."

"Does she?"

"My daughter? Definitely. The teacher, too. I like people with attitude. She defected, right?"

"1981, did a Baryshnikov in Toronto, asked for asylum."

"She a citizen now?"

"Oh yeah, that's all square. The Russians didn't make much of a fuss. Not a *big* star."

Orwell attacked his six ounces of rare beef and, for appearance's sake, a few bites of salad. "What's the interest?"

"She confessed to a homicide."

Orwell blinked. "She did? When was this?"

"Six years ago. In the city. Before she moved up here. Somebody dead in High Park. She was questioned."

"Why?"

"Routine. She lived close to where it happened. She was seen in the park, walking in the park, no big deal, she wasn't a suspect, we were questioning people in the neighbourhood, just routine, and out of the blue she confesses."

"To you?"

"It was a follow-up interview after the uniform cops had canvassed the neighbourhood. Uniform made a note that she'd acted a bit weird and might be worth a second visit. My partner and I knocked on her door, she comes to the door with a drink in her hand, sees the badges and says, 'Ah, there you are at last.' We give her the just routine ma'am, follow up visit, in case you may have remembered something, and out of the blue she says, 'I know what you are talking about. I know the man you are talking about. I killed him.'"

"Holy cow."

"Well, ah yeah, but it didn't check out. Everything was wrong with her story. She said she shot him, the guy was strangled, big guy, strangled, she's a small woman, no way she strangles somebody that size. The body had been moved, no way she *moves* a guy that size. She took a polygraph, she lies about everything. Nothing checks out. She didn't have a gun. She had an alibi but she didn't use it, the super in her building says she was moving furniture, tying up the service elevator, he saw her five, ten times that day. She's a loon."

"I know she's seeing a psychiatrist," Orwell said. "Dr. Ruth." Delisle raised his eyebrows. "That's her *last* name. Lorna Ruth. Anyway, Lorna's in the medical building near the campus. Evangeline Street."

"She won't tell me anything, probably."

"No, she won't. I just mention it. You saying she was a loon. You want coffee?" Delisle nodded, distracted. "Doreen, couple of coffees?"

"Got Dutch apple pie, Chief."

"Temptress. But I am strong. Maybe next week. You want dessert?" Delisle shook his head, his thoughts still elsewhere. "Where's your partner in all this?"

"What? Oh, Dylan? He's retired. Six years ago. O'Grady. Black Irishman. Literally. Afro-Irish. Big guy, your size, used to play tackle for the Argos. Dylan O'Grady. Know him?"

"Vaguely. Don't think he played very long."

"Broken toe did him in. Believe that? Worked out in the end. Did his twenty as a cop, went into politics. He's a city councillor now, but I hear he's running for a vacant seat in Ottawa."

"The big time."

"Yeah, he's a go-getter." Delisle sounded dubious.

The coffees arrived as well as two bite-size portions of Dutch apple pie on saucers. "Just so's you two know what you're missing." Doreen walked away, fluffing her hair again. Orwell savoured the single bite. "The guy in the park," Orwell said, licking the corner of his mouth. "You ever find the real killer?"

"Oh sure we did, not for that one, but we found a strangler, a big gay dude, eight months later for another one, and for one more that the guy didn't finish off and the victim lived to testify. Messed up his life, but he stood up, testified, give him that."

"You should try the pie," Orwell said. Delisle shook his head. Not interested. Orwell popped Delisle's sample into his mouth. Be a shame to let it go to waste. "So you closed the first case, too," he said, wiping his lips.

"Not officially, he wouldn't cop to the guy in the park but we're pretty sure it was him."

"So if she didn't do it, what's the interest?"

"Well, we've got this other case, still open, two years previous, guy got himself shot, out in the Beaches. I was checking her out and her name pops up in this other file. She confessed to that one, too. Said she strangled him."

Orwell shook his head and stifled a laugh. "So she's on record of having confessed to two different murders, only she got the methods wrong?"

"Or backwards."

"Got anything else?"

"Oh yeah. Turns out we've got a file on this woman four inches thick. From September 13, 1987, to October 27, 1995, she called 9-1-1 fifty-four times. Prowlers, assaults, stalkers, rapists following her, assassination attempts. Fifty-four."

"How many responses?"

"Actual investigations? Maybe seven. Patrol logs, maybe another fifteen. She wasn't ignored, at least not at first, but after a couple of years she was kind of established, a crank, not to be taken too seriously, paranoid delusion, persecution complex, chronic confessor, that kind of evaluation."

"Sounds like she was going through a bad patch," said Orwell. "She seems to be functioning all right in Dockerty. Opened a dance school, teaches ballet to the kids, ballroom dancing for the grownups. Never any trouble as far as I know."

Delisle looked away from the river and the bridge and wherever his mind had travelled. "She says she did something in her homeland that will never be forgiven, they're going to send assassins after her to make her pay."

"The body in the park, guy was an assassin?"

"Not hardly. Stockbroker. Riverdale. Wife and kid. He had coke in his system. Some white collar putz taking a walk on the wild side, got himself into a dangerous situation."

"So what are you up here for?"

"Well, another guy turned up dead. Last week. On the Queensway. In a motel room."

"She didn't confess to that one, did she?"

"Far as I know, she was up here. But here's the thing, this guy was Russian, he was a defector, he was a scenic designer for a ballet company and he was carrying her picture in his wallet."

She had recognized him immediately as he drove by — not the sort of man you forget, so tall, that preposterous red hair, and there he was again, on the sidewalk across the street. He was even walking in rhythm with the music, Rimsky-Korsakov, *Schéhérazade.* The children in the room behind her were fighting the tempo, but the tall man below was floating along in perfect time. She wondered if he could hear it. The windows were closed, no traffic noise. Maybe it was a sign. A good sign. A sign that would cancel out a dead crow. It was possible, was it not? Of all the people looking for her, he was the one she always hoped would find her again. From that first time, when he came to the apartment on Quebec Avenue with that huge black man, that first look, standing in the hall, offering his badge toward her like a sandwich. Viktor had been there, getting drunk on her vodka, smoking her cigarettes, badgering her, hiding in the corner. Unlike Viktor, she had been happy to see the policemen, welcomed them into the apartment, offered them drinks. She didn't like the big black man. He was too friendly, and he crowded her with his big smile and sexy voice, acting like her uncle, the one who always stood too close. But the red-haired man, she liked him, standing by the door, not leaning, but giving the impression that he was lounging, so relaxed. He had an easy smile. He had a nice voice. She wanted to get his attention.

"Yes, the man in the park. I know who you mean," she said. "I killed him."

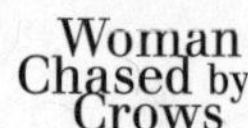

They hadn't believed her, they took her to the police station for questioning and that was all she really wanted, to get away from Viktor who was drunk and getting crazier every day, to ride in a car with the red-haired man, to have him pay attention to her for a while. And he drove her home as well, insisted even. She turned down a ride with the big black man, but she went home with the red-haired one. When she invited him inside, he demurred, but so charmingly, with a smile almost rueful, a smile that suggested *another time, another place, ships that pass in the night, if only we'd met last week*, and never that she was too old for him. He was a charmer. And courtly. A private part of her, the tiny part that wished for things, had prayed he would return some day.

"Mademoiselle?"

It was the tall girl, the graceful one, perhaps a model some day. But not a dancer. "Class is over now. I am tired today," Anya said. "I will not charge your parents for this class. Go home."

She heard them changing, leaving, still she watched the street, hoping for another glimpse of him. And there he was, coming out of the National Bank, talking to a pretty girl who kept fluffing her hair. Tsk. Such a flirt. Him, too. She watched him fold his cash and slip it into a pocket. He had such beautiful hands.

Her own hands were not attractive. Short fingers, the palms square and knuckles prominent. Her thumbs especially were distasteful to her, a heavy callus where she habitually bit her knuckle instead of chewing her nails. And to hurt herself. She knew how use her wrists to make her hands appear beautiful from a distance, to an audience, but offstage she held her cigarette inside a cupped palm like a convict in an exercise yard.

Maybe he will visit me tonight. That would be nice. I'll wait for him. And if he is to be my assassin, I will welcome him.
